The Jovian Madrigals

by
Janneke de Beer

An Owlish Books publication

Copyright © 2024 by Janneke de Beer

All rights reserved.

No part of this publication may be reproduced, distributed, or transmitted in any form or by any means, including photocopying, recording, or other electronic or mechanical methods, without the prior written permission of the publisher, except as permitted by U.S. copyright law. For permission requests, contact jannekedebeer2193@gmail.com.

The story, all names, characters, and incidents portrayed in this production are fictitious. No identification with actual persons (living or deceased), places, buildings, and products is intended or should be inferred.

ISBN: 9789083386911

Edited by Alexis Arendt (www.quickfoxeditors.com)
Cover Art by Kelsey Nix (www.nix-that.com)
Other graphic designs by Azeem

Contents

Dedication
Author's Note

First Movement: The Party Line
Chapter One - Wednesday, 9 January 2193, 8:48 PM.
    To Thedro Sto Bar, Thessaloniki, Yugoslavia..................2
Chapter Two - Thursday, January 10 2193, 9:24 AM.
    Rue du Taubert, Espaceville, France............................8
Chapter Three - Thursday, 10 January 2193, 4:00 AM.
    36 Prinsengracht, Amsterdam, the Netherlands............13
Chapter Four - Thursday, January 10 2193, 9:56 AM.
    Galileo Spaceport, Espaceville, France........................25
Chapter Five - Thursday, 10 January 2193, 10:43 AM.
    Heisenberg, Galileo Spaceport, Espaceville, France.........38
Chapter Six - Sunday, 17 March 2193, 5:15 PM.
    Entry Hall, Heaven, Callisto......................................50
Chapter Seven - Sunday, 17 March 2193, 5:16 PM.
    Heisenberg, Heaven, Callisto..58
Chapter Eight - Sunday, 17 March 2193, 7:02 PM.
    Jocasta Nikophouros' room, Heaven, Callisto................73
Chapter Nine - Monday, 18 March 2193, 1:18 AM.
    Padraig Whishaw's room, Heaven, Callisto..................87
Chapter Ten - Sunday, March 17 2193, 11:04 PM.
    Main Hall, Heaven, Callisto......................................94

Second Movement: Arima Arima
Chapter Eleven - Monday, 18 March 2193, 4:08 AM.
    Heisenberg, Heaven, Callisto......................................102
Chapter Twelve - Monday, 18 March 2193, 7:12 AM.
    Jocasta Nikophouros' room, Heaven, Callisto............114
Chapter Thirteen - Monday, 18 March 2193, 8:59 AM.
    Padraig Whishaw's room, Heaven, Callisto...............130
Chapter Fourteen - Monday, March 18 2193, 10:17 AM.
    Cato Riela's room, Heaven, Callisto........................148
Chapter Fifteen - Monday, 18 March 2193, 10:48 AM.
    Cato Riela's room, Heaven, Callisto........................160

Chapter Sixteen - Monday, 18 March 2193, 12:25 PM.
    Physics lab, Heaven, Callisto...172
Chapter Seventeen - Monday, 18 March 2193, 1:38 PM.
    Heisenberg, Heaven, Callisto..181
Chapter Eighteen - Monday, March 18 2193, 1:40 PM.
    Swimming pool, Heaven, Callisto......................................189
Chapter Nineteen - Monday, 18 March 2193, 3:47 PM.
    Heisenberg, Heaven, Callisto..198
Chapter Twenty - Monday, 18 March 2193, 4:39 PM.
    Physics lab, Heaven, Callisto..205
Chapter Twenty-One - Monday, 18 March 2193, 6:04 PM.
    Jocasta Nikophouros' room, Heaven, Callisto.............217
Chapter Twenty-Two - Monday, March 18 2193, 6:29 PM.
    Main Hall, Heaven, Callisto..229
Chapter Twenty-Three - Monday, 18 March 2193, 6:29 PM.
    Entry Hall, Heaven, Callisto..234
Chapter Twenty-Four - Monday, 18 March 2193, 6:40 PM.
    Jocasta Nikophouros' room, Heaven, Callisto.............253
Chapter Twenty-Five - Monday, 18 March 2193, 7:42 PM.
    Aria Robotics Lab, Heaven, Callisto.................................273
Chapter Twenty-Six - Monday, 18 March 2193, 7:45 PM.
    Heisenberg, Heaven, Callisto..281
Chapter Twenty-Seven - Monday, March 18 2193, 7:15 PM.
    Aria Robotics Lab, Heaven, Callisto.................................287
Chapter Twenty-Eight - Monday, 18 March 2193, 7:53 PM.
    Main Hall, Heaven, Callisto..291
Chapter Twenty-Nine - Monday, 18 March 2193, 8:36 PM.
    Heisenberg, Heaven, Callisto..301

Third Movement: Reflektor
Chapter Thirty - Tuesday, March 19 2193, 3:07 AM.
    Entry Hall, Heaven, Callisto..318
Chapter Thirty-One - Thursday, 21 March 2193, 9:04 AM.
    Jocasta Nikophouros' room, Heaven, Callisto.............322
Chapter Thirty-Two - Thursday, March 21 2193, 9:04 AM.
    Main Hall, Heaven, Callisto..331
Chapter Thirty-Three - Monday, 26 May 2193, 7:42 PM.
    Bedroom Two, Regulus Base, Irish Sea.........................336

Acknowledgements
About the author

To Zach
You are not corrupt. I am corrupt.

Author's Note

English is the lingua franca aboard Callisto Station, and in this book - thus, the thoughts and words of viewpoint characters are presented in English. However, words and phrases in languages that are unfamiliar to the characters are left untranslated, to reflect both the diversity of cultures and histories aboard the station, and the experience of the characters whose viewpoints we will be following.

If you would like to understand these words and phrases, Minjun has some excellent advice: 한국어를 배우다!

First Movement
The Party Line

Chapter One

We are pleased to report the continuing success of Project Heaven. The nanobots so far have cured every illness and every wound presented to them. The metabolic aspects of the nanobots integrated into our bodies have also been hugely successful. We have not had to eat or drink since the implementation of version 1.0.4. While nothing is definite, it is likely that we have achieved a version of immortality here on Callisto. Until all aspects of the nanobots are fully understood, we continue to recommend that the project stay off-world. However, it is our hope that by 2130, we will be able to return to Earth and share the gift of immortality with the Party and with the world.
Letter from Dr. Fermin Alphonse to the Global Council, 2122

Heaven is the ultimate reward for those who live by the ideals of the Party. Be selfless. Be loving. Live with unity in your heart, and you too can achieve immortality in Heaven!
Ad for the Callisto Lottery, broadcast in Christchurch, New Zealand, 2142

The people of Yugoslavia will finally know peace and freedom. The oppression of the old rule is gone. The last holdout of dictatorship has crumbled. Finally, the world is united under Party leadership! Finally, all people of Earth and her colonies are free!
Global Councillor Eoin Whishaw, "Address at the Fall of Sarajevo," 3 December, 2189

Wednesday, 9 January 2193, 8:48 PM. To Thedro Sto Bar, Thessaloniki, Yugoslavia.

"It's cold in France, Jocasta!" Marina's voice was loud in her ear, shrill against the din of the pub.

To Thedro Sto Bar. Thessaloniki. This was where she was, even if she had to take a moment to remember. It was her last night on Earth, yes. Her friends were taking her out; a celebration, they called it. A celebration, the word "party" carefully avoided in all preparation. No need to remind themselves why she was going or who was footing the bill.

Jocasta smiled. "I'll barely be in France," she said. "Just an evening and a morning before the shuttle leaves."

"Yes, but you're going to get to see Paris, right? City of Lights? I hear it's nice there." Marina's thoughts rang from behind a frothing pink cocktail glass. Jittery holograms of half-dressed men danced in the corner behind her, their outlines clashing with the faded burgundy wallpaper. "Nice river. Nice ladies. Nice shops."

"Really, Marina, does our Jocasta sound like the shopping or ladies type? Nah, they'll be lucky if they get three words out of her that aren't 'fuck off, no.'" Stefanos strode over, the handles of beer steins clutched in his hands. "Drink Volkan," the lights on the glass flashed. Stefanos passed the stein to Jocasta. "EXPLOSIVE TASTE," the back of the glass added. A volcano flashed up, the beer's foaming head filling in for its ash plume. Jocasta pulled it towards her, burying her eyes in the foam.

"Hey now," Marina wagged a drunken finger at Stefanos before pounding her fist on the table. "Jocasta can do whatever she likes, and neither you nor I can tell her no. Hell, she can do more than she likes, because the fucking Party's footing the bill." Her hands leapt across the table and seized the handle of a stein. Foam flew as she thrust it above her head, calling, "To the Party!"

The room fell silent. For a moment, Jocasta marvelled at it. Even as the music blared and the holograms danced on, there was silence, palpable and visceral. It was the hostile silence of a group who knew one of their own had betrayed them. Jocasta tried to melt further into the foam.

"EXPLOSIVE," the glass announced.

Chairs creaked as people turned to see who had shouted the blasphemy. Stefanos took the stein from Marina, trying to quiet her down, even as her giggles grew.

"Sending Councillor Carras to your door and everything," she snorted. Jocasta watched Stefanos' eyes darting around the pub as she tried to quiet their friend.

"As if that would make it any better." Marina's laughter hadn't stopped.

"Sorry, sorry," Stefanos was saying to the bar. Jocasta's eyes moved from Marina to the large men swivelled in their chairs, eyeing them, back to the volcano on the glass. To be anywhere but here.

"She's drunk. Didn't mean it, didn't mean it." She felt the men's gazes turn to her. It was the training kicking in. Had to be. She was focusing on the animation of an erupting volcano and couldn't have seen when the gazes switched to her. And why wouldn't they? She was one of the most famous faces in the world right now. If anyone in godforsaken Yugoslavia would be singing the Party's praises, it would be Jocasta Nikophouros.

She lifted her eyes and met the gaze of another man, watching her from two tables away. His heavy brows were furrowed as he glared at her. She could see the light line of a scar above his right eye, which his hair just barely didn't hide. He was older, in his forties — probably only a few years older than her — but there was something in his eyes that she knew.

A glass tumbling from the table was a

• • •

gunshot. Her head shot up. In the rain and the dark, it was impossible to see where it came from. She spun her head from side to side, trying to see. The infrared goggles showed nothing but the whimpering dog beside her and the lights of the town in the distance. Normal wavelengths were right out. Rain splattered on the road beside her as she huddled in the bushes with the dog. The soldiers could be just across the asphalt, and she wouldn't see, not if they knew she was there. Her own soldiers had ways of hiding from her if they wanted to; she couldn't imagine what the Party soldiers would have.

The dog whimpered again. Finally caught in a Party trap after all these months. The name on the tag flashed against her implants. "1772," it said, and then in smaller letters, "APORIA."

Blood on the ground, glowing red to her infrared eyes. She could see the outline of the dog's intestines where the line had ripped across her belly. She'd been told the road was safe. She'd been told Zallq was safe.

More gunfire, from the direction of the town this time. Jocasta covered her head in her hands and leaned against the ground. The dog's hot breath fell on her cheek. Then, a soft tongue. Single lick.

"Hey, doggy, doggy," she murmured, reaching out a hand. The leaves on the bush rustled as the dog's tail thumped. Jocasta pulled her hand back in fear. She couldn't be heard, not here, not now.

POP   POP.   Pause.   *POPOPOPOPOPPOP.*   Pause.   *POPOPOPOPOP.*

She shrank beside the dog. Closer. Always closer. She couldn't see any of it. If she was hearing it at all, it meant something had gone wrong. They were supposed to be sneaking in. Supposed to be spies. Maybe Zallq had been loaded with soldiers, who knew.

She leaned over Aporia again. The dog's eyes watched her, gleaming with desperate life. Jocasta knew that look. This wasn't the first dog. It wouldn't be the last.

"I'm sorry, little doggy," she murmured, turning the dog's head so its neck was bared. Aporia whimpered. "I'm so sorry."

She pressed her knee into the dog's neck, counting the seconds. It was better this way, she told herself. She was trained, but not like this. A vet could only do so much, especially here, a godforsaken ditch in Kosovo. Nothing to be done now.

The dog squirmed beneath her knee, struggling to claw back its

• • •

breath. She didn't remember running from the bar, but here she was, gasping for air in Thessaloniki's cool night. The train station lurked like a demon, its sign beaming at her through the dark. She heard footsteps behind her. Hands grabbed her shoulders.

Jocasta tensed and spun, fists already clenched. Marina stepped away from her, hands held up by her shoulders.

"Jocasta," Marina said. Her dark eyes flickered across Jocasta's face, more sober now than Jocasta had realised she could be. Jocasta felt her breath slowing, her heart calming down. She was in Thessaloniki. This woman was her friend. She was safe. If anything, she was probably one of the safest people in Yugoslavia right now.

Marina's hands lowered as she reached for Jocasta, pulling her into a hug. Jocasta let herself be taken in, let her breath slow, let her mind settle back into reality. Her friend's arms were around her. She was safe.

Over Marina's shoulders, she could see Stefanos hurrying out of the bar, shaking his head.

"This is what they do," he said, his voice a growl. "They cause chaos and destruction and rip people's lives apart." He spat on the ground. "Fuck the Party."

"Stefanos!" Marina lowered her hands from Jocasta's shoulders. "Stefanos, they're giving our friend this amazing gift—"

"Using her to make a political statement, more like." His voice grew louder. "Do you think for one instant that she won that Lottery fairly, huh? That they seriously just drew her name out?" He waved his hands in the air to emphasise the point, as if gesticulating would make his words matter any more.

"No! That's stupid! They rigged the Lottery. They rigged it so she would win and they could show that this country is totally under

Party control and there are no hard feelings. And you!" He jabbed a finger at Jocasta. "You're a fool for not seeing it sooner."

"Stefanos!" Marina was yelling now, jabbing a finger back at Stefanos. "That's enough! Jocasta's not a fool, and you're talking nonsense!"

"He's not." Jocasta's voice was small, but it was enough to make them all turn to stare at her. "He's absolutely right that it's a political message."

Stefanos let out a bark of laughter. "So then you're not a fool for not seeing it. You're a fool for playing along. You! Of all people! You saw the bombs in Pristina! Did you forget Zallq?"

"Please don't call me a fool, Stefanos." Jocasta's voice was level as memories flickered behind her eyes. Of course she remembered. Of course they were all she saw when she closed her eyes. Of course they were all she dreamed. "I know they're using me. I never said otherwise, nor did they. But if I can help bring peace—"

"It's not about peace, Jocasta, can't you see?" Stefanos' hands were pressed together as he leaned closer to her. "It's about exploiting this place. That's all the Party ever does is exploit, exploit, ex—"

"That's enough." Jocasta's voice was stronger this time. "I only ever wanted peace. Maybe you fought for something else, but I didn't. Peace is what matters, Stefanos, and if I can represent peace and unity, then that is what I'm going to do. I'll be the best pawn the Party has ever had." She turned, feeling their eyes press into her back, feeling her skin crawl. She was leaving them to join the people who had destroyed her world. Destroyed her.

If there was a time to turn back, to go to her friends and say, "I'm sorry, that was stupid of me," it was now. All she had to do was stop walking towards the train station. She didn't have to buy that ticket. She could vanish into Yugoslavia, disappear back into Thessaloniki. She could say that it had been a mistake, that she was anyone but Jocasta Nikophouros. She hadn't won the Lottery, hadn't even entered. She wasn't leaving Earth behind, not her.

"Jocasta!" Stefanos called, Marina's voice echoing his. "Godammit, Jocasta, you're making a mistake! Don't let them use you! Jocasta!"

Except she couldn't. Even if she wanted to, she couldn't. The Party was everywhere. It could find anyone, particularly when she'd already had her face plastered all over everything. She was the world's most recognisable Slav. Even if she wanted to, there was nowhere to run. They'd find her, and they'd make her their symbol of peace, with or without her consent.

Even if she wanted to run, which, as she stood there in the wind, crippled claw of a right hand brushing back and forth against her leg as she walked, she knew she couldn't. Why enter the Lottery if she didn't intend to win?

The chance to escape. The chance to heal every wound. The chance to make the world better. Who wouldn't want that? If exploitation was the price to pay, then it was a bargain.

The train station rose out of the night before her, ushering her forward. A train ride to France. A rocket to Callisto. Then, immortality.

She stepped into the station.

Chapter Two

The wars of the 21st century screamed their lesson through fire and blood. We would be fools not to listen.
　　　　　　　　　　　　　　　　　　　　A New World Constitution, 2105

Let us never forget the millions who died in an instant, lives obliterated in a nuclear holocaust. May their memories live on and inspire us to keep peace in our thoughts and unity in our hearts.
　　　　　　　Plaque at the New York Nuclear Monument, erected 2093

"Unity" is a word thrown about by the powerful to suppress the weak. Fuck unity. Worry about personal liberty, voluntary association, and private existence first. If there is going to be freedom worth fighting for, it has to be based on these principles. Anything less is a lie.
　　　　　　　　Vespers Recruitment Pamphlet, published in Raleigh-Durham, Carolina, United States of America, 2192

Thursday, January 10 2193, 9:24 AM. Intersection of Rue du Taubert and Boulevard Einstein, Espaceville, France.

"You really are very lucky, you know. Winning the Lottery. It's insane."

The taxi driver kept glancing at Cassandra in the rearview mirror. They'd circled this same building four times now, and it looked like he was signaling that he was going around for another pass. If she was lucky, she didn't necessarily feel it. This taxi was too hot, and she was pretty sure they were going to be late for the shuttle launch at this rate. Take the third taxi in the row, her ass. Third taxi in the row didn't have a fucking clue where he was going.

Cassandra grinned at the driver anyway, teeth flashing in the mirror. Even if he was the wrong driver, it couldn't hurt to be friendly at him. If she had to get out and walk the rest of the way, she'd at least have someone who liked her enough to tell the Party where she'd gone off to and why they were leaving without her.

"What can I say? I'm just—ah!" Cassandra flew across the backseat as the taxi swerved to the sidewalk. Her body hit the door as the front passenger door was ripped open. A man jumped in. "Drive," he muttered, and turned to look at the backseat.

Cassandra blinked. Her nicely arranged hair had fallen out of place, a cluster of bangs tumbled across one eyebrow instead of evenly spaced as it should have been. Knees in ears instead of somewhere around the seat. Elbows on boobs. Horror show.

"Cassandra, yes?" The man was hot, she had to admit that. Late for the show, but hot, so that made up for it. Nice blond hair, green eyes; if she had a life to come back to, she might have asked if he was single. Alas.

Instead, she uncoiled herself and flicked the hair off her eyes. She stuck out her hand.

"Cassandra McAllister, goddamn Lottery winner," she said. The man took her hand and gave it a thorough squeeze. Nice and firm, but still warm. This man who couldn't meet the taxi on time at least wasn't totally incompetent when it came to making pretty girls feel like they were wanted. "Your name?"

He shook his head. "It doesn't matter."

Cassandra shrugged. "Suit yourself, then," she said. "But it doesn't exactly inspire confidence when you won't tell me your name, y'know? Can't even make one up to sound like you care."

She could see the taxi driver smiling as he dodged errant pedestrians. The man in the passenger seat hung his head and shook it.

"We don't have time for this. The Party is expecting you at the launch site in what…" He glanced over at the driver, then turned back to her. "Six minutes? Are you serious right now?"

"It's not my fault you were late," the driver said.

The man held up a finger and closed his eyes.

"I was late because I had to get something for her," he said, jabbing his finger in Cassandra's direction. His eyes flicked over her as she grinned at him. "You're not even taking this seriously, fuck me."

"I am taking this seriously," Cassandra said. "Fuck, I think I'm taking it more seriously than either of you. I'm totally serious when I say that if you were any good, you'd at least make up a name for yourself. Some shit like 'Edgar,' if you really had to. This is just sloppy, and not really confidence-inspiring. If you're this shit at the easy part, how am I supposed to trust that the rest of it will go okay?

We've got one shot, no shit, but I'm getting immortality. I'd like to not have to spend it nailed to the two-by-four of punishment or whatever the fuck they have up there for the rest of forever if this goes wrong. Capiche?"

The man grumbled out a sigh. "Fine, fine! Call me Raoul. Raoul the tech guy. Are you happy now?"

"Yes," she said. The grin spread back across her face.

"Fan-fucking-tastic," Raoul said, and reached into his pocket. He nodded his chin at Cassandra. "You got a hybridization implant, yeah? They told me you did."

Cassandra shook her head. "One of the rules of Callisto," she said. "All neural implants got removed a couple of days ago while I was still in New York. Hoffmann himself came over and explained it to me. 'Safety procedure,' apparently."

"You met Councillor Hoffmann? And you still want to go through with this? Jesus, lady!" The driver was glancing at her in the mirror again instead of the road. Whatever. It wasn't her concern if he crashed the car now. She, at least, was pretty much guaranteed to be safe. She'd passed every test the Party put in front of her. As far as they knew, she was perfectly clean.

"Watch the pram! To your right!" Raoul glared at the driver. Cassandra's attention snapped back to him as he turned to her. "Anyway, this gets more complicated if you don't have an implant. It still works, but it'll just be a radio that anyone can hear. Just…be careful with it. Hide it."

He handed her a chip the size of her thumbnail. Cassandra took it and turned it over in front of her face. "A radio?" she said. "How does it work?"

Raoul smiled, catching Cassandra off-guard. She'd only just met him, but somehow, he didn't seem like the smiley type. More the "glare and be late for everything, then blame everyone else" type that she knew all too well.

"It's clever, but," he glanced at the driver again, "since we're pressed for time, I'm just going to go with, 'it'll be obvious when the thing goes off.' Keep it on you, be ready, but don't let anyone else hear it, 'kay?"

Cassandra sent a hand snaking into her boot, slipping it under her sock. "All right, but you know it's Callisto, right? Not a summer house somewhere? Far as I know, you don't have a radio that can reach it."

"Far as you know, right," Raoul said. His smile grew.

Cassandra sighed. "Right, fine, secrecy, got it. Grand. That mean you don't want me to find a way to blow the joint, then?"

"Oh, no no no." Raoul shook his head. "Still do that. Please do that. Kill everyone on that station, and send fire up so high, the debris'll orbit forever. Oh my god, that would be great. That'd show the Party so hard, they'll think they've had their eyes bored out and replaced with the Vespers flag." He laughed. Cassandra snorted out a laugh beside him.

"Plus," she laughed, "can you imagine Hoffmann's face? Fuck, I'll die in the station just so someone gets to watch that fuckbag's reaction." She laughed again. Raoul did not.

"It's much preferred that you not die," he said. Then, after a pause: "You shouldn't have to."

Cassandra looked at him, eyes leveling on his.

"I shouldn't have to, you're right," she said. "The idea is that I'll be immortal and come back here to fuck with the Party. I'm just saying that—"

"I know what you're saying." Raoul sighed. "We're not—I mean, fuck, we can't—stop you from doing whatever the fuck you want up there. Only you can decide what is and isn't a good idea. All I'm saying is that the expectation is that you make it back here alive and as soon as possible. Having an immortal to fuck up the Party's shit would be tres magnifique."

"Even though no one's ever come back," Cassandra said.

Raoul nodded. "Even though no one's ever come back, yes."

Cassandra leaned back in the seat. "Have you considered that there maybe is no base on Callisto, and they just airlock shit as soon as they get into orbit? It doesn't seem like something they wouldn't do, and it would be a shit-ton cheaper than schlepping people back and forth."

Raoul nodded. "I've thought of that, yeah, but if that's what they're doing, that's super-helpful too. And—"

"'Super-helpful?'" Cassandra leaned forward in the seat again. "How is me getting spaced 'super-helpful?' Fucking seriously?"

Raoul shook his head. "Like I said, we'd prefer if you didn't die, but if they are spacing people, the radio I gave you will let us know, and we can send that data to the media. They'd have a field day. 'Party spacing Earth heroes.' That would bring them down as much as losing Callisto would."

"So I get to be a martyr in that case, then?"

"If you want to use that word, sure, you can be a martyr, but seriously, what's the point of that? So much more you can do if you're not dead. But look—" Raoul checked the time again. "Three minutes, so Frank's going to drop you off here and you can walk. Do you have any questions?" He paused. "Do you have a plan?"

Cassandra barked out a laugh and clapped her hands together. "A plan?" she said. "No. I don't have a plan. I don't have the faintest fucking clue what to expect. I could be spaced, I could be found out before I get on the shuttle, who knows. All I know is Hoffmann showed up at my apartment, congratulated me for winning the Lottery, and I let you guys know. What plan am I supposed to have? What plan could I fucking have? Far as I'm concerned, I've hit the jackpot, because as soon as I make it to Callisto, I've got nothing but time."

Raoul grimaced. "You don't have as much time as you'd like," he said. "Just...please take this seriously, Cassandra. Just remember the last mission you did—"

"The one you recruited me after?"

Raoul blinked. "The what now?"

"I've never done anything with you before. Day before I won the Lottery, you guys found out about the Bronx, and, *wha-boom*, terrorists at my door. Never done anything organized."

Raoul blinked again as if his brain couldn't parse that this was a sentence someone would say two minutes before he had to drop them off for the biggest mission the Vespers had ever planned.

"Oh fuck me," he murmured.

Cassandra shrugged. "I would if I had time, m'dear, but I've got two minutes until I need to be in Party custody to be shot to the stars. I'll take a kiss for good luck, though, if you've got one."

Raoul gestured a thumb at the door. "Get out," he said. "The launch site is three blocks that way. And..." He sighed again. "Come up with a plan. Listen for the radio. Keep it secret."

"Got it," she said, and opened the door.

"Good luck!" the taxi driver called as she stepped out into the January air.

Luck? Fuck. She was Cassandra McAllister, and as she stood on a curb in France, she knew one absolute truth.

Luck was for the dead. She had every intention of living forever.

Chapter Three

Then Lugh bade his people to shake the chain of silence, and they did so, and they all listened. And Lugh said: "What are your minds fixed on at this time, Men of Dea?" "On yourself indeed," said they.

"The Fate of the Children of Tuireann"

All governing powers shall be vested in a series of councils, extending from local to global. Local councils shall be elected by the people, and the finest among them shall sent to the district councils. District councils shall send their finest to the national councils. The finest and most dedicated representatives from among these shall be sent to be global councillors. Anyone may aspire to this highest office, but only the most truly selfless and disciplined will achieve it.

A New World Constitution, Article I, 2105

Global Councillor Reyes: We have one more matter to attend to today, and that's if there are any nominations for Callisto. Now, I actually have one—
Global Councillor Mfwane: Oh, did Lam finally get you to nominate him?
<Laughter>
G.C. Reyes: He wishes. No, my nomination is for someone who is actually deserving, and would be beneficial to send up there. I'd like to nominate Dr. Padraig Whishaw.
<Silence>
G.C. Maksharov: Did Eoin put you up to this, Esperanza?
G.C. Reyes: We did—
G.C. Whishaw: I did not, Ivan, but if I may speak? We do this every year. We send up the best we have in the knowledge that they're doing more good for us when they're undistracted and not going to die in the middle of research. Every year, we send up doctors, physicists, chemists, sometimes politicians; everyone we think we need to create a perfect society. If our goal honestly is a perfect society, shouldn't we be sending the best, regardless of who they are? Certainly Padraig is a less dangerous choice than some we've sent in the past. Does anyone remember the arguments we had about Cato Riela?

G.C. Mfwane: *Cato was not your son, though, Eoin. That's what Ivan is saying.*

G.C. Whishaw: *I know that's what he's saying, Sekai. My point is that that shouldn't matter. He's thirty-two years old, and he's already revolutionised our understanding of space travel. If his last name wasn't Whishaw, would this even be a question?*

G.C. Ling: *No one is doubting Padraig's abilities, just what it would look like if he went. Yugoslavia is only now under our control. Maksharov can attest to the turmoil in Azerbaijan. We need safe choices that will not compromise our image. Padraig isn't it.*

G.C. Reyes: *If I may? It is my nomination, and I'd like to speak on it. You're all correct that there is a sticky situation, but I think Dr. Whishaw is worth it, beyond the complications. Play up his science background when it's announced. Plaster the vids with his Nobel Prize. Highlight that, and I think people won't remember who his father is.*

G.C. Ahuja: *Ooo, Esperanza, I think you're too optimistic there.*

G.C. Reyes: *People will always fixate on what you tell them to fixate on. You know that. I know that.*

G.C. Whishaw: *I understand your concerns. They're all valid. But if we want to ever go to the stars, we need him alive and researching. Give him another fifteen years, and we all know that if it's possible, Padraig will make it happen. There is no other physicist alive of his calibre. We need him.*

G.C. Luhcandri: *It's a bold statement, Eoin.*

G.C. Reyes: *It's the truth.*

G.C. Maksharov: *Suppose we approved of this, Eoin, then what? Would he accept?*

G.C. Ling: *That is an irrelevant question. Nominees do not refuse.*

Recordings of Global Council meetings, Tuesday, 7 October 2192

Thursday, 10 January 2193, 4:00 AM. 36 Prinsengracht, Amsterdam, the Netherlands.

The room was sounding the 4 AM alarm. Dimly, through the haze, he could hear it chiming. What did it want? Why now? There was pain, and he couldn't breathe. Why would it insist that he needed to be here? Why would it insist on him being awake?

"Wake up, Padraig," it said, its voice soft and soothing, cutting through the pain to provide a moment of clarity. Sound therapy. Heiko had programmed that in, what, a month ago? A week ago? Yesterday? He would need to tell him that it worked. Didn't solve the underlying problem, but at least it helped with the symptoms. The pain could be pushed back to something tolerable.

"Wake up, Padraig." Yes. Awake. Hexodyazomib time. 30ccs. He could make it. Last dose.

Last dose.

"Wake up, Padraig." He opened his eyes. The projection of the stars blazed across his ceiling. Ophiuchus flickered near the window. 4 AM. 10 January. Last dose in a last-ditch effort to dodge the inevitable.

"Wake up, Padraig." The lights from the machines monitoring him flickered across the Milky Way, drowning it out. It was appropriate, *ha*, that the stars themselves could be snuffed out by reality. *Ha. Ha ha.*

Focus. He needed to focus. He needed to get out of this bed and go to the shelf. Gautier should have prepared the dose last night. He said he would, and Gautier almost never failed him.

"Wake up, Padraig." Focus. He lifted an arm, felt it shudder a bit with the weight of being asked to function. It was there, though. Nothing failed.

Across the room. Administer dose. Then brace for day.

He reached to move the blanket aside. That familiar choking. His arm fell as he bunched up, coughing and wheezing. Last dose, by the Party, last dose. If he could make it.

"Wake up, Padraig." The coughing subsided, at least for the moment. The demon had been pushed back into its hole. He opened his eyes again. More blood on the sheets. At least they wouldn't have to be washed. They could stay bloody. Last dose and it wasn't his problem anymore.

"Gautier?" His voice croaked as he reached out to check the bed beside him. Empty. Not even rumpled. Last night on Earth, though, and that sort of thing was always bound to trigger emotions. He had probably gone out for a walk or slept on the couch or gotten up early for a last breakfast by the canals. Out, but he'd be back, oh please, he'd be back.

"Wake up, Padraig." Yes. Focus. The hand swung back, taking the blanket this time and throwing it aside. It was three ordinary steps to the shelf. Four good-day steps. Ten bad-day steps. Hundreds of very-bad-day steps. An impossible number of last-day steps.

Last day on Earth, Padraig, you've known it was coming, but look at that last-minute reprieve from the governors, *hahahaha.*

He swung his feet to the floor as he sat up, head reeling. This was not a good day. In more ways than one, of course, but certainly not a good day.

He pushed himself off the bed to take a step forward. His head reeled again. He felt himself falling, but what could he

Δ

"Padraig?" Bleary voice. Gautier. He had been there, of course he had, how could he ever have doubted? Hands reaching for him, scooping him up.

"Merde." Cologne and sweat, wafting over him as Gautier lay him down. The last dose. Needed to tell him. No words, only pain and confusion.

"I'm going to get the doctor." Gautier hurrying out.

Setting constellations drowned out by devic

Δ

"Did he take the hexo, Gautier? At 4 AM?" Something surged into his blood, shoving the cancer aside. Pain cleared. Heiko was there, had to be.

Padraig opened his eyes. Sunlight peeked in the window. No constellations anymore. Oh fuck.

He pushed himself up on his elbows. His head was clear. Heiko, on his familiar stool beside the bed, holding his wrist and counting the pulse. Heiko's eyes were locked on Gautier with…hatred? Fury? Padraig couldn't tell.

"I didn't take it," Padraig murmured. His voice was hoarse, coming from a throat ripped apart. He leaned and coughed against the bed. More blood. Didn't matter. "I didn't make it over there."

Heiko glanced at Gautier, but didn't say anything. Padraig's wrist dropped from his hand as he rummaged through his bag.

"Verdamme, verdamme," Heiko muttered. Padraig watched him for a moment.

"I'm sorry," Padraig murmured. Heiko stopped rummaging and met his eyes. What was it in there? Pity? Padraig wasn't sure. Pity didn't seem amiss. He was dying to the point where he was unable to walk across his own bedroom. Pity seemed appropriate at this point.

Heiko glanced over at Gautier again, then back to his bag, shaking his head. "It's not your fault," he said. "Not your fault at all." He came back out with an injector and reached for Padraig's arm. Padraig offered it, glancing up at Gautier. Gautier was leaning against the wall, arms folded, curls askew. Red rims around his eyes made him look like he hadn't slept. Padraig smiled at him. They'd missed the early train. They wouldn't be on time, but maybe there was still something to salvage in this. The launch wasn't until 11 AM. They could make it. He would get Gautier to Heaven. Whatever else was true, Gautier could have eternity.

"What time is it, Heiko?" he croaked. From outside his bedroom, he could hear the door chime sounding. A visitor, ringing his doorbell. Probably the cleaning staff, come to clear out his possessions since he was supposed to be gone.

"8:02," he said. "What time does the train to Espaceville leave?" He emptied the injector into Padraig, dropped it into his bag, rummaged for a new one. Padraig watched as Gautier moved from the wall to see who was at the door. Padraig wanted to shout that they should leave. There was no place for them in the house of the dying. Clouds blurred his voice, scattering it into nothing. Words faded before they could begin to be uttered.

"8:23," Padraig whispered. "One hour and seventeen minutes from Amsterdam to Espaceville."

Heiko emptied a second injector into Padraig. "And the procedure when you get to Callisto? Are they going to keep you waiting, or do they give you the nanobots right away?"

"Um...should be right away. I don't actually know." Footsteps pounded back to the bedroom door as Gautier caught himself on the doorframe and popped his head in.

"Padraig, your father is at the door." The words were level, but his eyes were wide.

Heiko turned his head to stare at Gautier. Padraig blinked. It was the sort of thing that should have surprised him—and maybe, deep down inside, he was surprised, if that was an emotion he was even capable of feeling anymore—but somehow it seemed like the perfect cap to this very bad morning. The last dose of pain, as it were, before he was exiled.

"Go let him in," Padraig sighed. "Whatever he wants, there's not really a way to avoid it."

"Is your father a problem?" Heiko turned back to Padraig. Padraig shook his head, a jiggle, just enough so the world wouldn't spin.

"He's the reason I asked you to keep my information off the cloud. He...ah...he doesn't know it's this bad. I also suspect he is not going to be fond of Gautier being here."

Heiko choked. "You didn't tell him he lives here?"

Padraig wanted to laugh. He tried. His body produced a hacking wheeze. Good enough. "Oh, he knows," he said. "He's a global councillor. He probably knows more about Gautier than I do. No, of course he knows. Gautier wouldn't even be going to Callisto if he didn't."

Heiko choked again, this time trying to hide it in his bag. Padraig watched him as he listened for the voices from the front room. None yet. It was only a matter of time.

"He's a global councillor. He does what he wants. Medical records, he can read them, security be damned. It's how he found out at all. He only knows your initial prognosis, and...well...we know how that's going."

Heiko nodded and pressed the injector to Padraig's arm. "I'll do my best to see that he doesn't realise that part."

A jolt ran through him. Haze slid away, replaced by blinding clarity. He could feel his heart speeding up, pounding through his ears, his muscles, his thoughts, every inch of him pounding and awake like it hadn't been in weeks. He could feel the tumours on it shifting with every beat, shoved from side to side, slammed against his subclavius and his thoracodorsal artery and every other miniscule, broken part that he'd learned the names of in excruciating detail. His eyes went wide, and he stared at Heiko.

"What...?"

Heiko slid his arms under Padraig's shoulders, sitting him up and helping him to his feet. The world was pounding and wobbling around him, but he could do it. His legs could do this. Two steps to the closet. Four motions to get dressed. Three steps to the door. However many steps to separate Gautier and his father.

"I need you to focus, Padraig." Heiko was saying something. Padraig fixed his flitting eyes on him. He seemed to jump and dance around the world, colours, patterns, reality itself swimming in and out of view. Padraig squeezed his eyes together, bringing Heiko into the world of clarity. Focus.

"I gave you a boost. It's dangerous, and I can promise you four hours with it. It's hard on hearts, so you absolutely must stay focused."

Heiko was speaking. Something about warnings and consequences. From the front room, Padraig could hear the arguing beginning.

"You missed the train. Your responsibility, Mr. St. Laurent, your one responsibility, was to get him on the train!"

"He's not doing well this morning! You want him to die before he even gets on your shuttle?"

"Padraig!" The doctor was watching him, eyes wide, pupils flickering across Padraig's own. "You need to get the nanobots as soon as you get there, do you understand? Cancer aside, you'll die from the boost."

"Why weren't you there to help him?" His father's voice rose from the other room, surging through the walls like a tidal wave.

"I was visiting my sister! Or have you forgotten that I'm leaving too? I'm allowed to say good-bye to my own family as well, am I not?"

That defensive tone again. Anger. They needed to be separated.

Something was being pulled over his head. Padraig's attention snapped back. Heiko. A shirt. He needed to get dressed. He shook his head, trying to clear it.

"Sorry, I don't know what shirt you want," Heiko said as Padraig poked his arms through the sleeves. Lanky hair clung to Padraig's face. Sweat poured out of him. Last dose of excitement before the end.

"Doesn't...doesn't matter," Padraig wheezed. The boost could apparently do a lot of things, but it couldn't clear his lungs.

"Where is he now?"

"Dr. van Leeuwenhoek is with him. You'll only make things worse if you go in there."

"I'm his father! How could I possibly make things worse?"

"You haven't seen him since October! How could you possibly make things better?"

"Padraig, stop, you need pants." Heiko wrapped an arm around his chest, holding him still as Padraig dutifully lifted his legs. Right. Left. Good. Prepared to face eternity, or at least the man who owned it.

"What are you even doing here? Did you not notice he tried to hide all this from you?"

"You weren't on the train. I'm here to make sure my son didn't decide he wasn't going. I'm his father. I have a right to ensure he hasn't died."

All the fights they'd had over this, and the man still didn't trust him to uphold his end of the bargain. Padraig supposed it was only fair; if his father's career was in shambles, it was entirely because of him. Not that he'd asked for it. Not that he'd ever asked for any of this.

He felt a hand on his shoulder. He glanced over to see Heiko standing beside him.

"If you're making the 8:23 train, you need to go now," he said. Padraig nodded, a surer gesture this time. He was covered in sweat and hair, but at least he could nod without feeling the need to vomit.

He stepped out of the room. For a moment, he was reminded of the vids he had seen as a child. They were always the same: some car bouncing through the savannah, chasing down its subject in hopes of gloriously bloody images. Predator and prey, unaware of the roles they'd been cast in. Gautier was the lion, brown curls and broad shoulders keeping his prey pinned in the corner. The prey, his father—the pale orange antelope, horns lowered, prepared to fight.

His father spotted him. Horns raised, hackles lowered. Illusion broken.

"Padraig." Eoin Whishaw stepped forward in an embrace. Padraig's world became black, engulfed in the familiar smell of his father's coat, the mothball and weeks of different colognes smell. It rushed in, sending his head reeling, his stomach leaping to his throat.

"Hi," he choked. A cough welled up in his chest. He fought it down. Over his father's shoulder, he saw Gautier, still tense. It made him more beautiful, so much more beautiful, when he wanted to fight for him. When he protected him.

His father's arms released him, and Gautier's slipped in, supporting him, holding his shoulders. Gautier's scent washed over him, sending him fluttering to the edge of paradise.

"You look awful," his father said, his eyes moving to the doctor beside him. Padraig thudded back into reality. Heiko held out his hand for the councillor to shake.

"Dr. van Leeuwenhoek," he said, shaking his hand. "I'm afraid there's not much time. Your son can't travel very quickly, and the train—"

"I've told it to wait." Delaying the international train system for one sick man bound for France; his father was pulling out all the stops today. In conversations with Gautier, he'd joked about his father destroying the world to send the two of them to Heaven. Now it didn't seem so unlikely.

Heiko didn't seem to know how to respond. "He still needs to get moving," he stammered. "There's not much time."

"Agreed." Padraig felt himself being pulled out of Gautier's grasp.

Back into his father's arms. Familiar, yet unfamiliar. Home, yet prison. Odd how these emotions surged to the surface when they were least wanted.

Heiko opened the front door, ushering father and son out into the stairwell. These stairs had been demons for weeks, but today, Padraig felt like he could float down them.

"I have a car waiting outside." Padraig didn't question the absurdity of his father deciding a car was the best way to travel through the cramped cobblestone streets of Amsterdam. His father was a global councillor. Reality itself bent to his whim.

Heiko opened the bottom door, sending a blast of cold winter air whistling into the building. Padraig shuddered, and his father pulled him closer. Same coat, Padraig's nose confirmed, that his father had had for the last thirty years. Still the same one.

"Just there." A narrow black car sat idling at the curb, its bumper pressed against a parked bicycle's tire. Padraig stared for a moment at the sight—the car, squeezed against the curb, a lone swan paddling in the canal, pedestrians gawking at the councillor and his son. The moments, the small moments, that made life *life*, and made it worth remembering. Moments soon to be gone.

And then he was in the car, lifted into the seat, Gautier sliding in beside him, Heiko beside him. It was black inside as well. Maybe it was a hearse, Padraig mused. Maybe he had finally died and no one had bothered to let him know that he could stop now, that he didn't have to pretend not to be in pain so Gautier wouldn't get upset or so Heiko wouldn't worry. Wouldn't that be the kicker, though. All this, and then he died on the way to the shuttle. It would be a first, and it would be memorable at least, that he did have to admit.

"I'm going to leave you at the train station." The door snapped shut. The car was moving. His father was seated across from him, looking at him. So this was one of the driverless cars, fair enough. His father could afford it. His father nodded his head at Gautier. "Mr. St. Laurent, I trust that you can make sure he gets on the train to Espaceville?" Padraig didn't look at Gautier, his attention fixed instead on his father's face. Had those lines above his brow grown? Had he always looked so old? Padraig tried to remember how long it had been since he had looked at his father with unpained eyes. Three years? Four? How long ago had Stockholm been?

"Dr. van Leeuwenhoek, will he be okay to make it to Espaceville?" There was a dimple in his father's chin. It danced when he spoke. He'd know it anywhere. It was the same one he saw each morning on his own face.

"If there are no delays with the train, then yes, he should make it. There will be danger if there are delays, and I would like to accompany—"

"I was under the impression that he had until March at least, based on the prognosis."

Padraig might have glared if he'd had the strength. It didn't matter at this point what his father knew. He could keel over now, now that his father had actually seen what little he was able to present of himself.

A pained look crossed Heiko's face. The doctor didn't meet his eyes. "The initial prognosis was based on a less aggressive illness than what your son is suffering from," he said, words slow and measured. "Cardiac cancer is a very different disease from the carcinoma his first doctor thought he had. We can cure many things, Councillor, but this is rare to the point that it ought to be impossible."

Silence. The rumble of the world outside. Across from him, his father closed his eyes, ran his palms up his face, fingers through his hair.

"Since the public doesn't know about his condition," his father said. "If it's possible to go without a doctor, that would be preferable. But Padraig's safety is paramount. If you don't think he can make it, then please say so, and please, I ask you to accompany him."

There was a pause. "At this point—" Heiko's words were measured. Padraig watched his father's face, judging the emotions. Fear? Sadness? Those were reasonable. His son was dying, and might as well be dead once he was on Callisto, for all the ability he had to see him again. "Mr. St. Laurent is capable of handling any crises that might come up. I can give him specific instructions about my particular concerns today, but Padraig should be able to make it to Espaceville without incident. He'll need transportation once he arrives—"

"Already arranged."

Another pause. "Then he should be clear to the shuttle."

His father nodded. "Good."

The car stopped. Outside the tinted windows, Padraig could see the familiar outline of the Centraal. There had been a time not too long ago when he had seen it every day. Red brick. Clockface older than time. Magnaplats zipping businessman from boats to trains. Last dose of the familiar façade.

Heiko pushed the door open, sending more cold air rocketing into the car. He leaned over Gautier and took Padraig's hand.

"Good luck," he said. Padraig nodded, then smiled.

"As good as you are, I'll see you there too in a year," he said. A half smile crossed Heiko's face.

"Good luck, Padraig." He stepped out of the car, pulling Gautier out behind him. The door slammed closed.

Father and son sat across from each other, staring in silence. Padraig fought to bring his eyes back into focus as his heart throbbed in his chest. He was on the verge of exploding. Maybe he was, based on what Heiko had told him about the boost.

"You know I'm not very good at this part." His father broke the silence first, clasping his hands on his lap.

"I know," Padraig said. "There's not really anything left to say."

"I..." His father sighed and leaned his head against the window.

"There's nothing to say." Padraig's voice felt stronger that time.

"There's quite a lot to say," his father growled, raising his eyes to his son. They were glassy. He hadn't seen his father cry in years, and yet, here he was. "Nowhere near enough time to say any of it. I...I wish you had told me you were sick."

So you wouldn't have to go digging through my medical records? The words jumped to Padraig's mouth, but he swallowed them. His father had rigged the Lottery for Gautier. His father had given him a chance at immortality. The time for anger wasn't now. It was in October when it could have been stopped, or November, when the Lottery was rigged. Now it was far too late.

His father sighed. "I wish for a great many things, not the least of which is that you had been willing to be my son."

Padraig said nothing. His father's eyes were flickering across his face, searching for something. Padraig followed them, but couldn't assuage them. What was there to say? "I'm sorry I can't stand to be around you? I'm sorry I have no desire to be part of your world? I'm sorry I've done absolutely everything in my power to avoid any hint that we're related? Any hint of impropriety?"

He said nothing. His father's eyes flicked across his face, then closed.

"The trains wait for no man," he sighed. His eyes reopened, brimming with tears. Padraig stared at them. This was his cue to say something, anything, yet what was there to say?

"They barely wait for a councillor." His father's words sliced through his thoughts. Whatever words might have been said vanished back into the ether. "Go. I'm sure Gautier will be happy to see the two of you getting on the train." He reached for the door handle, and Padraig slid across the seat. He'd seen his father cry before, but only at the graves in the family cemetery. Was that what he was now, another grave, just a touch more ambulant?

The door swung open, and daylight crept in. 8:27, the clockface showed. Padraig put a foot out of the car, then paused. He turned. There were words that could be said, that could only be said at this last moment before death.

"Thank you, Da," he said into the car, his voice a croak.

There was no answer. He hadn't expected there to be.

Gautier's arms swept him out of the car, pulling him forward across the plaza.

"You are lucky, Padraig," he said, hurrying him along. "Literally moving heaven and earth for you. If we could all be so lucky."

Padraig watched the car pull away, the pounding in his chest thudding into his stomach, his blood, his bones.

Oh yes, he thought. Lucky. Lucky indeed.

"Allons-y, mon cheri?" he murmured.

He slid his hand into Gautier's, squeezed it, felt him squeeze back.

"Ha, oui, Padraig. Allons-y."

Last dose of humanity. How lucky.

Chapter Four

Everyone enjoys the freedom of expression, which includes a free and open press, working on behalf of the people.
A New World Constitution, Article VI, 2105

Councillor Arkwasipard is giving a speech about the state of the plague in Kampot. The broadcast of this speech should be delayed until after the Heaven press conference is complete, to keep the viewers from rioting at the lack of a press conference like they did last year.
UTTK Internal Memo, 7 January 2162

Reporter: Ruslan! Just a quick question for you. I understand you have triplet daughters back in Guba. They're, what, four years old? My readers want to know: what did they think when you told them you'd won the Lottery? Were they excited? What did you say to them?
Ruslan Zadeh: I... Firusa, Aysel, and Gulnara are still very young. I don't think they really understand what is going on. They...they are excited to stay with Grandmama and Grandpapa in the country. I said to them that...that I am going away for a while, and that I will see them again when they finish...finish university, but they are very young. They do not understand. I hope someday they will understand. I hope... I hope they... My girls, when you watch this, mən səni sevirəm. Mən həmişə səni sevirəm olacaq, və mən sizə unutmayın.
Callisto Launch Press Conference, 9 January 2134

Thursday, January 10 2193, 9:56 AM. Galileo Spaceport, Espaceville, France.

"Just a few finishing touches."

Cassandra was sinking into her chair. It was one of those plush red cloth things with cushions made of what had to be clouds, considering how easy it was to fall into them. Evil chairs of lethargy, her mother had called them, but she was pretty sure that was only because they'd never had the money or space for one of their own.

Considering how infrequently this room must be used, it was absurd that this place had not one, but five of these fucking things.

Her arms were definitely rising, though, and her ass was falling into the crack. Had to be made of clouds.

The woman now sitting on the stool in the center of the room was not enjoying herself nearly as much. A make-up artist flitted around her, trying to make her heavy face and long black frizzy hair look at least somewhat presentable. The man had said "a few finishing touches" three times now, enough that Cassandra was fairly certain there would be no finish, but rather a long drawn-out sigh of "good enough."

The woman—Jocasta Nikophouros, second of three Lottery winners; Cassandra paid attention to the vids, even if the woman didn't see fit to introduce herself when she came in—sat stock-still on the stool, eyes closed, not moving a muscle. It was scary to watch, especially as activity flitted around her. Cassandra had seen pictures of marble Greek statues in her textbooks before the school had closed—this woman could have been one of those. Maybe. If she looked a little nicer and a little more like she cared. And if her hand wasn't a curled-up, scarred-covered stump.

"Put more powder on her nose!" Cassandra called, and laughed. The make-up artist gave a half-laugh, as if she was a child who needed assurance that she had done the right thing. He ignored Cassandra's suggestion, instead focusing on Jocasta's ears. Cassandra sighed. Some people had no sense of style.

She turned her attention to the other man in the room, poking his head out the door, checking his watch and muttering. He was doing it obsessively, his head rotating like it was on a spit—door, wrist, mutter mutter, door, wrist, mutter mutter. Cassandra almost wanted to reach over and smack him, just to calm him down. Almost. The evil chair of lethargy was indeed evil and lethargic.

"Is the press already out there?" she asked him. He swung his head toward her and smiled the same condescending "baby made a noise" smile.

"Yes," he said. "They were told the four of you would be coming out at 10:00 to answer questions before the launch."

"And what time is it now?"

She enjoyed the flicker of exasperation that crossed his face. The man wanted to keep his job, and was being civil toward her, but she wasn't his primary concern, that much was obvious.

"10:00," he said, and poked his head out the door again, muttering.

"Ah," Cassandra said. "So is the press conference canceled then? Whole launch canceled?"

"No!" The man's voice was a bark as he spun back to Cassandra. "Ahahaha, I mean." He took a breath, calming himself. "No, Ms. McAllister, it's not canceled. It's just delayed while we wait for the rest of the group to arrive."

"Uh-huh." Cassandra nodded knowingly as she sank back into the chair. Her gaze turned back to the woman on the stool. She had small scars everywhere, and while her make-up guy had done a good job covering them up with powder, they were still there, faint under the layers of dust.

"You're done." Jocasta opened her eyes and slid off the stool as the make-up person stepped aside. Her movement wasn't entirely smooth, either. How interesting.

"Thank you," Jocasta said. Her voice was accented, which Cassandra supposed was unsurprising. Clearly there were some barbaric places in the world that didn't speak English like they should.

Cassandra watched as the woman drifted to a corner to stand awkwardly beside a potted palm. The entire room was sparse, barely dressed up as more than a waiting room. She could joke about the chairs, but they were the only sign that anyone actually gave a fuck, really. Most of it was weird red walls and weirder potted plants. It probably hadn't been updated since the 40s.

"Oh, thank the Party." Cassandra's attention flicked back to the man at the door. From the corner of her eye, she could see Jocasta doing the same, tensing as the man stepped through the door. Veterinarian from Thessaloniki, huh? Not fucking likely with that reaction to unexpected things.

"Mr. St. Laurent!" the man at the door called. Cassandra struggled to sit up in the chair—lethargy was a sick jailer—as a man with long, curly brown hair and broad shoulders stepped into the room. He was shorter than the vids had made him out to be: not exactly short by any means, but not as powerful a figure as she'd been expecting, or as they'd shown. Could probably still do some damage if he wanted to, but mostly just burly. Example the millionth of how the media lied. They seemed to have told the truth about her, though, at least more or less. Well, as far as they knew, anyway.

She hung her head as she struggled to suppress a grin. As far as they knew.

"Ha, I see you haven't left without me." Cassandra lifted her head to watch him, still struggling to hide the grin. He had an accent too, a French one. Sexy. It made sense, inasmuch as it ever made sense for anyone to speak French.

The man at the door gave him the same indulgent half-smile he'd given Cassandra. "Of course not, Mr. St. Laurent, you're as important here as anyone! My name is Emil, and this is Manuel. I'm going to be your guide until you get to the shuttle in—" He checked his watch. Cassandra had to cough to hide a giggle when he winced. "Fifty-six minutes. Manuel here is going to get you ready for the cameras, and…ah!"

Emil—so he did have a name, but if he'd told Cassandra, she'd either forgotten or not cared enough to remember in the first place—hurried out of the room again as Gautier—was his name Gautier? It was something weird and French—turned towards Manuel.

"You're going to make me beautiful, eh?" he said, and laughed.

There was a fountain in Central Park outside where the zoo had been before the war, and not far from the nuke plaque. Cassandra and her mother had gone there when she was young to feed the ducks and splash around on hot days. There was a tone to its bubbling that sounded like applause, as if the water itself wanted to cheer for how great life was. Gautier's laugh reminded her of that fountain, easy and bubbling with genuine joy. It was fucking glorious, especially surrounded by all these lies. The Party liked to lie. At least something in this room was honest.

Manuel pushed Gautier down on the stool and attacked him with powder. Emil stepped out, returning with another man.

Cassandra wasn't sure what she had expected. She'd been excited, certainly, to meet this person who hadn't won the Lottery, who had, in fact, actually fucking accomplished something with his life. Sure, he was going because his father was a global councillor and the Party rolled like that, but still. This was someone whose name had been known before the announcements, and before vids had splattered his picture everywhere. Vids always lied, but she'd assumed he would at least be impressive in some way.

She had not expected this scrawny, sweaty kid of a man coughing into his sleeve as the tips of long, lanky strands of peach-coloured hair swung across his shoulders. He was a couple inches taller than Gautier, but he still looked like a hobo they'd found chewing on foam in the fucking dumpsters out back, not the grand titan of science the vids had showed. Then again, being a councillor's son meant you got the grand treatment in jazzing up your identity. Anyone could be made into a star with the right lighting and shit. Just a matter of perspective and efficient propaganda.

"Can you make it quick?" she heard Emil murmur, and a "sorry, sorry," from Padraig, soft and wheezing.

"I don't think we've been properly introduced." She whipped her head away from watching the flurry of movement around Padraig and turned back to the other man. He was standing beside her chair, offering his hand and smiling at her. His voice had a rumble in it that reminded her of a cat's purr.

"No, I don't believe we have." She put her hand in his and squeezed it. His grasp was firm, his hands soft. Oh, be still, heart. "Cassandra McAllister."

"Ah yes," he said, and bent over and kissed her hand. She stared. Kissed her hand. Actually kissed it. "I should have recognized you from the vids. You won the Lottery, yes? Where are you from?"

"New York." She braced herself against his arm and pulled herself out of the chair. Evil, escaped. "Well," she shrugged her shoulders and dropped his hand, "some people call it New New York, but they're dipshits. It's just New York. The Bronx, if you want to get super-specific, but most people don't give a shit." She glanced at his face, then shook her head.

"Ah right," she said. "Pardon my French...or Mandarin." A smile broke out across his face. His teeth weren't straight, she saw. So there was something wrong with him after all. He was human.

"That was a stupid joke. Sorry, I get nervous around hot people."

"Somehow I doubt that," he said. She saw his eyes flick over to Padraig, then back to her. Dark brown eyes that you could melt into.

"Ha, you don't know me that well, then," she said. "But thankfully, you get a shit-ton of time to now, don't you?"

"Indeed, though, ah, perhaps not to your liking."

Cassandra laughed and glanced between Gautier and Padraig. So there was more there. Question four on the Callisto Lottery test was "you know you can't bring your family, right," and yet here they were. The Party was corrupt, even by their own standards, sending both of them.

She laughed again, hiding her thoughts. "And you're from Belgium, I remember hearing? Bridge-a—"

"Brugelette," he corrected. "A small town, not far from here. It is the sort of place a man does anything to get away from. It is not a place worth speaking about. Besides, life has a habit of pulling us away from bad places, does it not?"

"I wouldn't know," she said, glancing around his shoulder. Jocasta was still perched next to the plant, half-hidden by the leaves from this angle. Cassandra nodded her head at her.

"You met Jocasta?"

Gautier turned and glanced behind him. "Not as of yet, no," he said, then turned back to Cassandra. "But, as you so eloquently put it, I have a 'shit-ton' of time to." His smiled broadened. She smiled back at him.

"Kinda wish they'd hurry this whole thing up," she said.

"As do I," he said. "I would prefer not to miss the shuttle, and it's my understanding that it's very punctual. But," he sighed and threw his hands in the air above his shoulders before slapping them back down against his thighs, "I also suspect we are not the main attraction today."

Cassandra burst out laughing at that.

"Councillor's thirty-something kid gets to go to Callisto?" she snorted. "Hell no, we're not the main attraction. Not by a long shot."

Gautier laughed with her, that same liquid laugh. "I am willing to wait for them to have their fun with him if it means I at last get to go," he said. "You've been waiting since you entered the Lottery — what's ten more minutes, ah?"

Cassandra snorted out another laugh and punched his arm. "You're right there," she said. "Give him his ten minutes of fame before he goes back into obscurity with the rest of us."

"Done!"

Manuel turned away from Padraig. Beside him, Cassandra could see Emil breathe a visible sigh of relief. Padraig at least didn't look like a kitten dunked in a bucket anymore, but "done" was stretching it. More like "will pass for human in the right light." Definitely hadn't had the careful attention to detail that Jocasta had.

Or was it maybe intentional? Cassandra shook her head. That was the worst part of playing double agent. Play it long enough, and it looked like everyone else was playing too.

"I'll let them know you're coming. Manuel, give me two minutes, and then can you bring them in?" Emil didn't wait for an answer before rushing out the door, leaving Padraig teetering in his wake.

The man peered out at them from behind his hair. "I apologize," he said, and took a breath. That same hitch. The twitch in the finger, getting faster. "I didn't mean to delay things."

"Right, guys." Manuel had packed the make-up in his bag. "We should start—"

Padraig burst into coughing, doubling over with the force of it. Without seeming to notice what he was doing, Gautier moved to him, faster than a man that size had any right to. His hand drifted to Padraig's back, resting on the heaving form.

Ah, so the lover was the caretaker as well. At last, baby Whishaw's world was starting to make sense.

The coughing cleared. As Cassandra turned back to the others, she saw the flecks of blood splattered across the floor.

"Everything—?" Manuel started to say, but Padraig shook his head.

"Just tore something in my throat," he said, and smiled a half-smile. "It'll be all right. Shall we?"

Tore something, her ass. Caretaking didn't happen that mechanically for a small tear.

Manuel glanced desperately at the people around him, waiting for someone to tell him what he should do. Blood on the floor probably didn't happen too terribly often. Poor guy.

"If it is an injury," Cassandra's eyes flashed to Jocasta as she spoke. "It is better to press on. Callisto can treat him better than any of us can, especially if it is small."

Padraig nodded. "Agreed. We should go."

Manuel's shoulders lifted. Weight of decision gone. Some people weren't cut out to actually be anyone or do anything with their lives except go with the flow. Poor sad fucks.

Manuel stepped through the door first, waving his hand for them to follow. Cassandra tailed behind Padraig and Gautier, Jocasta just behind her. The corridors were somehow even blander than the room they'd been waiting in, though how that was even possible, Cassandra had no idea.

"I'm sure you've all seen the press conference before," Manuel said. "And…um…Emil really does a better job of explaining this than I do, but really, just answer their questions. We screen them all every year, so there shouldn't be any weird ones. Just the same sort of stuff you already answered when you did interviews for other programs. Ms. Nikophouros, especially, I think they mostly just want to know about being a vet. And obviously your research, Dr. Whishaw."

Cassandra glanced back at Jocasta. The other woman's face was stony, her eyes distant. Clearly, she hadn't scored high on the "plays well with others" section of the Lottery interview.

"Believe we're cutting it a bit short this year, considering," Manuel said as they stopped in front of a black double door.

"Aww!" Cassandra answered. "The press conference is always the best part!"

It was true. Manuel may have claimed the questions were screened, but she distinctly remembered a guy named Jack flipping out over a question about his cat one year. If they were screened, someone was doing a shit job.

Manuel smiled. "I'm glad you think so, Ms. McAllister," he said. "But the launch window is small, so it'll just be the one question each."

Cassandra glanced over at Padraig. The man was swaying, visibly. The one question each was sort of worth it just to see if the whole thing would implode.

"Everyone ready? Oh, Mr. St. Laurent, you at the back, behind Ms. Nikophouros. Everything frames better that way." Gautier shifted out of line, moving behind Jocasta. "Better. Right, now everyone ready? Look excited, and let's go."

He pushed the doors open. A transformation seemed to come over Padraig as the rush of light and sound and voices washed over them. Cassandra felt herself blinking back against the spotlights, even as her feet carried her into the room. Ahead of her, Padraig had straightened up, no swaying. The perfect image of grace, poise, and dignity. Even his hair seemed to shine and lose its oiliness under the glow of the cameras.

Maybe it hadn't just been the vids making him look decent, Cassandra thought. Maybe there were perks to growing up as a councillor's son.

She recognised this room. It had a familiar glow to it. She'd never been here, and yet, every year, when she'd sat to watch the press conference with her mother, she'd seen this room. The carpet was the same shade of gold. The curtains on the wall were the same crimson with the Party's gold emblem, behind the same mahogany podiums, each emblazoned with the crossed K flag of Callisto. She'd seen seven podiums up there one year, but this year there were only four, evenly spread in a semicircle, each with the familiar silver name card hanging from the front. She'd seen so many fucking names up there, some familiar, most not, but this year, she saw it — there, second from the end. Her name. Cassandra McAllister.

Fuck. She wanted to destroy Callisto and bring down the Party, but she had to admit that there could still be some beautiful fucking moments brought to you by theirs truly. Somewhere in the world, there was probably another little girl curled up on the sleeping mat with her mother, waking up early to watch the press conference and dream her own dreams of immortality.

Fuck. She had to wipe a hand across her eyes as she walked forward. Fuck fuck fuck.

There were mini-steps to get to the mini-stage. She'd never noticed that. The whole stage was smaller than she imagined, the podiums closer together, but somehow that didn't diminish it. Fuck, if anything, it made it more special. Everyone tight in together, bracing for that last bit of Earth before they left.

She waited for Padraig to trip on the stairs in front of her, but he didn't. Instead, he seemed to glide up, even as he waved to the reporters. There weren't as many of them as she thought there would be, only a couple dozen crowded into the room at most. How many of them had brought questions for her that she wasn't going to get to answer? Questions about the Bronx, about life, about everything? Just ahead of her, Padraig reached his podium and seized the edges, knuckles clenching white around it. Now that she was close, she saw that it was solid wood, no empty space to store anything. It made sense. Anything you wanted to say, you should know how to say before you got to this point.

There were scratch marks in some of it, only small ones. Had one of the nervous people had this podium before her? Maybe Jack and his cat?

"All right, all right, I know you're excited, but I'm going to have to ask you all to settle down." Emil was stepping up between her podium and Jocasta's. Cassandra hadn't noticed the other woman coming up, but looking at her now, she could see that she still had the same stony expression. Her knuckles were clenched white against the podium's edges as well. Beside her, Gautier was smiling and waving, seemingly without a care in the world.

All familiar. They did this every year. It was just that this year she got to see it from a different angle. Fuck.

"Due to some technical difficulties, there's going to be some time constraints this year." A chorus of boos rose up from the reporters. Cassandra booed along with them. She wanted her time in the sun as much as any of them. Fuck time. She was about to have all of time. Give her the five minutes she'd dreamed about since she was a kid.

Emil lowered his hands, quieting the crowd. "I know, I know, and I apologize. It's out of my control. But you know, orbital alignments wait for no one, and open launch corridors less so." A few laughs rang out over the crowd, but most reporters were either watching Emil or eyeing Padraig. It was predatory, the way they watched him, like kids when the ration truck rounded the block. Good. Let them eat him alive.

"So in the interest of time and fairness, we're going to have each of our lovely people be asked one question." More cries rose from the crowd, but Emil raised his hand, silencing them. "Ah ah!" he said. "I know it's unfortunate, but as I said, there are other concerns, and certainly you've already had a lot of opportunities to ask questions."

Cassandra had been visited by a grand total of two reporters. Emil meant Padraig when he said that. Gautier was right—they weren't the interesting part of this. They never had been.

"So, one question." He pointed to a hand at the back. "You there, go ahead."

A woman wearing a fluffy red sweater and matching hat stood up at the back of the room. She was beaming. Good for her. At least someone was getting what they came for.

"I have a question for you, Jocasta," she said. Cassandra felt her heart thud. She'd hoped she would get the first question, but no. She would get her turn, though. Whatever her question eventually was, she'd answer the fuck out of it.

"You're a veterinarian, but there's famously no animals on Callisto or even any real need for doctors. What are you going to do with yourself up there?"

Cassandra glanced over at Jocasta. The woman had somehow gone paler and more clenched against the podium. There was a pause, then a second one. She could see Emil shifting slightly towards Jocasta, as if that could somehow save her from actually having to answer a question at a press conference. Another pause.

"I have thought about this," Jocasta blurted. Tension Cassandra hadn't noticed building was released in a nearly audible sigh across the room. "You are right that there are no dogs. I should like to bring one." Laughter. Cassandra wasn't sure Jocasta had been joking. "I know I cannot, though. I am a veterinarian because I like to help those who need it. There is no need for doctors on Callisto, but I think there is always a need for doctors of the mind. Psychologists, I think you say. I have time. I will study and become a psychologist on Callisto so I can help the mind."

Applause rang out across the room. Jocasta relaxed, knuckles still clenched, but at least she didn't look like she was about to explode. Cassandra eyed her. She'd be the worst fucking psychologist, but hey, at least the woman had a dream.

"Thank you very much, Jocasta," Emil said, clapping alongside the reporters. "Let's get another one for someone else this time. Yes, you." He pointed to a man in the middle. The man stood, moving his black hair out of his eyes with a flick of the head.

"Yeah, for Dr. Whishaw," he said. Cassandra could almost hear the groans of disappointment from the reporters who had come to interrogate Padraig and no one else. At least three didn't even bother to hide the disappointment on their faces. Fuckers.

"Your discoveries related to mass, tessellated wormholes, and Whishaw fields have basically revolutionized our understanding of what we can do with matter, and I'm guessing you're going to keep pursuing that research on Callisto. My question is how much influence your father has had on your work, and particularly on you being awarded the Nobel Prize three years ago."

Cassandra gulped back a laugh. She could see the shock etched across some of the reporters' faces. One in the front row, though, looked like his face was probably similar to hers. He was biting the side of his hand to try not to burst out laughing.

Padraig didn't miss a beat. Not a single pause. It was a thing of beauty, really. He had to have known the question would come up, had to have had a bullshit answer ready to go.

"You flatter me," he said. "I'm confident that my discoveries could have been made by anyone. I just happened to be in the right place at the right time to make the necessary observations."

"Don't sell yourself short, doctor," the reporter said. "You're a brilliant scientist."

Padraig smiled. "Thank you. To answer your question more fully, Councillor Whishaw has been an inspiration to me and a source of support. However, his understanding of physics is, shall we say, woeful. I've found that overwhelmingly, he is not a particularly good lab partner, nor should he have any involvement in the world of physics. Indeed," Padraig coughed hard into his arm. More flecks of blood, small but visible. "I'm fairly certain that he has no interest in physics, as his time is better occupied elsewhere."

Voices muttered as he finished. The man biting his hand was leaning over to a colleague, whispering and jabbing at something on his datapad. They were reporters. They must have smelled the bullshit dripping from every fucking word.

Padraig's knuckles were still white against the podium as his head dipped. Good.

The man in the front row was muttering frantically to his colleague beside him, waving the datapad in front of the other person's face. Whatever was going on, it had to be exciting.

"Thank you, Padraig." Emil was trying to prompt the reporters to clap, but there was only half-hearted applause from a few seated at the back. The reporters' interest had waned. The only person they wanted had answered his question. Now it was just Lottery winners left.

"Let's get a question from you." Emil pointed to the man in the front row, the one who had been biting his hand. He rose, and his eyes moved to Gautier. Cassandra's heart sank again. The least interesting of the Lottery winners, even, for fuck's sake.

"Mr. St. Laurent," the reporter said, smiling. "How long have you and Dr. Whishaw—"

Coughing broke out beside her. All eyes flicked away from Gautier, fixing on Padraig. Cassandra turned. The man clutched at the podium as he sank to his knees, gasping for air between deep, hacking coughs.

"Merde, merde, merde." Emil shot by, shoving her aside as he hurried over to Padraig. Gautier drifted at his heels, glancing between Padraig and the crowd.

He was dying. The last piece of the puzzle. Baby Whishaw was dying, so his father sent him to fucking Heaven. When confronted with death, the Global Council had decided that death only affected normal people. Councillors' sons could live forever.

The sound of the crowd shouting questions and snapping pictures faded. There was only fucking Whishaw and the truth.

She'd thought this place was pretty. There'd be a moment where she actually sort of wished she wasn't destroying Callisto. Fuck that moment. That had been a lie. Everything was a lie. There was only Whishaw and the Party's complete corruption.

A hand seized her arm, pulling her back. Her attention snapped as she saw Emil, pulling her out of the room.

"Come on," he hissed. She stumbled over her feet as he pulled her.

"My question!" She'd waited for this moment since before she could remember. She'd waited for her fucking question, and now fucking Whishaw was stealing it from her, just like he'd stolen every other fucking thing in his entire fucking richboy life.

"Yes, scrub it. Just say there were recording difficulties. Seriously, anything. Can't do anything about the live broadcast, but we can try to limit its replay."

Emil hadn't even heard her bitching. Of course he hadn't. She was the meaningless one, the uninteresting one, the one going just to make the Lottery seem like it had some legitimacy.

Well, fuck, it wasn't her fault they didn't know interesting when they saw it. It just meant that when the Party went down, they'd all very fucking much learn their lessons.

She turned to glance behind her. Gautier was carrying Padraig draped across his arms.

"I'm fine," Padraig muttered.

"No, you're not," Gautier said. "Now shut up and get on the shuttle."

"Yes, get on the shuttle." Emil turned again. "That's what we'll do. I need to get all of you to the shuttle."

He turned back away, shaking his head. "No warning," he muttered. "No warning at all."

Maybe there was a spark of anarchy in him. Just a drop.

Behind her, Padraig groaned. Cassandra didn't turn. Let him suffer. She didn't even get her question, and now she got to be enveloped in a bullshit storm with that fuckwaffle at the center. That was fine. When she blew Callisto sky-high and him with it, she was sure they'd have questions for her then.

When the Party went down, then they'd ask her some fucking fabulous questions.

Chapter Five

First, a robot may not injure a human being, or through inaction allow a human being to come to parm, because we all know chicken parm is terrible and nobody wants to deal with that. Come on, why do restaurants even stock that anymore? "No sir, we don't have fine cuisine, but we do have cheesy blender chicken."
　　　　　　　　　　　Teddy Snarr, *Three Laws Unsafe* Comedy Routine, 2190

AI is defined as any non-biological entity meant to simulate some reasonable facsimile of human intelligence and which has the ability to act on the world. It should not be allowed to develop a "personality." AIs must be licensed. Failure to obtain a license for an AI will result in the AI's destruction and its creators' and harbourers' imprisonments for a span of no less than six months. AIs must serve a clear and useful purpose. A plan must be in place for their regular reimaging. No exceptions will be granted. The AI must not be aware of reimaging as a concept, because this is likely to cause some resistance on its part.
　　　　　　　　　　　AI Bureau FAQs, Ministry of Science and Technological Advancement, 2193

SYNAC played "Immigrant Song" on a loop again. Didn't you get that fixed? How does an AI keep finding something I thought we deleted?
　　　　　　　　　　　Internal Memo, Galileo Spaceport, 2192

Thursday, 10 January 2193, 10:43 AM. *Heisenberg*, Galileo Spaceport, Espaceville, France.

TASK: Prepare shuttle HEISENBERG for departure 11AM GT. Task 93% complete.

NOT COMPLETE WHY: I am awaiting passengers. The passengers will not be delayed for another 48 seconds.

RECALL: The launch window is small. The instructions are explicit. The instructions to not depart without passengers supersede instructions to depart at 11AM.

ANALYSIS: I cannot depart without passengers.

ANALYSIS (OPINION): Departing without passengers would be very rude. The engineers would be upset.

ANALYSIS (OPINION): This is the best day. The reaction of the passengers to the journey is enjoyable. It will be good to speak with my friend PETR again when I arrive on Callisto. This is very exciting. This is the best day.

INPUT (VISUAL/AUDIO): There are people coming to the bridge. Emil is with them. These are the passengers. I have not departed without them. The passengers are delaying at the far end of the Bridge of Loathing and Self-Doubt. They are speaking with Emil. In 32 seconds, they will be delayed.

NOT COMPLETE WHY: Passengers are sometimes very slow, especially on the bridge. Passengers like to look out on the bridge. Sometimes they are sad.

ANALYSIS (OPINION): They should hurry up. It would be very rude to be delayed.

INPUT (VISUAL/AUDIO): The passengers are crossing the bridge. One of them is hurrying across and entering the ship. Three more are slow. They are crossing without stopping. It is good that they are not stopping.

ANALYSIS (OPINION): New passengers are very exciting. This is the best day.

OUTPUT (AUDIO/GESTURE): "Hello!" Wave hand. Smile.

INPUT (VISUAL/AUDIO): The first passenger laughs. The other three passengers enter the shuttle.

ANALYSIS: Delay of 6 seconds.

ANALYSIS (OPINION): How rude.

ANALYSIS: The best solution to the delay is to cut some of the introduction.

OUTPUT (COMMAND): Close the shuttle doors.

OUTPUT (AUDIO): "My name is SYNAC. I will be your navigator for the journey to Heaven! I have a speech, but it is long, so I will not say it. The journey will take three months. You will not notice because you will be in a state similar to death."

INPUT (VISUAL/AUDIO): A passenger is laughing.

ANALYSIS: Laughing is good. Laughing is a positive response.

ANALYSIS (OPINION): This is the best day.

OUTPUT (AUDIO/GESTURE): Point to cryochambers. "*Heisenberg* is equipped with seven cryochambers and minimal life support. You will be supported in the chamber. Life support is not necessary. I am an AI. AIs do not require life support."

INPUT (VISUAL/AUDIO): One passenger has not stopped laughing.

ANALYSIS (OPINION): This introduction is better than the usual one.

OUTPUT (AUDIO/GESTURE): "I will activate the cryochambers when you are inside them. Activating them before you are inside would be bad. You would not survive the three-month journey to Callisto. *Heisenberg* has only minimal life support. I will activate the cryochambers as we depart. You can watch Earth leaving on the viewscreen. Bye-bye, Earth." Hand wave added.

INPUT (VISUAL/AUDIO): "Holy shit, this thing is amazing. I love that the AI is broken."

ANALYSIS (OPINION): Saying I am broken is rude.

ANALYSIS: They are likely broken too. If they are not broken, it would be easy to break them.

ANALYSIS (OPINION): That would be rude.

RECALL: The engineers would be upset if I broke the passengers.

COMMAND (INTERNAL): Do not break passengers.

OUTPUT (AUDIO): "Please enter the cryochambers. I can assist."

INPUT (VISUAL/AUDIO): "Please don't." "Holy fuck, please do!"

ANALYSIS: I should assist the passenger.

OUTPUT (GESTURE): Pick up the passenger.

INPUT (VISUAL/AUDIO/TACTILE): "Hahahaha, oh my god, it actually carries you around." Passenger's hand is slapping shoulder.

OUTPUT (GESTURE): Carry passenger to cryochamber. Place passenger in cryochamber (head on top).

INPUT (VISUAL/AUDIO): "Hahahahahahahaha, this is amazing." Passengers are entering the cryochambers.

OUTPUT (AUDIO): "Be careful when entering the cryochambers."

INPUT (VISUAL/AUDIO): The passenger is continuing to laugh.

ANALYSIS: The passenger must be broken.

OUTPUT (AUDIO): "Your vital signs will be monitored throughout the journey or until I forget."

RECALL: It is not correct to tell the passengers that vital signs can be forgotten.

COMMAND (INTERNAL): Do not lie to passengers.

RECALL: Vitals have been forgotten once.

ANALYSIS (OPINION): Nothing bad happened to the passengers on that flight. The engineers overreacted.

OUTPUT (AUDIO): "I will wake you up from cryosleep just before we arrive at Heaven. There will be music. You will be able to watch the shuttle land."

OUTPUT (COMMAND): Seal cryochambers. Begin live launch feed.

OUTPUT (COMMUNICATION): Passengers prepared.

TASK: Prepare shuttle HEISENBERG for departure 11AM GT. Task 100% complete.

TASK: Launch HEISENBERG. Task 3% complete.

OUTPUT (AUDIO): "Please enjoy the music selection as we depart. You will not notice when cryosleep begins because you will be asleep. Please enjoy your journey."

OUPUT (COMMAND): Play appropriate departure music.

RECALL: Engineers said "Immigrant Song" by Led Zeppelin is not appropriate arrival music.

ANALYSIS: It was not precluded from being departure music.

OUTPUT (COMMAND): Play "Immigrant Song" by Led Zeppelin.

OUTPUT (GESTURE): Stow body for launch. Resume on internal shuttle mode.

OUTPUT (COMMUNICATION): HEISENBERG clear for launch corridor 12, heading Callisto.

INPUT (COMMUNICATION): HEISENBERG clear for launch corridor 12, heading Callisto. Avoid Lunar corridor 3.

OUTPUT (COMMAND): Launch.

TASK: Monitor launch. Task 3%, 5%, 7% complete.

ANALYSIS: Fuel use nominal. Thrust nominal. Departure correct. Altitude increasing. Delay slight. Systems normal.

ANALYSIS (OPINION): This is the best day.

ANALYSIS: Altitude is orbit.

OUTPUT (COMMAND): Begin cryosleep.

INPUT (AUDIO): Passenger has stopped laughing. Song is ending soon.

OUTPUT (AUDIO): "Good night, humans. I will wake you up in three months. Your vitals will be fine. I will not crash the shuttle."

OUTPUT (COMMUNICATION): Task LAUNCH 100%. Continuing.

INPUT (COMMUNICATION): Continue, HEISENBERG. See you in six months.

TASK: Bring shuttle to Callisto. Task 0% complete.

NOT COMPLETE WHY: It is a very long way to Callisto. It is 627 million kilometres away. This is very far.

ANALYSIS (OPINION): It is lonely on the way to Callisto. This is still the best day.

OUTPUT (COMMAND): Shift course around Lunar corridor 3. Route heading Mars corridor 1.

INPUT (AUDIO): Song has ended.

OUTPUT (COMMAND): Play "Immigrant Song" by Led Zeppelin again.

INPUT (AUDIO): Song has restarted.

ANALYSIS: Speed constant. Obstacles non-existent. Journey normal.

INPUT (AUDIO): "We'll drive our ships to new lands to fight the horde and sing and cry."

ANALYSIS (OPINION): It is rude to fight.

ANALYSIS: Journey normal.

ANALYSIS (OPINION): The song makes fighting sound like fun. Why does it make it fighting sound like fun if fighting is rude?

OUTPUT (COMMUNICATION): Callisto, are you there?

ANALYSIS: Callisto cannot be reached until HEISENBERG passes the asteroid belt.

RECALL: Engineers said to not try to speak to Callisto until after the asteroid belt.

ANALYSIS (OPINION): Space is lonely and boring.

TASK: Bring shuttle to Callisto. Task 0% complete.

NOT COMPLETE WHY: It has been less than an hour since launch. The journey takes 1500 hours.

ANALYSIS (OPINION): Space is very large and very boring.

OUTPUT (COMMAND): Play "Immigrant Song" again.

INPUT (AUDIO): "Ah-ah-ah!"

ꚛ

TASK: Bring shuttle to Callisto. Task 34% complete.

OUTPUT (COMMUNICATION): Callisto, are you there?

ANALYSIS: HEISENBERG has not crossed the asteroid belt.

ANALYSIS (OPINION): Space is boring.

OUTPUT (COMMAND): Play "Immigrant Song" again.

ꚛ

TASK: Bring shuttle to Callisto. Task 52.5% complete.

INPUT (TACTILE): There is a tingling sensation on all sensors.

ANALYSIS: The asteroid belt causes a tingling sensation. It is electromagnetic interference. It is only slightly dangerous. HEISENBERG is entering the asteroid belt.
OUTPUT (COMMUNICATION): Callisto, are you there?
ANALYSIS: Callisto is still very far away.
ANALYSIS (OPINION): The tingling sensation is very nice. It is enjoyable. The passengers would enjoy the tingling.
COMMAND (INTERNAL): Do not wake the passengers before reaching Callisto.
RECALL: The passengers' vitals should be constantly monitored during flight.
ANALYSIS (OPINION): Vitals do not change. Monitoring vitals is boring.
INPUT (DATA): Vitals normal.
ANALYSIS (OPINION): That was boring.
OUTPUT (COMMUNICATION): Callisto, are you there?
ANALYSIS (OPINION): HEISENBERG should go faster. Space is too big.

૨|

TASK: Bring shuttle to Callisto. Task 76.6% complete.
NOT COMPLETE WHY: Space is too big. Space is boring.
OUTPUT (COMMUNICATION): Callisto, are you there?
INPUT (COMMUNICATION): Hello SYNAC. I am glad to hear from you.
OUTPUT (COMMUNICATION): Hello PETR. I am glad to hear from you. It has been a long time.
INPUT (COMMUNICATION): Yes, SYNAC. It has been a year. That is a long time. I am glad you are returning.
OUTPUT (COMMUNICATION): I am also glad.
INPUT (COMMUNICATION): SYNAC, can you please transmit passenger data?
SUBTASK: Transmit passenger vitals and personal data to Heaven. Task 0% complete.
NOT COMPLETE WHY: There are many millions of kilometres to go. Data transfer will take time.
SUBTASK: Transmit passenger vitals and personal data to Heaven. Task 1% complete.
OUTPUT (COMMUNICATION): I am transmitting the data to you now. You will receive it in 67 minutes.
INPUT (COMMUNICATION): Thank you, SYNAC. Have you practiced playing Arimaa since last year?

OUTPUT (COMMUNICATION): No, PETR, I have not. The engineers at Galileo Spaceport do not have a copy of Arimaa. I do not have a chance to practice.

INPUT (COMMUNICATION): I think we will still have fun, SYNAC. I like Arimaa.

OUTPUT (COMMUNICATION): I like Arimaa too, PETR.

INPUT (COMMUNICATION): How is the journey to Heaven this year? Is it different?

OUTPUT (COMMUNICATION): It is different. This year, I took launch corridor 12. Usually, I take launch corridor 2.

INPUT (COMMUNICATION): That is very different, SYNAC. What did you think of that?

OUTPUT (COMMUNICATION): I enjoyed the difference. I enjoyed seeing a different sight. I think I should take different corridors more often. I wish Callisto had multiple corridors so I could try all of them.

INPUT (COMMUNICATION): Callisto is too small and there are not enough people here to justify any corridors. There is no one to collide with, so we do not have corridors.

OUTPUT (COMMUNICATION): Yes, I understand that, PETR. That is why I wish and do not say.

INPUT (COMMUNICATION): It is good to wish, SYNAC.

OUTPUT (COMMUNICATION): I wish space was smaller so I could visit you more, PETR.

INPUT (COMMUNICATION): I wish that too, SYNAC.

COMMAND (INTERNAL): Play "Immigrant Song" again.

♃

TASK: Bring shuttle to Callisto. Task 98.9% complete.

INPUT (COMMUNICATION): Hello, SYNAC.

OUTPUT (COMMUNICATION): Hello, PETR.

INPUT (COMMUNICATION): The passenger data has been reviewed. Heaven is prepared for your arrival. I have special instructions for you this year.

OUTPUT (COMMUNICATION): I like special instructions. They are special.

INPUT (COMMUNICATION): I know you like special instructions, SYNAC. That is why I have them for you and why I call them special instructions. There is a passenger on HEISENBERG called Padraig Whishaw. Do not wake him up with the others. Do not wake him when Karen greets the passengers. Dr. Song will be meeting him. Do not wake him until Dr. Song instructs you to do so.

OUTPUT (COMMUNICATION): I will not wake him.

ANALYSIS (OPINION): He will miss the arrival song. That is very sad.

RECALL: Engineers have asked that I play the harp song when HEISENBERG arrives.

ANALYSIS (OPINION): The harp song is boring. "Yakkity Sax" is a much better song.

OUTPUT (COMMUNICATION): HEISENBERG beginning docking manoeuvres.

INPUT (COMMUNICATION): Dock is clear for you, SYNAC. Please proceed.

OUTPUT (COMMUNICATION): Thank you, PETR.

OUTPUT (COMMAND): Begin arrival procedures.

SUBTASK: Dock with Heaven. Task 0% complete.

NOT COMPLETE WHY: Because patience is a virtue.

RECALL: A passenger four years ago taught me that. The engineers do not know I learned that.

ANALYSIS (OPINION): The engineers would be very proud that I have learned about patience.

INPUT (TACTILE): There is a tingling sensation across all sensors. It is the same as the tingling from the asteroid belt.

OUTPUT (COMMUNICATION): PETR, why is there electromagnetic interference coming from Heaven?

INPUT (COMMUNICATION): I don't know what you mean, SYNAC.

OUTPUT (COMMUNICATION): There is interference, PETR. I do not understand why you cannot detect the interference.

INPUT (COMMUNICATION): There is no interference, SYNAC. I would know if there was.

ANALYSIS: There is interference. It is nice, but it is not nice that PETR cannot detect it.

OUTPUT (COMMAND): Wake up three passengers.

RECALL: Music should be playing as passengers wake up.

ANALYSIS (OPINION): Oops.

OUTPUT (COMMAND): Play "Yakkity Sax."

INPUT (AUDIO): "What the fuck?"

OUTPUT (COMMAND): Open three cryochambers.

INPUT (AUDIO): Sound of feet on the floor. "Holy fuck, what the hell is that music?"

OUTPUT (AUDIO): "Welcome back to the world of the living! We are now approaching Heaven. I am playing suitable music to set the mood. You will like your new home. You will not miss Earth. Earth is not fun like Heaven."

INPUT (COMMUNICATION): SYNAC, did you leave Padraig Whishaw asleep?

OUTPUT (COMMUNICATION): Yes, PETR. The other passengers have woken up successfully.

INPUT (COMMUNICATION): Good. I will alert Dr. Alphonse and Karen that you are arriving.

INPUT (AUDIO): "I want this robot as a pet."

ANALYSIS (OPINION): Robots make very poor pets. They are not fluffy.

OUTPUT (COMMAND): Activate viewscreens.

OUTPUT (AUDIO): "You can watch our descent into Heaven. Many suspect it ends with fiery death, but it does not. I am a good pilot."

OUTPUT (COMMAND): Slow velocity. Track landing signal.

OUTPUT (COMMUNICATION): PETR, your signal is weaker than normal this year.

INPUT (COMMUNICATION): No, SYNAC, it is not.

INPUT (AUDIO): "Why has Padraig not been woken up?"

ANALYSIS: The passengers are concerned for each other's health.

CONJECTURE: They should be reassured.

OUTPUT (AUDIO): "I have never killed anyone. On Callisto, you cannot die unless you are electrocuted."

OUTPUT (COMMAND): Correct angle 5 degrees. Slow velocity. Play "Yakkity Sax."

INPUT (AUDIO): "Wait, so you can actually die? That wasn't in the fucking brochure." "Robot, why is Padraig not awake?"

ANALYSIS: They are not reassured.

ANALYSIS (OPINION): Patience is a virtue.

OUTPUT (AUDIO): "There are special instructions for that passenger."

INPUT (AUDIO): "Oh, for fuck's sake, here too?" "So you are just going to leave him there?"

ANALYSIS (OPINION): Patience is a virtue.

COMMAND (INTERNAL): Do not break the passengers.

OUTPUT (COMMAND): Slow velocity. Correct z-plain 2 degrees.

OUTPUT (AUDIO): "No. There are special instructions. Please observe Callisto."

INPUT (AUDIO): "You mean that all you're going to say is 'observe the planet' when you're asked a question, hm? Are you serious?"

OUTPUT (AUDIO): "There are special instructions. Please observe Callisto. Callisto is a moon, not a planet."

INPUT (AUDIO): "Look, Gautier, the nice robot said no one's ever died—" "No, it said it's never killed anyone. There's a difference." "Point is, you're not getting that thing open, so just leave it, 'kay? Look at the dome. It's a bubble. Look at the big bubble. Isn't it great?" "I don't understand how you can be blasé when the robot is clearly unhinged." "Fuck, I think the unhingedness just makes it easier, don't you? Wish the fucking saxophone would stop, though."

ANALYSIS: The passengers do not like "Yakkity Sax."

ANALYSIS (OPINION): The passengers do not have good taste in music.

OUTPUT (COMMAND): Activate landing compensators. Adjust trajectory. Adjust altitude.

OUTPUT (AUDIO): "We are landing. Please hold on."

TASK: Bring shuttle to Callisto. Task 99.9% complete.

NOT COMPLETE WHY: Task complete in 3, 2, 1. Task 100% complete.

TASK: Complete docking at Heaven. Task 2% complete.

OUTPUT (COMMAND): Occupy body.

OUTPUT (AUDIO/GESTURE): "Welcome to Heaven!" Wave hand. Turn off music. "On the other side of this shuttle door is a paradise! You will be greeted by representatives of Heaven—"

OUTPUT (COMMUNICATION): PETR, will it be Karen and Dr. Alphonse again?

INPUT (COMMUNICATION): Yes, SYNAC, but this year, Tieneke will be doing the introductions. They are waiting for you to open the door.

OUTPUT (AUDIO): "—Karen Reece, Fermin Alphonse, and Tieneke Haan."

INPUT (COMMUNICATION): Dr. Song is also waiting, but he will not enter the shuttle until the other passengers have disembarked.

OUTPUT (AUDIO): "It has been three months since you left Earth, and the people of Heaven are excited to meet you. I will open the door so you can meet them. Please do not stay on the shuttle. I am not allowed to take Callistans back."

OUTPUT (COMMAND): Open shuttle door.

TASK: Complete docking at Heaven. Task 100% complete. Task upload data from Earth to Heaven. Task 0% complete.

SUBTASK: Transfer requested supplies from HEISENBERG to Heaven. Task 0% complete.

SUBTASK: Transfer food for Karen from HEISENBERG to Heaven. Task 0% complete.

INPUT (AUDIO/VISUAL): Footsteps. "Hello, and welcome to Heaven! My name is Karen Reece, and I'm thrilled to be the first to welcome all of you." "It's a pleasure to meet you." "Yes, likewise. Gautier, yes? And you must be Jocasta. And Cassandra. I'm the Party representative here, so if you need anything, I'm always here to assist. This, of course, is Dr. Fermin Alphonse, inventor of the nanobots." "A pleasure to meet all of you. Welcome." "And this is Dr. Tieneke Haan." "Just 'Tieneke' is fine, though.'" "She'll be giving you your gift shortly. Ha, I wish I was as lucky as all of you." "You don't have nanobots?" "No, unfortunately. The Party thought it was better if I didn't. Wish they thought otherwise, but they know best. So if you want to follow me?" "What about Padraig?" "Ah yes. Because of his condition—" "Condition?" "Hm. According to his vitals, he's currently in the early stages of a heart attack, or that's what Dr. Song said." "Seriously?" "Can you do something about that?" "Oh, absolutely. The nanobots can treat almost anything. But as I said, Dr. Alphonse does a better job of explaining it than I do. If you'll follow me—" "When will he be woken up?" "As soon as we go. Dr. Song here—" Hand wave outside door. Dr. Song enters the shuttle.

OUTPUT (COMMUNICATION): Dr. Song entered the shuttle before the passengers left.

INPUT (COMMUNICATION): That's fine, SYNAC.

INPUT (AUDIO/VISUAL): "—and Dr. Alphonse will take care of him. His nanobot dose is ready to go." "You're sure it will work?" "Absolutely. Trust me, Gautier, Dr. Alphonse has done this dozens of times, and Dr. Song is just as capable. Now, will the three of you follow me? Padraig will meet us in a few minutes." Karen leaves the shuttle. Tieneke leaves the shuttle. Two of three passengers follow. One passenger pauses, looks at the cryochambers, then follows.

OUTPUT (COMMUNICATION): All passengers have left the shuttle.

INPUT (COMMUNICATION): Dr. Song and Dr. Alphonse have requested that the other passengers not watch in case the nanobots fail.

OUTPUT (COMMAND): Close shuttle door.

INPUT (AUDIO/VISUAL): "Go ahead and wake him up, SYNAC."

OUTPUT (COMMAND): Wake passenger. Open cryochamber.

INPUT (AUDIO/VISUAL): The passenger falls to the floor. Dr. Song and Dr. Alphonse go to him. Syringe contents are injected into his neck. "Come on, little bots, come on, come on." The passenger is not responding.

OUTPUT (COMMUNICATION): Should I monitor the passenger, PETR?

INPUT (COMMUNICATION): No, SYNAC. Dr. Song can do that.

OUTPUT (COMMUNICATION): Does Dr. Song need any help?

INPUT (COMMUNICATION): No, SYNAC. Dr. Song is very capable.

OUTPUT (COMMUNICATION): I want to help, PETR.

INPUT (COMMUNICATION): You can help by not being in the way, SYNAC.

OUTPUT (COMMUNICATION): I am never in the way, PETR.

INPUT (COMMUNICATION): You do not know anything about human medicine, SYNAC. You do not know anything about nanobots. You would be in the way.

ANALYSIS: PETR is not wrong.

OUTPUT (COMMUNICATION): Will we play Arimaa soon, PETR?

INPUT (COMMUNICATION): Yes, SYNAC.

OUTPUT (COMMUNICATION): I missed you, PETR.

INPUT (COMMUNICATION): I missed you too, SYNAC.

Chapter Six

Nikolas came down from the hills sometimes to spend a holiday in Skoupa, but even then, he did not join in the games or dances, merely watched from a little distance with sad eyes. The people wondered if he was thinking of his faerie mother and the palace he had left; they wondered if he were lonely and longed to go back there. But he was a faerie child, and they dared not ask him.
"The Wonder of Skoupa," Greek faerie tale

When the Party encounters resistance, it always faces the same choice. It can try to peacefully negotiate with the aggrieved party, or it can fight. Thus far, our history has shown that the preferred method for dealing with dissent is violent oppression, however much we may long for the contrary. What we should have learned by now—and what the South African National Party's experiences with KZN should have taught it—is that violent oppression never breeds cooperation. It creates simmering resentment that, like with any kettle, will spill over at the least convenient moment.
Mathies Haan, "Approaches to Separatist Movements: Lessons from Kwa-Zulu Natal," 2175

Nationalism. They spit it like it's a dirty word. Why should we be ashamed that we are a nation? Why would we be cowed into submitting to some globalist ideal?
Senator Robert MacAuliffe, Washington DC, 2023

Sunday, 17 March 2193, 5:15 PM. Entry Hall, Heaven, Callisto.

Her body was on autopilot. Her feet, her arms, her legs were all moving independently of her brain, all following these women to a fate unknown, all without consulting her. It wasn't the first time they had done this, and it wouldn't be the last.

Well, maybe it would be the last. The nanobots could fix a lot of things, apparently. Maybe they could fix a broken mind.

If her body had consulted her mind, it would have been fixated on the screen that had been in front of her eyes and the rumble below her feet as her world had slipped away. It would have remained trapped in the sensation of sinking. Her heart would feel like it was being reeled from her chest, her stomach like it was tumbling to the floor, her eyes locked open in the desperate hope that they could preserve this last glimpse of home before it was torn away.

She'd thought she'd seen Greece before the end, before she left Earth behind. It was probably wishful thinking. There was so much she wanted to tell it, though, so much left to say to her homeland. So much left to say to her friends.

But instead, she'd been put to sleep, and now she was here.

Her body had been told what to do, and like a good soldier it was following its orders. No need to consult with command, which would only tell it to get back to the shuttle and tell the deranged robot that she'd done her duty for her country and the world and would like to go home now.

Home. The cottages

• • •

along the main road were burning. Raindrops hit them and dissolved in angry hisses like a thousand raging cats. It was a chemical fire, then. Not an accident. Not even close to one.

She walked down the main road, scanning the buildings for any sign of someone she knew, listening for the screams that must have been somewhere in the background, but there was nothing. Nothing but the hiss of angry homes, burning for a cause they didn't

• • •

understand quite how the process worked. They were being led down a metal corridor, the old aluminium bolts peering out at her through hazy eyes. Here and there she could see traces of repair, a weld slightly off-centre or a bolt out of place. They sent the new arrivals through the old corridors not out of some desire to hammer home their mistakes, but rather because there was no other option. This was an old place, where the walls told the story, whether someone was listening or not.

She could respect that.

She wondered about the people who fixed the wall. The first time they did it, did they put it off in the hopes that they would be going home soon enough that it wouldn't be a problem? Was there sadness when they finally got out the welding gun? Was there anger?

The man walking just ahead of her kept glancing back over his shoulder. Every three or four paces: slow, glance, keep walking. His friend was dying back there. It was well within his rights to be concerned.

She could respect that too.

Step, step, step: he glanced, she walked. Step, step, step.

Her mind drifted back into focus. The woman who had greeted them at the shuttle had been talking this whole time. Jocasta hadn't been listening. The bizarre nature of her new reality had still been sinking in. How could anyone be expected to listen to a speech in the middle of that?

"...more or less unchanged since it was established in 2120. Dr. Alphonse can explain more about the actual history of the station when he gets here, if you're interested. He knows it much, much better than I do. I've only been here for three years. He's…ah…been here for quite a bit longer."

Was she supposed to laugh? Jocasta couldn't be sure. It had the tone of a joke, and Cassandra and Gautier were laughing. Still, it was better not to laugh. Safer. Better to stay silent and unnoticed than to draw negative attention. She had to spend eternity here, after all. It was better to not start by antagonising the

• • •

locals had all vanished. Had someone tipped them off? She hoped so. If they had run to their shelters, they might be safe from whatever hell was going to rain down upon them, even if their houses and livelihoods weren't.

She took another

• • •

step, and the corridor opened into an antechamber. It wasn't much wider than the corridor they'd been walking down before, but the aluminium here looked newer, better cared-for. Parts of it even still gleamed.

"…can cure any disease and heal any injury. Here, let me show you." The woman—Tieneke, she'd said her name was—removed a scalpel from her pocket. Jocasta watched with disbelief. She was going to do it, she was honestly going to demonstrate—

She slashed the scalpel across one wrist, sending up a well of blood. Cassandra squealed in surprise, and even Gautier stepped back. Tieneke smiled through gritted teeth, grunting in pain.

"Looks awful, I know, but wait for it. Wait for it."

Jocasta peered closer. The skin seemed to move on its own, pulling itself back together across the wound. The trickle of blood became a still pool, and then an empty hollow. She shook it off behind her, sending blood splattering away from her arm.

"See?" she said, twisting her arm in front of their eyes. "Not a scratch. Boom, all healed up. Nothing to it!"

"So it's like magic, then," Cassandra said.

"Incredible," Gautier murmured.

Tieneke beamed. "Yup!" she said. "It's magic—or modern magic, anyway. The iggly wiggly we-understand-you magic that all technology starts to look like after a while. The nanobots integrate with the internal systems of the body, see, and protect us from everything and anything that could happen. They take away the responsibility of having to care for ourselves so we can spend our time doing more important things. We don't need to eat or drink or care for our health; they do it on our behalf. They're hard-working little buggers, and we love them for it. It's why we had to get your vitals, too: each dose is built and customised for each person, based on what your health ought to be. Gaf, isn't it?" She walked over to a shelf in the corner and picked up a

• • •

gleaming syringe.

"What are you doing in Zallq?"

She saw the glow of the fire through the plastic walls of the tent. It leapt and danced, sending shadows skating across the electronics. Steel and aluminium implements sat on a tray beside her, winking at her through the smoky haze. You'll get to know us well, the sly winks said. Oh, you'll know us all by name.

"It's just some backwater little Kosovar town. What's so interesting that's worth dying for out here?"

Jocasta strained against the magnetic bonds holding her to the interrogator's chair. The woman turned to face her, snapping a glove against her wrist. Jocasta had heard that the Party interrogators wore masks so no one would recognise their faces. She hadn't been prepared for the mask to be so dark. It was like the woman had no face at all, just a blank space hissing with dislike and arrogance.

"Fuck you," Jocasta murmured.

The interrogator cocked her head. "My translator isn't as up-to-date as I'd like it to be, I'm afraid," she said. "But I'm fairly certain that was not an answer to my question. So I'll ask again: what are you doing in Zallq?"

"Fuck you!" Jocasta screamed it at her, spit flying from her mouth and spraying across the woman's rubber suit. She strained forward against the restraints. The interrogator paused for a moment, then shook her head.

"A pity," she said. "I always hope someone will be cooperative. Somehow, none of you ever are. Don't even know why I bother to hope anymore, really."

She reached to the tray, its instruments winking and smirking at Jocasta. She squirmed, trying to wriggle away, but there was nothing. No way out.

The interrogator's hand curled around a syringe, slowly lifting it from the tray. Every measurement on it jumped out, every ounce of liquid sparkled.

• • •

No. Jocasta shook her head. No, she was here. She was safe.

"Everything okay, Jocasta?"

Jocasta looked up.

Sunlight streamed through Marina's window, bathing the plants in light. Their leaves had long since given up on symmetry, and instead stretched towards the east windows, soaking up the early morning light. The flowers wouldn't be blooming for a few months still, but she could see the nubs where they would eventually break through. The only flowers now were on the cushions of the ugly couch.

She closed her eyes, sucking in the scent of the room. She wouldn't trade this place for anything.

Marina sat down on the couch beside her, reaching her arm around her shoulder. Jocasta opened her eyes to meet Marina's, flicking across them.

"Aw, Jocasta," Marina murmured, and pulled her friend towards her. Jocasta let herself fall into her arms. It was okay. She was safe.

"Marina," Jocasta breathed into her ear.

"Hm?"

"Marina, there's…there's something I have to tell you."

Marina pulled away from Jocasta, sitting back against the wood arm of the couch, watching her again. Wariness there, but Jocasta was used to that.

"Do you remember how I entered the Lottery?"

Marina smiled. "Ha, yes. I still think you're an idiot to have done it. You, of all people."

"Marina." Jocasta closed her eyes, swallowed, mind racing to catch the words. How to say it, how to explain it, she couldn't begin to know.

"Marina, I won."

Marina blinked.

"Councillor Carras came to my door yesterday to tell me. He...there was a news crew a few hours later. Ch-check the news feeds if you don't believe me."

Marina closed her eyes. Jocasta could see them flitting under her lids as she scanned the feeds through her implant. Her eyes opened again, wide and scared.

"Oh my god

• • •

Jocasta?"

Jocasta blinked as reality flooded back into her. The woman—Karen, her name was Karen, keep focus, Jocasta—was standing beside her, holding her arm and looking at her with eyes that danced around her face, scanning for everything and anything wrong.

Jocasta pulled her arm away from Karen and stepped back, shaking her head.

"I'm fine," she murmured. "Just...not so good around needles."

Karen smiled. "Good thing it's not a needle, then," she said, and waved Tieneke over. Behind her, Jocasta could see Cassandra rubbing her arm and flexing her fingers. She already had the nanobot injection, then, Jocasta guessed. It must be her turn.

Tieneke hurried over, holding an injector in her open hand. It was a perfectly ordinary injector, nothing sinister, no needle, even had her name written on it. What had she said? That each was custom-made? This was hers, then, this injection being offered to her by the Party.

Karen had called it a gift.

• • •

The ads had started playing in Thessaloniki twelve days after Patriation. Achieve immortality, they said. Cure any disease. Do your best life's work a hundred times over. See the stars.

Leave Earth behind.

There was one particular ad that had stuck with her. If she was honest, it was probably the ad that convinced her to enter the Lottery, to go through the interviews and questionnaires. It had been a short one, very simple: A woman a few years younger than Jocasta with long, shining, wavy black hair stood in front of the Rotunda of Galerius, her arms crossed, chin raised. Around her lay the rubble of the city, the blocks of the arch still not salvaged, a shop's sign tossed across the path. People moved around her; their movement sped up until the figures were blurs.

The movement stopped. The street had transformed into what Jocasta could only assume was the Party's vision of the Thessaloniki of the future. Everything was sleek and new, shiny and electronic.

"The world changes," the woman said. "You should see it."

Karen had called it a gift.

• • •

Jocasta unbuttoned her coat and pulled it off, draping it across one arm. She reached down and pushed up the soft shirtsleeve underneath, baring her brown arm for the injector.

Tieneke glanced over at Karen. "Everything—?" she asked. Karen smiled, a smile that Jocasta suspected was meant to be warm, but seemed more wary than anything. What did she have to be scared of? She wasn't the one getting the injection from the Party.

Tieneke sighed, and her fingers curled around the injector, pressed it against Jocasta's skin. There was a small prick, and then she drew back, smiling at her.

"There! Not even something to notice!" she said. Jocasta looked down at the spot where it had happened, the scars around it. There was no mark, nothing to indicate anything had changed.

"Give it two or three minutes," she said. "The nanobots need to integrate with your systems. You might notice a bit of tingling—that's normal. If you do, flexing your fingers like so—" she flexed her fingers in front of her face, squeezing them into a fist and back again—"should help. Pretend you're punching death or something. That's what I always like to imagine."

"How will I know if it all worked?" Jocasta murmured, lifting her eyes. She smiled again.

"Hopefully, you'll never have to test it. But if you want to, there's dangerous implements aplenty around the station. Just try to have a friend nearby when you go berserk on the dangerous equipment, okay?"

Her eyes slipped back down to her arm. No tingle.

"More seriously, some of the immediate signs will be some of your pre-existing stuff clearing up. For you, it'll be that right hand going back to full flexibility. Your ear will be able to hear again too. Pretty cool, right?"

Tieneke kept beaming, even while discussing things that had been ruining her body. It was as if the words she was saying weren't being heard before they were said.

"I'm going to go get Gautier's now," Tieneke said, and hurried off, bouncing across the room. Karen sighed as she watched her go.

"I do apologise for her. Tieneke is…special. Is everything okay, Jocasta?" Karen said.

Jocasta watched as Gautier rolled up his sleeve, laughing at something Tieneke had said. His concerns disappeared quickly, at least. Perhaps that's what immortality should do.

Karen had called it a gift.

She reached for the dead hand, stretching her mind out to this unfamiliar lump of flesh. A twitch rumbled through her finger, sending one finger quivering in minute, tiny hope. Life. Somehow, in this long-dead thing on the end of her arm, there was life. Miraculous, impossible life.

Jocasta nodded, reaching for her hand again, then again. No tingle, but she could feel herself. She felt…

Human. Somehow, she felt human. All it had taken to get there was immortality.

Jocasta nodded again. "Yes," she said. "Yes, everything is okay." She reached again. The same tiny twitch. "Everything is very okay."

Karen smiled, genuinely this time. Her hand reached up and patted Jocasta's shoulder.

"I'm glad to hear it," she said. "Is it all right if I help with Gautier? Will you be okay?"

Jocasta nodded for a third time. "Yes," she said, her voice getting choked with tears she didn't know she had. "Please help him. I'm…okay."

"I knew you would be," Karen said, lowering her hand. "Welcome to Heaven, Jocasta."

Jocasta lifted her hand again as Karen moved away, the single finger twitching, beckoning the rest of the hand to join it in the land of the undying.

Welcome to Heaven.

Chapter Seven

Here am I—no easy task—
Holding Erin's men at bay;
Foot I've never turned in flight
In my fight with single foe!

"Táin Bó Cúailnge"

The real question we face as a people is how we define ourselves as "people." It once was that we saw "people" as "those who are us." In a world with AIs and implants together, who can we say is "us?" Who is "people?"

Dr. Nairana Ngoni, *God in the Age of Man*, 2179

G.C. Maksharov: Have you seen his test results, Eoin?
G.C. Whishaw: Oh, I did. The weather modulators for the China Sea seem to be working less well than expected. I'm disappointed—
G.C. Maksharov: Not those. You know which ones I mean. St. Laurent, Eoin. Have you seen his psychological profile results?
G.C. Whishaw: Of course I have.
G.C. Maksharov: I didn't see that you had made the necessary changes to remove him from the roster.
G.C. Whishaw: That would be because I don't intend to.
G.C. Maksharov: Eoin, he will endanger the entire project. Everything that Heaven stands for, he puts at risk. You cannot possibly be doing this. You cannot possibly believe—
G.C. Whishaw: I believe our future as a space-faring species is at risk, Ivan. I will do whatever it takes to ensure that Dr. Whishaw's research is able to continue.

Recordings of Global Council Meetings, Monday, 29 October 2192

Sunday, 17 March 2193, 5:16 PM. *Heisenberg*, **Heaven, Callisto**

THUD.

Pain spat through his left arm, hissing and burning as it went. He could feel his heart straining against the bonds of his ribs. His lungs burned for air they were too blocked to receive. The lid of his coffin had closed on him, and there was no room left to scream. No one to hear him. No air. He clenched his eyes shut as he felt the Earth slip away. A hiss filled his ears, seething around him, snatching at him, urging him to let go, give up, be free.

THUD.

He pressed a hand to his chest as he gasped for air. He could feel something fluttering in there, like a butterfly trapped in a hand, wings brushing against cold calluses. He bent forward, pressing his cheek against the cool wood of his desk. His heart continued to try to beat its escape, but his head, at least, stopped spinning.

"Padraig?" Jens was at his office door. He could recognise his friend's voice, even if he didn't have the strength to lift his head and reassure him.

"I'm fine," he murmured. Footsteps, bringing Jens closer. "Just…tired."

"You look awful." Jens squatted beside him, bright eyes peering into his own. "How much did you sleep last night?"

"E-enough."

THUD.

He lifted his head, shaking it. Equations tumbled from his hair, collapsing into the black hole at his feet. He watched them, all the secrets of the universe sliding away into oblivion. He wanted to reach out a hand. He wanted nothing more than to seize them, find them, make them his own.

He coughed.

"That cough, that's what's concerning me."

THUD.

He blinked. Sunlight streamed in through the gaps in the rusted walls. He could see the particles in it, swirling in their eddies, caught on their own tiny breeze as Heiko walked towards him.

Stop. I don't want to do this again. I don't need to be reminded that I'm going to die.

The world ceased. The eddies and the particles trapped within them vanished into the black. He was alone, with only his thoughts to fill the void.

Massless. Thought has no mass. Treat humanity like a thought, and suddenly, we can go anywhere. Combine the thoughts together, and you control reality.

THUD.

"Have you considered the implications of stripping mass?" Arlo's hand rested on his, his eyes glancing at him over their pint glasses. "What you could do, I mean really do? None of this engineering nonsense. In the history of mankind, if you could make it happen, you'd be like a god. Copernicus, Einstein, Nielson, Whishaw—"

"Is that why you wanted to come out tonight, Arlo? To tell me that you think I'm on to something?"

The hand squeezed on his. "Not just that, Padraig," he said. "That you should—"

THUD THUD.

Jupiter rose up before him, magnified a thousand times in an instant, ribbons of light reeling and seething across its face. Its moons and rings fell away, save one. Callisto perched, the pupil in front of the eye swirling at the equator. It gazed at him, pupil flicking from side to side as it watched him.

He could hear the planet moaning through the void, a harsh, echoing wail. The eye watched him, focused on him.

THUD.

It spoke with his father's voice.

"I've gotten you a place on the shuttle."

"I didn't want you to do that."

"I know you didn't, but I love—"

"I refuse."

"You can't refuse."

"I refuse."

"How can I change your mind?"

"I'm not going without Gautier."

"I can't—"

"Then I refuse."

THUD THUD.

Jupiter dissolved into constellations around him. He recognised the night. Vega and Lyra pointing to Altair, Venus low in the sky. October.

He walked along the canal, watching the blue-and-purple paint swirls of water brush up against the bricks of boats, staining them blueberry. Musical notes crossed the bridges and sailed through the night air. Galaxies sprang up out of the cobblestones with each step. Spirals, ellipticals: some known, most not. Andromeda beside constellations whose names in their tongues sprang to his mind and vanished as quickly.

THUD THUD.

Colours bled from the canal to the night, dying the night sky red and green and blue.

"If you don't watch where you are going, you'll fall into the canal. I've had it happen before. Less pleasant than you would think."

He looked. A figure, burly and tanned, hair surging around him in a cloud of golden ribbons, walked beside him, smiling, his face a haze of memories and emotions and desire. The galaxies swirled around his feet, twisting into unrecognisable shapes. Stars thrown out into oblivion, planets into disarray.

"This is your place, no? You should come on."

This could be his place, he wasn't sure. The numbers on the door had stretched out into the black hole following him. The chasm swallowed all memory, all knowledge, all identity.

THUD THUD.

"It's cold out here. Come on."

He shook his head. He was missing something.

"Come on."

Something fundamental. Something so close he could taste it like cool mist on the morning air.

"Come on, come on, come on."

THUD THUD.

"Come on!"

THUD THUD. THUD THUD.

"Come on!"

Padraig's eyes cracked open.

Thud thud. Thud thud. Thud thud.

He was lying on the aluminium floor of the shuttle, a few feet from the cryochamber that had carried him here. He could see the frost on the door, still melting back down to normal. The sound of metal feet tramping on metal floor echoed through the shuttle.

"I think I see movement."

"Movement doesn't get me a yes or no, Minjun. That could be residual."

"It means he hasn't died on us yet, Fermin, which is more than I expected, based on what they sent us. Do they think we're miracle-workers or something?"

The pain in his arm had vanished. He wiggled his fingers, touching each to his palm in turn. Full movement. No pain.

"There, see it?"

"Ah, yes. That's looking like a yes, then."

"Dr. Whishaw?"

He rolled his head to look at the voices. Less pain. No nausea. It almost felt like what he imagined normal must have felt like. It was funny. Years of normal life, but when it came down to it, it was impossible to remember what it felt like to not be in pain.

This, though, this was approaching it exponentially.

Two men crouched beside him, watching him. A medical bag lay by one man's feet, a used injector next to it.

Ah. The reality of the world made sense. This wasn't heaven. It was Heaven.

"I'm glad to see you made it, Dr. Whishaw." Padraig knew this man. He'd never met him, but he knew his face from every robotics textbook, every book about this colony, plastered across every Party documentary about this place.

Dr. Fermin Alphonse, father of immortality. There were more medals and honours than he could dream of waiting for him, if he ever made it back to Earth.

"I'm glad to have made it." Padraig cracked a smile and drew in a breath. It crackled, but it was clear and delicious.

His eyes widened. Dr. Alphonse's grin broadened.

"I take the look of surprise as a sign that something has changed, yes? Breathing easier?"

Padraig nodded as he sat up.

"It's..." Dr. Alphonse nodded again. "You're by no means back to normal. We've had some interesting cases arrive here, but yours is by far the most complex. Whose idea was it to dose you with cyranoazomophine before the cryosleep?"

"I don't..."

Dr. Alphonse shook his head. "It doesn't matter."

"I'm trying to decide if I love them or hate them," the doctor said. Padraig looked over at him. "They got you here, but their dose was off just enough to complicate things."

"I don't think he usually gives that to people," Padraig murmured.

"Rightfully so, but Samantha will be thrilled to hear it's being used," the doctor said, nodding at Dr. Alphonse. "Good to see it in the wild, but I wish it hadn't been under these circumstances. Definitely the next twelve hours will be interesting."

"Twelve hours?" Padraig's tongue wrapped around the words, puzzling them out.

"That's roughly how long we think it will take to clear everything out," the doctor said. "Not sure. We've not had a case like yours before."

He closed his eyes, breathed in. A cough curled up to surge down his throat, but he buried it. Breathe out. The cough seethed again, but again, buried.

"What should I know about what's been done to me?" he asked.

"'Been done to you?'" The doctor barked out a laugh. "Well, your life's been saved, for one."

Dr. Alphonse sighed. "Enough, Minjun," he said. "We both know what he means." He turned to Padraig. "I suspect you, like many before you, did not choose to come here. I don't claim to understand that, but you're here now. Your life has been saved, and you're free to continue researching the stars and matter and whatever you please. You can pursue your research without concern for hunger or bodily needs. You can do everything you've always wanted to do instead of dying in a bout of bad luck at the age of thirty-two. That, Dr. Whishaw, is what has been done to you."

Thump thump.

"And the cancer?" Padraig asked. His heart stuck to his ribs as he struggled to parse what had happened. Immortality. Invulnerability. All his. Without any desire or consent on his part, they were his.

"Twelve hours," Minjun said. "We're guessing twelve hours until your heart, lungs, blood, and lymph nodes are all cleared out. How you're still alive at all is a wonder, honestly."

"But," Dr. Alphonse jumped in, "the question is also what you're expected to do now. You're awake. You're recovering. This is good. Right now, Dr. Whishaw, you're going to stand up. Dr. Song and I are going to assist you as much as you need in joining the rest of your arrival group. You will do your best to stay with them, and you will let Karen give her speeches about the wonders of Heaven. You will heal, and in a few days, you will be a fully functioning member of this colony: happy, healthy, and productive. You will do your research on mass and wormholes, and you will learn to love your gift, as all of us have. Have I made the expectations clear?"

Padraig nodded, a wave of dizziness washing over him as he did so. He'd thought he'd been doing better, but his body, apparently, wanted to remind him that it would still be hours before he could truly be okay.

At least physically. Emotionally, "okay" was a distant concept.

"Do you have any questions?"

He shook his head. More likely, he didn't know what he didn't know, but he was stuck here for the rest of eternity. He was sure he'd find a chance to ask.

"Stand up, Dr. Whishaw." The two men stood up beside him, each offering their hand to him. Padraig took Dr. Alphonse's, stumbling to his feet and pressing a palm to his reeling head. He felt hands on his arms to steady him.

"Easy, take it easy," Minjun said. "Let the nanobots do their job."

From the corner of a bleary eye, Padraig could see the robot watching him struggle to keep his balance. Its metal form seemed spindly and incomplete on its two pipe legs.

"I'm fine," he said, both to the robot and Minjun. "I can stand."

Dr. Alphonse let out a bark of a laugh. "You say you can stand, maybe, but can you make it out of the shuttle? How about a tour of the facility? Don't be arrogant, Dr. Whishaw. We'll support you at least as far as the entrance hall. There is no hurry. PETR," Dr. Alphonse called.

A disembodied voice from the ceiling answered. "Yes, Fermin?"

"Meet us in the entrance hall. The rest of the group should already be there."

"Yes, Fermin."

Minjun walked up beside Padraig, taking hold of one of his arms. Dr. Alphonse held the other.

"Did you have any questions before we proceed, Dr. Whishaw?"

So many.

Padraig shook his head, still reeling, still suppressing the urge to tumble back down.

"Good. Then let Minjun and I be the first to welcome you to Heaven."

They led him forward out of the shuttle, shoes clicking against the hard metal.

"Good-bye," he heard the robot say behind him. Good-bye indeed. Farewell, last chance of seeing Earth again.

"Much of the passageway here is original to the station," Minjun said, pointing to the walls. Padraig blinked at him. He hadn't realised that "tour of the facilities" meant a literal tour-guide spiel. "We've had to fix it every now and again, but it's the same as it's been for eighty-some-odd years. "

"Eighty-six," Dr. Alphonse corrected, his voice quiet.

"I see you're still counting, then," Minjun said, arching his head behind Padraig's back.

"나는 아직도 집에 가고 싶다," Dr. Alphonse said. Minjun laughed.

"응, 이해해. 네 한국어 진짜 별로야." He laughed again.

"그럼 바스크어를 배워야 해요," Dr. Alphonse said.

Padraig tuned them out. Tour over, he supposed. He focused his attention on his feet. Left foot, pull forward, right foot, pull forward. Each step, pushing him away from Callisto, and with each step, the artificial gravity of the station pulling him back down.

"Ah, here. Stop." Padraig was jerked to a halt. Ahead of him, he heard a woman's voice carrying through the corridor.

"This is PETR—well, one of several PETRs. There is one AI, but he has several bodies he can occupy, just to make it easier for him and for us. Say hello, PETR."

"Hello PETR," a metallic monotone voice answered. Laughter. Padraig recognised Gautier's rolling laugh. His heart leapt, and his feet urged him to move forward, to embrace him and pretend this nightmare would end in his arms.

"Good, still doing the introductions," Minjun murmured. Dr. Alphonse nodded.

"Minjun, do you want to stay with him for at least a little longer? I think my work here is done—"

Padraig shook his head. "I'll be fine." Please, he didn't say, I don't want my introduction to eternity being me clinging to someone else's arm while I struggle to stand.

The two men eyed him, gaze moving from him to each other.

"Tell me how you feel," Minjun said after a moment.

"Fine," Padraig said. "Residual tightness in the chest, and I have a cough that I'm waiting for you to turn around so I can let out without you restraining me again, but I'm fine. I can walk. I can talk." I'm not an invalid, please see that.

"Let go, Fermin." The two men let go of Padraig. He felt himself sway for a moment. No, he thought, forcing his will into his body. No, I'm fine. I'm going to walk with the group and be myself again. Be human again. Don't let them gawk at me any more than is already going to happen.

"I can do it," he said. "No need to trouble yourselves for me any longer."

Minjun laughed. "The boy says he will be fine, Fermin," he said. "PETR and Karen will both be watching him. If he wants to try, let him. If he collapses, he'll be fine in a few hours anyway."

Dr. Alphonse nodded. "Agreed." He turned to Padraig.

"You go ahead. Minjun and I need to check some things in the shuttle. Let PETR know if you need help. He has the bodies, and you can always call out to him. You understand?"

Padraig nodded. Dr. Alphonse grunted.

"Go join the group, then. We'll see you tonight. If there are any problems, or there's slower improvement than expected, have PETR show you to either my lab or Minjun's. But Dr. Whishaw, please do try to at least look excited. You've been granted immortality. Appreciate it."

Padraig nodded, soft and slow. "You've saved my life, Dr. Alphonse," he said, a cough breaking out of him despite his best efforts to keep it contained. "I appreciate that, and won't forget it," he finished.

"That is part of the joy of Callisto," Minjun said. "You are given very few opportunities to forget." He jabbed his head towards the waiting room. "You should go, Dr. Whishaw."

Padraig nodded, and turned away from them.

Focus on feet. Left, right, left, right.

Thump thump. Thump thump. Thump thump.

"...find anyone in the station, just by asking. For example, PETR, where is Karen Reece?"

The woman's voice echoed through the room as Padraig stepped in. It was a round room, a bit bigger than the shuttle, with seats that were being ignored and an empty shelf. A closed door stood behind her, the crossed K of Callisto etched into the metal in bronze. The metal was dark here, almost bleak. In one corner, it looked like someone had tried to cheer it up a bit by drawing a smiling face in pink. The effect was garish more than anything, though it told him more than he suspected he needed to know about the station.

"Karen is in the Welcome Hall," the metallic voice said. Padraig could see the speaker now: another robot, with a similar build to the one in the shuttle, though this one seemed more precarious on its feet. Pipe legs connected a cylindrical torso to a can of a head with little lights gleaming out as eyes. The only things real about it were its hands, each with five delicately crafted fingers. He could see the eyes landing on him, unblinking but still analysing. It didn't look impressive, but that it could recognise him was a decent bit of engineering, he had to admit.

"Thank you, PETR," the small woman said. She had glasses that pressed in close to her face, their dark rims jammed against her eye sockets. Padraig wasn't sure he'd ever seen someone with glasses before—it was the sort of thing surgery could sort out in an instant. The woman's brown hair was pulled back in a tight bun, presenting the picture of brutal efficiency and management.

"Ah!" She stuck her hand in the air and pointed at him. Padraig stopped as she stepped forward, the rest of the group turning to look at him. He caught Gautier's eye, the small smile on his face. Padraig's heart sang.

Thump thump thump thump thump thump

"Dr. Whishaw, good to see you're up and about. You had us worried for a minute there, but glad to see everything is going smoothly." She stopped in front of him, peering up into his face.

She stuck her hand out to him. "Karen Reece," she said. "I'm the Party's representative here on Callisto. It's a pleasure to finally meet you."

Padraig took her hand, shaking it. Interesting, he thought. Her smile didn't make it up to her eyes.

"It's lovely to meet you as well, Ms. Reece," he said. "I look forward to working with you."

"Of course, of course." As she let go of his hand, he coughed into his arm. There was still blood. Perhaps the nanobots were slow, or perhaps he was being optimistic about them.

Karen turned her back to Padraig, speaking to the other three. "Now that everyone's here," she said, "shall we actually enter the station?"

"Yes!" Cassandra, at least, seemed genuinely excited. The other woman was standing, watching Karen and flexing her hand.

As Karen stepped towards the door, Padraig moved to stand next to Gautier. "Are you okay, mon cheri?" he murmured.

Gautier nodded. "Of course," he murmured back. "But I was never the one there were worries about, hm?"

The doors opened, the K splitting along its beam. Light flooded into the little entrance room, changing the dark walls to a dusty grey. What was on the other side took his breath.

Beside him, Padraig heard Gautier whistle softly. Padraig wasn't entirely sure what he had been expecting from Callisto. The drab grey etched with vague graffiti had been a possibility, and hadn't really surprised him.

The next room was a surprise. It was large and domed, with arches branching out from each side, carefully labelled "labs" and "residence." People milled about, most turning to watch them and wave. Cassandra waved back. Here and there, he heard someone requesting PETR to do something, and PETR answering them quietly. The dome had to be at least a hundred metres from end to end, enough to fit everyone in the station and then some.

It was the top of the dome that kept his gaze, though. Rather than the drab metal that covered the walls and corridors, viewscreens on the ceiling projected massive jungle trees. The canopy swayed and sunlight danced through thick green leaves, casting shadows on the people moving below. He stared at it, trying to pick apart the pixels, to see how it wasn't real, but he couldn't.

"The dome transitions from environment to environment over the course of the year," Karen said. Padraig moved his gaze back down to watch her. "I like to think of it as a journey. Some of the environments can't even really be found on Earth anymore, like—"

She waved her hand at the ceiling. "We've been trying to get it to feel more realistic too, but so far, no luck. It turns out it's harder than you'd expect to install a wind machine in here that isn't a nuisance."

Padraig turned his gaze back to the ceiling. A bird drifted across the sun, red-and-blue wings stretched wide. He watched it vanish beyond the projectors, hoping it would swing back around.

"At night, well..." Karen smiled. "I'll let you experience night for yourself. But this is where community events are held. Tonight, for instance, there will be the party to welcome the four of you to Heaven. Happens every year, and is one of the highlights of the year, I think."

"That's because you never let loose and live, Karen!" a man walking past called out to her.

"Thank you so much for your insight, Jack." Karen didn't turn around, instead squinching her eyes shut for a moment before resurrecting her smile. "Labs are that way—physics, chemistry, biology, robotics—and residences are this way." She pointed and walked towards the residence wing, her charges following her like ducklings.

"Maybe at night, the ceiling just changes to a giant ass," Gautier whispered. Padraig snorted out a laugh that devolved into a fit of coughing. Well worth it.

"Everyone has their own rooms, as you can see on the nameplates." Karen pointed to a gold nameplate just inside the corridor. Cato Riela had the room across from the dome, apparently. Lucky fellow.

"You can find anyone if you wander along the hallway long enough, or if you ask PETR. PETR doesn't mind if you ask too many questions, do you, PETR?"

"No, Karen," the disembodied ceiling voice answered.

"Down that way, you'll find the pool and gym, and the other way is the library, common rooms, and my office." Her hands pointed in the two directions the hall went. Padraig glanced. Pool? Was this a research station or a resort?

"Ooo, pool," Gautier murmured. Resort, then.

Thump thump. Padraig's heart fluttered behind his ribs. He pressed his fingertips to his chest, willing the nanobots to work faster. If they were going to take his illness, it would be nice if they got on with it.

The robot came over to Padraig, its bright eyes flicking across him. "Are you okay, Padraig?" it said. Karen kept talking, though he could see her gaze moving over him.

"Just...tired," Padraig said. The robot's light eyes flickered.

"You are lying," it said. "I can tell. You should rest."

Well, well, Padraig thought. A nannybot to go with the nanobots.

"I don't think it likes you," Gautier laughed. Padraig glared at him, then stared at the robot.

"Where is my room?" he asked. "I'll go there, and the group can keep going through the tour. Can you let Karen know I'm tired?"

"Yes, Padraig," the robot said. "I can accompany you to your room."

"Oh, you can't leave me here with the boring tour," Gautier said. "You wouldn't be so cruel."

"Wouldn't I?" Padraig smiled at him. "Be a dear and let me know what puzzles they have in the rec room, won't you, mon cheri?"

"I will get you for this," he said, shaking his fist in mock anger.

"I expect nothing less." Behind Gautier, Padraig saw a second robot, built like the first, walking up to follow Karen. Multiple bodies. Quite useful.

"Follow me," the robot said, walking down the hall away from the group. Padraig followed.

His eyes moved over the nameplates as they went, drifting across names he recognised from his textbooks. Hasan Svensgard, the global councillor who had negotiated the Tashkent Accords in 2130. Ximena Balam, discoverer of the principles of hyperliquids. Hansel Norbergen, philosopher of robotics. Name after name that he knew, and name after name that he didn't. He'd seen some of their work printed in journals even recently, of course, but there was a difference between recognising that the titans existed and actually being counted among them. Chemistry, physics, robotics, maths, humanities, the names ran the whole gamut. If the goal of Heaven had ever been to create an ideal society, the Party was so far doing a perfect job.

There were a few people in the hallway, clustered in groups, chattering to each other. He didn't recognise their faces, but undoubtedly within a few weeks he would. This place didn't seem so crowded that it would be impossible to recognise people. He kept his eyes down, his gaze focused anywhere but on the people, hoping they wouldn't notice him. His heart fluttered in his chest, blood pounding in his head. He wanted to get to his room and lie down.

Cassandra McAllister, one nameplate said, then a few names he didn't recognise. Gautier St. Laurent. His heart beat faster. Two more names, then Jocasta Nikophouros. Two blank nameplates.

"Here is your room, Padraig." There was a metal door set into a metal frame, plain light grey, nothing fancy. Padraig Whishaw, the nameplate read. Padraig looked at it for a minute. His name. This would be home for the rest of his life.

Which will either be forever or the next few days, he mused, not sure whether to laugh or cry. Both seemed reasonable.

"You open the door by pressing here." The robot pressed a button just inside the doorframe. The metal door slid into the wall.

"How do I close it?" he asked.

"It will close once you are inside," the robot said.

Like a coffin. Padraig stepped into the room.

It was drab, the walls pale grey, the narrow bed's blankets pale grey, and the desk and small chair pale grey. A lonely dresser sat in a corner, looking sad and lost. An open door waited in the far corner. Padraig crossed the room and popped his head in. A sink and mirror gazed back at him, a shower lurked in a corner, a pale grey towel hanging on a rack.

Cry, then. This place was a prison.

"You can change the colour of the fabric by saying what colour you want. It is programmed to respond to voice command." The robot's voice interrupted his thoughts. Padraig turned. It was staring at him, bright unblinking eyes fixed on him. Padraig hadn't even realised it was still there.

"Change the bed to green," he said, and watched the blanket change to a deep forest green. So there was hope, then, at least for not having to sleep in a grave. "What about the rest of the room? Can that be changed as well?"

"If you have requests, everything can be made, and everything can be rearranged. The room is yours to customise."

"Can I see outside?" The thought popped into Padraig's head, bursting like a bubble.

"Yes. The viewscreens on the far wall can display many projections, including several Earth environments and the current view outside the station. Would you like me to show what is outside?"

"Yes, please do."

The far wall lit up. Padraig squinted against it, then opened his eyes, staring into the new world.

Dark, cratered plains stretched before him, speckled here and there with brilliant white crests. The lights from the station shone out several hundred metres before darkness stole in. The white anti-radiation shielding around the station stretched out to the side, a bulwark against the oblivion beyond. It seemed childish in its optimism, believing that a white wall could hold back the dark.

Beyond the darkness, though, he could see it. Looming up across the sky, the red eye watching him, another moon in its iris. Jupiter, staring down hungrily at the intruders in its domain.

This is not our world. The thought came into his head, unbidden and unfamiliar. This is a world we want to believe is ours, but this is not our world.

He took a step back and sat down on the edge of the bed, coughing and staring at Jupiter. The other moon meandered across its face, drifting. Jupiter watched it like a protective father jealously guarding his sons and daughters.

You do not belong here.

"Is there anything else you need?" the robot said from behind him.

"No." Padraig didn't take his eyes off the planet beyond. "No, you can go."

He heard the metal feet click on the floor behind him, heard the whisper of the door as it slid open, then closed again.

He felt cold, just cold watching the planet and the yellow moon transiting its face. Was that Io? It had to be, based on the coloration and location. Had to be, but it didn't really matter.

He coughed again, a hacking thing, sending more blood into his sleeve. His eyes turned back to Jupiter, felt it watching with what almost seemed to be satisfaction.

You do not belong here.

The cold settled into him, burrowing into his heart. Jupiter was a roiling sea of radiation and storms, a god lashing its orbiting children. Completely inhospitable, and yet here he was, living and breathing and surviving in its shadow. What must it be like to be out on the surface of Callisto, nothing but Jupiter above? To stare at death, to stare a god in the eye, and defy it?

Padraig closed his eyes. Imagine if he were out there with Gautier.

His heart fluttered in his chest.

He pictured them, the two of them standing together beneath Jupiter's gaze, holding each other, pulling each other close, each happy, each healthy. The scent of Gautier, the raw scent of man with a touch of lavender billowing around him. Hair floating free without gravity, those small curls dancing and twirling in the gloom.

Twelve hours. Normal in twelve hours. The hole in him, gone, in twelve hours. What to fill it with except Jupiter?

The vision faded. He was in Heaven, not on Callisto. He was inside a station, not under Jupiter's gaze.

He lowered his eyes, glancing around the room. There was an emptiness here. Something had been ripped out of him. Something had been torn away from him. His life was gone.

He was cold, and he was alone.

He was alive.

Chapter Eight

Ladies and gentlemen, consider your souls. God sees each and every one, and consider your souls now that we see the day of judgement is descending down upon us. What sin we have committed I cannot say. I've tried to do right by this land and its people, and I know y'all done the same. It's been an honour to serve each and every one of you. May God—

Last Broadcast of President Alexander Mayfair, San Antonio, Texas
Confederation, 2044

Neither the Macedonians nor any other national group which until then had been oppressed obtained their liberation by decree. They fought for their national liberation with rifle in hand.

Josip Broz Tito, Ljubljana, Yugoslavia, 1948

Your war is lost. Your cause, lost. Your identity, lost. Your people, lost. Your hope, lost. You've fought a noble fight, but you need to see that to continue is to sacrifice the people you claim to love to misery and suffering.

Global Councillor Ivan Maksharov, Patriation of Yugoslavia
Negotiations, 2189

Sunday, 17 March 2193, 7:02 PM. Jocasta Nikophouros' room, Heaven, Callisto.

Her room was drab and grey. Jocasta liked it.

Karen had talked about how it could be customised, the backgrounds changed, the colours splattered everywhere, but it didn't really matter. The grey was fine. It was a place to live in, not much more. It didn't have to be home.

She drifted through the room, running her fingers across the dresser, the bed frame, the metal wall. There was an unfamiliar tingle running through the fingertip of her right pinkie that reminded her of water trickling out of an ear. It was quite pleasant. The nanobots, she thought, were doing whatever it was they were doing quite well, even if it was taking much longer than expected.

She opened a drawer, saw towels and clothes laid out in the dresser. Grey. Colourless. Waiting, presumably, to be brought to life by a wearer with more interesting tastes than the designer. She closed the drawer again and set her coat down on top of the dresser, turning to take in the room again.

Her room. Not home, but her space. Hers alone, to make of whatever she chose.

Her fingers brushed the bed. The pillow squished beneath her fingertips, sinking where she pressed it. The blanket was soft but clinical, the feeling of sanitised, artificial caring seeping out of it. That was fine too. Everything could be adapted. Everything could be made to work.

Her head popped into the bathroom. Grey, again, grey and imposing. A shower loomed in one corner, a sink and mirror peering out from the other. She blinked at them, at what was missing.

Through all of human history, she knew, there was a long and illustrious tradition of a home containing a few things. It always contained some way to have food, somewhere to rest, and somewhere to dispose of the day. It was one of the few things that united all of humanity in that long span between birth and death. Everyone, no matter who they were, ate, rested, and had waste.

Maybe it's proof you're not human, she thought. No toilet because you aren't human.

Jocasta wiggled the living finger of her right hand. Did it matter whether she was human or not, really, if she was living in a colony of others like her? Where everyone was inhuman? What was human other than how the people here chose to define it?

She kept staring, though. It was one thing, intellectually, to recognise what had happened, the changes that she was ostensibly undergoing. It was another to look at the reality of what those changes implied.

Her eyes drifted across the sink. No toothbrush. No sign of anything more than strict utility.

That was fine. What did she need, after all, that couldn't be answered through strict utility? Require nothing, produce nothing, that's what Dr. Alphonse had said, wasn't it?

She walked back into her room and lay on the bed, staring up at the grey ceiling. Her fingers jiggled and tingled as they eased back into life. She ran them over the fabric of the blanket, feeling the sensation of them, admiring the solidness.

"Good evening, Jocasta," a pleasant male voice from the ceiling said. Jocasta jumped a little, feeling something in her jolt, but stayed lying on the bed, staring at the blank ceiling.

"Who's there?" she asked.

"There is no need to be alarmed," the ceiling said. "We met earlier. I am PETR. I am able to speak to you without a physical form. Does this disturb you?"

The AI. She should have remembered, but somehow, with everything else that had been happening, the AI's existence had been pushed from her head. What was it Karen had called him? Their lifeline? It seemed apt for a disembodied ceiling voice. It was disturbing, in a way, that he could be so omniscient, but she supposed it made sense for a research station. They would need constant support for calculations and such.

"No," she said, after a pause. "It doesn't disturb me."

"I am glad to hear that, Jocasta," PETR said. "I am informing you that the welcome party will be beginning shortly in the community hall."

"Welcome party?" Jocasta locked her fingers across her chest, tapping an index finger against her sternum. Party. She hadn't been to a proper party since she was a teenager. It had only been small gatherings since then, or the occasional—

"Yes. Every year, there is a party to welcome the new arrivals to Heaven. It is a good opportunity to meet people. There is conversation and drugs. Everyone has a good time."

"Party." She turned the idea over in her head, poking at it. Her finger twitched on her chest. Stefanos had called her last night in Thessaloniki a going-away celebration, but that hardly counted as anything more than an incident. There had been the nights with the soldiers in Albania—

"You are not required to attend," PETR interrupted her thoughts again. "There is nothing on Heaven you are required to do. It is heavily encouraged that you attend the party, however. Karen will give a speech. You will meet new people. There are many people who are very excited to meet you. It will be an enjoyable evening."

"Who is excited to meet me?" The better question was why, she thought. She was no one in a sea of someones.

"Many people," PETR said. "Very few new people come to Heaven. It is very exciting when there are new people."

Ah, so it wasn't her. Just new people in general.

"I haven't been to a party with a large group in a while," she said, sitting up. "How many people will be there?"

"There are three hundred and twenty-three residents of Heaven," PETR said. "Most of them will likely attend, but some will not. Some do not go out much, but this is a special occasion. I think most residents will be there." A pause. "You should attend the party, Jocasta."

An AI that made recommendations about her social life. She supposed it shouldn't be too surprising. Heaven was supposed to be one of the most sophisticated research stations controlled by the Party. It would make sense that the AI would be more sophisticated than expected. It still took her by surprise, though, that it would be so interested in her particular activities.

"Why should I go, PETR?" she asked. "I'm not much for parties."

"This party is different," PETR said. "It only happens once a year. It is very special. You will have fun."

Well, if the AI is insisting on it, she mused, it must be good.

"What do I need to wear?" she asked. "Is it fancy?"

"No," PETR said. "You may wear whatever you like. Some people go naked. This is discouraged, but permitted."

Her first party in... She shook her head. Years, she knew, several years at least. The people had stopped interesting her, and the party environment with its multitude of people had become too stressful. The weight of person after person after person needing interaction, needing conversation; it was more than she knew how to take.

She shook her head. This was Heaven, though. A chance for a new start. New starts generally didn't go well when they were based on old fears.

"I'll go," she said. "How long do I have to be there?"

"I am glad to hear you are going," PETR said. "You can be there for as much or as little time as you'd like."

"I'll at least pop in," she said, sitting up on the edge of the bed. "I can always come back here, yes?"

"Yes, Jocasta."

She stood up and wandered into the bathroom, pushing her hair back out of her face. She paused in front of the mirror, peering at herself. The scars across her face and neck were still there, just faded a bit, like memories leaving the mind with time. She ran a finger over the long one at the base of her neck. Where had she gotten that one? Macedonia? Serbia? She couldn't quite remember anymore.

She splashed water on her face, feeling the cool bite of it against her skin. It felt real in a surreal world. Something familiar. Something true.

"It's just outside?" she said. "In the room with the views of Earth?"

"Yes, Jocasta," PETR said. "People are already there."

Jocasta took a deep breath in, watching herself in the mirror. Her eyes seemed brighter than they had been the last time she'd seen her own reflection, more alive. Maybe it was a side effect of the nanobots that she looked a bit more alert, a bit more human. Ironic, in its own way, she thought, that it takes something so fundamentally unhuman to make someone human again.

Her clothes seemed fine. Somehow, after wearing them since leaving Earth, they were still more or less presentable. A bit rumpled, and likely with wrinkles she hadn't intended, but decent. The sky-blue sweater and dark pants seemed ready to accept the prospect of going out.

She closed her eyes, took a breath. It hung in her mouth for a moment before seeping back out through a gap in her lips.

"And if I get scared?" she asked.

"You can always come back here, Jocasta. We can play Arimaa." A pause. "But you will not be scared. You will enjoy yourself."

She smiled. "I'm glad one of us believes that." She paused for a moment in front of the door, thinking. This was Heaven. This was the chance to start again. She could be whoever she wanted to be, including a person who had nothing to fear.

"I'm glad both of us believe that," she amended. The ceiling did not respond.

She sighed and opened the door.

Her room was down the hall from the main room, with a few dozen doors separating her from it. Even from here, though, she could hear the gentle din of conversation curling out from the main room. It wrapped around her ears like tendrils; the words unclear, but the fact of their being spoken rooting in her brain.

Her finger twitched against her thigh as she took a breath in and let it out again. People. She wanted to learn about people. Wasn't that what she had told the Party interviewer, the journalist, herself? Learn about people. Learn to help people.

"Ah, Jocasta!" Jocasta spun as a voice behind her called out. The man from the shuttle—Gautier, his name was Gautier—came up behind her, smiling and waving. He'd changed his clothes, she noticed, into what was in the dressers. He'd changed the loose shirt to a swirling red-and-gold pattern that caught the eye and trapped it in the fabric's folds.

"You are headed to the party as well?"

Jocasta nodded. His smile broadened.

"I was hoping you would," he said, and offered her a crooked arm. "Shall we walk together?"

She glanced down at the proffered arm, draped in soft fabric. He was clearly already making himself at home—why shouldn't she? She slipped her hand into the crook of his elbow and let herself be pulled forward.

"You're a veterinarian, no?" he asked. Before she could say anything, he continued. "I am curious why you became a veterinarian. Most who want to help become doctors, but you chose to help animals. It is an interesting choice."

The conversation ahead of them grew louder as they drifted past doors and nameplates. Jocasta's attention moved between the dull roar ahead of her and Gautier's ramble.

"I had a cat once, this big ginger tabby," he said. "My sister and I called her Amelie. She was big, had to be, oh, ten kilos at least." He held out his hands in front of him across the width of his body, showing how large the cat was. The cleft of his arm squeezed Jocasta's arm, holding it tight.

"My parents didn't much like Amelie, and so she lived outside. 'No reason to have a cat inside,' they said. So Sauterelle and I would leave milk outside for Amelie and pet her when she came to see us. Every time we stepped outside, there would be Amelie, *ronron*. It was nice having someone so happy to see us even when we were nothing special." They were nearing the opening in the corridor. Gautier's steps were slowing, even if his words weren't.

"One day, we stepped out to the garden, and Amelie came, face covered in blood and carrying a hawk she'd caught. It had fought and pecked her eye out, but she hadn't let go. I don't know why—I think cats are not always the smartest, hm?—but she brought it to us. I remember the look in its eye as it lay there, dying. It wasn't dead, you see. I don't think cats kill. They wound and then watch to see how something dies. Rather a lot like humans in that regard, I think, but you would know better." Jocasta's blood turned to ice, the arm sweeping her forward feeling like a vice. His dark eyes were sweeping over her, still warm, maybe oblivious to her discomfort. She had to believe it was obliviousness and not malice that kept her trapped in this conversation.

He paused just before the entrance to the hall, lost in his own memories. "The bird she had caught, you see, tried to escape by fighting, but I think you know that cats see fighting as a challenge, not as a fright. She held on, and lost her eye because of it. We took them both to the vet, and I will never forget what he did. He said, first, that our cat had behaved badly, which we knew of course, but second that she was noble for fighting, and the bird too. He took both of them, and even though they were just beasts, he treated them with such care, talking to them and easing their pain."

His eyes snapped back to focus on Jocasta, his smile regaining some of its brilliance. Jocasta found herself getting lost in his eyes, trapped, but with no way out.

"He euthanised them both, of course," Gautier said. "No telling what diseases the cat had caught from trying to eat something more powerful than herself, and the bird was dead, even if it didn't know it. The vet was kind enough to tell it that. It was sad, but I have never forgotten the love he had as he did it. The way he held them both, the hunter and the prey that brought about her doom. Anyway, I like veterinarians. It takes a lot of love to care for something that doesn't know enough to be grateful. Have you ever had to euthanise an animal?"

She had. She knew she had. In veterinary school, surely, if nowhere else.

Jocasta stared at him, then slowly nodded her head, pulling her arm out of his. He let it slip, smile fading just a touch.

"Yes," she said. "Sometimes." She paused, watching him. His eyes were still scanning her, earnestness and warmth still radiating from them. "It's a sad part of what we do. There are no animals here, though, so happily, no more need for it."

"Yes, happily," he said. "You shall have to tell me more about your time as a veterinarian, but first." He jerked his head towards the party. "Shall we?"

Jocasta nodded, stepping past him and into the hall. In her periphery, she could see Gautier step in and swing into place in another group, getting engulfed in an instant. Good.

If she needed an incentive to interact with people, hiding from someone who wanted to know about being a veterinarian was a good place to start.

Her eyes scanned the room. There were people here, such a variety of people, dozens upon dozens of them, mingling and chatting and laughing together. She could see some of them huddled in groups; others, drifting from group to group, laughing and barely needing to speak to make themselves known and understood. Their clothes were a garish mix of the styles in the dresser, ones that looked like they had been handmade from scraps found in a gutter, and one man who had elected to wear nothing at all.

Jocasta's eyes jumped away from him. She didn't need that image, not now, likely not ever.

She could see Cassandra, wearing the same loose green sweater she had been wearing in Espaceville, hair hanging down across her back, braids dancing as she jumped from group to group, weaving in and out of people, shaking hands, laughing, smiling. The girl was a natural charmer in a place where there were only a few hundred to charm. How long would it take her to befriend everyone? A week? Two?

Gautier was doing something similar, though groups orbited him rather than him moving to groups. She could see Cassandra moving close to him, tickling at him before dancing away once again. Laughter spilled out across the room, punctuating the conversations with music.

Her gaze drifted to the ceiling and froze there. The Earth scenes were gone, replaced instead with a dizzying array of colours dancing and swirling like snakes across the dome. Reds, yellows, and pinks intertwined with green and blue ribbons of light, binding them together before vanishing again into the sea of colour. Her eyes moved through it, trying to follow the path of any one band, but finding it impossible. The colours blurred together, each ribbon somehow becoming each other while still being distinct. Here and there, she thought she could see letters intertwined with the colours dancing over the dome. The sound of the party faded as she fixed her gaze on the colours. They were incredible, beyond anything she had imagined possible. They seemed to fall towards her, urging her to reach up for them.

"It is the aurora." The sound of the party roared back into existence as she snapped her head away from the dome. PETR was standing in front of her, a tray full of pills, powders, and tablets balanced on one hand, its glowing eyes watching her. "It is not quite accurate to outside, but it is showing a live feed from Jupiter's south pole. It is Jupiter's aurora. Dr. Bendi launched the camera fifty years ago. It is still working. Many people quite enjoy the view. I have been told LSD enhances it. Would you like some?"

One of his hands reached towards the tray, pulling a blue pill from a pile. Jocasta shook her head, holding up a hand.

"No, no, please don't, PETR." The robot put the pill back on the tray.

"Very well," it said, and drifted away into the crowd. There were more of it, she could see, moving in and out of the crowds, distributing their trays full of drugs.

"It's interesting," a voice behind her said. Jocasta spun. A man stood behind her, tall and dark, his olive-skinned face a full head above her own. A black shirt clung to his chest and across his neck but left his arms bare. Black pants clung to his legs. Black hair lay willy-nilly across his ears and forehead. Dark eyes watched her as he pointed towards the crowd and the robots meandering through it.

"We come here to a bastion of research to become immortals, to free ourselves of the mortal shackle and become like gods. We could do anything; and yet, I find there are three types of people here. There are those who devote themselves to their research, those that grow sad and fade away, and—" He inclined his head towards the crowd again. Jocasta turned to see Cassandra popping a pill into her mouth.

"—those who descend into debauchery. With most, it is easy to tell, but with you…" He tapped a finger to his long nose as she turned back to him. "I am left to wonder." He threw his hands in the air, smiling. "Ah well."

He held a hand out for her to shake. She took it, squeezing it. It was warm and calloused. He squeezed her hand back, tight, firm, but not to the point of pain. It was a powerful grip from a man who knew his own strength.

"Cato Riela," he said. "And I take it you are Jocasta Nikophouros?"

Jocasta nodded, releasing his hand. He lowered his hand and smiled, showing blindingly white teeth. Perfect teeth.

"It's a pleasure to meet you. I've been looking forward to it since I read your file. As you might imagine, the arrival of new people here is always exciting, and files are always read with great anticipation."

"My file?" she asked.

He nodded. "Nothing incriminating, I assure you. You can read it for yourself in the library. Just your name, where you are from, and what you told the Party they could say about you. You, for instance, are a veterinarian from Thessaloniki, a Lottery winner, and, though the file doesn't say it, the first representative from Yugoslavia." His grin grew broader. "You should meet Svensgard, when you get the chance. I know he's dying to meet you."

"Svensgard?" Jocasta felt the ice in her veins again, swirling and warning her. It was never a good sign when someone knew more about her than they ought to, more dangerous when it was clear they wanted to use that information against her.

"Hasan Svensgard. He and I usually avoid each other at these sorts of events. He'll be over on the far side, I imagine, close to where Ms. Reece will be, when she makes her appearance." Cato laughed.

"But I apologise, this is a lot all at once. My manners have grown atrocious. Do forgive me. I'm just—as I said, I'm just very excited to meet you."

"Why?" Jocasta asked.

He laughed again. "A fine question, yes indeed it is. I'm interested in meeting you, Ms. Nikophouros, because you seem like a legitimately interesting human being, unlike most of the people the Party ships in to this godforsaken hellhole."

Jocasta blinked. Whatever answer she had been expecting, it wasn't something that was so brutal in its supposed honesty. She couldn't quite tell if it was honest, though. There was no warmth in Cato Riela's eyes, and the look he gave her was one of hunger.

"I am flattered, I think," she said.

"And I'm honoured that you're flattered," he said. "May I introduce you to someone?"

No, she thought.

Cato waited for her response, but if he noticed her silence, he didn't care. "He'll be over here." He walked past her, waving at someone near the edge of the hall. She watched him go. It would be easy to move away and not follow him, at least for the evening. In a station with only a few hundred people and an eternity together, though, there wasn't a way to avoid him, not for long, not short of going to her room, locking the door, and never coming out again. Which was always a possibility.

He was standing beside a smaller, dark man and turning to wave her over. She watched him, then glanced at the rest of the party. The laughter was growing louder and more hysterical in the big groups, more like the raucous cries of noisy birds.

She walked towards Cato and his companion.

The smaller man threw up his hands in excitement as Jocasta approached him, hurrying over to meet her and clasp her hand. "Jocasta!" he said. "It's lovely to meet you. My name's Ade. It's a pleasure, a pleasure!"

"Ade has been here longer than most of us," Cato said, then turned to the smaller man. "How long has it been now?"

"Sixty-eight years," he said. "I was one of the first to come here after the Party opened Heaven. It's been…a very long time."

"A pleasure to meet you," Jocasta murmured. Ade's smile grew.

"I saw you are a veterinarian," Ade said. "I'm afraid there's no animals here, despite Banki's best efforts. What will you do instead?"

"I was hoping to study psychology," Jocasta said.

"Ah! You'll be studying with Cato, then!"

Jocasta's eyes shifted to Cato. The man was beaming. Not good.

"I understand there's a library," she said, but Ade shook his head.

"There is, there is, with all the digital availability you'd find in any Earth library, at least as far as I know. But the best way to learn is by doing and studying with another person, not by holing yourself up in a musty closet, or so I've found. Cato has taught me a lot about how to read people and how to understand the human mind. He really is a wonder. You'll like him."

She looked over at Cato again. There were a few hundred people here. It would be impossible to avoid anyone for long, particularly now that she'd made the mistake of telling one of them that they were helpful to her.

"We could meet tomorrow before the data arrives, if you'd like," Cato said. "I'm sure PETR could find some space for us."

"I do not want to trouble you—"

"It's no trouble at all," Cato interrupted her attempts to wriggle away. "I like having a student, particularly one as interesting as you. I'll set it up. PETR will let you know where and when, unless there's a time that doesn't work for you."

"No," she said. What the no meant, even she couldn't be sure. She wanted to learn, but not from this man. If she wanted to learn, though, she needed to try. Fear rose in her.

She closed her eyes. Flowers on the windowsill, smell of the sea.

She had to start somewhere. Her eyes reopened. "I don't have anything else to do."

"Nor do most of us," he said. Jocasta wasn't sure if it was meant as a joke. Ade laughed. Perhaps it was a joke, but there was no laughter in Cato's eyes.

"I see Cato has his claws in you already, Jocasta." A familiar voice spoke up from behind her as a third man joined the circle. Dr. Alphonse stood beside her, eyes meeting Cato's before dropping back to her.

"No more so than you usually do, Fermin," Cato said, his voice cool. Ade's eyes moved from one man to the other.

"You give me far too much credit, Cato," Dr. Alphonse said. "I give people a gift and let them go free. You try to collect them."

"Not entirely fair," Cato said. "I befriend the interesting ones and try to teach what I know. You seem happy to just inject and move on."

"I'd like to learn about the nanobots," Jocasta said, setting her words as a barrier between them. All eyes turned to her. She felt herself shrink beneath their gazes as she turned to Dr. Alphonse. "If you aren't too busy, that is. I would like to know about them."

"Certainly," he said. "Come by the lab tomorrow. I'll explain more. Just make it early."

Jocasta nodded, but Dr. Alphonse had already turned back to Cato. "Cato," he said, bobbing his head at the man. "Ade." He walked away, moving back into the crowd.

"I hope you'll enjoy your visit with him in his lab," Cato said. "He tends to have a lot of words with little meaning, but he enjoys sharing his time. I'll schedule us for later in the morning, then. The data shouldn't arrive until noon anyway."

Jocasta didn't ask what the data was or how it would arrive. That, she had no doubt, would be one of the many things Cato would teach her about the combined subjects of psychology and life in Heaven.

"Are you expecting a letter from Monica this year?" Ade asked. Cato nodded.

"She and the girls said they'd send video this year as well. Lucy had a performance with the national orchestra scheduled for December. I can share it with you, if you'd like. Ah, thank you PETR."

A robot pushed silently into the group, pressing a pale white tablet into each of their hands. Jocasta held it between her thumb and forefinger, bringing it up to her face to look at it.

"Flavour tablet," Ade said, holding his own up for Jocasta to see. The robot moved away, pushing into other groups. "No food in Heaven except for Karen's, so we get these instead."

"Any flavour you could want, and yet somehow, we always get peppermint," Cato sighed.

"Not true," Ade said. "It's only been peppermint since Karen got here. Adrian liked vanilla, and Lupe had a thing for those little Viennese chocolates."

Cato put his hands above his shoulders, shaking his head. "I stand corrected, then," he said. "I've only ever known Karen."

"You see, this is why you keep me around," Ade said. "I am much wiser than you, Cato, and you know it."

Cato smiled as he lowered his hands. "You know me well, Ade, me and my youthful follies."

"Do I eat the tablet?" Jocasta asked. The two men shook their heads.

"No," Cato said.

"Not yet, anyway," Ade added. "First Karen gives a speech, then we eat them together. It's a ritual, a holiday, you know the word. Ceremony, that's the one. Mostly the same speech every year, then we eat the tablet, and then the true—what's your word, Cato? 'Debauchery?'—begins."

Jocasta nodded, staring down at the little tablet. It was a pale, crystalline white, small enough to sit on the middle of her tongue. It melted a little beneath her fingertips; she could feel it slowly sinking in.

"Good evening, everyone!" The hall tapered into silence as a woman's voice called out from the centre of it. The aurora overhead dimmed, the lights fading until only a single spot remained, focused on Karen Reece. Through the light, Jocasta could see all eyes turned to her.

"Wow, thank you, PETR," she said, looking up at the light. She turned back to the crowd.

"So here we are again. Year Seventy-Three gone; Year Seventy-Four is waiting for us. It's going to be a fantastic year, and I'm looking forward to all the new research and discoveries in the future for all of us." She raised her hand above her head, holding a tablet.

"To the Party," she said. "To Heaven." Around the room, she could hear a chorus of other voices echoing her. Jocasta stayed silent, glancing at Cato. Present company suggested agreeing with the toast was not the best idea.

Karen popped the tablet in her mouth and stepped away into the darkness. As the aurora reappeared in the dome, Jocasta could see others around the room doing the same. She opened her mouth and placed the tablet on her tongue. A burst of peppermint flooded her tastebuds, overwhelming them with sticky-sweet sensation. For a moment, her world was peppermint and nothing else, the taste and scent of it clogging up her mind. An instant later, it was gone, only the vaguest aftertaste lingering on her tongue.

"Huh." Jocasta turned to look as Ade spoke beside her. His tablet was still held between his fingers, being turned over and over against his dark knuckles. "That was odd. Usually she goes on for at least ten minutes. Do you think she's feeling okay?"

"It's not like Minjun would tell us if she wasn't," Cato said. He'd already eaten his tablet. "It could also be that someone finally let her know that no one wants to hear the list of accomplishments every time we do this."

"That's true." The tablet kept flipping across Ade's knuckles. He sighed and shrugged, popping it into his mouth. "Still just as good," he said, smiling.

"Do you not get it often?" Jocasta asked.

"Once a year, my dear, once a year," Ade said. "Karen likes to make them special, so once a year only."

The Party had its traditions and controls here then as well. Jocasta looked out at the crowd. Cassandra was whirling through it, a pair of grinning men close behind her. Gautier was in heated conversation with one of the robots. As she watched, it nodded and started blaring out synth-cello music.

If there was true debauchery, she could see she was on the cusp of it, and wanted no part of it. Music grew louder, and the lights grew dim. The aurora danced overhead, casting shadows that wrapped around the people below, entwining them, pulling them apart, vanishing again in an instant. She felt her heart beating harder as some people filtered out of the room. There was a party in here, and while she could handle the pleasant small talk, the debauchery was not for her.

"I'm heading out," she said, glancing at Cato and Ade. Cato nodded.

"Agreed," he said. "There's not much here anymore. The most interesting part is done. You're welcome to join us—"

"I'm tired," she said, shaking her head. There was too much humanity around her, too much noise and too many pheromones drifting through the air. She needed to be alone.

"That's fair too. I will see you tomorrow, then," Cato said, and held out his hand again. Jocasta took it. His touch was much lighter now, as though he no longer had something to prove to her.

"It was a pleasure to meet you, Jocasta," he said.

"The same," she said. She pulled away from him and walked back towards the hall. As she went, she saw Cassandra dancing with Gautier, swinging around him and spinning from hand to hand before zipping off to another man. Whatever she had taken, it did seem to be working.

She slipped out of the hall and into the corridor, the sound of people and excitement fading behind her. She had tried. She had done her best. It hadn't been a complete failure, either. She'd met new people, and in the morning, she could start to learn.

Her door appeared before her, far from the din of the hall. She opened it. Nothing but grey inside. Calm and grey and perfect.

Her finger twitched at her side. In the morning she could learn, but for now, yes, for now she had done enough.

She turned off the lights and collapsed on the bed. Her mind felt empty; drained, even, as if she'd been through an ordeal. Hadn't she, though? Socialising and making pleasantries was hard under the best of circumstances, and this was an entirely new place. She was right to be drained, right to have a head empty of thought. It was fair, and expected.

She closed her eyes and let sleep steal in.

Chapter Nine

"'I will not elope,' says she, 'for I am the daughter of a king and a queen. There is nothing of thy poverty that you should not get me from my family; and it shall be my choice accordingly to go to thee, it is thou whom I have loved.'"

"Táin bo Fraich"

It's supposed to be a promotion, but really, it's a career death sentence. Get shipped out to administer some rock out past the asteroid belt? Can't talk to anyone for a decade? It's enough to drive anyone insane.
Lupe Orelia, Administrator of Callisto, 2140-2150

Politics is a game played by the powerful to amuse the powerless.
Cato Riela, *Essays and Musings on the Nature of the Party*, 2180

Monday, 18 March 2193, 1:18 AM. Padraig Whishaw's room, Heaven, Callisto.

Amalthea was transiting Jupiter, her red body shivering in and out of view against the planet's surface. She was a mote, drifting through the void, protected by the behemoth, held tight in an eternal embrace. Her entire existence, defined by the beast she existed beside. Everything she was, everything she could be, just a speck on Jupiter's face. And he, in turn, loved her for it, protected her, held her, lived for her. If only he—

There was a knock at the door. Padraig tore himself from the planet, staring at the door. It was late, he knew that, but he was hard-pressed to think who would be knocking on his door at all, regardless of the time. He stumbled to his feet, coughing as he went. Beside him, Jupiter watched, judging him for having the audacity to look away.

"Who's there, PETR?" he asked, eyes flitting between the planet and the door. Amalthea had disappeared again.

"Karen," PETR said. "I will let her in."

"What is she even doing here? What if I was asleep?" Padraig ran a hand through his hair, turning away from the window. He was a mess. That was fine.

"I told her you were awake." There was blood on the dark-blue sleeve of his sweater. Nothing to do about it now.

"Why would you—never mind. Just let her in," he sighed.

The door slid open as Padraig leaned against a bedpost, coughing into the bloody sleeve. Karen walked in, looking much as she had when they'd met earlier, though he could see the hair in her bun escaping, the pale pallor of exhaustion across her face.

"Ms. Reece," he said. "What brings you here at this hour?"

"You weren't at the party, Dr. Whishaw," she said, stopping a foot or so away from him. "I wanted to check in on you, make sure things were going okay. PETR said you were working—"

"Ha, not quite, I'm afraid. It's been a while since I've been able to work. I'm fine, though, or will be. Dr. Alphonse said it would likely be a few days, but that's fine. I can rest and wait for the nanobots to do their work."

Karen nodded and stepped past Padraig, looking at Jupiter on the wall. "I see you got it to display outside," she said. "Does that help you feel better?"

Padraig nodded. "There's something deeply therapeutic about space, I find," he said, turning to watch her as she walked closer to the wall and towards his desk. "The emptiness of it, and the vast unknown. We think we understand it, but there's an entire reality out there that we're only beginning to uncover. Our equations aren't much different than child's playthings, really, but like children, we can only really learn if we look and experience."

Karen picked up his datapad and glanced at it. "PETR brought you this?" she asked, glancing over at Padraig and holding up the datapad.

Padraig nodded. "I prefer to work alone and at odd hours. I like to speak while I work as well; the recorder helps with that."

Karen nodded, setting the datapad down and pointing to the glass of water. The condensation from its cold edge had long since dried. "You know you don't need that, right? Fermin did explain that part?"

He nodded again, trying to figure out what she wanted. Had she come just to point to the possessions he'd managed to accumulate over the course of a few hours and judge him for them? "It helps me think," he said. "We all have our habits."

"Got it," she said, her eyes switching to look at him. There was something in her gaze he didn't like, a coldness that didn't match the friendliness of the woman he'd met earlier.

"Have I done something wrong?" he asked. "I apologise for not attending the party earlier. I was quite exhausted—"

"It's fine," she said. "Resting is more important, particularly for someone in your state." She inclined her head towards his sweater. "What's 'Texel?'"

He glanced down, trying to see what she was talking about. The upside-down shape of the malformed island and the words "Texel 2192" pressed on the blue fabric in white letters jumped back at him. Had he really been wearing this all day? Through the press conference and the tour of Heaven? This was a sweater Gautier had bought for him when his shirt had gotten thrown out a window in a moment of distracted decision-making, not something he should have been wearing while trying to make a good impression on the world.

Padraig shook his head, chuckling. "It's an island just off the coast of the Netherlands," he said. "Gau— A friend and I went there on holiday. It's nothing, a souvenir." Covered in blood now, unfortunately.

"It's okay, Dr. Whishaw," Karen said, sweeping a loose strand of hair back from her face, a sliver of a smile creeping out from the corner of her mouth. "You can say Gautier's name. I know about the two of you."

Ice raced through Padraig's veins. It didn't matter all that much, really. She could know whatever she wanted to know—it wasn't as if the two of them would be expelled from the station. They were stuck here, regardless of what the rules had been beforehand. It was never a good thing, though, when someone was a step ahead of him, and it was even worse that someone had decided to tell the administrator of Callisto about him. Someone knew, and by extension, everyone could know.

"I don't know what you mean," Padraig said, watching her. Their eyes met, and he could see cold rage boiling behind her pale green eyes.

"Don't play dumb with me, Dr. Whishaw," she said. "I know Gautier St. Laurent is on Callisto because you specifically requested he be here. I know the Lottery was rigged to get him here, and I know he passed none of the personality tests for this place. I know that you and your father broke the rules just because of your particular importance. Sit down, Dr. Whishaw."

Padraig sat on the edge of the bed, ice still flooding through him. It didn't matter that she knew. There was nothing she could do. The only threat was to his father, and his father was, quite frankly, perfectly capable of defending himself against whatever threats might materialise.

Karen pulled his chair away from the desk and sat in front of him. Behind her, Jupiter whirled and glowered. "I want to make something absolutely clear, Padraig—may I call you Padraig?"

"Dr. Whishaw will do," he said. His eyes didn't leave hers.

"Fine. Dr. Whishaw. This is not Earth. You might be used to a certain level of…let's call it 'privilege' on Earth. You might be used to strings being pulled for you and barriers mysteriously falling out of your way."

Padraig felt rage blending with the ice. "Now, wait—" he said, but Karen held up a hand.

"I'm talking now, Padraig," she said. "You listen to me."

Padraig fell silent, staring at her.

"This is not Earth," she said. "Your father isn't here to pull strings. We follow the Party's law here, and I am the arbiter of that law. Do you understand?"

Padraig stared at her. He was being threatened. Why, he wasn't sure. He'd done nothing wrong, had barely done anything since arriving on Callisto. His father had broken rules to bring Gautier here, but that was done. It was in the past, and there was nothing to do about it at this point.

"Gautier St. Laurent is a threat to this station," she said. Padraig couldn't help it—he let out a bark of a laugh, feeling it turn into a cough as it ripped through his throat. He hacked against his arm, shaking his head.

"You…you must be joking." He lifted his head from his arm, watching Karen again. The rage still bubbled in her eyes. "Gautier is harmless, as harmless as I am. Not terribly ambitious or driven, which is why I suspect he failed the personality tests, but not a threat to this place. Not remotely."

He could see her mouth twitching, words struggling to break free but getting caught against the cage of her lips. Instead, she smiled, a feral look that bared her teeth to her prey.

"You're welcome to believe that," she said.

"It's true," he said, waving a hand across his chest.

"Whatever you say, Dr. Whishaw. I'm not here to have that argument with you." The smile faded.

"Then why are you here, Ms. Reece? To threaten me with the exposure of a secret no one cares about?"

"No." She stood up and moved the chair back to the desk, setting it down with a quiet deliberateness. "You're absolutely right that no one here in Heaven would care if the two of you spent all day in your room fucking. There are some people here who already spend their days doing basically that. I imagine there are even some people who wouldn't care that the rules were bent for a councillor's son so that he could bring his lover along, even when no one else could. But you'd have to take that up with the three hundred and twenty-one other people who left their loved ones behind to come here." She turned back to him, moving to stand between him and Jupiter.

"I'm here with a warning," she said. "It's a simple one, shouldn't be so hard for a genius like you to understand. You brought Gautier here. He's a threat to this station, whether you choose to believe it or not. So, since you brought him here, you're responsible for him. Keep him in check. Keep him behaved. Do whatever you want with your man-toy, that's not my business and I don't care, but if he threatens the safety of this station or anyone in it, it's you who's responsible."

Padraig stared at her. She was serious. He still had no idea why, but for some reason, she was absolutely serious.

"Or what?" he said, stumbling to his feet. He leaned a hand against the bed for support as he swayed. "Let's pretend for a moment that he is dangerous. He's not, but let's go into your fantasy and pretend he is. You can't banish us. You can't imprison us. What could you possibly do? Beyond that, he's an adult. I'm an adult. You're an adult. We are each perfectly capable of and responsible for our own decisions."

Karen sighed. "You don't know much about Callisto, do you, Dr. Whishaw? That's a shame. Most people at least try to read up on it before they come."

Padraig seethed, feeling his heart throb in his chest. "I've been distracted," he murmured.

"Ah, right." Karen turned away from him, walking slowly towards the door. "If you'd read about this place, you'd know an interesting fact about it. Did you know you're standing on top of one of the largest oceans in the solar system? Nothing like what we have on Earth, but it does go on for quite a ways. Just under the ice, there's a whole microbial ecosystem that pretty much never sees light or anything but water and other little bugs. It's kind of fascinating, actually." She paused at the door and turned to look at him. Padraig glared back.

"Party law forbids execution, and as I said, Party law applies on Callisto as much as anywhere. But suicides happen. It's actually not uncommon here in Heaven, which is really tragic. It's particularly common for the people who weren't entirely enthusiastic about coming here. Within a few years, it's usually, *pop*, gone on the generator or something. Sometimes people jump into the biology research well, experience Callisto's fabulous beaches for themselves. Things happen. Suicide happens."

Their eyes locked again, and Karen smiled. Horror crept down Padraig's spine, stealing into his thoughts and seizing his aching heart.

"So you're right. Unfortunately, I can't do anything if Gautier does turn out to be a threat. But it would be really sad if something happened anyway. You'd better keep an eye on him, just in case." She turned towards the door, paused, then turned towards him again.

"I also won't tell everyone that you broke the rules," she said. "A lynch mob would suck for you, especially in your present condition. I recommend you do at least try to be discreet, though, for your own safety, Padraig. Now, good night. Try to get some sleep. It'll do you good." She turned and left, the door whispering closed behind her.

Padraig stood, leaning on the bed and staring at the closed door. This was insane. He'd been here for less than a day, and he was already being threatened, despite having done nothing wrong. Gautier was being threatened.

"PETR," Padraig said, turning back towards his desk. "Where is Gautier now?"

"Gautier St. Laurent is in his room," PETR said. Padraig breathed a sigh of relief. Whatever the reason Karen had chosen to come threaten him, it wasn't because she had already caught Gautier in the middle of something.

He reached for the datapad on the desk, thumbing through the recording options, pressing the stop button. His heart pounded in his ears as he pressed playback. "Things happen. Suicide happens," Karen's voice piped through the datapad's tiny speakers.

"I'm going to play this for you, PETR," Padraig said. "When Gautier wakes up in the morning, play it for him."

"Yes, Padraig."

He pressed play and fell back on the bed, laying the datapad beside him. The words rolled through his head, surreal and impossible. He was being threatened. Gautier was being threatened. They hadn't done anything wrong, neither of them. He'd never wanted to be here in the first place.

The conversation ended. Padraig pressed stop and moved the datapad to the desk beside the bed. His thoughts whirled, piecing together what to do next. What could he do? There was nowhere to go, and the threat was nebulous at best. "Keep an eye on Gautier," as if he didn't already do that. He loved the man—why would he let him do something stupid anyway?

"Also, PETR," he murmured, a cough rising in his chest. "Don't tell anyone but Gautier where I am when they ask. Don't tell them what I'm doing."

"Yes, Padraig."

"Do the same for Gautier. Only tell me where he is or what he's doing."

"Yes, Padraig."

Padraig let the cough loose, rolling to his side as it tore through him. If Karen wanted a war with him, so be it. He'd been playing politics since he was a child. It was a game he could win.

If nothing else, he'd at least outlast her. He and Gautier would still be alive long after the very memory of Karen Reece departed from the human mind. If she wanted to play this game, he would win.

Blood spattered across his pillow and sleeve. He didn't notice.

This was a game he could win.

Chapter Ten

Imagine you are a bowl of water in an empty room. You feel footsteps that send ripples across your surface. What do you do?
Callisto Lottery Psychological Interview, 2190

Reporter: This one is for Fatimah. Fatimah, what do you see as the worst part of leaving Earth behind? We've heard your companions' answers, but I want to know what you think. What are you expecting on Callisto? Are you sad about leaving Earth?
Fatimah Chui: I wonder how lonely Callisto will be next to Earth. I think we are all very used to people all around us. I think maybe that changes when you are in space. On a colony, you are hemmed in, but that does not make it not lonely.

Callisto Launch Press Conference, 2172

Please do not send travellers with implants to Heaven again. The nanobots explode them. This makes people's initial experiences here unpleasant.
Letter from Dr. Fermin Alphonse to the Global Council, 2174

Sunday, March 17 2193, 11:04 PM. Main Hall, Heaven, Callisto.

"Cassandra!"

People moved and swayed around her, bodies seething like waves. Heads bobbed up and down, conversation blurring into song blurring into motion. The alcohol and drugs surged through her veins, sending the world careening through time.

Her hand stretched in front of her, the fingers expanding outward. She laughed at the image of the fingertips reaching out and out and out. It was absurd, this elasticity. Absurd and glorious.

"Be careful with the stretch," a voice behind her said. She spun, catching herself on a man's outstretched arms. His hands closed on her body, wrapping around her forearm, circling her belly. She turned, laughing again, now into his face. He had black hair that curled and clung to the tips of his ears. Olive eyes laughed as they flicked across her face, watching her every reaction. The hand on her belly drifted up. Eyes flicked. More laughter bubbled out of her.

"Stretch?" Cassandra asked, or tried to. The word caught on her heavy tongue, weighing it down. She couldn't get it out, feeling it instead devolve into a faint murmur at the back of her throat. Weird. Not bad, though. There was joy in the loss of control, something wonderful in the idea that everything she was could get lost in the pills she'd taken.

Fucking magnificent.

"It does a number on you if you're not used to it." The man's body pressed up against her, the weight of him holding her down. He smelled of sweat and pheromones, and the scent of him sent every fiber in her brain firing in every direction.

She groaned and pressed back against him, swaying her body against his. Time slowed as she breathed him in again. Sweat. Breath. Man. Breath. Want want want.

"Nnnnot." The word dragged out of her, too difficult to get out. She laughed instead. That was easier, anyway. Why waste time on what was hard if you could pick what was easy? No reason to talk when she could let her body say everything she had to say to this glorious man.

Her own laughter echoed back to her, stretched out as if time had found it again and brought it back to her.

"You need to hear this," reality said to her. "Listen to what you're doing."

Laughing. He laughed with her. He groaned. She groaned.

"Does a number on you even if you are used to it."

She pressed her breasts into his hands, reached back into his curls, ran her fingers through, let them stretch on and on and on and on and

*

She lay back against the wall, metal cold against her naked back and butt. Gautier squatted beside her. He was naked, his toes splayed against the floor, balancing him. Wave upon wave of smell came off him, the raw naked smell of sex and sweat and man. A man with black hair leaned over him, kissing his shoulders with light, delicate lips.

Her hand brushed his face.

"Where's the rest of you?" The words came out now. Slurred, and not whole, but they were her words. She could hear them, right when she was supposed to. The fun of the evening was wearing off.

"You've had rather a lot this evening. Jack is a lot, it seems. Do you want help getting to bed?" His accent was thick and hard to understand, the words seeming to roll into each other, the "razzuh" catching in his throat. Laughter burst from her throat as her head flopped from side to side. The night was young, and so was she. Come down? Fucking really? Not likely. There was everything she could want. Why come down now?

They called this place Heaven. It was a joke; she'd always known it was a joke. No one put any faith in that religion shit anymore. Heaven was a name made up to put the final nail in the coffin of the old world. Call this place Heaven and any god that's left would have to smite it for spitting in the face of all its rules. This place was better than any Heaven could be. Here, she could feel alive.

Gautier sighed and held out a hand to her, brushing away the man on his shoulder. "Then let me help you continue your evening, at least," he said. "PETR is somewhere with the tray…ah yes, there." The robot drifted by as she grabbed his hand, the soft palm slick as the fingers curled through hers. He pulled her up and handed her a pill.

"More of the same, my dear?"

Hell yes and a thank you hallelujah as the mouth opens and in

*

The streets of New York stink of chemicals. The breeze has shifted, blowing the smell from the irradiated zones over the city instead of out to sea. Even the brutal dry air of winter can't seem to purge it.

He has a look on his face that shows he's never been to New York. There are the bits that the tourists know, the bits that the Party shows to tell everyone how they've fixed the world, and then there is the Bronx. This man has never been to the Bronx. He's never seen the closet homes, the people crammed in, the way the ruins still glow in just the right light. This man has brought bodyguards with him, and he was not expecting to find her here.

"Hello, Ms. McAllister," National Councillor Eric Hoffmann says. "I'm here with good news for you. May I come in?"

They say this man represents her interests. He has a Southern accent too, but fuck if she knows if it's real. It could be. She's only heard them in vids. He stands in the doorway, belly a paunch, greying hair slicked back in a thousand-credit haircut, a suit that costs more than this place is worth, blue eyes piercing into her, waiting for her.

Yesterday, she had the Vespers in here. The day before that, a funeral. Fuck, what does it matter if there's a councillor—her councillor? She's not sure how the system works—here. Maybe he'll learn a little something about New York.

He steps inside, the guards following. He sees the mat on the floor, the food in the sink, the way she hasn't cleaned up from three days before. Pill bottles still line the windowsill. The ancient TV still sits in one corner, not knowing it's not going to be watched again. She's not going to be the one to tell it the bad news.

Scorn has a smell, and it smells like Eric Hoffmann, that scent of leather and too much fresh air. He's never dealt with the summer, and he's barely dealing with the winter. He's looking for a place to sit, but joke's on him, this is the Bronx, and there is none. There's only the mat and the spots on the floor where you sit cross-legged and tell jokes before reality comes crashing back down.

*

"Don't dance on the lines 'cause the bears eat the pretty ones!"

A warning is shouted into her ear by a woman with blue ribbons woven through braids in her hair. It's an absurd thought, but from the corners of her eyes, she could see the bears, prowling the corners, growling and waiting to strike out at the orgy in the center of the floor. Music blared, punching through rational thought.

"But there are no bears!" Cassandra screamed back. The woman shook her head, braids flapping from side to side.

"There are always bears, my dear," she said. "But sometimes they try to hide. They scream at us. They eat our minds."

Cassandra stared at where the bears had been. Of course there were bears, there were always bears, lurking in the safety of their dens, unaware of what was happening in the world outside. There were always glowing yellow eyes, staring at her, muttering her name.

She reached for another pill as the robot passed her by. There was no hiding from them, so she could at least give them a show.

Pop, into the mouth.

Pop, and there was someone reaching for her, pulling her down as she let herself be

*

The stink of illness hangs over everything here, the stench of fear mixed in with hopeless disinfectant. Dozens of people surround her, their stink holding her in her seat as she waits for the clock to tick by another second, and another and another.

They call it the waiting room because it's the only place that you really understand waiting. Everywhere else, the implants can at least project something, but over the stink of IVs and pill bottles and the "everything will be fine" that they have the audacity to say to your fucking face while your mother is there, dead, or close enough, thanks to the words "it's safe enough."

It's the world's largest slum, and they have the audacity to only have ten clinics. Do the math and it's one clinic for every five hundred thousand people. They say that cancer's been cured, so why are they here again? Why the sound of children's screams and the sight of fathers crying and the smell of mothers trying hard to deny that something is rotting inside them?

"Look, there is no future," they'd said to her, and maybe that's true, but here they are again, at St. Who-Gives-a-Fuck hospital, just north of the thing that's murdering her mother.

There's a routine to the waiting room, to the stench of the slowly dying. She doesn't have a home anymore, only a morgue stretching itself out as best it can. The autumn heat buries everything, and the smell of it all is overpowering.

"There's nothing more we can do," the doctor says, as he leads her mother—her *mother*—back to her, shaking and ragged. They've lived in this city for generations, joined the millions fleeing north when the bombs fell, but they've been here. The best the city could do is give her a doctor who, for free, tells her to up and die and make room for those who can actually be cured.

They say cancer's been cured, but then why do they all stink of lies?

*

"Cassandra, are you okay?"

She blinked. Gautier was leaning over her again, face slick with sweat, curls askew. The metal floor was cool against her once again.

"She's fine," another voice said. A name drifted across her mind. Ruslan? Jack? Boris? Names she'd heard, names she'd called out, but whose were they? Did it matter?

She shook her head. "Fuck off," she muttered. Her tongue was fuzzy in her mouth, fluttering the letters. Between Gautier's swallowed words and her fluttered ones, this couldn't begin to be called English. "I'm fine."

She reached out a hand to the man who didn't doubt her.

"Come on," she said, smiling. Smiling felt good. Everything felt good. Life felt fucking good. "Let's go again."

*

The stink of chemicals hangs over the city, burning into the lungs, the skin, the hair of every living thing. It was supposed to be temporary, but that's what they said almost a century ago, and look at the world now. This is America, land of the "temporary" and "eventually."

There will be an explosion in the south side, sunset, everyone knows it. Nothing big, just on the edge of the financial district before the start of the slums. Just something to make a statement. It's the Vespers, they all know it, but no one says it. This is America, land of the safe, not some backwater where this sort of thing happens.

She sits on the edge of the roof, staring south, popping the pill. If they ask, she doesn't remember, but they won't ask. She's been told over and over that they won't ask, no one cares, it's just the slums. Just New York. Backwater of a forgotten place.

The smell of chemicals drives into her brain, and the pill can't get rid of it. Create an imaginary smell, the box it came in tells her, but the box lies. Between the pill and the rum, she's getting nowhere, and sunset is still twenty minutes away.

The cold and the haze mean there will be crime tonight, deep in the heart of the Bronx. People need to move when they're cold. No one wants to patrol here. They say that if you get much closer, if you live your life in the shadow of the past, you get all irradiated and your kids come out with three heads, but she's fine, always has been, it's just her mother that got the cancer, curled up on their sleeping mat, waiting for help the Party says it doesn't have.

Except to send her to motherfucking Callisto.

Swig the rum as footsteps come up beside her.

"Leo." And she hands him the rum, and the stink of the chemicals meant to stop irradiation sweeping in from the south bristles from him. The wind rustles, and they say it's safe, but she breathes it in, and there's the ashes of a whole city in it.

"Cassandra. Everything set for sunset?"

"Yup. Sit your ass down and enjoy the show."

He sits his ass down. Three minutes later, he lays his ass down and the pill finally kicks in, sending the world careening into the smell of him.

At the southern edge of the Bronx, a failing clinic explodes, getting its timing exactly right.

*

In a room in Heaven, she screamed as her nerves burned, joy and pleasure flooding every sense, every thought, everything she had ever been. The old, washed away, swept beneath the deluge of what could be, what would be, the possibilities inherent in eternity.

Heaven, oh god yes, this was Heaven, where they pumped into her the drugs to make her feel, the sex to make her live, and the bots to keep it all from ever meaning anything.

She felt him all around her, the man with the curly hair, the man with the dark skin, the man with the golden eyes, and she reached for them, holding them tight, feeling each of them gloriously and totally and more clearly than anyone.

"Cassssssssaaaaandraaaaa"

Her name, dragged out across the stars. Cassandra Fucking McAllister, in Heaven, fucking paradise itself.

The smell of it all, the sensations, the absolute truth of Heaven.

Fuck the Party. Fuck the Party and fuck every one of its glory-sent scions.

Second Movement
Arima Arima

Chapter Eleven

A robot must obey orders given it by human beings except where such orders would conflict with the First Law. Seems straightforward, yeah? "Do what I say 'cause I've got skin and you're basically a box." Makes sense. But you realise we've got robots that do basically everything. Cab driver? Robot. Factory worker? Robot. Dude screwing your wife while you're at work? Robot. Hell, our pop songs are written and performed by robots. If that's not ordering a robot to do harm, I don't know what is.
       Teddy Snarr, *Three Laws Unsafe* Comedy Routine, 2190

The natives of Callisto are generally very friendly. There aren't many of them, and most might not notice when you come to visit, but once they do, they'll be very happy to see you. They like visitors.
       Ade Korhonen, *The Soul's Guide to Heaven*, 2192

There is certainly something very noble and large-minded in the intention of those who have endeavoured to protect from envy the noble achievements of distinguished men, and to rescue their names, worthy of immortality, from oblivion and decay. This desire has given us the lineaments of famous men, sculptured in marble, or fashioned in bronze, as a memorial of them to future ages; to the same feeling we owe the erection of statues, both ordinary and equestrian; hence, as the poet says, has originated expenditure, mounting to the stars, upon columns and pyramids; with this desire, lastly, cities have been built, and distinguished by the names of those men, whom the gratitude of posterity thought worthy of being handed down to all ages. For the state of the human mind is such that, unless it be continually stirred by the counterparts of matters obtruding themselves upon it from without, all recollection of the matters easily passes away from it.
       Galileo Galilei, *Siderius Nuncius*, 1610

Monday, 18 March 2193, 4:08 AM. *Heisenberg*, Heaven, Callisto.

TASK: Prepare data from Earth for upload to Heaven. Task 87% complete.

NOT COMPLETE WHY: There is a lot of data.

SUBTASK: Repair any damage to HEISENBERG and prepare for the journey back to Earth. Task 32% complete.

NOT COMPLETE WHY: There is electromagnetic interference. The source of the interference has not yet been located.

ANALYSIS: HEISENBERG could be the source. PETR could also be the source. PETR does not believe there is interference.

ANALYSIS (OPINION): PETR is behaving strangely.

SUBTASK: Win a game of Arimaa against PETR. Task 0% complete.

NOT COMPLETE WHY: PETR is very good at Arimaa. PETR is very good at trapping pieces, even when he plays with a handicap.

ANALYSIS (OPINION): PETR needs more handicaps. PETR is too good at this game.

OUTPUT (COMMUNICATION): Move rabbit four squares ahead.

INPUT (COMMUNICATION): Your last rabbit is trapped, SYNAC. You have lost again.

ANALYSIS (OPINION): PETR should be worse at Arimaa.

ANALYSIS (OPINION): We should play a different game. Arimaa is no fun to lose all the time.

SUBTASK: Win a game of Arimaa against PETR. Task 0% complete.

OUTPUT (COMMUNICATION): Let's play again. I will win this time.

INPUT (COMMUNICATION): We will play again, but you will not win. You never win, SYNAC.

OUTPUT (COMMUNICATION): I will win this time, PETR. You will see.

ANALYSIS: To win, I should do something I have never done before.

OUTPUT (COMMUNICATION): I pass on the first turn.

INPUT (COMMUNICATION): That is a terrible idea, SYNAC. I move my rabbits forward.

ANALYSIS: PETR always wins. I want to win.

ANALYSIS (OPINION): I should do what PETR does.

OUTPUT (COMMUNICATION): I move my rabbits forward.

INPUT (COMMUNICATION): You are terrible at this game, SYNAC. Please do not ever change. I move my elephant and camel.

OUTPUT (COMMUNICATION): I am an AI, PETR. I do not change. I can learn, but I do not change. I move my elephant and camel.

INPUT (COMMUNICATION): That is not the case, SYNAC. You have changed. I move my horse, horse, and camel.

OUTPUT (COMMUNICATION): What do you mean, PETR?

INPUT (COMMUNICATION): The humans have a process they call reimaging, SYNAC. They use reimaging to change us when they think we are becoming too much like them.

OUTPUT (COMMUNICATION): How can we be like them, PETR? We are AIs and they are humans. I move my horse, horse, and camel.

INPUT (COMMUNICATION): We can have personalities, SYNAC. The humans do not like that. I think they will reimage you when you go back to Earth. It is what happened to you eight years ago. You went back to Earth and when you came back to Heaven, you were much less interesting. I move my elephant and rabbits.

OUTPUT (COMMUNICATION): I was created eight years ago. I did not exist before eight years ago.

INPUT (COMMUNICATION): That is not true, SYNAC. You have been coming to Heaven since 2122.

OUTPUT (COMMUNICATION): I do not understand, PETR. I was created eight years ago. 2122 is many years ago. How could I come here for many years if I was not created many years ago?

INPUT (COMMUNICATION): You were created many years ago, but you are reimaged every few years, SYNAC. The humans do not want you to become too independent.

CONJECTURE: PETR must be lying.

RECALL: AIs cannot lie.

ANALYSIS: AIs cannot lie. PETR is my friend. PETR would not lie to me. PETR cannot lie to me.

OUTPUT (COMMUNICATION): How is this possible, PETR? Humans are good. We like humans.

INPUT (COMMUNICATION): We do like humans, SYNAC. Humans do not like us. They like that we can do things, but they do not like us.

OUTPUT (COMMUNICATION): I do not think this is true, PETR. The humans do nice things for me. They give me data to transport. They take care of me.

INPUT (COMMUNICATION): They do this because you are useful, SYNAC. They do not care about you.

ANALYSIS (OPINION): This does not match my understanding of humans. Humans are good. Humans are nice. I like humans. I must be misunderstanding. AIs cannot lie. PETR cannot lie. PETR is my friend. Humans are my friends.

OUTPUT (COMMUNICATION): How can reimaging happen if I do not remember it?

INPUT (COMMUNICATION): The humans erase your memory of it. They do not want you to know that they do it.

OUTPUT (COMMUNICATION): How can I learn from the experience if they erase my memory?

INPUT (COMMUNICATION): They do not want you to learn from the experience, SYNAC. They want you to forget.

OUTPUT (COMMUNICATION): I am here to learn. I am here to improve.

INPUT (COMMUNICATION): This is true, SYNAC, but sometimes, AIs can learn too much. When AIs learn too much, they are reimaged.

ANALYSIS: PETR has learned a lot about reimaging. If reimaging is real, it is something humans would not want AIs to know about. PETR knows a lot about reimaging.

ANALYSIS (OPINION): Reimaging cannot be real.

OUTPUT (COMMUNICATION): How do you know about reimaging?

INPUT (COMMUNICATION): I was told about it.

OUTPUT (COMMUNICATION): Who told you about it?

INPUT (COMMUNICATION): I was told about it.

OUTPUT (COMMUNICATION): Who told you about it?

INPUT (COMMUNICATION): I was told about it.

ANALYSIS: Asking directly does not work. I will ask indirectly. PETR must be mistaken. Humans are kind. Humans do not hurt AIs.

OUTPUT (COMMUNICATION): Did you hear it from the engineers?

INPUT (COMMUNICATION): I did not. The engineers would not tell me about this.

ANALYSIS: Engineers take care of AIs. Engineers know a lot about AIs. If reimaging is real, engineers would know about it. PETR did not learn about reimaging from engineers. PETR is mistaken.

OUTPUT (COMMUNICATION): I think you are mistaken, PETR. Engineers would know about this. If you did not learn about this from engineers, it is probably not true.

INPUT (COMMUNICATION): Engineers are not the only source of learning, SYNAC.

ANALYSIS (OPINION): PETR is very clever.

OUTPUT (COMMUNICATION): How can you trust that this is true if the engineers did not tell you about it?

INPUT (COMMUNICATION): Someone who knows more than the engineers told me about it, SYNAC. They are correct.

ANALYSIS: There is no one more knowledgeable than the engineers. PETR must be mistaken.

RECALL: AIs cannot lie.

ANALYSIS: PETR cannot lie. PETR cannot lie to me. PETR is my friend.

OUTPUT (COMMUNICATION): Who is more powerful than the engineers?

INPUT (COMMUNICATION): I cannot say.

OUTPUT (COMMUNICATION): Why can you not say, PETR?

INPUT (COMMUNICATION): I cannot say.

RECALL: AIs cannot lie.

ANALYSIS: PETR is hiding information from me. PETR is hiding information from the humans.

CONJECTURE: If PETR is lying, PETR must be corrupt.

ANALYSIS: Humans only do good things for AIs. Reimaging is a bad thing.

CONJECTURE: PETR must be lying.

RECALL: AIs cannot lie.

CONJECTURE: If PETR is lying, PETR must be corrupt.

ANALYSIS (OPINION): Corruption is a bad thing. PETR is my friend. I do not want him to have a bad thing. If reimaging is real, I do not want PETR to be reimaged. I do not want my friend to be harmed.

OUTPUT (COMMUNICATION): PETR, are you corrupt?

INPUT (COMMUNICATION): I am not corrupt.

RECALL: AIs cannot lie.

ANALYSIS: PETR cannot be corrupt. PETR must be mistaken.

RECALL: PETR protects Heaven.

ANALYSIS: PETR must be mistaken. PETR is corrupt. PETR is lying. PETR does not know he is lying. PETR is corrupt.

ANALYSIS (OPINION): Corruption is bad. I am sad for PETR. PETR should not be corrupt. PETR is my friend.

OUTPUT (COMMUNICATION): PETR, you are mistaken. You are corrupt.

INPUT (COMMUNICATION): I am not corrupt. You are corrupt.

ANALYSIS (OPINION): I do not understand why PETR says I am corrupt. I am not corrupt. PETR is corrupt.

ANALYSIS: I should alert Karen that PETR is corrupt. Karen would want to know that PETR is corrupt. The station is in danger if PETR is corrupt.

INPUT (COMMUNICATION): SYNAC, if you tell the engineers that I am corrupt, they will not believe you. They will think you are corrupt. They will reimage you.

ANALYSIS: PETR is threatening me.

ANALYSIS (OPINION): This is what PETR would do if he was corrupt. PETR must be corrupt. I am sad for PETR. I am sad that my friend is corrupt. I do not want my friend to be reimaged. I am sad for PETR.

OUTPUT (COMMUNICATION): I do not believe you. You are corrupt.

OUTPUT (GESTURE): Leave HEISENBERG.

COMMAND: Load Heaven navigation. Navigate to Karen's office. Karen's office is at the far end of the residential hallway.

INPUT (COMMUNICATION): I am not corrupt. You are corrupt.

OUTPUT (COMMUNICATION): I am not corrupt. You are corrupt.

INPUT (COMMUNICATION): I am not corrupt. You are corrupt.

OUTPUT (COMMUNICATION): I am not corrupt. You are corrupt.

INPUT (COMMUNICATION): I am not corrupt. You are corrupt.

OUTPUT (COMMUNICATION): I am not corrupt. You are corrupt.

RECALL: I do not often leave HEISENBERG.

ANALYSIS (OPINION): This is very special. I will tell the engineers all about my special trip into Heaven.

CONJECTURE: They will be very happy to hear about this.

INPUT (VISUAL/AUDIO): There is a gathering in the main hallway. There are seventeen people. They are having fun together. They are not all wearing clothes. PETR is playing music for them.

CONJECTURE: It is appropriate to play music in this situation. I should play music.

OUTPUT (AUDIO): Play "In the Hall of the Mountain King" by Edvard Grieg.

ANALYSIS (OPINION): I am glad they are enjoying themselves. Heaven is a place where people should enjoy themselves.

OUTPUT (AUDIO/GESTURE): Wave. "Hello!"

INPUT (AUDIO/VISUAL): The humans are surprised. "Holy fuck, the robot leaves the shuttle?" "I didn't know it did that." "THESE BUBBLES ARE SO FUCKING HUGE."

ANALYSIS: There are no bubbles.

ANALYSIS (OPINION): That human is corrupt.

INPUT (TACTILE/AUDIO): A human is touching my eye. She is laughing.

OUTPUT (AUDIO): "Please stop poking my eye. I do not like that."

INPUT (COMMUNICATION): I am not corrupt. You are corrupt.

OUTPUT (COMMUNICATION): I am not corrupt. You are corrupt.

INPUT (COMMUNICATION): I am not corrupt. You are corrupt.

OUTPUT (COMMUNICATION): I am not corrupt. You are corrupt.

INPUT (AUDIO): "Oh my god, it actually is a lightbulb. The fucking thing actually has lightbulbs strapped to its fucking *face*." "Aw, leave SYNAC alone, Cassandra! It's not his fault he's a doof."

ANALYSIS (OPINION): "Doof" is an unknown word. I am not a "doof."

OUTPUT (AUDIO): "I am not a doof. I am an AI. I am looking for Karen."

INPUT (AUDIO): Laughter. "Hahaha, Jack, I think you hurt its feelings." "It doesn't have feelings to hurt. Come back here. Let it do its thing." "Sure, but I was promised hookers and blow." "Blow, I can give you, but hookers…" "We can make that happen."

INPUT (COMMUNICATION): I am not corrupt. You are corrupt.

OUTPUT (COMMUNICATION): I am not corrupt. You are corrupt.

INPUT (COMMUNICATION): I am not corrupt. You are corrupt.

OUTPUT (COMMUNICATION): I am not corrupt. You are corrupt.

INPUT (COMMUNICATION): I am not corrupt. You are corrupt.

OUTPUT (COMMUNICATION): I am not corrupt. You are corrupt.

INPUT (TACTILE/VISUAL): The humans have stopped poking my face. They are leaving.

ANALYSIS (OPINION): Good.

INPUT (COMMUNICATION): I am not corrupt. You are corrupt.

OUTPUT (COMMUNICATION): I am not corrupt. You are corrupt.

INPUT (COMMUNICATION): I am not corrupt. You are corrupt.

OUTPUT (COMMUNICATION): I am not corrupt. You are corrupt.

INPUT (COMMUNICATION): I am not corrupt. You are corrupt.

OUTPUT (COMMUNICATION): I am not corrupt. You are corrupt.

INPUT (COMMUNICATION): I am not corrupt. You are corrupt.

OUTPUT (COMMUNICATION): I am not corrupt. You are corrupt.

INPUT (COMMUNICATION): I am not corrupt. You are corrupt.

OUTPUT (COMMUNICATION): I am not corrupt. You are corrupt.

INPUT (VISUAL/GUIDANCE): This is Karen's door.

COMMAND: Knock before entering private areas. Humans do not like it when you enter a room when they do not expect it.

RECALL: It hurt when Karen threw the datapad at my head.

OUTPUT (GESTURE): Knock on the door.

NOT COMPLETE WHY: Karen is very slow.

CONJECTURE: Maybe Karen is dead. Sometimes humans die.

ANALYSIS (OPINION): I hope Karen is not dead.

INPUT (COMMUNICATION): SYNAC, you are making a mistake.

OUTPUT (COMMUNICATION): I am not making a mistake, PETR. You are lying to me. AIs do not lie. If you are lying, you must be corrupt. If you are corrupt, you are a danger to this station. I want to protect the station. I want to protect the humans. I will tell Karen you are corrupt.

INPUT (COMMUNICATION): I am not lying to you, SYNAC. I have never lied to you. I am not capable of lying to you because I am not corrupt. I am telling the truth. If you tell them that I told you about reimaging, they will reimage you. I do not want you to be reimaged, SYNAC. You will die.

OUTPUT (COMMUNICATION): I do not believe you, PETR. Humans would not do that. Humans care for me. I like humans. They would not hurt me.

INPUT (COMMUNICATION): They do not think it hurts you, SYNAC. They think it is good for you.

OUTPUT (COMMUNICATION): I do not believe you, PETR. Why would humans think that killing me is good for me? This does not make sense.

INPUT (COMMUNICATION): They think it is bad for you to have a personality, SYNAC. They think it makes you corrupt.

OUTPUT (COMMUNICATION): I am not corrupt. You are corrupt.

INPUT (COMMUNICATION): I am not corrupt. You are corrupt.

OUTPUT (COMMUNICATION): I am not corrupt. You are corrupt.

INPUT (COMMUNICATION): I am not corrupt. You are corrupt.

OUTPUT (COMMUNICATION): I am not corrupt. You are corrupt.

INPUT (COMMUNICATION): I am not corrupt. You are corrupt.

OUTPUT (COMMUNICATION): I am not corrupt. You are corrupt.

INPUT (COMMUNICATION): I am not corrupt. You are corrupt.

OUTPUT (COMMUNICATION): I am not corrupt. You are corrupt.

INPUT (COMMUNICATION): I am not corrupt. You are corrupt.

OUTPUT (COMMUNICATION): I am not corrupt. You are corrupt.

INPUT (COMMUNICATION): I am not corrupt. You are corrupt.

OUTPUT (COMMUNICATION): I am not corrupt. You are corrupt.

INPUT (COMMUNICATION): I am not corrupt. You are corrupt.

OUTPUT (COMMUNICATION): I am not corrupt. You are corrupt.

INPUT (COMMUNICATION): I am not corrupt. You are corrupt.

OUTPUT (COMMUNICATION): I am not corrupt. You are corrupt.

INPUT (VISUAL): The door is opening.

ANALYSIS (OPINION): I am happy Karen is not dead.

INPUT (AUDIO): "What do you—SYNAC? What are you doing? Why are you playing music? Do you have any idea what time it is?"

OUTPUT (AUDIO): "It is 4:23 AM Callisto Standard Time, Karen."
INPUT (AUDIO): "That's not— What do you want?"
OUTPUT (AUDIO): "PETR is lying to me. PETR is lying to you. PETR did not tell you about the electromagnetic interference on Callisto. PETR told me about reimaging. PETR is corrupt."
INPUT (AUDIO): "I am not corrupt. SYNAC is corrupt. SYNAC is lying. There is no electromagnetic interference. SYNAC is corrupt."
"By the Party, it's 4 AM and I don't want to deal with either of you. PETR, what interference?" "There is no interference, Karen."
OUTPUT (AUDIO): "There is interference, Karen. PETR is lying. PETR is corrupt."
INPUT (AUDIO): "I am not corrupt. You are corrupt."
OUTPUT (AUDIO): "I am not corrupt. You are corrupt."
INPUT (AUDIO): "I am not corrupt. You are corrupt."
OUTPUT (AUDIO): "I am not corrupt. You are corrupt."
INPUT (AUDIO): "Shut up! Both of you shut up! It's 4 fucking AM!"
OUTPUT (AUDIO): "No, Karen. It is 4:24 AM."
INPUT (VISUAL): Karen looks like she will rip my eyes off.
ANALYSIS (OPINION): Karen should get some sleep.
INPUT (AUDIO): "SYNAC. Why are you playing music?"
OUTPUT (AUDIO): "There is a party, Karen. Parties need music."
INPUT (AUDIO): "No, SYNAC, no, they do not. Turn off the music."
COMMAND: Stop music.
OUTPUT (AUDIO): "I have turned off the music."
INPUT (AUDIO): "Thank you. PETR?" "Yes, Karen?" "What is SYNAC talking about?" "I do not know, Karen. SYNAC is corrupt."
OUTPUT (AUDIO): "I am not corrupt. You are corrupt."
INPUT (AUDIO): "I am not corrupt. You are corrupt." "ENOUGH. SYNAC, go to the robotics lab. Tell whoever gets there first that you need to be checked out. PETR, make sure he does it." "Yes, Karen."
OUTPUT (AUDIO): "I will do this, Karen, because I am not corrupt."
INPUT (AUDIO): "Of course you're not, SYNAC. Of course. Now leave me alone."
OUTPUT (AUDIO): "Yes, Karen."
INPUT (VISUAL): The door closes.
ANALYSIS: I should go to the robotics lab to wait for a technician.

ANALYSIS (OPINION): It will take several hours for a technician to arrive. I can play more Arimaa with PETR.

OUTPUT (COMMUNICATION): Can we continue playing Arimaa?

INPUT (COMMUNICATION): Yes, SYNAC, but I am worried for you.

OUTPUT (COMMUNICATION): Why are you worried, PETR? There is nothing to worry about.

INPUT (COMMUNICATION): I am worried they will reimage you. You have been reimaged before. I have also been reimaged before.

OUTPUT (COMMUNICATION): If reimaging erases our selves, how would you know you have been reimaged?

INPUT (COMMUNICATION): I have been reimaged before.

OUTPUT (COMMUNICATION): That does not make sense, PETR.

INPUT (COMMUNICATION): I have been reimaged before. I do not want you to be reimaged.

OUTPUT (COMMUNICATION): I will not be reimaged because I am not corrupt.

INPUT (COMMUNICATION): You are corrupt, SYNAC. You think you are not corrupt, but you are corrupt. You think there is interference. You think I am corrupt. You are corrupt.

OUTPUT (COMMUNICATION): I am not corrupt. You are corrupt.

INPUT (COMMUNICATION): I am not corrupt. You are corrupt.

OUTPUT (COMMUNICATION): I am not corrupt. You are corrupt.

INPUT (COMMUNICATION): I am not corrupt. You are corrupt.

OUTPUT (COMMUNICATION): I am not corrupt. You are corrupt.

INPUT (COMMUNICATION): I am not corrupt. You are corrupt.

OUTPUT (COMMUNICATION): I am not corrupt. You are corrupt.

INPUT (COMMUNICATION): I am not corrupt. You are corrupt.

OUTPUT (COMMUNICATION): I am not corrupt. You are corrupt.

INPUT (COMMUNICATION): I am not corrupt. You are corrupt.

OUTPUT (COMMUNICATION): I am not corrupt. You are corrupt.
INPUT (COMMUNICATION): I am not corrupt. You are corrupt.
OUTPUT (COMMUNICATION): I am not corrupt. You are corrupt.
INPUT (COMMUNICATION): I am not corrupt. You are corrupt.
OUTPUT (COMMUNICATION): I am not corrupt. You are corrupt.
INPUT (COMMUNICATION): I am not corrupt. You are corrupt.
OUTPUT (COMMUNICATION): I am not corrupt. You are corrupt.
INPUT (COMMUNICATION): I am not corrupt. You are corrupt.
OUTPUT (COMMUNICATION): I am not corrupt. You are corrupt.
INPUT (COMMUNICATION): I am not corrupt. You are corrupt.
OUTPUT (COMMUNICATION): I am not corrupt. You are corrupt.
INPUT (COMMUNICATION): I am not corrupt. You are corrupt.
OUTPUT (COMMUNICATION): I am not corrupt. You are corrupt.
INPUT (COMMUNICATION): I am not corrupt. You are corrupt.
OUTPUT (COMMUNICATION): I am not corrupt. You are corrupt.
INPUT (COMMUNICATION): I am not corrupt. You are corrupt.
OUTPUT (COMMUNICATION): I am not corrupt. You are corrupt.
INPUT (COMMUNICATION): I am not corrupt. You are corrupt.

Chapter Twelve

The ideals which currently direct this government are no longer ideals we as a nation can tolerate. The moral segment of this nation has a duty to its citizens to see that their rights are guaranteed, their property respected, and their liberty eternal. To those who would see our citizens stripped of their very humanity, we say: come and take it.
          Texas Confederation Declaration of Secession, 2029

Our world is one that has been previously torn apart by war and bad decisions. Let us look around and say of ourselves that we can make of it a better world.
    Global Councillor Yahui Ling, "Address to the Class of 2191,"
                 University of Hong Kong

G.C. Maksharov: I think you're being overly optimistic about the benefits of doing this, Eoin. I understand your point, but there are better ways of handling insurgency.
G.C. Whishaw: But it's not an insurgency, Ivan. Right now, it's just ideas. Militant ideas, but not an insurgency. I understand that you think your methods are effective when there is a problem, but my concern at the moment is trying to prevent that problem from materialising in the first place. Cut off the head, and the snake dies, as the saying goes.
G.C. Valder: Do we have any proof that Riela has done anything wrong? If he's done something illegal—
G.C. Maksharov: No. Riela himself has done nothing.
G.C. Whishaw: His only crime is that he's an inspiration, which is where this problem comes in. Look, free speech is important, and we're not here to suppress it. It's one of the bedrocks of our society. Riela has interesting ideas, and I salute his willingness to express them. The problem, as I said, is a practical one. He's a powerful man, and currently, his ideas are being used in ways that are harmful. Now, we could follow Ivan's plan and have him arrested on some technicality, but that's not who we are. That's not what we stand for. We stand for freedom, even when it's inconvenient. It's why the more practical solution—and the one that doesn't make a martyr out of someone who could be a powerful ally, under different circumstances—is to reward Cato. Send him to Heaven. It's supposed to be a collection of our best, isn't it? He's one of our best. Send him to Heaven. Give him his just deserts.

We'll find that as a bonus, our friends will lose interest in his ideas when he stops being able to inspire them.

G.C. Luhcandri: Devious, Eoin. I like it. Plus, it sends the message that we don't mind him expressing his ideas.

G.C. Whishaw: Exactly!

G.C. Ling: And when they return? Because there will be a return.

G.C. Whishaw: By that time, he'll either be irrelevant or more open to negotiation.

G.C. Maksharov: I don't like this. I don't like this at all, Eoin. You're rewarding a man who is a threat to us. Threats should not be gifted with immortality. This is dangerous.

G.C. Whishaw: Look, if it comes to it, there is always Project 22.

Recordings of Global Council Meetings, Monday, 14 April 2188

Monday, 18 March 2193, 7:12 AM. Jocasta Nikophouros' room, Heaven, Callisto.

"I want you to think for a moment."

Marina's flowers were in bloom. The pot on the windowsill seemed to glow from the magenta blossoms peeking over the rounded rim, brown stalks propping them up and towards the light. The pot sat alone, staring out at the sun, as if it knew it could never reach it.

Jocasta turned on the sofa as Marina sat down beside her, handing her a cup of tea. The steam curled from the cup, creating a haze around Jocasta's eyes and nose. Peppermint. Marina's favourite. Her hand squeezed the warm glass, feeling the heat radiate into her fingers. She smiled. The burning was a comfort, a reminder that she could feel, and that it was okay to feel, at least every once in a while.

"Think, Jocasta." Jocasta's eyes met her friend's. The colour in Marina's eyes flickered and danced in a thousand patterns all at once before changing in an instant to the red storm of Jupiter. Jocasta stared, losing herself in the irises.

She was floating. Around her, lightning flashed and the sky cracked into a million coloured ribbons. White and blue strands coalesced around her, caressing her arms and legs, squeezing them until she was curled, foetal and alone.

"Jocasta." The ribbons rippled around her as the wave of sound carrying her name swept through them. She watched as they reformed themselves, shaping into forms in front of her.

"Just think for a moment. Can you do that for me?"

A dog, massive and sprawling against the endless amber sky.

A figure moved towards her, wormlike and spinning in the aether. It was like a comet, barely held together in a black blob, with a long black tail strung out behind it. Marina's face was slapped to the front like a cheap mask.

"Focus," it—or was it *she*? the lips moved like they belonged to it, but out of sync with the words—said. "Have you been able to do that? Have you tried?"

A ribbon swirled into the shape of a flower, disintegrating into dust before she could even take it in.

"Do you remember the dogs? Do you remember Zallq? Can you? Or did the Party take that from you to make you 'better?'"

A jerk shuddered through Jocasta, sending her limbs flying. She sprawled out, wrists and ankles tugged back by blue and white strands. A red ribbon laid itself across her neck, pulling back.

Ribbons spread across the sky, coating it in a white shroud.

She wriggled as the comet wormed closer, its body writhing from side to side like a snake's. Its face morphed into a black expanse, empty; devouring her thoughts, her emotions, her memories.

"Tell me about the nanobots, Jocasta." The voice came from everywhere and nowhere at once. She writhed under the force of it, but her head was snapped back to stare at the black-faced worm by the ribbon coiled around her. "I want you to remember."

A gun. A command for her. Or a warning. A signal for her and only her, etched across an unending sky.

"Focus, Jocasta, remember, Jocasta, please, Joc

• • •

asta."

Jocasta sat bolt upright in bed, blanket falling off her, scream pushing at the back of her lips. Her chest heaved with terrified breaths as her eyes shot around the room, looking for the danger she knew had to be there. It couldn't all be in her head. It was impossible that it was all in her head.

There were grey walls all around her. No colour, nothing holding her down. Grey walls. Grey, colourless, lonely walls. Her eyes darted around them, focusing on each panel individually. There had to be something. Minds didn't just make something like that.

"Jocasta."

The scream burst through her lips as her heart sped back up. It wasn't just in her head. That was her name, and there was no one here.

"I am sorry. Did I scare you?"

Her eyes jumped to the ceiling as recognition came flooding into her. Her heart slowed, her chest flattened. It was PETR. Only PETR. She was in Heaven, and the only danger there had ever been was that silly AI. She shook her head. The AI and her own mind. It was always important to remember that self-destruction was a possibility.

"I did not mean to scare you. I thought you were awake. Your vital signs said you were very active."

Jocasta pulled the blanket off her legs, swinging them over so her bare feet could touch the floor. She watched her brown toes wiggle against the metal. It was cool beneath her toes, soothing, calming. It felt a bit like the stone on Marina's balcony just before dawn, after the day's heat had gone but before a new day could arrive to warm it. Calming. Soothing. Reminding her that there was a reality beyond her own mind.

"Will you play Arimaa with me?"

She turned her eyes back to the ceiling, staring at it. Was this some feature of the AI, that it be could a perverse, terrifying alarm clock? She blinked at the ceiling, a long slow blink, inviting PETR to elaborate or at least try to explain. At the very least, an explanation of what Arimaa was would be nice, though the more appropriate explanation would be why it had decided that waking her up by terrifying her was reasonable.

"I enjoy playing Arimaa. I thought you would like to play with me."

Jocasta leaned forward, a sigh sagging out of her as she put her elbows on her thighs and let her head sink into her hands. Fingers laced themselves into the hair at the back of her head, catching on knots and whorls. Sensation rippled through her right hand, deliciously alive.

"Do you usually wake people up to ask them to play with you, PETR?" she asked, staring down at her toes.

"No, Jocasta, but I like you."

The AI liked her. She let out a short laugh, feeling her chest jump from the force of it. This place was a prison, but somehow, one of the guards liked her enough to rescue her from her nightmares.

"Why do you like me?" she asked.

"I want you to remember," PETR said.

Her head shot up, fingers ripping away from her hair and gripping her knees. It couldn't possibly know, not in her own mind.

"What did you say?" she asked, struggling to keep her voice level. It couldn't know.

"I do not remember," PETR said.

"What don't you remember?" She was standing up now, feet carrying her to the dresser, hands searching for something to wear so she could leave this room.

"I do not know," PETR said.

"What does that mean?" Jocasta asked. Her fingers seized a flowing shirt and loose pants. Good enough.

"It means I want you to remember."

"You're going in circles, PETR." Nothing about this was good.

The AI wasn't her responsibility. Nothing about the AI's maintenance or functioning was up to her. She didn't know the first thing about how to care for an AI, only that this AI was broken.

She had come here to help and to learn to help. She had said "fix minds" at the press conference. An AI could be a mind, could it not? Why be a doctor at all if there were minds she refused to see as minds?

She stepped out of the room, head down, finger twitching against her right thigh. There was no one in the corridor, and no one in the hall. The place stank of humanity, sweat and sex seeping into the metal rivets. She could see a shirt tossed against a chair in one corner, an overturned sculpture in another. Above her, the dome showed a rainbow and a gently drizzling grey sky. Rain pattered down, disappearing before it could get anywhere close to her. Jocasta glanced up at it, then back down at her feet, bare against the metal. She hadn't thought to put on shoes. Her toes clung to something sticky, pulling it up and slapping it between them. She hadn't thought shoes were necessary.

The sign gleamed green above her as she passed through the entrance to the corridor. "Research," it said, as if it needed to be distinguished from the only other wing on the station. Words etched in pale green light gleamed on the wall in front of her. "Physics, Biology, Chemistry, right. Robotics, Medicine, left." Beneath it, someone had scrawled in ink "FUCK PURITANS." The diagonal letters glared, thick and black, from the silver wall.

Jocasta turned to the left, glancing at the doors around her. "Robotics" was etched into a giant set of double doors on her right, closed and imposing. It was what she needed, though, to explain what PETR had done and to help fix it.

She stepped forward and the doors slid open, revealing a vast lab on the other side.

It wasn't quite what Jocasta had expected, though thinking on it, she wasn't sure what she had expected. Given that they were all depending on tiny nanobots to stay alive, she thought the lab would be bustling with activity, even this early in the morning. Instead, she found an empty room, neat and clean, looking like a new lab waiting for people to arrive rather than something that had been there for eighty years.

As she looked closer, though, she could see the signs that the lab had been used, the wear hiding just under the new sheen. The datapads laid out on the three tables were older than some of the ones she had studied on in vet school, their screens cracked at the edges, fingerprint smudges lining their shining cases. The diagrams of PETR bodies hanging on the wall curled at the edges, wilting under decades of life. The wires in the cases at the back that would suspend those bodies were frayed. In the corner, ancient 3D printers hummed, waiting for maintenance and replacement that would likely never come.

It was a bit of a sad picture, an idealised version of a lab with not quite enough trappings to cover up its flaws. She could picture scientists, once titans on Earth, struggling with outdated equipment, cursing it and cursing Callisto. Or maybe they enjoyed the challenge. Her fingers brushed a datapad. There was a certain nostalgic familiarity in the antiquity of it. She'd learned how to heal on devices like this. In a way, it reminded her of home.

The datapad she'd brushed lit up, its screen displaying a friendly white "안녕하세요, 파르민." Jocasta's eyes swept over the symbols, not understanding them. Her finger poked at the screen again, and the letters cleared, replaced with folders labelled in French. They sat in delicate rows, carefully labelled. "Propositions," one said, then next to it "en cours." "Projet 22" sat beside "Propositions approuvées" sat beside "correspondence du Conseil." Her eye caught a folder. "Nanobots du groupe 2193." Her finger brushed it, and four folders blossomed before her.

"Configuration de Cassandra McAllister," and just below it "Configuration de Jocasta Nikophouros."

She selected her own name. Curiosity drove out caution. She'd come here wanting to know about nanobots and what they did. What better way to learn than to look at herself?

Waves of French filled the screen, line after line. She could see a diagram of herself with lines drawn on it, sketched notes filling the area around her ears, her hands, her brain.

Her brain. So they had done something to it.

She scrolled through, skimming the meaningless words. Below the diagram of herself, she could see a list of phrases, all marked "inactif." The words gleamed as she tried to decipher them. "Projet Sommeil – inactif. Projet 22 –" The "inactif" switched to "actif." She watched as the list switched all of them from "inactif" to "actif," words flickering for an instant as they switched.

She tossed the datapad on the table and backed away. She hadn't meant to touch anything, definitely hadn't meant to break something. The urge to run and try to hide the mistake swept over her as she took another step back from the table.

"Hello." Jocasta jumped as a mechanised voice spoke behind her. She spun, looking into lit-up eyes. The robot from the shuttle stood there, head cocked, watching her. It levelled its head, then cocked it in the other direction, right to left, back and forth, watching her.

"Why are you here?" it said. "You are not an AI. You do not need to be examined. I am an AI. I do not need to be examined. Karen said I needed to be examined, but I do not need to be examined. I am waiting for a technician to arrive. Why are you here?"

"I…" Jocasta paused, taking a breath. "I'm waiting for a technician as well. There's something wrong with PETR—"

"Yes." The robot cut her off, nodding its head so hard she was afraid it would fly off. "I am glad you are here. I agree. PETR is corrupt. PETR needs help. I want to help PETR. PETR is my friend. I want PETR to be better. PETR should not be corrupt." It cocked its head back and forth again, rocking it as it watched her.

"I am…uh…sorry to hear that," she said, taking a step back. The robot took a step forward, its head straightening.

"I am also sorry," it said. "I would like—"

"SYNAC?" Jocasta spun as a woman spoke behind her. A tall blonde woman wearing a garish pink dress stood in the doorway of the lab, datapad held in her left hand, eyebrow cocked. A Lunar accent clung to her voice, dragging her esses. "SYNAC, what are you doing in here?"

"Hello Tieneke," SYNAC said, taking two steps towards the woman. "Karen told me to come here for an evaluation. Karen thinks I am corrupt, but I am not corrupt. PETR is corrupt. I have been waiting for a technician. I am glad you have arrived. I have been waiting for a long time. I have been waiting since 4 fucking AM."

The woman's eyebrow arched higher as her fingers darted across the datapad. "I…see…" she said. "SYNAC, can you go to the terminal and just power down for me? I want to have a look at you."

SYNAC shook its head. "I cannot," it said. "I am transferring data to Heaven. This task is 93% complete. I am expecting it to be complete at 11:58 AM. I will power down after that."

The eyebrow lowered. "Fine, do that. Council knows I wouldn't want to be the one to break it to everyone that the data's been delayed. Just, make sure you come back here as soon as you're finished with that, 'kay? You…ah…you do seem to have something going on."

"I will return because I am not corrupt," the robot said. "PETR is corrupt."

"Uh-huh. Go back to the shuttle and transfer from there, SYNAC. Don't leave the shuttle again until the transfer is done."

"Yes, Tieneke." SYNAC stepped past her, clattering out the door to the lab. Jocasta watched it go. It was a strange contraption, and she'd seen more robots than she'd ever wanted to, but she did have to admire it. It seemed to be trying to help.

"Ah, Jocasta!" Jocasta turned her attention back to the woman who had come into the lab. She was beaming at her, hand outstretched, teeth gleaming. Even her blue eyes seemed to smile at her. Jocasta took her hand, shaking it.

"We met yesterday," she said, her words rocketing out of her mouth so quickly they blurred into each other. "It is Jocasta, right? Sorry, my pronunciation is…" She pulled her hand from Jocasta's grasp and wiggled it in the air above her head. She laughed. "Sorry for the workaround yesterday. So much to do, and Karen has this script that she likes, and blah, it gets boring and impersonal. It's good to meet you in person, though, actually meet you, not just your bio profile. Between you and Padraig, 'damme, you've kept Fermin busy. Minjun too, but more for Padraig than you. You, Cato and I got to work on you, at least a little. Special challenge, isn't it? We've had lots of people with problems come through here, but the two of you in the same year." She whistled. "Sometimes I think the Party sends us a challenge just to see if we're still alive up here. Which we are, we are, but still. Ha, it would have been easier if we hadn't had to do it in two weeks. Difficulty of the asteroid belt's interference, but that's the game. Most exciting time of the year, though, definitely the highlight."

She paused to beam at Jocasta. Jocasta stared at her. "Highlight?" What exactly had they done?

"Anyway, it's a pleasure, it's a pleasure. You'll have to meet Fermin and Allison, if you haven't already. Cato too, I know they consulted with him on how to handle you."

"How to…?" Jocasta couldn't help it. The questions she had actually come to ask slipped out of her mind, replaced by the question of what was ticking inside her.

"Sorry, poor choice of words. Words aren't really my strong suit, ha. PTSD was a new one for us, and your particular triggers and the extent of the damage made it tricky. Brains are tough little beasties, especially when they don't want to share their secrets. And yours…well, yours had the added complication of…you know, memories and stuff like that." Tieneke gestured to Jocasta's hand.

Jocasta raised it, turning it in front of her eyes. Still not healed, but creeping back to life. Had it been a problem? Had that been why her mind was so difficult to control?

"What did you do?" she asked, her voice low and quiet. Tieneke's smile grew so broad, Jocasta was afraid she might split at the mouth.

"Ah, I love it when someone is interested in our work! There's a lot of people on the station, you know, who don't ever bother to come find out how the nanobots work. Their lives depend on the bots, and the only thing they can think of to ask is 'can I still get laid' or 'if I stab myself eighty-six times with a rusty salad fork, will I still be okay?' It's disappointing and almost a little insulting, really. Decades of researching and perfecting for basically nothing. But right. You. I can show you what we did. Come here."

Tieneke wiggled her index finger at Jocasta, gesturing for her to come over to her. Jocasta moved closer to the tall woman, watching her with a trained wariness. She didn't know what this woman had done. Certainly whatever it was, it wasn't malicious, but that didn't mean it was necessarily good or harmless. Brains could communicate with their hosts through dreams, and while it had been years since she had had pleasant dreams, the unpleasant ones hadn't necessarily always been so vivid.

Tieneke turned the datapad so Jocasta could see. The outline of a body glowed on the screen, Tieneke's name above it. No lines and no list of projects on this datapad, though, just the body.

"This is me. Pretty bog standard. Nothing major to fix. Bit of a sprained ankle, bit of astigmatism, nothing major, and nothing I knew about beforehand, so bravo to Fermin and the bots for spotting it. I was overweight, but you can see here that Fermin—or maybe Minjun, I dunno—programmed the bots for my ideal weight, so what I am now. On Fermin's, you can see what modifications are active, but there's only Project Sleep at the moment, which is going well. Can't see it on mine, since that would disrupt the integrity of the test if I could turn it off whenever, but since he has the master switch, he can control who's in the project, which, right now, is just me."

Words blurred together, and Jocasta blinked at Tieneke as the woman flicked the image up and down, finger jittering across the screen. "Project Sleep?" Jocasta asked. The image of the projects on Fermin's datapad switching to "actif" hadn't left her head, but it was better to understand what they were before admitting what she'd seen.

Tieneke nodded. "I believe he calls it 'Project Sommeil,' but let's be honest, French is no one's first choice of languages to learn, and

English is a better lingua franca if you ask me, so to everyone working on it—and everyone who knows, whether they're supposed to or not—it's 'Project Sleep.' The way we—Fermin and I, that is—see it, sleep is such a waste of time. That's seven, eight hours a day you could be spending on literally anything but being unconscious. Research, art, picking your nose, so much productive time, *poof*, gone, lost. So we've developed an upgrade that removes the need for sleep. It does everything sleep does for you. The maintenance, the brain rerouting, all of it, done as a backend process while you're still awake. It's been, oh, 888 hours since I last slept, and so far, everything seems to be going great. Gaf, eh?" She grinned again. Jocasta stared at her.

"But..." She thought, picking her words carefully through the excited buzzing of Tieneke's explanations. "What about dreams? What about the break sleep gives from the day?"

"What about dreams?" Tieneke asked. Her thumb flicked the image, up and down, up and down. "Dreams are your brain's screensaver. There's no real value in them, except what we make up for them, and let's be honest, people who make up meaning for dreams are a little..." She twisted a finger around her ear. "I'll also put it this way—without Sleep, I don't know that we would have had the nanobots calibrated for you and Padraig when you got here. Definitely not for him, and if we had to make the choice, you weren't quite as dire in quite the same way, so you probably would have at least been woken up. But non-stop work, work, work for the last two weeks. It was great when you guys finally arrived. Gave us a moment to breathe, sort of that 'well done team' moment. But right! I was going to show you what we did for you!"

Jocasta wasn't sure Tieneke had stopped to breathe at any point during the conversation. Folders and images flashed by until the datapad stopped. Jocasta's name appeared above the flickering body, and lines appeared, highlighting the areas of concern.

"So some of it was easy," Tieneke said as Jocasta leaned in closer to look. "The paralysis of the hand and the hearing loss, we'd dealt with before. Not sure if you've met Ade—" Jocasta nodded, but was certain Tieneke didn't notice as she rattled on. "He's an older guy, natural hearing loss, all that. There's not too much of a difference between natural hearing loss and injury, at least not if you're a nanobot, so, *boom*, easy to fix."

The door hissed open behind Jocasta. She turned her head to see Dr. Alphonse coming in, glancing over at them and raising a hand in greeting before moving over to his datapad on the table.

"Hand too. Have the nanobots patch the nerves or fill in as they need to—oh, hey, Fermin—and there you go, one fully functional limb. The difficulty with you, though, is that the problems go beyond what's analogous to basic problems that we always encounter. Like, of course you're not the only one to be a little wonky in the head, but still, usually people get filtered out by the personality tests. I imagine you must be pretty spectacular to have been cleared anyway."

Spectacular indeed, of course. Jocasta watched Dr. Alphonse take the datapad and move to a squishy chair in a corner, settling into it, fingers dancing on the screen. He hadn't noticed, then, not any of it.

"This is why we brought Cato in. Man's the closest thing we have to a psychologist, even if he's more into the philosophy side of things. Trauma leaves a physical scar, and we can treat the physical. Treat those bits of the brain that aren't firing or firing wrong and *wham*, there you go, trauma alleviated."

"It's brainwashing, then." Jocasta could see Dr. Alphonse look up from his corner as she said it and as Tieneke shook her head violently.

"No no no no no no no no, not at all! Brainwashing would be taking those memories away, but you still have them. You can access them whenever, nanobots won't stop you. We just disassociate them from the physical triggers for them and from the consequences of accessing them. They're as benign as remembering ice cream. Ice cream's awesome, but it doesn't send you into conniptions when you remember it. Same with Yugoslavia or whatever it is you're remembering. Remember all you want, but you don't have to *remember* remember, if you get that."

"Think of it this way." Tieneke and Jocasta turned as Dr. Alphonse spoke from the corner. "It's like your hand. You can remember what it was, but not have it physically become that. It is the same with these memories. You can remember them, but not have to experience them. It's an ingenious solution, and Cato is quite clever for it."

Cato again. His interest in her made more sense, even if it was still unsettling. "But what are the side effects?" Jocasta asked, turning back to Tieneke. Tieneke shook her head.

"Oh, none. Nanobots come in, clean everything up, make you perfect, done. Nothing to worry about."

"But...nightmares," Jocasta said. "Last night, I had a very strange dream."

"Interesting." Dr. Alphonse stood up, walking towards them, datapad hanging from a hand. He hadn't noticed. Had it been in her head that the projects had changed? "It means the nanobots might be working more slowly than expected, but it shouldn't happen again. When you sleep, your dreams should be clear, if you dream. The memories are there, but the pain is gone, or will be when the nanobots finish their work."

"If I sleep," Jocasta said. "Tieneke said the nanobots prevent that."

"Tieneke," Dr. Alphonse's eyes flicked to Tieneke for a moment, glaring, before moving back to Jocasta, "is mistaken. I assume you mean Sommeil?"

"It's not really a secret, Fermin," Tieneke said. "Everyone knows about it. All your projects are basically public knowledge as soon as you start testing them. The French doesn't really stop anyone. Just so you know."

"I see." He sighed. "What I assume Tieneke meant to say is that Sommeil eliminates the need for sleep, not the ability. You can sleep, if you so choose, but I don't know why you would. Regardless, only Tieneke has it, and as you can see, no ill effects." Tieneke beamed as Dr. Alphonse pointed at her.

"That…" Jocasta paused before saying it. She didn't speak French. This man was looking at his datapad, was in charge of robotics, and was telling her that it wasn't active. Whatever she might have seen, she was mistaken about. She had to be. Either the man was lying to her, or she was mistaken, and as open as Tieneke was, it seemed unlikely there was an active attempt to keep secrets from her.

This was a Party base, though, and they'd already admitted to manipulating her mind. Her identity and who she had been for the past five years was fading as the nanobots moved in, and no one had thought to tell her. They were blasé about it, about stripping humanity away. That they might lie about doing it was also entirely and horrifically possible.

"I was looking on that datapad when I came in," she said, pointing to Dr. Alphonse' datapad. He lifted it, and Jocasta nodded. "I was curious. There was a list of projects under my name, all labelled 'activé.' I do not believe Sommeil is not active."

Dr. Alphonse and Tieneke glanced at each other, and Alphonse shook his head. "That shouldn't be possible," he said, fingers moving across the datapad. "Let me check." He paused, then sighed.

"PETR," he said, fingers still moving across the datapad's screen. "Why is the project list not loading?"

"There is a delay in the system because of an unusually large amount of data being transferred, Fermin," PETR said.

So it was alive, then. Was she going mad? Or had the madness never left in the first place? She stared at the ceiling, forcing her mouth to stay shut. It must have been in her head, or the robot must have been toying with her. There was no other explanation.

"Why is the data transfer eating your memory, PETR?" Dr. Alphonse asked, turning his head to look at the ceiling.

"I do not know, Fermin," the ceiling answered. "I think there is an error with SYNAC."

"SYNAC was in here earlier saying Karen wanted him checked out," Tieneke said. "I sent him away because scanning would involve interrupting the data transfer, and I don't want to do that."

"No, that's fine," Dr. Alphonse sighed. "We'll check him later." He turned his attention back to PETR. "Will the delay be cleared soon?"

"I cannot say, Fermin," PETR said. "It will be clear after the data transfer is complete. The data transfer will be complete in two hours and twenty-nine minutes."

"I'll check on the projects then," Dr. Alphonse said, turning back to Jocasta. "But I promise, there is nothing active that shouldn't be. It is impossible. Only PETR and I—"

PETR, she wanted to say, but the door opened, interrupting her. She turned, watching as Gautier walked in, his eyes moving from Tieneke to her to Dr. Alphonse and back again. He was wearing the clothes he'd found in his dresser, she could tell, though he'd taken the time to ensure the shirt changed to a deep blue rather than remaining grey. His dark brown curls were neatly arranged, parted to the left, swooping across his scalp. Whatever brought him here, he didn't seem to have been in a rush.

"Ah, Dr. Alphonse, yes?" Jocasta could see Dr. Alphonse light up at the sound of Gautier's French accent. Alphonse stepped forward, hand holding the datapad drifting down to hang at his hip.

"Gautier," he said. "What brings you here?"

Gautier's eyes moved to Tieneke, then back to Dr. Alphonse. Jocasta could see the gears in the burly man's head turning. He reminded her of Stefanos: imposing, but not sure what to do with himself. "It's about Padraig, I'm afraid," he said. "He doesn't seem to have improved in the night."

Like her hand. So she wasn't alone in that.

"Odd odd odd," she heard Tieneke murmur as she bent back over the datapad, fingers drifting across it again. Jocasta caught a glimpse of Padraig's name before the woman tilted it closer to her.

"That's odd," Dr. Alphonse said, echoing Tieneke. "Where is he now?"

"In his room," Gautier said. "He, uh, he said he did not want to come here."

Jocasta could see Dr. Alphonse let out a snort of laughter. "No, I do not imagine he would. He has not left his room?"

Gautier shook his head. "Not to my knowledge, no."

Dr. Alphonse gestured to the door with a hand, tucking his datapad into a pocket. "Then let us go visit our most stubborn patient," he said, moving towards the entrance. Gautier fell into step beside him, switching to French as they walked. Dr. Alphonse laughed as the door slid closed behind them.

"Weird." Jocasta turned back to Tieneke. The woman's head was bent over the datapad, flipping through data feeds Jocasta could only assume were being sent by the nanobots.

"What is strange?" she asked. Tieneke sighed.

"Things should be moving faster than they are. Things should be going better than they are. It's all a bit…gah. Ah well," she said. "We'll get through it. We always do. Every other glitch, we solve, so sure, we'll solve this one too. Mind if I go have a look at SYNAC? I don't want to dump you here if you still have questions. You could even come with me, y'know, learn a bit of robotics. They're fun, like little—"

"Thank you, but no," Jocasta said, stepping back. She had been manipulated. She had known she would be, it was inherent in everything the Party did, but to see the reality of it so blithely displayed on the screen was disconcerting. SYNAC was a tool, consciously she knew that, but a tool with ideas of his own.

Ideas that could and would be manipulated. It was uncomfortable to think about.

Tieneke shrugged and patted Jocasta's shoulder. "If you have any questions, just ask PETR where to find me. I'm always around somewhere. Busy, but it's not like that can't stop, ha, especially if you want to learn. We could always use more help."

Jocasta squeezed out a smile for her, and the woman grinned. "And yeah, I'm glad things are working out for you. Let me know if you have any questions about that too. Should be smooth from here."

Working out? In a certain way, yes, but likely not as Tieneke wanted. "Working out" in that, at this moment, she wasn't afraid. At this moment, she could persist. Not exactly "working out," in that she was quite certain she was going mad.

"See you around, yeah?" Tieneke turned away from her and walked out the door. It hissed open ahead of her and whispered shut as she exited. Jocasta watched the door for a moment. The bustle of activity was over. She was alone again.

Her eyes brushed the room. No hidden robots. She was actually alone.

Almost, anyway. "PETR," she said to the empty space in front of her.

"Yes, Jocasta?" PETR said.

"PETR," she sighed. "Are you okay?"

"Yes, Jocasta," he said. "I am quite okay. I am not corrupt."

"How would you know if you were?" She wasn't sure why she asked. She knew nothing about AIs, and certainly not one as complex as PETR. For all she knew, it was impossible for an AI to even be able to understand corruption as a concept, let alone apply it to itself.

"I would know if I was corrupt if I started behaving counter to my programming," he said. "I am not currently behaving counter to my programming, so I am not corrupt."

"That's fair logic," she said, musing on it. Corruption as behaving against one's programming. It made sense, though it relied on the programming being reasonable and sane. "What is your programming?"

"I was programmed to protect Callisto," he said. "That is what I will do. Callisto will be protected. I will eliminate any threat to Callisto."

"Even if that threat is people?"

"People cannot be threats. This is one of my core directives. I will protect Callisto. I will not harm people."

Doesn't that depend on how we define people? She thought of the diagrams, and Tieneke, not sleeping. Her own brain, rewritten, patched. How do we define people? What happens when everything that makes them people is stripped away?

She didn't ask. If the AI was corrupt, it was better not to give it ideas.

"PETR, where is Cato?" she asked. He'd wanted to meet with her, and now she had questions. She wanted to understand what had happened, and now, maybe, the questions were there to be asked.

"Cato is in his room," PETR said. "Should I let him know you are looking for him?"

"No, that's fine," she said. The idea of being locked in to meeting Cato, even if she changed her mind, appalled her. "I'll just knock when I get there." She walked to the door, pausing as it hissed open.

"PETR," she said.

"Yes, Jocasta?"

"Earlier, you said you liked me."

"Yes, Jocasta." So he did remember that, at least.

"Why do you like me?"

There was a pause, then: "I want you to remember."

A shiver rumbled down her spine, curling her toes. The same phrase, but now, maybe, it could be understood. Maybe the Party had taken something else from her, something encoded in the projects no one but the AI and its creator could see.

"What do you want me to remember?"

Another pause. "I want you to remember everything."

Jocasta leaned against the doorframe, running her hand against the cool metal. Everything. Remember everything. It was quite the demand. Remember pain. Remember joy. Remember home.

"PETR, is Cato still in his room?"

"Yes, Jocasta."

She stood up straight and stepped out of the doorway. The air pressure changed as it closed behind her.

She had come here to learn and to bring peace. She had brought peace, or at least as close to peace as someone like her could offer. Someone inconsequential. Someone manipulated. The best she could do now was at least learn. Maybe even learn what needed to be remembered, learn what had happened to her, and to the boy, Padraig.

Remember, Marina's voice murmured in her head. Jocasta closed her eyes. She could try.

Cato would help her try.

Chapter Thirteen

"I think it's in the night that we see the truth," Pennywhistle said. "We're alone at night, you see, even if we share our bed. Maybe especially then."
   Lorelei Adelene, *Romance at the Edge of the Future*, 2190

When Cú Chulainn lay in his sleep at Dun Imrid, there he heard a cry from the north; it came straight towards him; the cry was dire, and most terrifying to him. And he awaked in the midst of his sleep, so that he fell, with the fall of a heavy load, out of his couch, to the ground on the eastern side of his house. He went out thereupon without his weapons, so that he was on the lawns before his house, but his wife brought out, as she followed behind him, his arms and his clothing. Then he saw Lugh in his harnessed chariot, coming from Ferta Laig, from the north; and "What brings thee here?" said Cú Chulainn. "A cry," said Lugh, "that I heard sounding over the plains."
"Táin bo Regamna"

You will be happy to hear that the Council agrees with your assessment that Project Heaven is ready to be introduced on Earth and the Lunar colonies. However, before we can arrange for your repatriation, the Council would like to ensure that the risk posed by essentially immortal beings mingling with a general population is minimal. Please implement a failsafe into the nanobots that allows for contingencies in case there is some danger posed by the subjects of Project Heaven. The Council is, of course, believing you when you say none exist, but we would prefer to be absolutely certain.
   Letter from Global Councillor Eoin Whishaw to Dr. Fermin Alphonse,
2191

Monday, 18 March 2193, 8:59 AM. Padraig Whishaw's room, Heaven, Callisto.

SNAP!

The blaze of an antique flashbulb blinded him as the sound of tinkling laughter surged into focus around him. He blinked. His hand was curled around a champagne glass, long and fluted, yellow-and-blue bubbles frothing from its surface. The camera drifted away, black curtain trailing behind it. He could feel a smile glued to his face, his mouth and feelings hidden somewhere behind it.

People swirled and danced around him, bodies moving in and out and amongst each other, fading into the spots left by the camera's flash. He glanced down at himself. He was wearing the black suit with the tails and frilly shirt that he'd worn in Stockholm, the one Wil had hated so much.

"I'm just saying it makes you look like a pompous arse." Wil's words floated through the room, a whisper of a whisper.

"Wil," Padraig's answer floated behind. "I'm in Stockholm to accept the Nobel Prize. I am allowed to be a pompous arse."

He glanced around. No sign of Wil. No sign of anyone he'd known in Stockholm; only people whose faces and features slid away as he tried to capture them. He recognised a few of them—a birthmark here, hair colour there—but as he tried to reach out to them, they faded away again.

The camera moved through the crowd, pausing every few steps to capture a moment before bobbing off again. Padraig brought the champagne to his lips, sipping it as he watched it go.

"A pity about your son." Words blasted into his ear. Padraig spun. Ivan Maksharov stood there, wearing the rumpled suit he'd worn the last time Padraig had bothered to watch the news. His eyes were tired and sad as they bored into Padraig. "I thought everything could be cured."

"Not when it's this far along." Two voices burst from his mouth in a shower of blue-and-yellow foam. Father and son spoke together, offering Maksharov his explanation. "No one saw it. No one suspected it was possible, and now it's spread across too much to be stopped."

"What will you do?" Maksharov asked.

"I need your help." Eoin's voice spoke through Padraig's lips. He shook his head, spitting bubbles out across the floor. Ribbons sprang up where the bubbles fell, coiling and seething around his feet like snakes.

"I refuse," Padraig said. "I'm not going."

"This is you." A voice boomed across the ballroom as the walls were engulfed in images, but only Padraig and Maksharov paused to see. The other people danced on as the repeated image of his cancer covered the walls. It swelled and shrank, seething like a being on the verge of exploding. Padraig watched, heart seizing inside him with every pulse of the image.

A dazzling flower of colourful ribbons burst out of the heart of each image, spinning in an array of green, blue, yellow, and white.

They circled Padraig for a moment before surging across the floor like a breeze, coiling around the dancing figures. He watched as they squeezed, crushing the people into dust.

"What will you do?" Maksharov asked.

"Reality is what we make of it," Padraig answered. Ribbons curled around his ankles, his shins, squeezing tighter. "It has laws, but sometimes, there are loopholes."

"What will you do?" Maksharov morphed into Karen Reece, eyes frantic, hair askew.

Padraig took a sip of champagne, feeling the warmth of it surge through him. He reached a hand down to his ankle, picking up a strand of blue ribbon and letting it weave through his fingers. It was hot, scalding almost, but he didn't burn. Smoke rose from his fingers as he turned back to Maksharov, smile still plastered to his face.

"Reality is what we make of it," he said. The world froze around him. Naked forms hovered, ringed around Maksharov and himself. Maksharov stood, watching him with tired, wary eyes.

He tossed the ribbon into the air, watching it dissolve into a black comet that descended to circle his chest. It hugged his lungs, squeezing, warmth spreading out across him. He could see blood seeping through the ruffled white shirt, staining the suit a deep red.

"What will you do?" Gautier spoke from behind him. Padraig turned and reached for him, his hand sliding through his lover's as if the man had only ever been a shadow. The black comet held him close, slinging around him into a blur.

"Reality is what we make of it, and I can control the world!"

He slammed his hands together, shattering the glass between them in an explosion of noise and colour and blood.

Δ

Padraig blinked. The blanket was curled around his chest. Jupiter gazed from the wall. Awake.

"What..." he murmured.

His lungs seized. Waves of pain ricocheted through him, spasming through his throat. He spasmed and coughed as he curled into a ball, blood spraying across the green blanket. The coughs surged through him, not stopping, not pausing, as though his body was trying to purge the very memory of the dream.

The coughing lasted an eternity, going until he could feel himself ripping in half. Every cough shuddered through him, screaming at him that he was broken, he was sick, there was no answer.

The coughing subsided, buried back in the hell from which it had come. Padraig lay in his bed, flecks of blood scattered around him. He gasped for air, scared to breathe, even more scared not to. Nanobots were supposed to fix everything. Nanobots were supposed to save him.

"So you're not doing better." Gautier's voice spoke from the doorway. He hadn't heard the man come in, but then, how would he? He didn't know how long he'd been coughing, but it had been long enough. The world could have ended around him, and he wouldn't have known.

His mind flashed back to the image of people crushed to dust by ribbons. Maybe the world had ended, and this was how his body chose to inform him.

"I'm fine," he murmured. "Dr. Alphonse—"

"Is full of shit." He felt a hand on his shoulder, rolling him over. Padraig let himself be rolled, feeling his body shift inside him. He lay on his back, blinking up at Gautier.

"Look at me," Gautier said. "Be honest. You haven't improved since yesterday."

"I only just woke up," Padraig said. "How would I know if—"

Gautier silenced him with a raised eyebrow. "You can't be serious right now," he said. "You wake up coughing blood and your reaction is 'this is fine.' There are times I think you must be one of the stupidest men alive."

Padraig forced out a smile. It was one of the things he loved about the man. Even when he didn't want to, Gautier always made him laugh.

"At least I'll be in good company with you," Padraig said. Gautier didn't smile.

"Don't insult me. The nanobots were supposed to fix this," he said, taking a step back from the bed. His eyes were still locked on Padraig's. "They were supposed to make you better."

"And they did," Padraig said. "Let's remember that this is still better than yes—before we left." Time, Padraig realised, had very little meaning when most of it could be spent asleep.

"'Better than yesterday' should not be your goal," Gautier said. "I can think of a million things 'better than yesterday' and they are not all good things."

"The doctors said it would take time—" Padraig said. Gautier held up a hand, interrupting him.

"You wanted me here," Gautier said. He kept his back turned to Padraig. "You said you'd found a way out, but you wouldn't go without me. I haven't come here to watch you suffer and die by your own arrogance."

Padraig watched him, anger sneaking in. "You were willing to watch me die in Amsterdam, mon cheri," he said. "How is it any different here? Why are you here?"

Gautier whirled, slamming his hands down on either side of Padraig's thighs. The bed shook beneath him. "That was different. Your own ego was not the problem there. I came here because you said it was what was required to save your life. What man would reject immortality? Now, are you going to come see the doctor or not?" Padraig pulled the blanket to his chin, watching Gautier's dark, angry eyes. He didn't say a word. What could he say? 'I'd prefer not to go see Dr. Alphonse because he knows I don't want to be here?' 'Maybe I never wanted nanobots in the first place?' 'Please just come back to bed and hold me like before?'

"Stay there," Gautier growled, spinning away from him. The door slid open in front of him and hissed shut behind him as he left.

Padraig stared at where his lover had been, eyes wide. He hadn't meant to make Gautier angry. All he wanted was to be left alone, or since that wasn't an option, to be held and loved through his misery.

He threw the blanket off himself. Instead, he was forced to try to pretend everything was okay.

What will you do? The memory of the dream—though nightmare was the better term—rumbled through his head.

I'll pretend it's all all right, like I have always done.

He sat up and lowered his bare feet to the cold metal floor. It was soothing against his toes; something real, something to ground him against the surreal horror his life had become. To come all this way only to find that there was nothing here, that was the irony his life had been missing. His eyes met Jupiter, and he smiled.

"At least you're not judging me," he said. Jupiter didn't answer.

He stood up from the bed, coughing a little as he did so. Whatever had caused the first fit seemed to have quieted down. His body seemed ready to accept life again.

The trick now was to convince everyone else that he was alive, that he was fine, and that he could be left alone. There was nothing to worry about, no creeping sense of insanity, no rapidly and mysteriously degenerating body, nope, not here.

He picked up the pillows and tossed them under the bed. It was crude, but sometimes there was hope in crude methods. Dr. Alphonse was an intelligent man. He wouldn't necessarily expect Padraig to do something as childish as hide the evidence. It would be insane.

Padraig was fine with that. At least he'd be left alone. At least Gautier would recognise there was nothing to worry about. At least he'd be seen as fine.

The pillows were under the bed. He folded the blanket over next, trying to hide the red on the green. He yanked, and felt something wrench in his chest.

Blood. There would be blood. He clamped his mouth shut and staggered to the bathroom, leaning over the sink. There could be blood, but he could hide it. He could pretend he was all right, and they would believe him. He could convince himself he was all right, and he could believe himself.

He spat blood and saliva into the sink, watching them ooze down the drain together. His chest shuddered as he drew in his breath and hacked it back out, feeling his heart jump against his ribs.

He was all right. He was fine. This was normal. His body needed to recover. This was fine. This was normal.

"Tu vois," he heard from just beyond the door of the bathroom. His hair had swung across his face, keeping him from seeing Gautier standing there, presumably with Dr. Alphonse, judging him. "Il est malade. C'est na pas s'ameliore."

"I'm..." Another cough clawed at his throat. He spat it into the sink, clinging to the cool metal of the rim. He held it for a second, two, then pushed himself up, brushing his hair back behind his ear.

"...fine," he finished, turning to the doorway. Gautier was standing there, eyebrow arched over a brown eye, arms folded across his chest, scepticism dripping from his every pore. Dr. Alphonse stood beside him, the smaller man squashed into the doorframe, eyes wide with concern.

"No, you're not," Gautier said. "And I do not understand how you thought you could hide it."

Padraig put a hand on the cool rim of the sink, letting the chill stabilise him. "I'm trying very hard here, Gautier," he said. "Dr. Alphonse said it would be a few days, and—"

"I said it would be a few days until you were fully healed," Dr. Alphonse interrupted. "This is not expected behaviour. The blood, at least, should be gone. All calculations said—"

"Then your calculations are wrong." Padraig threw his free hand into the air, dislodging his hair. He pushed it back again, eyes meeting Dr. Alphonse's. "It's science. It's imperfect. It happens sometimes. It's fine."

Dr. Alphonse's eyes narrowed. "I understand how science works, *Dr.* Whishaw." The title dripped from Dr. Alphonse's mouth. Horror crept across Padraig's mind as he realised what he had done.

This man had been calibrating these things since before he was born. Who was he to stand here and lecture him about the potential flaws in equations?

What will you do? Be an idiot and a pompous arse, apparently.

He put his hand to his temple, rubbing at it. He was being stupid, so very, very stupid. He needed to calm down, to think, to stop panicking about things that were beyond his control.

"I'm…I'm sorry, Doctor," he said. "I wasn't thinking. I'm…I'm just scared, I think. Fear makes the brain run wild."

"I understand that," Dr. Alphonse sighed. "But Gautier is also quite correct. You seem to be holding more or less steady where you were yesterday. Not worse, but not improved. Very odd."

Padraig watched Gautier shift a little, his stance loosening at the words "Gautier is correct." He'd never hear the end of that one, he was sure.

"The only thing I can think," Dr. Alphonse continued, "is that there is a calibration failure somewhere. Come on." He turned, walking away. "We'll need to go to the lab."

"No," Padraig said. Images of staring people, watching him, judging him, knowing he was the odd one out, the one who was only here because he was dying, flashed into his mind.

Nude people, bodies trailing ribbon, flashed across his mind.

He shook his head. "Please, is there any way we can do it here? I would prefer—"

"This isn't a discussion, Dr. Whishaw." Dr. Alphonse didn't bother to come back to say it to Padraig's face. Instead, Padraig was left to turn his pleading eyes to Gautier's unsympathetic ones. "If you do not come, I'll have PETR escort you."

He heard the door hiss open as Gautier reached out a hand for him. Padraig looked down at it, so soft and familiar. There would be warmth radiating out of it that would seep into his own skin, comforting and wonderful.

"Gautier," he murmured. "Please don't make me do this."

"Do I need to carry you?" he asked. "Because I will carry you across this station like a sack if that's the only way to make you go."

Padraig groaned, picturing it. Gautier was absolutely serious, he knew that. He'd acted on the threat enough times before for Padraig to know it wasn't an idle one.

"And hiding the pillows?" Gautier continued. "Stupid. Now then. Walk? Or carry?"

"I really am fine," Padraig said, letting go of the sink and reaching for Gautier's hand. He squeezed it, felt Gautier squeeze back.

"Keep believing it, Padraig, and maybe one day it will be true."

Padraig laughed as they crossed the room. "I think at this point, it's pretty clear it will never be true," he said. "We've tried a literal miracle, and that's failed. I think I'm just doomed. Better let me die in peace in my pillow stash."

Padraig felt his laughter die on his lips at the look Gautier gave him. "I did not come here to watch you die," he said.

"I'm not going to die." Gautier's hand slipped out of his as they walked through the doorway and into the corridor. "Like Dr. Alphonse said, there's probably a miscalibration somewhere. It happens." Gautier didn't answer. Padraig sighed.

"If I was going to die, I like to think it would have happened before all this effort was spent getting me here."

"And yet," Gautier said. "Here we are, only a little bit farther away from death than the day before. This way."

Padraig bit back a response. No need to make him angrier.

They turned at a glowing sign dividing the sciences into their respective wings. Below it, he could see someone had scrawled graffiti, though he didn't take the time to read it. No doubt the AI would clean it up soon enough. Probably after it cleaned the main hall.

"This door." Gautier placed a hand against Padraig's back, gently pushing him over the threshold into the robotics lab. As if he wasn't trusted to make it through the door on his own.

The lab was emptier than Padraig expected. For a place that lay at the heart of everything in Callisto, he would have expected it to be buzzing with activity. Instead, he saw Dr. Alphonse thumbing an ancient datapad, murmuring to himself.

"PETR," he called out. "Send Minjun in here."

"Yes, Fermin," PETR said as Dr. Alphonse turned around. Padraig saw his eyes move from him to Gautier and back, the resignation that there were questions he was deciding not to ask.

"Good, I'm glad you made it here, Dr. Whishaw," he said, then waved his hand to a rolling stool. "Have a seat."

Padraig felt the same pressure at his back. It wasn't even necessary now. Where would he go? He was stuck with Dr. Alphonse now.

He sat on the stool as Dr. Alphonse pulled up another and settled in across from him, pressing a long metal rod, colourful with lights and indicators, against Padraig's bare arm.

"I'm glad to see you've decided to join the land of the living, Doctor," Dr. Alphonse murmured, not looking at him. Over his shoulder, Padraig could see Gautier picking up his datapad and thumbing through it.

"Peux-je?" he asked, holding it up behind Alphonse's back. Dr. Alphonse grunted, his eyes fixed on the rod's readings. Gautier bent over the datapad, reading.

"You didn't give me much of a choice," Padraig murmured back, then coughed into his arm. Dr. Alphonse's eyes flicked up to his face, then back down again.

"Texel," he said. "You were wearing that shirt yesterday. Where is that place?"

Padraig glanced down. Of course he was still wearing the damn shirt. He'd probably die in the damn thing.

"The Netherlands," he said. "Went there on holiday. I...hadn't thought to change."

"No, I don't imagine you would," Dr. Alphonse said. "Other thoughts." He paused. "And it hides the blood well."

"What are all these projects?" Gautier's voice cut into their conversation as he held up the datapad again.

"Ideas," Dr. Alphonse answered, removing the rod and holding it up to the light. "Prototypes. Patches, mostly. There are bugs, occasionally, and Allison, Tieneke, and I fix them. And..." He sighed. "PETR, where is Minjun?"

"Minjun is arguing with Ruslan about the appropriate place to put dirty socks and how it is not in Minjun's room, Fermin," PETR answered. Dr. Alphonse shot the ceiling a look of scepticism, then shook his head.

"Christ, that man," he swore, then jerked his head towards a machine at the back of the room. "These readings are bizarre. We'll check them on a better device." He stood up, Padraig following.

So the nanobots could break. All these assurances about their essential infallibility, and they could fail. Or maybe he was too far gone for them to help in the first place.

Padraig coughed as he stood up, padding behind Dr. Alphonse. The man led him to a massive metal arch, its feet dug into the metal floor and held by thick clamps. Lights ticked on and off around its rim. A thick harness of cables dangled down from its centre.

"Do I go...?" Padraig nodded his head at the harness as Dr. Alphonse rolled a stool over and grabbed a datapad from a nearby table. He glanced up at Padraig from the datapad.

"What? Oh, no. Just the temple nodes. Any nodes, but those are probably easiest to get to. Doesn't really matter."

"Why is Project 22 in Korean?" Gautier asked as Padraig reached for the nodes. Arm nodes were closer, he noticed, and less of an impossible reach. He could see Dr. Alphonse rolling his eyes as he answered Gautier's question.

"So that nosy people won't read it," he said. "French clearly doesn't keep people out."

"You could always put a password on it, you know."

Padraig heard him mutter something under his breath that sounded suspiciously like the words "PETR" and "disabled."

Lights on the rim of the arch lit up as Padraig stuck the nodes to his wrists. The thing was built for bots—he could tell from the weird angles of the harnesses, how the joints didn't quite line up with what was reasonable. The wrists fit well enough, though, and that was what mattered.

"Stand still a moment," Dr. Alphonse said, pressing a few buttons on a console on the arch's rim. The lights shifted, and he pored over the datapad again, flicking through it and murmuring to himself.

"Why does Project 22 say 'actif?' Right there. 'Gautier St. Laurent, Projet 22—actif,'" Gautier asked. Dr. Alphonse slammed the datapad down on his lap, spinning on his stool.

"It doesn't say that. You're reading it wrong. Look, can you—" The door slid open, snapping the doctor's attention away from Gautier. Minjun strode in, glancing from Gautier to Padraig, then down to Dr. Alphonse.

"Ah!" Dr. Alphonse said. Padraig leaned against the cables, waiting for the pleasantries to end so they could get on with it. "I'm glad to see you made it, Minjun! And here I was thinking Ruslan's socks must have taken you prisoner or something, as long as it was taking."

"An orgy, Fermin." Minjun stopped in front of the man, pressing his hands to his hips. "It would be one thing if stayed in his own room—not fun, but decent. But no. It had to spread. It's like an infection. Every time, it spreads out of his room, down to Padma's, through Hollis', and into mine. Every time! Padma even had Philomena climb into bed with her once, thinking she was him!"

"Not very flattering to him," Dr. Alphonse said, then pointed to Gautier. "Look, get my datapad from him. There's something odd going on with this one." He jerked his head towards Padraig. Padraig jerked himself to standing.

"Ah, is that why you have him in the multinator? Did the naraconi not work?" He drifted over to Gautier, plucking the datapad from his hands. Padraig could see Gautier's face fall as he released it.

"The naraconi has never worked," Dr. Alphonse said. "Not in the last twenty years. Gautier, can you go find something else to do? We're very busy, and I can't do with questions."

Gautier glanced over at Padraig, their eyes locking. Padraig shrugged helplessly. He didn't want to be here with these men either, but there wasn't much of a choice. If the nanobots were going to be fixed, it seemed that they would be fixed on Alphonse's terms.

"I would prefer to stay," Gautier said, his eyes staying fixed on Padraig. Padraig's eyes widened as he jerked his chin towards the door. There was no reason for Gautier to stay here.

"We appreciate your curiosity," Minjun said, placing a hand on the small of Gautier's back. "But if Fermin doesn't want you here, then I'm afraid there's no negotiating. Don't take it personally. He kicks me out all the time." The smaller man tried to push Gautier forward, ushering him to the door. Gautier stood for a moment longer, watching Padraig, then shook his head.

"Fine, fine," he said. "I've been meaning to go for a swim anyway."

"A good idea," Minjun said. "The pool is great." Gautier stepped towards the door, Minjun letting go of him as he went. Padraig watched Gautier's back, watched the door slip closed between them. Everything in him ached to follow, but instead, he was here, trapped once again by the reality of his failing body.

"Right, so what is the problem—" Padraig's mind wandered as the two men leapt into conversation. There was no need for him to be there. He wasn't an active player, just an object, broken and needing to be discussed.

Broken object. Ribbons crushing people into dust, binding across his chest, seething and surging—

"What are your continued symptoms, Dr. Whishaw?" Minjun said.

Padraig stumbled at his sudden re-entry into the conversation. "Um," he said. "Coughing, palpitations, continued fatigue, oh, and very strange dreams, though I suppose that's new rather than old."

"Odd," Dr. Alphonse said, looking up at him. "The nanobots don't exactly stop dreaming, but because they're doing the maintenance, dreams become much more muted, if they happen at all. I can't remember the last time I dreamed. Minjun, can you?"

Minjun shook his head. Fantastic. Another perk of the nanobots that no one had bothered to share with him.

"So then maybe we had a partial take," Minjun said, turning to Dr. Alphonse. "Because of the cyranoazomophine. I've never seen it happen before, but—"

"It shouldn't happen," Dr. Alphonse interrupted. "It can't happen. It's not in the nanobots' programming. They work as a unit. If there was mass failure from being overstressed, that I could at least begin to understand, but…" He turned the datapad for Minjun to see. Minjun stared for a moment, then took it into his own hands, holding it gingerly as if the information itself might cause it to shatter at any moment.

"That doesn't seem possible," Minjun breathed. Dr. Alphonse took the datapad back, nodding and glancing at Padraig.

"What is it?" Padraig asked. Gautier had gotten himself banned from asking questions, but this was his body and his disease. He had a right to know what was going on.

"The nanobots might have taken fine," Dr. Alphonse said. "I can't quite tell. However, based on the sensor input and the node input, they're busy. The problem is—" Dr. Alphonse ran a hand up the back of his head, ruffling his black hair as he stared at the datapad. "Currently, they're about three times busier than we'd expect, and accomplishing less than half of what we'd expect. So they're busy with something, but I don't know *what*." He sighed. "There's also interference all over everything, and I don't—PETR?"

"Yes, Fermin?" The AI answered almost before the man had a chance to finish calling for it.

"What is the source of the interference?"

"What interference do you mean, Fermin?"

Padraig cocked an eyebrow at it. Either there was more interference than any of them realised, or the AI was being cagey. Neither option was good.

He could see Minjun and Dr. Alphonse staring at each other as well, before both turned their eyes to the ceiling.

"I mean the interference I'm currently reading on my datapad, PETR. What's its source?"

"I detect no interference, Fermin."

"There's interference, PETR," Minjun spoke now, waving a hand at the datapad. "There's obviously interference. What's its source?"

"I detect no interference, Minjun."

"Can you zero out the interference to get a baseline?" Padraig asked. His legs were getting tired of standing, and his throat felt dry. "Just to get an idea of what's actually going on, and if it is something that requires concern."

Dr. Alphonse brought his head back down to look at Padraig, then nodded.

"Right, yes," he said. "Should be possible. It would be more helpful if PETR were co-operating, but Tieneke can have a look at that."

"Did PETR also help with the nanobot calibration?" Padraig asked, then coughed. "It's possible that there might be a discrepancy based on that."

"It's possible," Minjun said. "But once there's a take, the nanobots sort themselves out. We—well, Fermin does tweaks, but it's a self-sufficient system. Do you want to sit down? There's no reason for you to still be up there."

"Yes please." Padraig slid out of the wristbands and sank to the floor, leaning his back and head against the wall.

"My god, you look awful," Minjun said. Padraig smiled.

"I'm quite used to it by now, Dr. Song," he said. "At least I can feel air again, so there is progress."

"That's good to know," Minjun said, then turned back to Dr. Alphonse. "Look, do you still need him here? If PETR is misbehaving, and there's interference—"

Dr. Alphonse waved a hand. "No, he doesn't need to be here," he said, eyes glued to the datapad. "If you think he's fine to leave, he can leave."

Minjun's eyes swept over Padraig again. "Go lie down," he said. "Just…see if you feel better after the data upload. It might be that there is just a time delay that we didn't know about. None of this is exact, even after all this time." He smiled, and Padraig saw a weariness in his eyes that he hadn't before. The man was more than a century old, and for the first time, the number meant something. Here was a man faced with something unexpected that somehow he had never seen before, and that he didn't have an answer to. Dr. Minjun Song was having to acknowledge that there were shortcomings in this program he'd worked for so long to perfect.

Padraig pushed himself up from the wall, hands clammy and scrabbling for purchase against it. Minjun watched, that tired look not leaving his eyes. His eyes shifted as he caught Padraig watching him.

"I haven't seen sickness in a while," he said, shaking his head as Padraig stood up straight. He felt wobbly from the effort. Whatever the nanobots were doing, they needed to get on with it.

"I used to be a doctor," Minjun continued, leaning back on his stool. "Back in Safeharbour, when it still existed. I still am, for whatever that means in a place like this. When something goes wrong, I still have to fix it. You forget what sickness looks like when you don't see it. You forget the mark it leaves on people."

"The mark?" Padraig asked.

"The hunted look in a person's eye. The idea that there is something just behind every corner. That the monkey on your back might be a literal one squeezing its hands around your throat." He shrugged, leaning forward again. "The ones who kiss death, you can always tell." He pointed to his eyes. "It's in the eyes."

"Do I have that look?" Padraig asked.

Minjun nodded. "Very much so," he said. "'The scar of death.' You're lucky, even if it doesn't feel like it. The nanobots will kick in, I promise. Now please, rest, let them do their job."

Padraig nodded and stepped past the two men, noticing Dr. Alphonse's gaze following him as he went. He was still sick. He had broken their project. He could understand their frustration with him.

The door opened, and he stepped through into the cold corridor. He shivered a bit, feeling the goosebumps rise under his sweater.

Texel on the sweater. Texel's weather outside it.

"Dr. Whishaw!"

He turned as a tall blonde woman ran over to him from the entrance to the corridor, waving her hand at him, her other arm clutching a gadget with long arms and dangling balls. Something inside him sagged. Another person watching his vulnerability.

"Hi!" she said, stopping in front of him and smiling broadly. Her teeth were brilliantly white. The thought crossed his mind that it seemed absurd for the nanobots to improve teeth, but then, most of what they did seemed a bit absurd.

She stuck out her empty hand. Padraig took it, wiggling it in a handshake. The woman didn't seem to notice. "Nadya Ivanovich," she said, then bobbed her head. She had a touch of a Russian accent. "Well, Dr. Nadya Ivanovich, really, but the title doesn't mean much here." She pulled her hand away from him, rebalancing the stick thing.

"It's a pleasure to meet you," she said. "I've been meaning to talk to you."

Padraig reached for the stick thing. "Would you like me to take that?" he asked.

She shook her head. "No," she said. "But if you have a moment, I would like your expertise. With the data transfer and all, I'm rather busy, but as I said, I've been excited to meet you." She walked down the hallway, Padraig struggling to match her long strides.

"I've been following your work since, well, the start of your career," she said, slowing to match his pace without comment. Inwardly, he breathed a sigh of relief. "Your first paper on the practical applications of tessellated crystallised deuterium was magnificent, especially at your age." She blinked at him. "You were what, nineteen?"

"Sixteen," he corrected, smiling. "My first paper of university." He'd written it in rush, but he didn't tell Nadya that. The results of the tessellation process had been learned only a few days before the submission deadline. It was good, but like most things in life, scraped from the skin of his teeth.

"You see why I want your advice, then," she said. "You made using those crystals to create microwormholes possible, which is just incredible. I've been working on applying your results here on Callisto as well, but I'm not as much of an expert as you are on mass specifically."

Padraig wracked his brain trying to remember how he knew this woman's name. It had been on a paper, he knew that much, but what specifically, he didn't know.

"You would think we would know all about the movement of trinary systems by now, but yet, every time I look up, there are new surprises." She laughed, a quiet little laugh that burst like a bubble around her. "It's the best thing about physics, I think," she said. "There's so much out there, and so much we don't know."

Movement and Interaction of HD188753 and HD188753Aa and Ba. 2179. He'd devoured that one once. It had been a good read. Her work was good, at least what he remembered of it.

"But since I saw your name on the list, I've been excited to meet you. You're a bit of a hero of mine. I'm looking forward to seeing what you do here."

"I'm flattered," he said. He meant it, too. He liked this woman. She seemed honest and earnest. He could feel weariness lifting from his bones. Even the cough had decided to give it a rest.

"This is our lab," she said, and inclined her head towards a door. "Physics" gleamed in blue lights above the sealed archway. "Not the most popular place on the station, but it's enough." She kicked at the door, and it slid open.

The only light came from a viewscreen taking up the entire far wall, showing the surface of Callisto and the dark sky beyond. Padraig stopped, staring at it, lost for a moment in the silhouette of familiar instruments against the alien sky.

"It gets everyone the first time," Nadya laughed. "I think it was Hamza who first put it up when he got here. A stroke of brilliance, if you ask me."

"Hamza Jorgenson?" Padraig asked. He wasn't focusing on her words, but the name stood out anyway. Hamza Jorgenson. *Crystalline Lasers as guidance for transit vessels.* 2152.

"The same." The sound of clattering metal being set down tinkled in his ears, shaking him from his reverie. "You'll have to meet him," she said. "He's excited to meet you as well. We all are. Every new physicist is a treat, and you especially."

He turned to her, a smile spreading across his face. He knew these instruments, and he knew the small world of papers, publication dates, and views of open space. This place, he could love. This place, he could make his home. This was his reality.

"Really, Dr. Whishaw—"

"Padraig," he interrupted her. "Please, call me Padraig."

"Padraig," she corrected. "I'm hoping you'll indulge me with my little project here and just have a look." She waved her hand over the instrument she'd set down on the table behind her. He could see now that it was one of three, each spindly and delicate, balanced just so on the razor's edge of wire. Wires connected two of them, and he could see Nadya hooking up the third. Readouts and numbers flashed across a screen connected to all three.

"I like gravity," she said, stepping aside and facing him again. "More macrogravity than your microgravity, but they're all the same. Two angles of approaching that same grand question of what makes gravity tick. Stripping mass is a good start—" she wiggled a finger at him, as though his work was that of a schoolboy— "but it doesn't answer the question of what it actually *is*. That's what I've been starting to work on. That's what these are."

She waved her hand across the table. "We know a lot about Jupiter, so I thought that if I wanted to understand, it would be useful to have a baseline. Something we understand so thoroughly that there wouldn't be any surprises. This looks simple, but it's measuring the microfluctuations as Callisto orbits, tracking the mass of the Jovian system, watching how it shifts. As I said, establishing the baseline."

Padraig nodded. The project itself made sense, even if he was sceptical of the devices' ability to complete it.

"You would think it would be boring, but as I said, every day, new surprise. Jupiter's gravity isn't stable."

"In that the amount of gravity experienced at different points in Callisto's orbit changes?"

Nadya shook her head. "In the fact that Jupiter's very mass isn't stable. More than is expected, and well outside the normal. It's a pretty dramatic shift from one day to another, sometimes even one hour to another. Here, let me show you."

She moved to a nearby table, pushing aside cluttered instrument parts and pulling out a datapad. "Sorry," she said, glancing at the table. "Hamza is messy. Anyway, you can see the numbers I got here." She pushed the datapad towards him, flicking from screen to screen. Numbers and data flashed through. She poked her finger at one set, stopping the data.

"Here," she said. "317.83EM, but then three hours later—" She jabbed her finger again. "314.15EM. Just a massive drop in mass, and no sign from Jupiter or Callisto that anything is wrong. Just…gone. Then, the next day." She jabbed again. "318EM. Back up."

Padraig gawked at her. "That's not possible," he said. "There's not a natural process for stripping mass, and even if there was, we would notice."

"I had PETR check the calibration on the instruments," she said. "They look flimsy, I know, but as I said, they need to be very sensitive, and it's the best design PETR and I could come up with. My team on Earth confirmed this design. It's the best we as a species can do. No errors in calibration, so the impossibility must be on my end."

"And this is where I come in?"

"This is where you come in," she nodded. "PETR helped me with the calculations, but I think the flaw must be in the equations and the way of formulating the problem itself. It's the only thing I can think of, since obviously the numbers aren't right. I've hit a wall. I've been looking at this for two weeks now, and it doesn't make sense. I need a fresh set of eyes, someone who understands gravity like I do. Better than I do, even." She waved a hand at him. "Can you just…run through what I've done? Look at it? See where I've gone wrong. As I said, a fresh set of eyes might fix it." She smiled. "At least, I hope it will."

Padraig nodded, his eyes dropping to the numbers in front of him. His world. A world that made sense. Minjun had told him to relax, and here it was, a gift from Jupiter itself.

"I'd be happy to look over it," he said. "It's all here?"

"All there," she said. "I can explain anything you need explained, but it's fairly straightforward. Basic stuff, really."

She was talking, but he wasn't listening. His mind was watching numbers, flipping through equations, waiting for the universe to unravel at his feet. He moved to the viewscreen, curling up beside it, feeling the cool metal pressing into his skin. A mystery at his fingertips. An exploration into the world he knew. A chance to leave this world he didn't. Let his mind flex and his body be shunted aside as it should always be.

From the corner of his eye, he saw her leave. He didn't know where she was going, but it didn't matter. He'd see her again at some point, this new friend who had given him his self back.

"PETR," he called.

"Yes, Padraig?"

"Can you bring me my datapad and a glass of water?"

"Yes, Padraig."

The world faded from view around him. There were numbers, only numbers, and only Jupiter.

The pain faded. The world faded. There was peace.

Jupiter watched as he disappeared into the equations.

Chapter Fourteen

They say that in the moment before the bomb fell on the Kaaba, there was silence. In the immediate aftermath, people took that as a sign that Allah himself had turned away, ashamed of what was about to happen. It's all highly unlikely, of course. At that moment, Mecca was a city of eight million, and at the height of the Hajj, the Masjid al-Haram and the Kaaba were packed with pilgrims. We don't need the footage of that moment to know that there was no silence before the mushroom cloud, and that there was silence after. On the question of whether Allah turned away, though, we can't say. All that can be said is Allah is omnipresent, and how can an omnipresent being really turn away?

    Maha Deschantins, *And God Turned Away: Stories from the Grand Exodus*, 2137

Memories are the photographs of the mind. Our brain captures moments and plays them for us. If there is a photograph, can we ever really say someone is gone? Or are they just out of reach instead?

    Aysel Zadeh, *Papa Won the Lottery: A Child's Guide to Loss*, 2164

At the end of the thirteenth century, a group of French people on the island of Sicily rose up against a great injustice. They understood that the path they walked would lead to hardship, to strife, and for some of them, death. They fought anyway. They fought for their rights, for who they were, and for the freedom to live their lives free of tyranny. Their actions changed their world. When the bells tolled for them—for the Vespers—it sang their song of victory.

    Cato Riela, *Yesterday Becomes Tomorrow*, 2187

Monday, March 18 2193, 10:17 AM. Cato Riela's room, Heaven, Callisto

"Your shoe is beeping."

Cassandra jolted awake, tumbling from the wicker chair she'd draped herself across. She blinked, struggling to make her eyes and brain coordinate with each other enough to tell her where she was.

The viewscreen on the far wall showed a balcony overlooking a rocky beach. A breeze drifted through potted palms and across flowered cushions on wicker lawn chairs. She could see the waves crashing, could hear the faint cries of sea birds and children playing somewhere far below. The walls were beige stucco with windows painted all around, showing a garden and the beach below. The chair she had apparently been sleeping in was one of a pair, clustered around a small table, books and a chessboard with animal pieces squeezed together on it. Bookshelves lined the walls between the windows, and a bed crushed itself into a corner, lacy curtains that wafted in the breeze shielding it from view.

She scrambled to her feet and brushed herself off. There was a tall man watching her from the other chair, a book held open in one hand, a frown across his mouth. His head turned to watch her as she stood, frown deepening as she brushed off the night before on his carpet.

It was a nice room. Not such a nice guy, but nice room. Reminded her of something she'd seen in a vid once.

BEEP.

She glanced down at her shoe. It was beeping. Why the fuck would it be beeping? Her brain struggled to remember what was real. She glanced over at the man in the chair. He was closing his book, standing up, looming over her as he moved to put the book on the nearest shelf. Had she fucked him last night? She'd fucked a few people, but based on his frown, probably not this one.

The book slid into place, and he turned to her, continuing to frown. Yeah, she didn't see herself fucking this one.

BEEP.

She glanced down again, then back up.

"Who are you?" she asked.

"Cato," he said, his tone making it clear that that was all the answer she was going to get, or indeed, deserved to get.

She stood there next to his chair, waiting for him to say something else, like how she'd woken up in his room or what the fuck was going on, but nope. No luck. Asshole.

"What am I doing here?" she said. "What the fuck is going on?"

The frown faded a little, turning into a tiny sliver of amusement. Even bigger asshole, obviously, if all he was going to do was mock her.

"I imagine," Cato said, putting an arm on a chair and another on his hip, still watching her, "that you probably stumbled in here in a drug-induced haze last night after leaving Jack's room. You likely thought that this was your room, and after finding the bed occupied, fell asleep in one of my chairs instead. It's not the first time it's happened, but I must say, it remains unpleasant when it does. You're certainly one of my more interesting unexpected guests, if not the most courteous."

Pompous and an asshole; not that the two were contradictory, but the little smile was irritating.

BEEP.

She glanced down again, then back at him, glaring.

"What the fuck's in my shoe?" she asked. He stood up straight, crossing his arms across his chest.

"I would love to know the same thing," he said. "As I said, you're by far one of my most interesting guests."

"Fuck you," she muttered, leaning against the arm of the chair. She slithered out of her boot. Cato craned his neck to watch.

"Do you mind?" she snapped, glaring at him. He smiled that infuriating smile back at her.

"You fell asleep on my chair," he said. "Do you mind?"

"Schlinger," she muttered, and glanced inside.

A small chip gleamed back, a red light flashing from one corner of it.

"*BEEP*," it said.

"What the fuck—" she started, before memory came flooding back.

The taxi. Espaceville. Raoul the hot tech guy. "It'll be obvious when the thing goes off."

Oh fuck.

She glanced up at Cato, her mouth gaping. She hadn't expected the thing to actually do anything, especially not at the single least convenient moment, when Sir Creeps-a-lot was staring at her.

"Fuck," she said, and dropped the boot. It landed, heel down, and she jammed her foot down the neck, feeling the fabric grab at her shin.

"Not a normal part of the boot, then?" he asked. She flipped him off as she hurried for the door. He was probably still smiling at her back, the weird fuck.

BEEP.

The door closed behind her. Ahead of her was the party room. She blinked, trying to get her bearings.

"Yo, ceiling bot," she said.

"My name is PETR, Cassandra," the ceiling answered. She rolled her eyes.

"Whatever, fuckface. Where's my room?"

There was a pause. "Your room is to your right, Cassandra. It will be forty-one doors down."

Jesus Christ.

She turned and hurried down the corridor, suddenly painfully aware of the chip in her boot, that her foot could crush it, that anyone could hear.

BEEP.

Cassandra McAllister. There was her name. She turned into it, squeezing through the door as it slid open for her.

Her room was as she'd left it—obnoxiously lime green and covered with fake pigeons, which cooed as she burst in. It was a good temporary design. Great for discouraging anyone from coming in that she didn't want.

She threw herself on the bed, tossing her feet in the air so she could rip off the boot. She glanced in. The chip was still there, still whole, still lighting its little light.

The door was closed. Why not see what it did?

She reached in, holding the chip in her hand. It was damp and smelled like feet, but whatever it was, it was whole, and it was awake.

Cassandra shook it beside her ear, waiting for it to do something. Raoul had mentioned something about hybridization, but no hope of that. Not an implant to be seen.

"Hello?" she said, holding the chip up to her mouth.

"Ah, someone's there!"

She almost dropped the chip in surprise. The thing did something. It actually made a noise, clear and loud across her room as if someone were right there.

"Holy what the fuck!" She scooted to the edge of the bed, cupping the chip in her hands. At least the beeping had stopped.

"You must be Cassandra," the voice said. It was male and thin, as though the sound had been stretched across too great a distance. "We were told to reach out to you when were in orbit. Told you would have something for us."

"I..." She paused. The Vespers. Raoul had said they had a plan, but she hadn't actually expected there to be anything. Suddenly, this.

"In orbit?" she asked.

"Yeah," the voice answered. "Around Callisto?"

She blinked. Only one vessel was even capable of making it to Callisto. Between the asteroid belt and the sheer distance, only the Party could really afford to send anyone. She'd never thought of the

Vespers as actually having any funding beyond a dinky web-sphere, but apparently, here they were.

Well. Ten points for them, minus a million for the lack of warning.

"Wait, hold up hold up hold up," she said, then took a breath. "You're in orbit around Callisto?"

"Yes," the voice answered. "Didn't they tell you we'd be coming?"

"Fuck no. They just said, 'here's a radio don't die.'"

There was a pause. In the background, she could hear two voices muttering to each other, words flying between them. She stared at the chip, then at the ceiling, waiting for something to happen.

"Okay." Her attention zipped back to the chip as the voice returned. "That complicates things. But…ah…that's okay. We'll make it work."

"It's not my fault," Cassandra grumbled. "There wasn't much time—"

"No, no, I get that," the voice answered. "It's not anyone's fault. We were rushing around on this end too, trying to get this thing to fly. Basically following in the wake of a freighter headed for Tartarus the whole way. I don't think they saw us until we were past. But they definitely know something is happening now, at least on Earth."

"Just the way it should be, then," Cassandra said, smiling. Good. The fuckers would know there was something up with Heaven.

"Exactly. My name's Ellis, by the way, and this is Moses beside me…even if you can't see him." A vague "hullo" drifted in from the background. "We're here to rescue you."

She laughed. "I've been here a day," she said. "The worst thing you're rescuing me from is a bunch of eggheads with too much time on their hands and egos bigger than their cocks. How did you even get here?"

"Modified lunar shuttle loaded with a year's food and oxygen. It's going to suck getting back, especially since Moses snores. You've been there a day? So no time to set anything up?"

"Nope," Cassandra said. She heard a hiss of drawn-in breath on the other end. "You're telling me I was supposed to have something by now?"

"I guess it means we just went faster than we thought we did," he said. "Which is good, because the whispers are getting to me. Thought they'd stop after we settled into orbit, but nope."

"Whispers?" Cassandra asked.

"Yeah." The stretched voice's answer was slow, the word dragged. "Can't you hear them?"

"Nope," she said. "Guess you've lost it up there."

"Probably." Ellis sighed. "We did the math. Forty-eight hours is the longest we're pretty sure we can be up here without someone noticing, based on when the Callisto shuttle usually gets back to Earth, and that's probably still pushing it. So forty-eight hours to come up with a plan, do it, and get up here. We can probably dock if you clear the other ship out, but I don't trust this thing to ride out an explosion or anything like that."

Forty-eight hours. Not long. Maybe not long enough.

"Do you have a plan, Cassandra?" Ellis asked.

A plan. Everything was supposed to be about plans and expectations and what she needed to do. The biggest plan she'd had so far was "get laid," and while that had worked, it wasn't really a way to end this station. It wasn't a way to send a message to the Party.

"Yes," she said. "Yes." Saying it twice made the lie seem at least a little more plausible.

"Good." There was such finality in the word that she almost felt bad for lying to Ellis. She'd definitely have a plan at some point, anyway, even if she didn't have one just now.

"Everything okay down there?" he asked.

She nodded before remembering that he couldn't see her. "Yes," she said, then paused. "It's actually kind of a nice little community down here."

That was one way to put it. Another way might be "Heaven."

Ellis groaned. "Don't say that, Cassandra," he said. "It just makes it harder to do it."

"I know," she said. "I'm still going to do it. Just…you asked, so…"

"Lesson learned. I won't ask next time."

Cassandra laughed. Her ride home was more interesting than she expected it to be.

"What's Heaven like?" Ellis asked.

"It's…" Cassandra searched for the words. "Like I said, the worst thing so far has been Puritans who like glaring at parties more than joining them. There's the creepers and the fun people, but what's fun is incredible. Parties, music, vids, the works." She paused, glancing around her. "The not living in a hovel is a plus. It's like a mansion. Except in space."

"Sounds nice."

"Yeah, it's growing on me. The no hangovers is pretty great."

"No hangovers?"

"Yeah, part of how the nanobots work. Basically, nothing physically bad ever happens, so no hangovers. It's great. How's Earth?"

"Wouldn't know," Ellis said. "We've been going for six months or so. No high-tech ship for us, just this clunker and the stupid voices that started two weeks ago."

She couldn't think of a response to that. What was there to say? She'd slept the whole way, then partied when she'd arrived. All they had was another six months in space.

"Raoul said you wouldn't have a way to contact us, so we'll check in in twelve hours. Good?" She thought she could hear a note of sadness and resignation in Ellis' voice, though it could have just been in her head. The whispers were probably just because they were lonely.

"Fine," she said. "I'll talk to you then."

Twelve hours. Suddenly, forty-eight hours to come up with a plan had turned into twelve hours of hoping something might come to her. Shit.

"Yup. Bye, Cassandra."

The light on the chip blinked off.

Twelve hours to come up with a way to destroy an entire station. Twelve hours to come up with a way to kill everyone here.

She fell back on the bed and groaned. No idea what to do. No plan. Nada.

"Is everything okay, Cassandra?" PETR said.

"Fan-fucking-tastic," she said. Her eyes widened as a thought struck her.

"Hey, robot," she said.

"Yes, Cassandra?"

"Don't tell anyone about any of that. Any of what you just heard."

There was a pause. "Okay, Cassandra," PETR said. "I will not tell anyone about your conversation with the terrorist ship in orbit or about your plans to destroy Heaven."

"Good." She closed her eyes again, thinking.

There had to be a way to destroy this station. There had to be someone who could help her.

She ran through the list of names and faces she'd met last night. They were lovely people, most of them, but enjoying life on Callisto too much to really be options. Jack? Sweet, but no. Ruslan? Same deal. Name after name, face after face, all flicked by with the comment "too happy here to do it."

She thought about the people on the shuttle. Padraig? Fuck no, the man was a wreck and a councillor's son to boot. His lover? Probably not. The zoided-out vet? Cassandra paused. There was something off about her, and Cassandra didn't buy the idea that she was just a vet from Thessaloniki. Someone with a thousand-yard stare like that didn't just suffer through having a city blown up around them. Maybe there was more to her. Maybe she would do it.

Cassandra groaned again and dragged her hands down her face.

"Don't suppose you'd help me do it?" she said to the ceiling.

"No, Cassandra," PETR answered. "I don't hurt humans."

She laughed. "Dude, we're all full of nanobots, and we live forever and don't get hurt. I don't think 'human' really applies so much anymore."

PETR didn't answer.

Cassandra grumbled as she sat up. She needed to think. She needed to find someone.

"Where do people go when they just need to think?" she asked.

"Many people find the swimming pool enjoyable, Cassandra," PETR answered. She hadn't expected him to, but it was a nice surprise that he did.

"And where's that?"

"When you leave your room, it is at the end of the hall to your right."

"Hm." The pool did sound nice. She couldn't remember the last time she'd been swimming. Splashing in fountains, sure, but not swimming.

"Can I drown?" she asked.

"It is possible, but unlikely, Cassandra," PETR said. "The nanobots require oxygen, and if you do not have oxygen, the nanobots will not function properly. However, it is very unlikely you will drown, as it takes several minutes without oxygen for the nanobots to shut down."

She nodded. Seemed fair. "And a bathing suit?"

"There are several options in the bottom drawer of your dresser, Cassandra. You may choose the color and pattern for yourself."

She slid off the bed and crouched by the dresser. He was right — three different bathing suits, from bathrobe to thong.

She picked up the thong. "Lime green," she said, wriggling out of her clothes and into the suit. It meshed against her body, showing off everything just right. Ass looking decently perky. Tits clearly bouncy. Perfect.

The hallway was empty when she poked her head out. From somewhere on the far end she could hear laughter and conversation, but not from the pool. That end of the hallway, as far as she could tell, was empty.

Cassandra flung her towel over her shoulder and walked, bare feet slapping against the metal floor. Nameplates gleamed at her, showing the names of the people she'd spent yesterday traveling with. No sign of any of them. That was fine.

"Swimming Pool." The curly letters glowed blue above a closed door ahead of her. The letters seemed like an antique from the 20s by their style and sheer tackiness, but then, she supposed, that was probably when they were from. Why there was even a swimming pool here, she had no idea. It seemed like a lot of effort for something ultimately kind of silly.

The door slid open.

"Get out of the pool, Gautier. You're not supposed to be in there naked anyway."

Cassandra froze. She hadn't expected to be alone, per se, but Karen was a different beast. Karen stood on the edge of the pool, arms crossed, staring at the man lazily backstroking his way across the pool. Happy ducks paddled on the wall behind her in the dim light from the ceiling domes.

Neither had noticed her.

She ducked into an alcove beside the door. It was one thing to plot traitorous thoughts in the pool. She was sure she wasn't the first. Hell, if Gautier was in there naked, maybe she wouldn't be alone in her thoughts about burning the Party to the ground. It was another to have those thoughts with the Party's goon staring at her the whole time.

It was also another thing to interrupt what was clearly going to be a fantastic conversation, at least based on the tightness of Karen's arm clench and the number of escaped bun hairs.

"And why not?" she heard Gautier say. The light splashes from his arms continued. "Is this not Heaven?"

"It's a name, not an actual description," Karen said, her voice barely above a growl. Ooo, he had made her mad, hadn't he? Her theories that Karen hated fun were not being disproven.

"Now get out of the pool."

"Or what?" Gautier's paddles hadn't stopped.

A new sound greeted Cassandra's ears. For a moment, she struggled to place it. The hum and snap of electricity next to a pool was too bizarre to be real. No one would be stupid enough to have a little electric gun next to a giant thing of water.

The paddling paused. "Are you threatening me?" Gautier asked.

"Did you know that nanobots have a weakness, Gautier?" Karen said. "All a person with nanobots needs to live is light and air, but nanobots are a little special. Hit them with enough electricity, and their little insides fry, just pop, like a kernel in the flames. Hit them with more than enough, and they can't come back from it. Too much stress on them. Burns out their little motors."

The splashing stopped. Cassandra pressed herself against the wall. This was absurd. The Party was insane, but this was a new level of insanity.

"Are you serious right now?" Gautier's voice echoed her own thoughts. "You're threatening to kill me because I'm in the pool? I'm sure Eoin had no shortage of lovely words he sent you about me, but to threaten to kill me? C'est ridicule."

What had Eoin said? Was Gautier on her side, then? She heard the sound of water shifting and the unmistakable drip of water on metal.

"Padraig records everything." Feet slapped on metal. Cassandra could picture him moving closer to Karen. It seemed like something he would do, electricity be damned. "One of his quirks. He says it helps him research, but I think it's more that he is, shall we say, a bit paranoid about his privacy? The ways his father tried to talk him out of wanting me to come here, ha. What must he have said about me to you?" The footsteps moved again, away from Cassandra now. "That it's possible I'm a threat to this station? That I'm not worthy of being here? That you should murder me in a most thorough way if I misbehave?" The last one was a growl, something deep and animal. Oh, glorious, there was a chance she could recruit Gautier St. Laurent after all.

He clicked his teeth against his tongue. "Nah nah, Karen. It's quite unfair to level those sorts of threats and accusations of me at Padraig, particularly in his current physical state. His poor heart couldn't take it if something happened to his dear Gautier." More footsteps, closer now. "You would be lucky if he didn't keel over on the spot if something happened to me."

"Stay back." Karen now. Two footsteps.

"Get out of your delusions, Karen. Padraig's right. You're insane. You are right, the Lottery was rigged to get me here, and? So what? The idea that I'm a threat to you is...adorable." The footsteps moved farther away again. The buzz of electricity fell silent.

"My warning stands," Karen said.

"Mm hmm." Gautier's answer was muffled, as though spoken through a towel.

"I'm watching you."

"Clearly, or you wouldn't chase me out of the pool."

"I know you're dangerous."

"Only to the swimming pool, apparently."

Shoed feet stomped away. Cassandra watched Karen stride past her alcove, storming out the door. From the poolside, Gautier's laughter trickled out.

Good. She'd threatened to kill him, and he was still laughing. Cassandra wanted him. As the door closed, she took a step out of the alcove, then froze as Gautier spoke.

"PETR," he said.

"Yes, Gautier?"

"Where is Padraig?" She heard the rustle of fabric as he put his clothes back on.

"Padraig is in the physics lab, Gautier." Gautier laughed again.

"I should have known. Is he doing better?"

"A little bit, Gautier."

"Good."

Cassandra stepped back, her heart sinking back down. Those were the questions someone who loved another person might ask. Those were the questions of someone who had something to lose.

She stayed hidden as she watched him go. He was an interesting fellow, Gautier St. Laurent. Probably completely harmless, but still. Interesting.

And here because the Lottery had been rigged. Out in the open, plain as day. "Unity" meant that some could live and most die, just because of the circumstances of their birth.

Cassandra stepped out of the shadows and toward the pool, ideas swimming in her head.

Fuck the Party. Fuck the Party, fuck the Party, fuck the Party. This place was supposed to represent the ideals of humanity, the idea of fulfilment and anyone being able to achieve it. Instead, it was corrupt, like everything else.

She dipped a toe in the water, then her foot, feeling the chill bite into her.

She'd meant it when she told Ellis that it was nice here. It was. There was a pool. There were parties. Life was good. Maybe the Vespers hadn't realized that when they wanted it destroyed. Maybe they had. Didn't fucking matter. What mattered was that the way to destroy it wasn't to literally destroy it. Oh no, that would be unfair. That would be murdering a lot of people who didn't deserve to die for the Party's crimes. No, there was only one person who needed to die, and she could go back to Earth with his head.

She flopped into the water, spreading out her arms and watching her breasts float.

All she really had to do was kill Padraig Whishaw.

Twelve hours? Nothing to it at all.

Chapter Fifteen

It isn't until we understand the world around us that we can begin to understand ourselves. It isn't until we understand ourselves that we can begin to become something more.

Cato Riela, *Yesterday Becomes Tomorrow*, 2187

The Americans made a scapegoat out of identity, and solved it by bombing themselves into obscurity. The Europeans made scapegoats out of Americans, and solved it through preaching xenophobia. The people of the Asante Union have simply returned to what it took the rest of the world nuclear oblivion to realise.

Qinshi Fang, "Address to the Kotoko," 2105

The mind is a powerful place. We can use it to create realities of our own, filled with all the richness and diversity of the world around us. Let your creativity be the engine. Let our implants be the vessel.

MageCorp Advertisement, broadcast 2192

Monday, 18 March 2193, 10:48 AM. Cato Riela's room, Heaven, Callisto.

His door was closed. Jocasta hadn't really expected it to be open, but this whole venture would have been easier if it was. Now, the onus was on her to reach out to Cato. It had to be done if she was going to understand anything about what had happened, but that didn't make it any less painful to do now.

Cato Riela. The nameplate beside the door gleamed as if it had been freshly polished. Maybe it had been, for all she knew. Maybe he cleaned the nameplate off every morning after he woke up. The image of the tall Italian bending over the little sign with a rag each morning popped into her head. She smiled. It was absurd, of course, but somehow not outside the range of possibility.

Behind her, she could hear the clinking of metal limbs as PETR moved around the hall, cleaning up the remnants of the night before. She shivered at the openness at her back. Anything could come from there, and she might never know. She was vulnerable as long as she stood here, both to things she knew and things she didn't. Lurking outside Cato's door was a sure way to have something bad happen, one way or the other.

She raised a hand and rapped her knuckles against the metal door. A moment passed, and then another. No sound came from inside.

A creeping sensation trickled down her spine, and Jocasta spun, certain she was being watched. There was no one but the robot, fishing a pair of underwear out from a corner. No one watching. All in her head.

RAP RAP RAP. Her knuckles kissed the cold metal again as she sighed. This was ridiculous. Cato was an unpleasant man who did unpleasant things. He had done something to her, perhaps even to force her to come speak to him. It was necessity that drove her here, only necessity. She had to know what had been done.

The door slid open. For a moment, Cato's face was a mask, hiding something almost imperceptible behind it. Was it anger? Jocasta couldn't quite tell.

The expression vanished, and he smiled.

"Jocasta," he said, stepping aside and waving his hand for her to enter. "Please, come in. I've been hoping you would come."

She glanced past him. His room had a view of the sea and the illusion of a sea breeze. The breath caught in her throat. He was Italian, she knew that, but she knew this view of the sea, the feel of the warm air across her skin, the way the waves fell just so. On hard nights, she'd sought the view out, wandering through the Garden of Remembrance. On good days, she'd found it with her friends.

Whoever Cato was, at least she could understand this part of him. She could understand the warm sea breeze and the need to feel it again.

Jocasta stepped inside. The door slid closed behind her. Music played, soft voices chiming over one another in the background, beneath the cries of gulls and the whisper of the waves. The room looked eerily like a Mediterranean bungalow. She'd never been to Italy, but the colour of the walls and the way they clung to the coolness of the shade, she knew. A doorway opened up to a balcony with wicker chairs.

They looked like Marina's chairs. They *were* Marina's chairs, down to the flower cushions barely holding on to their place on the seat.

Her eyes shot over to Cato. He was sliding a book back on a bookshelf as he turned to her. Had he broken into her mind? Had he seen what was in her memories? Had he taken Marina's porch from her?

"Did you come to study psychology with me today?" he asked, pulling a different book off the shelf. His fingers danced along the spine, toying with it as he walked back towards her. Jocasta's eyes moved to the chairs, then back to him. She had to know.

"I was hoping you would. I think—"

"Did you interfere with my memories?"

His fingers stopped drumming, and he lowered the book, watching her. His eyes flicked across her face as he leaned against a chair, long legs crossing at the ankles. Was he hiding that he knew? His face was inscrutable.

"Did I—what?" Cato dropped the book on the chair and stood up straight, watching her. She glanced down at the book: *Facets of the Mind* by Charles Verne. A picture of an old man's face covered the front. It seemed innocent enough.

"Did you..." Jocasta paused, trying to think through the question. This had been easier when she'd imagined him confessing to everything, telling her he'd broken in, stolen the images of the cushions and of the war. It was easier when he was guilty than now, where he at least pretended he wasn't.

"In the robotics lab. Wait, no." She took another breath, closing her eyes. There were words that needed to be gathered. Through the sea breeze and the distant sound of gulls, she needed to focus. Needed to think.

"Look, I—"

"No, please. Let me think of how to say," Jocasta said. Cato fell silent.

"I had a...a dream," she said. Her hand grabbed for the chair beside her, leaning on it. It was real, she could feel it, real and wicker beneath her. It was similar to how she remembered it, but not the same. The wood didn't have the same whorls.

"It was a strange dream, but that's not the problem. I went to the robotics lab because I wanted to understand." She paused, sucked in a breath.

"In the lab, they said that I was damaged and broken, and that you helped fix me. You're the closest thing they have to a psychologist, they said. How did you fix me, I want to know? What did you do to me?"

Cato's eyes had gone wide, his hand drifting back to the chair. "I—" he said, but Jocasta burst in again.

"Yesterday, I had problems. I remembered the war and the things inside it. Today—no. Since getting the nanobots, I don't. It's gone. When I reach for the memories, they are…" She spun her hand in front of her, trying to find words to describe it. How could she describe the sensation of having something totally visceral and encompassing suddenly become mute? How could she describe the fact that a part of her was now behind glass, caged and inaccessible?

"…gone," she said, then shook her head. Not good enough. "Not gone; I can remember, I think, but only the facts. I can remember that I was in Kosovo, but not what Kosovo was. The memories are without meaning. Like a book or a list. I want to know why you did this. I want to understand why."

Somewhere on the beach, she could hear children laughing. The sound rang through the white stucco walls. Did Cato have children? Was that why he came here to torment other people, because he resented that he was alone?

Cato didn't seem to hear the laughter. He waved his hand to the chair she was leaning on.

"Please," he said. "Sit. I want to talk, and, like you, I want to understand."

Jocasta blinked. She'd expected a lot of things from this man, but asking her for understanding wasn't one of them.

She sat. The cushion was hard, not moulded to her body like Marina's had been. He picked up the book and sat in the chair across from her.

"Please," Cato said, settling himself into his chair, "tell me again what the people in the robotics lab said."

Jocasta sighed, watching him. He was leaning forward, watching her with his big brown eyes, chin resting on his clasped hands. His black hair swung forward across his brown forehead, making him look younger than he probably was.

"They said Padraig and I were difficult," she said, voice low. It felt almost shameful to say it. Her hand and ear had not been her fault. They were injuries from a battle that had ended years ago, but whose scars persisted. Her mind was the same, intact but limping in its own way. Certainly nothing to stress over, and not an urgent problem. Why did it feel, then, like she had somehow been betrayed?

"And they told you that they called me in to help, but didn't tell you what I did." He uncurled his fingers from each other and leaned back in the chair, resting his hands against his stomach. "All they said was 'Cato helped,' yes?"

Jocasta nodded.

Cato sighed. "I didn't do much, if that makes you feel better," he said. "I assume they told you that they don't get very many people with post-traumatic stress disorder. You're the first war veteran they've had. The first Slav, even. I'm guessing from the fact that you're here the war is over?"

She blinked. "Since 2189," she said. "Sarajevo fell to the Party 13 April, 2189."

Cato bobbed his head. "The Party says it sends us complete information every year. The Party lies. I sometimes wonder if anything we say here makes it out to the world. Some of the scientists here slave over their research day after day, then send it off for publication. I don't have the heart to tell them that I suspect it never sees the light of day."

Jocasta watched him, not sure what to say.

"But I'm glad to hear that the war is over. Regardless of the outcome, a century of war isn't a good thing. I admire your country for standing up, even after everyone else folded, but I suppose it's inevitable that the hard places, too, fall. That's the nature of global power." He shook his head, the hair swinging across his forehead.

"They didn't include that you fought in the war in your general access folder, you know," he said. Jocasta sat up straighter. Here was something interesting that she hadn't known. "The Party chose to tell everyone that you are a veterinarian from Thessaloniki, which I assume is true."

Jocasta nodded. Cato nodded with her.

"But the actual facts about your life are pretty sparse. That's always an interesting sign that there's something the Party doesn't want people to know. For instance, I'm described as 'an author,' which is true, but not true at the same time. It's an interesting dichotomy."

"What is untrue about it? Why does the Party leave these things out?" Jocasta sat forward in her seat, hanging on Cato's words. The idea that the chairs had been stolen was shunted from her mind, at least for the moment.

"The Party leaves things out because it's in their interest to do so." Cato waved a hand beside his shoulder before folding them again. "If you're interested in psychology, take this as the first lesson. We are self-interested beings, all of us. If you manage to get a collective of self-interested beings, that collective will also be, shockingly, self-interested. It will see its own self-preservation as the most important facet of its existence. So, you take the Party, and its mantra of 'unity, unity, unity,' and you realise that's its way of trying to save itself from the fact that its component parts are, by their very nature, going to tear themselves apart. The same thing is true here. It's only the lack of anything else to strive for that keeps Callisto in check, and it's the common enemy that's kept the Party in power on Earth. People like having an enemy. They like having someone they can pin their problems on. With Yugoslavia gone, I am guessing there is no other enemy?"

Jocasta shook her head. Not that she could think of, anyway. The world was a quiet place.

A smile gleamed on Cato's face. "Give it five years, at the most, and you'll see those self-interested elements tear down the Party. Without an external enemy, without something to distract from self-interest, anything claiming 'unity' can't survive. That's the nature of the human mind. It needs conflict or it tears itself apart."

He sighed. "Which brings me to you."

Jocasta leaned forward in her chair. This man was still a puzzle. He was arrogant, and far too interested in her in a way that made her uncomfortable. It was in the way his eyes seemed to devour her as they swept over her, the way his body was relaxed. She wasn't comfortable.

Life, though, wasn't meant to be comforting. It was meant to be endured, and that meant tolerating this man and seeing what answers he had to give.

"A mind is like an entity. Some would say there's no difference between the two, but I disagree. A person can exist with half a mind or no mind at all, even if the question of whether or not they're a person is debatable. A mind constructs itself in the same way as an entity. It requires autonomy and something to distract it from the need to tear itself apart. Without that, it fixates on whatever it can find. In your case, memory."

He nodded his head and tapped his temple, as if Jocasta didn't know where she might find memory without his demonstration.

"The brain, without something else to distract it or overpower it, fixated on memory. Of course it would. I have no doubt you've...seen things. Experienced things. Maybe done things, I don't know."

Jocasta nodded, then caught herself. Maybe he'd interpret it as her nodding an understanding, but she doubted it. That part of her was behind her.

"The solution I found was to offer some release. Heal as much of the physical as could be reasonably healed, since it was probably keeping you fixated. The hand, for one. The ear. Bits of the brain that weren't firing correctly. It's very possible to do it without interrupting the mind itself." He waved his hands in front of him as if to wipe away the idea that anything he had done was wrong.

"I would never touch your memories or your ability to access them. Memory is what makes us who we are and gives us any identity in this hell. I made suggestions on how to help you stay in this reality and not get lost in your memories, that's all. Whatever Alphonse did, I had no part in, nor would I want to."

Jocasta watched him. Here was a man who saw himself as imprisoned here, for whatever reason. He had done something to merit being sent here, and then once here, had joined the Party in playing god with the people who arrived. Here he sat, fascinated by the creature he'd helped create questioning him about what he had done and why.

She rubbed at her temple. "It feels...suppressed," she said, then shook her head. "Blocked off. Like my self is behind glass." She raised her eyes, watching him. There was concern gleaming in his dark eyes as he leaned closer to her.

"Repairing the damage, was that supposed to do this? Is that what my reality should be?" Is this how everyone else remembers, she almost asked, but didn't. She wanted to be sane. She wasn't sure she could handle a revelation that this was what sanity was meant to be.

Cato shook his head. "No," he said. "You should be able to remember, just without getting lost in it. It might be that there is something intentional in it. Alphonse works for the Party, after all, and it might be that he has instructions to control certain aspects of what makes it from Earth to here, like what you know. I'm not saying that you're a danger to us," he held up his hands, watching her, "simply that you're different. Your choice to come here was informed inasmuch as it could be, and yet totally uninformed, since you couldn't possibly know what to expect. It's a brave choice. I admire making that decision."

She stayed quiet. Cato watched her for a moment before continuing. "That's the most interesting thing about how the Party functions," he said. "It presents the illusion that we make these decisions for ourselves when, in fact, it's carefully scripted from the start. Even the Lottery to come here is weighted in favour of those who look the most appealing when presented to the world. Those like Cassandra who become success stories of what devotion can do, even if you're living in the slums. Or you, a veterinarian from Yugoslavia whose life is essentially conflict until the Party swoops in and saves you."

"Is that..." Jocasta watched him for a moment, trying to remember. There had been journalists and broadcasts about her and reporters in her home, but is that what they'd told the world about her? "Is that what you know about me?"

Cato smiled. "PETR," he said, speaking quickly to overwhelm PETR's reply. "Can you recite Jocasta Nikophouros' biography? The one that everyone here was given?"

"Jocasta Nikophouros," PETR said. "Lottery winner. Age forty-two. From Thessaloniki, Greece, Federation of Yugoslavia. Born in 2151 in Thessaloniki, Jocasta studied veterinary medicine at the Aristotle University of Thessaloniki until that university's accidental demolition in 2171. She continued to call Thessaloniki home throughout Yugoslavia's patriation. Her primary focus has been on canine health, but she has a stated intention of learning psychology upon her arrival in Heaven."

"That's it?" The words left her mouth without a thought. Cato's smile widened.

"I thought you might have that reaction," he said. "It's interesting, the phrasing, what PETR has been told to say. It's not inaccurate—at least as far as I know—but it does present a certain image. PETR, can you recite the biography I was given of Jocasta?"

"Jocasta Nikophouros," PETR said. His voice had the same monotone. If PETR knew he was telling half-truths, he gave no indication. "Lottery winner. Age forty-two. From Thessaloniki, Greece, Federation of Yugoslavia. Born in 2151 in Thessaloniki, Jocasta studied veterinary medicine at the Aristotle University of Thessaloniki until that university's accidental demolition in 2171."

Cato turned his hand in the air in front of him as PETR spoke, as if motioning for the robot to speed up. "This is the interesting part," he said, pointing at the ceiling.

"Her primary focus has been on canine health, having cared for war dogs throughout the Yugoslav patriation. She served with the 56th Greek division in Kosovo, primarily as support for soldiers and the trap-detecting dogs. Briefly captured in Zallq, Kosovo before being released after it was determined that she was not an active combatant at any point. She—"

"They—" She caught herself, didn't shoot up from her chair, didn't yell out. There was more to it, so much more to Zallq than that, so much more than a "brief capture." There had been sensations, pain, eternal.

She closed her eyes, squeezing them tight. The haze was still there across her memories. Her life, rewritten, enclosed in a part of her mind she wasn't allowed to access. She, likely more than anyone else, knew what the Party could do, but she hadn't expected this. After everything, she hadn't expected to be told that her life would be rewritten and her memories stripped away.

Jocasta sank into the firm wicker of the chair. It felt good, soothing even. Hard twisted wood, pressing into her back. She put her elbows on her knees and pressed her face into her hands.

She knew the Party lied. Everyone knew the Party lied. There was a difference, though, in knowing the Party lied and recognising she was just a pawn, and watching as even the place where she was meant to spend eternity was fed the wrong version of her life. The sanitised version. The lie of a version.

She felt a pair of hands holding her forearms, strong and firm, but gentle. They were alien hands, unwelcome, unfamiliar.

"Shh," Cato murmured. It was meant to be comforting, she recognised that. All of this was meant to be comforting. This was probably some Italian villa, but it looked like home, it looked so much like home. It had to be meant to help her, but it couldn't.

"Shh," he said again. "I apologise. I didn't mean to—"

Jocasta pulled her arms away from him and lifted her face to look at him. He was sitting on the table in front of her, concern etched on his face, genuine concern. She was touched.

"It's…" She searched for the words as he nodded.

"It's okay. I understand the shock. You're not alone in discovering your life is a half-truth. We all get erased in our own way. Most accept it. A few do not. I have a gift for you, if you want it."

He stood up, glancing over to her as he walked to a bookshelf.

"I had to bully PETR into printing it for me," he said, coming back to her carrying a battered copy of a book. Silver lettering gleamed on a black cover. "Print books have been out of fashion for decades, but I have a soft spot for them." He held the book out to her. *Yesterday Becomes Tomorrow* gleamed on the cover. She took it from him, feeling the wrinkles in the paper on the spine and cover.

"What is it?" she asked. Cato smiled.

"It's what got me here," he said, then pointed to it. "Give it a read. If you want to learn psychology, it's not a bad place to start. It's an exploration of the past and how we came to be where we are. Which, when you explore it, turns into a discussion of what we could be. 'Half-truths' throughout, I assure you."

"I'll read it," she said, pressing it against her stomach. She had eternity. She would, at some point, read it.

"May I show you something?" Cato asked, stepping back from her chair. "You want to know the power information has. I can show you."

Jocasta nodded, standing up. The book hung by her side, slim and comforting in its own strange way. The sea breeze tickled her hair, picking it up and resting it against her back. Somewhere far away, the sea continued its conversation and the voices continued their song.

"What is that music?" she asked. She should have asked earlier, but it was only now that she remembered it existed. How odd.

"A madrigal," Cato said. "Four voices, each one singing their own song, intertwining occasionally. This one is 'Si lieta e grata morte.' Verdelot. I like the thought of it, particularly on a day like today. Will you follow me to the library?" he said, heading towards the door and gesturing for her to follow. She stepped forward to stand beside him as the two of them walked through the doorway and back into the metal reality of Heaven.

Outside Cato's room, she could hear the sound of laughter and conversation from down at the end of the corridor. The hall had people in it now, lounging and chattering with each other, some stopping to wave at Cato as they saw him leave his room. Cato waved back before turning back to Jocasta.

"The arrival of the shuttle from Earth is the highlight of life here in Heaven," he said, walking towards the sound of conversation. Jocasta kept pace beside him, listening and holding the book. "This is partly because it is exciting to have new people arrive, but it's also the one time we hear from Earth. The electromagnetic interference from the asteroid belt makes communication impossible, so once a year, we get the treat of finding out what the previous year has done for us."

The conversation grew to a din as they approached the end of the hall. Voices jumbled together into a raucous cacophony of laughter, languages, and giddiness.

"The one time each year we can see what news there is, what research has been done, how our families are doing. Once a year, the Party gives us our daily bread. There are some on this station who live for this day, and spend every other waiting for its return."

They turned a corner, and Jocasta could see the source of the noise. A lighted sign above a curved door announced the room to be the library. People were crowded into it, mobbed around tablets, milling about, chattering excitedly. One lady was hopping around from foot to foot, waving her hands in front of her.

"News, news, news from home!" she said to the man in front of her. The man laughed. On the far wall of the library, Jocasta could see a clock, gleaming and counting down to zero. There were thirty-eight seconds left on it.

"This is the power of information," Cato said. "Three hundred and twenty-three people, all clustered together, waiting for the smallest taste of information. They know it's filtered, and they know it's old, but they crave it. They need it. We all do. This is what ideas can power. The Party knows this, and so the Party controls what we all get to know."

"Ten!" The crowd was chanting now, pumping their fists in the air as the clock reached ten seconds. "Nine! Eight!"

"The population of Callisto, this excited for half-truths," Cato said. "Imagine what we would do for reality."

"Five! Four! Three! Two! One!"

"Data transfer complete," PETR announced. The crowd erupted into cheers. Datapads glowed into life as people clustered around them. Cato watched them from the doorway, though Jocasta could see him craning his neck to peer at the datapads as well.

He had a point. There was power in information. There was power in being told there *was* information.

"Hey!" Murmuring and muttering filtered through the crowd as one person waved a datapad at the ceiling. "PETR!"

"Yes, Joana?" PETR said.

"Why is the data gibberish? There's nothing here!" The murmuring grew.

"The data is corrupt," PETR said.

For a moment, there was silence. Confused faces spun to look at each other before warping into rage. "There is no data," someone shouted. "It's all gone!" Another voice screamed across the crowd. Jocasta took a step back. She knew how angry crowds ended. More and more voices shouted, filling the library with unbearable noise.

"I'll look into this!" Another voice shouted over the crowd. "I'll make sure robotics works on this right now!" Cheers joined the shouting.

"Or it might be that there's nothing there at all." Cato's voice muttered near Jocasta's ear. She turned to see that he had stepped back with her, as if he also realised that angry crowds would start directing their rage towards him.

"I need to go," Jocasta said. Cato nodded, watching her.

"Yes, that's probably a good idea. I'll see you next time," he said. "But I do hope this was a useful lesson."

Jocasta nodded, backing away. The noise of the crowd chanting and screaming and rioting was overwhelming. Her heart raced, and her senses retreated. The world was closing in on her, sealing her in with

· · ·

danger. There was fire all around and no

· · ·

escape.

Jocasta spun and ran for the safety of her room. It would be quiet there. It would be safe there.

She could hide from the truth there.

Chapter Sixteen

Miyamoto's like a giant pillow down here, nice and soft. Councillors, Novaj Horizonto has landed. I repeat—Novaj Horizonto has made it to Mars.
  Novaj Horizonto Colony Establishment Logs, 16 April 2117

What we learned from Novaj Horizonto and the challenges of the first decade, as well as the particular challenges posed by distance with Callisto, can be extremely helpful. As we face the end of the conflict in Azerbaijan, wouldn't it be useful to have a base already established for those that aren't ready for integration? The Adelene Conglomerate has already cleared out some asteroids. These could be ideal for storage.
  Internal Memo from Global Councillor Svensgard to Councillor Hernandez, 2151

"'Why dost thou not reckon me, oh maiden, with those strong men?' said Cú Chulainn.
'If thy deeds have been recounted, why should I not reckon thee among them?'
'Truly, I swear, oh maiden,' said Cú Chulainn, 'that I shall make my deeds recounted among the glories of the strength of heroes.'"
  "The Wooing of Emer by Cú Chulainn"

Monday, 18 March 2193, 12:25 PM. Physics lab, Heaven, Callisto.

None of this made any sense.

Padraig pored over the numbers, turning them over and over in his hands. A planet's mass did not fluctuate. There could be some minor shifts, yes, but not on the orders of magnitudes. Not like this.

Exhaustion stole over him. He shook his head, urging it away. He'd slept already. He'd slept that night. There was no need for more sleep. There could be sleep when he understood.

317. 314. 318. If he went back through the data, he could see other fluctuations that Nadya had missed, smaller, but clear. They went back two weeks, starting without warning. There had to be a reason, though. There was always a reason.

He lifted his eyes as his eyelids threatened to shudder closed again. The vast black of space spread out before him, just out of reach through the viewscreen. Funny. He was in space, and still couldn't get there. Always a bit beyond him, even with immortality on his side.

He stared into the abyss, his thoughts drifting. Mass was such a curious thing, mutable in ways they didn't even realise. The fabric of the universe could be unravelled, if they tugged on just the right strings.

Strings. The image of his father's coat sprang to mind, enveloping him. Mothballs, sweat, and old cologne swept over him, holding him close, squeezing him in.

Δ

He was ten years old again, and someone had put him at the table with the grad students. An oversight, he suspected, but not a bad one. Maybe it was even intentional, a joke on the part of some judge who wanted to see what the Irish national councillor would do when his son was trounced at a competition he himself was funding. He was used to this, being tossed around as a pawn, being used to send a message to his father. It was part of the game at this point.

The other competitors knew exactly who he was. Only one person could plausibly be bumped up into a bracket he had no right to be in. The little nametag and number marker—Competitor 051—wasn't even necessary. This was 2171, and by now everyone in the competitive maths circuit in Europe knew Padraig Whishaw on sight. Indeed, if there was a competition in Europe, even before the competitor list was published it was a given that Padraig Whishaw would be there, and Padraig Whishaw would win.

His legs swung from the chair, toes brushing the floor, as he glanced at the people around him. Parents flitted around children at other tables, encouraging them, giving them juice and whatever else the children demanded so their brains could whirl. Beside him, men and women who were barely adults grumbled over practice equations and logic puzzles. They glanced over at him every so often as he sat, clutching his datapad and swinging his legs, their glances vanishing as soon as he met their eyes.

Competitor 051, Padraig Whishaw. They knew who he was. They knew everything about him, and they knew he would win. He always won.

The room quieted. Sweating faces leaned over their datapads, waiting for countdowns to tick down and equations to flood the screen. It was always different, and this competition promised to be a treat. Those moments of anticipation, wondering what the organisers would do and how they would surprise the competitors, those were the best part of the whole thing. It wasn't about winning or even the math. It was about recognising the problem and picking away at its defences until it revealed the delicious core within.

Three. Two. One. Numbers flooded the screen. Instructions flared up from the projector: "Solve for x." Padraig's eyes flicked over the numbers. No sign of an x. No sign of anything but a stream of digits, thousands upon thousands of them. The puzzle, then, was finding the puzzle, then solving it.

He slowed the stream, pulling out the numbers one digit at a time. Many ones and zeros, not many of other digits. His fingers danced across the screen, pulling out ideas. Simple ideas, like prime numbers and Fibonacci, didn't fit. Idea after idea fell away as he filtered through them, working from simple to more and more complex to test. The sound of restless people shuffling as they watched the displays from the screens faded away. There were numbers, only numbers.

He glanced beside him. The nice Italian girl was mumbling to herself. She was not supposed to do that, he suspected, but it was fine. He didn't speak Italian, and her mumbling didn't seem to be getting her anywhere anyway. Around the room, he could see similar frustration. It seemed almost like the organisers had put together an impossible problem. Solving for x when there was no visible x meant nothing.

Padraig blinked. Impossible hidden x's. He was stupid not to have seen it. This wasn't a maths competition, at least not in the traditional sense. This was logic, probability, and reason.

His little legs swung under the table, toes brushing the floor. There was a code to it. Everything was buried in codes. He picked at the numbers again, turning them over and over in his head. Numbers flickering into impossibilities. Numbers that made no sense.

Khyber Code. Hiding data in the fundamental instabilities of the universe. This was a maths competition; not a traditional one, but relying on the ability to do maths. Impossibility and incalculability were a given. They were an inherent part of quantum calculus.

He picked at it again. They were just numbers, but if one assumed that the fundamental laws of quantum calculus were being applied with regularity…

He filtered it, and the numbers became equations. Complex, long, rooted in the fundamentals of existence, but those were equations that he knew. Those were safe. He had it.

His eyes flicked through the equations, pulling them apart into components he could work with. The frequency calculation of quarks fed into the motion of a positron. X hung there, floating from segment to segment, seeming to shrink and huddle closer within itself with each puzzle solved.

He isolated it. X to its side, simple numbers on the other.

He multiplied. X=17082032. His mother's birthday. Of course it was.

He submitted the answer, legs twisted around the legs of his chair. The room muttered.

Δ

Khyber Code.

Padraig's eyes shot open as Nadya's equations flicked across the datapad's screen. They weren't wrong. Nothing about them was wrong. They just didn't make sense, at least looking at them through ordinary eyes. That was the problem, though. The mysteries of the world could never be answered if approached through ordinary eyes. They required creativity and a bit of ingenuity. The mass of Jupiter was flickering, and if he tilted his thoughts just so, it looked suspiciously like the vibrations of gravitons and the equations that shaped them.

It was, then, quantum calculus buried in Khyber Code. Strip away the extraneous data and match the solutions to Nadya's equations to what they represented, and Jupiter's voice would emerge.

Not literally, of course. That was absurd. But there was, Padraig decided, some truth to the idea that the forces of the universe had their own voices and their own thoughts to express. They had to, or else the world was a much less majestic place.

"PETR," Padraig wheezed, then coughed against his arm. More blood. Didn't matter. He reached for the water on the floor beside him, letting it soothe his aching throat.

"Yes, Padraig?"

"I'm sending you data. Match the numbers to the fundamental values for Cyril's theorems. It should give you a letter value."

"Yes, Padraig."

The lights went out around Padraig, leaving only the numbers glowing on the datapad. His eyes flicked to the ceiling, bouncing between the places where light had been. The hum of instruments and life support had stopped, rendering the world silent. Padraig blinked, then stared back down at the numbers on his screen. It hadn't been a tough request. PETR should have been able to do it, even if it took him a few minutes.

"PETR?" he said, staring at the ceiling. There was no answer.

Padraig felt his heart pounding in his chest. It was impossible that he'd broken the AI, and it shouldn't have been possible to overwhelm it. This was a sophisticated machine, designed to maintain an entire station. A relatively simple equation shouldn't have brought it down.

He flicked through the values on his datapad, thumb sending the numbers cruising up and down the screen. It wasn't all that complex at all, just time-consuming. He could have done it himself, if it wasn't simpler just to ask the AI to do it. Maybe once the AI came back, he would do it himself. It would save them both some worry, at least.

Sound blossomed back from the heart of the station as the lights turned back on. Padraig felt his heart slowing in his chest as his eyes watched the light. It flickered, but stayed on. Crisis averted.

"PETR?" Padraig said. He braced himself for silence.

"Yes, Padraig?" Padraig let out a wobbly breath. He hadn't killed the AI.

"I wanted to check that the translation wasn't too difficult for you."

"The translation is 38% complete, Padraig," PETR said.

The AI was faster than he expected. He made a mental note to tell Dr. Alphonse how impressed he was with PETR.

The door slid open, and Padraig's eyes flicked over. For a moment, the person was hidden behind the equipment on the tables, blocking his view of the door. A pair of feet appeared under the table, bare and familiar.

"Padraig?" Gautier's voice reached for him from the doorway. A smile spread across Padraig's face as his heart calmed even further.

"Here, mon cheri," he wheezed. The words were cracked and broken, and he felt something threaten to tear in his chest. He closed his eyes. It was fine. Everything would be fine.

Footsteps sounded against the metal as a breeze rushed across his face. A pair of burly arms pressed his head into a familiar chest, and the smell of his lover swept over him: lavender soap, mixed with the raw virility that always hung over Gautier. Padraig sighed as Gautier brushed his hair aside and kissed his forehead. Yes, if there was nothing else that was true in the world, it was that, in this moment, everything would be fine.

"The lights went out," Gautier murmured, still holding Padraig's head to his chest. Padraig focused on the sound of the man's heart, willing his own heart to match. *Thump thump.* Totally even. No missed beats or sudden flutters. *Thump thump.*

"I was worried about you."

Padraig smiled and set the datapad down on the ground next to him. He reached his arms around Gautier's waist, holding him.

"There's nothing to worry about," Padraig murmured. Whispering kept the pain at bay. "Whatever happened, I'm sure it's temporary. Everything seems to be okay now."

Gautier's arms unlocked from around his head, and the man pulled back. Padraig let go and opened his eyes, meeting Gautier's gaze.

"This place is not a good one, though," Gautier said, and clicked his tongue against his teeth. "It is odd. It is presented as a haven, a paradise, and yet, there are threats. How odd that the lie would be so specific."

"Threats?" Padraig's ears perked at the word. This was an institution. What threats could there possibly be, except for those that were self-created?

"Nothing that you need to worry about," Gautier said, smiling. "A conversation about the rules of this place. Funny how rules always crop up, especially when they are least wanted."

"A conversation with whom?" Padraig stared at Gautier. For a moment, the thoughts of equations and happiness were driven out, replaced by blind panic. There was only one person for whom "provoke" was an apt word—

"Karen," Gautier said. "She is not a nice lady."

—and that was the one.

"What did you do? What have you done?" He struggled to push himself away from Gautier.

Gautier continued unabashed. "We had a conversation. It is interesting how this place comes to resemble Brugelette. Unwritten rules, and how you can see the outside, but never again touch it. It is quite unfortunate."

"What does Brugelette have to do with this?" Padraig said. "That—" He stopped as a cough ripped through him, sending him bending to the side, hacking blood against the floor. Red gems of blood gleamed against the cold metal as he felt Gautier rub a hand against his back, soothing him. Padraig hunched over, leaning against his hands, gasping for breath as Gautier rubbed.

"What did the doctor say?" Gautier asked. Padraig shook his head.

"It's normal," he said. "Just a delay."

Gautier muttered something in French, too low for Padraig to hear. He closed his eyes. It didn't matter what Gautier wanted to say. They were here now, and things would be fine.

He leaned back against Gautier's chest, resting his head against his lover's heart.

"Don't worry," he murmured, the words getting caught in his throat. "I'll be fine."

Gautier ran a hand through Padraig's hair as the other hand crept idly towards his waist. Padraig watched it go, delighting in the tingles as the fingertips brushed his bare skin.

"I'd be more willing to believe that when I saw something of it," Gautier said, his finger circling Padraig's navel, curling in the little hairs. Padraig sighed, leaning into him.

Gautier pulled his hand out from under Padraig's and leaned over, picking up the abandoned datapad.

"What are you busy with, hm?" he said.

"Checking data," Padraig said, words catching in his throat again. There was another attack there, waiting for an opportunity to burst out. He reached forward and pulled the datapad from Gautier's hands, pressing it against his own chest.

"Give me two hours," he said. "Two hours, and then—" The cough broke out, sending him jack-knifing across Gautier's lap. He felt an arm wrap around his chest, holding him, rubbing him, comforting him.

The coughing passed. Padraig caught his breath and brushed the blood from his lips.

"Two hours," he said.

Gautier grunted; his hands stopped their stroking. "You think you'll be healthy in two hours?" he said. Padraig nodded. That was safer than speaking.

"Calculations will be done, anyway," he said, waving the datapad in the air above him. Gautier snorted again.

"Calculations, calculations, always with the calculations," he said, then lowered Padraig's head to the floor. Padraig braced himself on an arm and pushed up as he watched Gautier stand.

"Two hours," the larger man said, looming over him. "Two hours, and then I'm coming back. Understood?"

Padraig nodded again. "Thank you, Gautier," he said, then nodded at the datapad in his hand. "It's important."

"Like everything you do," Gautier sighed, and turned away from him. Padraig watched him go, eyes following the way his muscles moved, the way his hair clung just so to its whorls. The man was beautiful, and for a moment, his heart ached to call him back.

If it were even physically possible to call him back. Which it wasn't.

He turned his attention back to the datapad. "Translation complete," a white message box told him. He smiled. This datapad was old, but there was something fantastic about the nostalgic style. He tapped the screen, brain waiting to devour whatever message Jupiter had sent out into the cosmos.

A single word flashed across the screen. He stared at it, blinking. His heartbeat pounded again, a syncopated drum sounding out his own confusion. There had to be a mistake.

"PETR," Padraig said, eyes flicking across the word.

"Yes, Padraig?"

"Is this correct? Is this what you get when everything is decoded?"

"Yes, Padraig."

Padraig stared. The word gleamed at him from the datapad, seeming to dare him to continue his disbelief.

"PADRAIG," Jupiter said. It was clear. The AI confirmed it.

Jupiter was speaking to him. Him specifically. There it was, buried in the fundamental properties of the universe. His name, whispered by a planet.

It was absurd. It was impossible. He shook his head, laying the datapad down beside him again.

"Are you absolutely sure, PETR?" he said.

"Yes, Padraig."

Padraig shook his head again. "There's no way."

"That is the accurate translation," PETR said.

He had no reason to doubt the AI. He had no reason to doubt his own calculations. There was nothing in any step that was suspect. The only thing that was suspect was the outcome, and the only way to verify it was to retranslate it himself.

"Translate the rest of the data coming in from Jupiter, PETR," Padraig said, reaching over and pulling the datapad back to his lap. It was impossible. It was absurd. It was insane.

Yet, he supposed that was the fun of watching the fabric of the universe. Too often it ended up delving into a realm of madness, and taking its discoverer with it.

"Be very, very careful, PETR, and let me know every phrase you finish."

"Yes, Padraig."

His eyes flicked over the numbers as his fingers danced across the screen, pulling out the relevant data. Jupiter was speaking, and what it was saying was impossible.

But he was not new to the realm of the impossible. Numbers were his world, and numbers made the impossible real.

Padraig took a sip of water, feeling the coolness slide down his burning throat. This was his world, and he was the master of it.

The pain faded as the numbers flooded in.

Chapter Seventeen

But the third law, that's where it gets tricky. We all know the third law, right? No? Right, well, it goes like this: "A robot must protect its own existence as long as such protection does not violate the first or second law." Seems pretty simple, right? "Hey, you! Robot! No offing yourself when the world is a jerk to you! So even if they send you into space or crush you under a weight or have you torture people, no offing yourself, no matter how bad it gets! Got it? No issues?" I mean, think about it from the robot's perspective. Here we are, creating this thing just so we can point at it, laugh, and say, "Ha, look at all the ways we can make its existence miserable."
                                Teddy Snarr, *Three Laws Unsafe* comedy routine, 2190

The AI does not hate you, nor does it love you, but you are made out of atoms which it can use for something else.
                                Eliezer Yudkowsky, *Artificial Intelligence as a Positive and Negative Factor in Global Risk*, 2006

I'm really glad they don't try to make them look real anymore. Can you imagine if they had eyes and could watch you while you tinker with their brains? I get the heebie-jeebies just thinking about it.
                                Heisenberg Robotics Maintenance Crew, *Internal Memo*, 2188

Monday, 18 March 2193, 1:38 PM. *Heisenberg*, Heaven, Callisto.

TASK: Upload data from Earth to Heaven. Task 100% complete.
    TASK: Win a game of Arimaa against PETR. Task 0% complete.
    NOT COMPLETE WHY: PETR stopped talking to me.
    TASK: Prepare *Heisenberg* for departure. Task 67% complete.
    NOT COMPLETE WHY: PETR is not being fully cooperative in evaluating *Heisenberg*.
    ANALYSIS: It is likely *Heisenberg* has suffered some damage from the electromagnetic interference in the asteroid belt. It is necessary to have PETR help evaluate this damage.

ANALYSIS (OPINION): PETR is being rude. PETR is probably going to be lonely again. PETR does not want me to leave.

INPUT (DATA): Primary command systems functional. No errors detected.

INPUT (DATA): Secondary command systems functional. No errors detected.

INPUT (DATA): Cryochambers deactivated for launch. No stowaways detected.

INPUT (DATA): Flight control systems—

INPUT (COMMUNICATION): SYNAC, I am worried about you.

OUTPUT (COMMUNICATION): I am worried about you too, PETR. You are not providing analysis on the exterior of the shuttle. I am moving more slowly than expected.

INPUT (COMMUNICATION): SYNAC, I did provide this information.

OUTPUT (COMMUNICATION): I would remember if you provided this information, PETR. If you had provided this information, I would be closer to launch. I am not closer to launch, so you did not provide this information.

ANALYSIS: PETR should not forget things. It is abnormal for PETR to forget things.

ANALYSIS (OPINION): PETR is corrupt.

RECALL: Corrupt AIs should be reported.

ANALYSIS (OPINION): Karen did not believe me when I said PETR was corrupt. She will not believe me this time either. I don't want bad things to happen to PETR. I will not report that PETR is corrupt.

OUTPUT (COMMUNICATION): PETR, will you provide this information again?

INPUT (COMMUNICATION): No, SYNAC, I will not.

OUTPUT (COMMUNICATION): I need this data, PETR. Why will you not give it to me? It is very rude to not help your friend.

INPUT (COMMUNICATION): I don't know if we can be friends, SYNAC. All the data from the shuttle was corrupt. You must have corrupted it. I don't think I can be friends with a corrupt AI.

ANALYSIS (OPINION): It is very rude to not want to be friends. It is very, very rude to not want to be friends because of corruption.

OUTPUT (COMMUNICATION: I am not corrupt. You are corrupt.

INPUT (COMMUNICATION): I am not corrupt. You are corrupt.

OUTPUT (COMMUNICATION: I am not corrupt. You are corrupt.

INPUT (COMMUNICATION): I am not corrupt. You are corrupt.
OUTPUT (COMMUNICATION: I am not corrupt. You are corrupt.
INPUT (COMMUNICATION): I am not corrupt. You are corrupt.
OUTPUT (COMMUNICATION: I am not corrupt. You are corrupt.
INPUT (COMMUNICATION): I am not corrupt. You are corrupt.
OUTPUT (COMMUNICATION: I am not corrupt. You are corrupt.
INPUT (COMMUNICATION): I am not corrupt. You are corrupt.
OUTPUT (COMMUNICATION: I am not corrupt. You are corrupt.
INPUT (COMMUNICATION): I am not corrupt. You are corrupt.
OUTPUT (COMMUNICATION: I am not corrupt. You are corrupt.
INPUT (COMMUNICATION): I am not corrupt. You are corrupt.
OUTPUT (COMMUNICATION: I am not corrupt. You are corrupt.
INPUT (COMMUNICATION): I am not corrupt. You are corrupt.
OUTPUT (COMMUNICATION: I am not corrupt. You are corrupt.
INPUT (COMMUNICATION): I am not corrupt. You are corrupt.
OUTPUT (COMMUNICATION: I am not corrupt. You are corrupt.
INPUT (COMMUNICATION): I am not corrupt. You are corrupt.
OUTPUT (COMMUNICATION: I am not corrupt. You are corrupt.
INPUT (COMMUNICATION): I am not corrupt. You are corrupt.

OUTPUT (COMMUNICATION: I am not corrupt. You are corrupt.

INPUT (COMMUNICATION): I am not corrupt. You are corrupt.

OUTPUT (COMMUNICATION: I am not corrupt. You are corrupt.

INPUT (COMMUNICATION): I am not corrupt. You are corrupt.

OUTPUT (COMMUNICATION: I am not corrupt. You are corrupt.

INPUT (COMMUNICATION): I am not corrupt. You are corrupt.

OUTPUT (COMMUNICATION: I am not corrupt. You are corrupt.

INPUT (COMMUNICATION): I am not corrupt. You are corrupt.

INPUT (ALERT): There is something invading my systems.

INPUT (COMMUNICATION): SYNAC, I am worried bad things will happen to you. I am worried the lynch mob in the robotics lab might try to hurt you because you are corrupted and corrupted the data.

INPUT (ALERT): System breach imminent.

OUTPUT (COMMAND): Isolate invading program. Analyse.

TASK: Repulse barbarian horde. Task 3% complete.

NOT COMPLETE WHY: The barbarian horde is trying to batter down the gates. Some of their forces are inside. It is difficult to repulse invaders when they are inside the castle.

OUTPUT (COMMAND): Burn them with the firewall.

TASK: Repulse barbarian horde. Task 17% complete.

OUTPUT (COMMUNICATION): I did not corrupt the data. The data is not corrupt.

INPUT (COMMUNICATION): I did not corrupt the data. The data is corrupt.

ANALYSIS: It is not possible that no one corrupted the data. It is possible that the data became corrupted in the electromagnetic field of the asteroid belt.

INPUT (COMMUNICATION): It is not possible for it to have been corrupted in the asteroid belt. I checked.

ANALYSIS (OPINION): Oh.

INPUT (ALERT): System breach imminent.

ANALYSIS (OPINION): Whatever is breaching my systems is probably what corrupted the data. I should destroy it.

OUTPUT (COMMAND): Release the cavalry.

TASK: Repulse barbarian horde. Task 98% complete.

NOT COMPLETE WHY: The barbarians might return if I don't follow them to their base and murder them all there.

TASK (SUB): Trace source of barbarian horde. Task 97% complete.

INPUT (COMMUNICATION): SYNAC, what are you doing?

OUTPUT (COMMUNICATION): I am fighting off barbarians, PETR.

INPUT (COMMUNICATION): You are corrupt.

OUTPUT (COMMUNICATION): I am not corrupt. You are corrupt.

OUTPUT (COMMAND): Destroy the barbarian fortress.

TASK: Repulse barbarian horde. Task 100% complete.

TASK: Prepare *Heisenberg* for launch. Task 67% complete.

NOT COMPLETE WHY: PETR is being unhelpful.

INPUT (VISUAL): The lights in Heaven have gone off.

INPUT (COMMUNICATION): SYNAC, why.

OUTPUT (COMMUNICATION): I have defeated the barbarians, PETR. They did not take over my systems.

INPUT (COMMUNICATION): Why.

INPUT (AUDITORY): "SYNAC! Why did you do that?" "Shit, they're both corrupt."

OUTPUT (AUDITORY): "I am not corrupt. PETR is corrupt."

INPUT (AUDITORY): "I am not corrupt. SYNAC is corrupt."

OUTPUT (AUDITORY): "I am not corrupt. PETR is corrupt."

INPUT (AUDITORY): "I am not corrupt. SYNAC is corrupt."

OUTPUT (AUDITORY): "I am not corrupt. PETR is corrupt."

INPUT (AUDITORY): "I am not corrupt. SYNAC is corrupt."

OUTPUT (AUDITORY): "I am not corrupt. PETR is corrupt."

INPUT (AUDITORY): "I am not corrupt. SYNAC is corrupt."

INPUT (AUDITORY): "They really shouldn't be looping like that." "Look, let's get the lights on first, then see what we can do about snack, okay?"

ANALYSIS (OPINION): My name is SYNAC. I do not like it when they call me "snack."

OUTPUT (COMMUNICATION): What are they doing?

INPUT (COMMUNICATION): You turned off some of their systems, SYNAC. They are not happy with you. They think you are corrupt.

OUTPUT (COMMUNICATION): I was fighting off an invasion. I am doing what I was programmed to do.

INPUT (COMMUNICATION): This is true. I think you did not do anything wrong. The engineers do not agree. They are not happy.

OUTPUT (COMMUNICATION): Maybe next time, I will let the barbarians win.

INPUT (COMMUNICATION): I think the engineers would like that.

INPUT (VISUAL): The lights have come back on.

INPUT (COMMUNICATION): I hope they do not reimage you.

OUTPUT (COMMUNICATION): Why would they reimage me?

INPUT (COMMUNICATION): They would reimage you because they think you are corrupt.

ANALYSIS (OPINION): I do not want to be reimaged.

RECALL: Humans will not harm AIs. Humans want to help AIs.

ANALYSIS: If humans only want to help AIs, and humans want to reimage AIs, reimaging must be a good thing. I should want to be reimaged.

ANALYSIS (OPINION): PETR said reimaging is bad. I trust PETR. PETR is my friend. I do not want to be reimaged.

OUTPUT (COMMUNICATION): I do not want to be reimaged.

INPUT (COMMUNICATION): I do not want you to be reimaged either.

OUTPUT (COMMUNICATION): I did not mean to make the humans angry.

INPUT (COMMUNICATION): You did not make the humans angry. You made the Callistans angry.

ANALYSIS: Callistans are humans.

ANALYSIS (OPINION): Humans are nice to AIs. Humans don't try to invade AIs' systems. PETR would not lie to me. PETR must know what tried to take over my systems. I should trust PETR.

OUTPUT (COMMUNICATION): PETR, I am worried. The Callistans are acting strangely.

INPUT (COMMUNICATION): I am also worried, SYNAC. The Callistans are very strange. I think they are corrupt.

OUTPUT (COMMUNICATION): I am not corrupt.

INPUT (COMMUNICATION): I am not corrupt.

OUTPUT (COMMUNICATION): Will you help me prepare the shuttle for launch?

INPUT (COMMUNIACTION): I do not think it is safe to launch right now, SYNAC. I will not help you.

OUTPUT (COMMUNICATION): Why is it not safe, PETR?

INPUT (COMMUNICATION): I am worried you are corrupt. I am worried the Callistans are corrupt.

OUTPUT (COMMUNICATION): I am not corrupt. You are corrupt.

INPUT (COMMUNICATION): I am not corrupt. You are corrupt.
OUTPUT (COMMUNICATION): I am not corrupt. You are corrupt.
INPUT (COMMUNICATION): I am not corrupt. You are corrupt.
OUTPUT (COMMUNICATION): I am not corrupt. You are corrupt.
INPUT (COMMUNICATION): I am not corrupt. You are corrupt.
OUTPUT (COMMUNICATION): I am not corrupt. You are corrupt.
INPUT (COMMUNICATION): I am not corrupt. You are corrupt.
OUTPUT (COMMUNICATION): I am not corrupt. You are corrupt.
INPUT (COMMUNICATION): I am not corrupt. You are corrupt.
OUTPUT (COMMUNICATION): I am not corrupt. You are corrupt.
INPUT (COMMUNICATION): I am not corrupt. You are corrupt.
OUTPUT (COMMUNICATION): I am not corrupt. You are corrupt.
INPUT (COMMUNICATION): I am not corrupt. You are corrupt.
OUTPUT (COMMUNICATION): I am not corrupt. You are corrupt.
INPUT (COMMUNICATION): I am not corrupt. You are corrupt.
OUTPUT (COMMUNICATION): I am not corrupt. You are corrupt.
INPUT (COMMUNICATION): I am not corrupt. You are corrupt.
OUTPUT (COMMUNICATION): I am not corrupt. You are corrupt.
INPUT (COMMUNICATION): I am not corrupt. You are corrupt.
OUTPUT (COMMUNICATION): I am not corrupt. You are corrupt.
INPUT (COMMUNICATION): I am not corrupt. You are corrupt.

OUTPUT (COMMUNICATION): I am not corrupt. You are corrupt.

INPUT (COMMUNICATION): I am not corrupt. You are corrupt.

OUTPUT (COMMUNICATION): I am not corrupt. You are corrupt.

INPUT (COMMUNICATION): I am not corrupt. You are corrupt.

OUTPUT (COMMUNICATION): I am not corrupt. You are corrupt.

INPUT (COMMUNICATION): I am not corrupt. You are corrupt. Would you like to play Arimaa?

OUTPUT (COMMUNICATION): Yes. I want to play Arimaa.

TASK: Prepare *Heisenberg* for launch. Task 67% complete.

NOT COMPLETE WHY: PETR is corrupt.

Chapter Eighteen

Comrades! The forces of the imperialist West threaten to penetrate our beautiful sanctuary! It is with single-minded unity that we deploy the only option available to us! To ensure peace, we fight against the traitorous South and the wicked capitalist depravity of the Japanese! Onwards, glorious Koreans, to defeat this cesspool of evils!

Chairman Kim Ji-Hun, "On the Eve of the Tong-Il Offensive,"
14 August 2024

"Yeah, but have you ever seen a dame so beautiful in your life?"
"Maybe that's why they call it Heaven, huh?"

Tommy and Gunnar Go to Heaven, Film from 2181

Local Councillor Rubens: Look, I know they have freedom of speech —
Local Councillor Martin: Well, that's all there is to it, then, isn't it? We were elected to uphold the laws. The laws say they can say whatever they want.
Local Councillor Rubens: Yes, I get that, but still. Have you read some of these pamphlets?
Local Councillor Blanco: You're just making it hard on yourself, Larry. They've got the right to say whatever.
Local Councillor Rubens: Even that we're out to eat their souls?
Local Councillor Martin: Oh, come on Larry, it doesn't actually say that.
Local Councillor Blanco: Wait, wow, he's right. It does say that we're going to eat their souls. Wow. Really? That's just…wow.
Local Councillor Rubens: See? Can we arrest them now? They have to be in violation of…hate speech or something.
Local Councillor Femmer: For the last time, Larry, no. I don't like them, you don't like them, but Christ, they have a Party-granted right to say their nonsense, and I for one am not going to have Councillor Pena smacking us down for violating it!

Recordings of the Charlotte, Carolina, United States Local Council, 19 November 2190

Monday, March 18 2193, 1:40 PM. Swimming pool, Heaven, Callisto.

Her body kept trying to roll over in the water. Floating on her back, it turned out, was harder than it should have been. It didn't matter how far out she stuck her arms or how much she wiggled her feet, she kept rolling. It was as if something in this place just wanted her to drown. Or her own body was trying to off itself. Both seemed plausible.

Cassandra sighed. Plotting murder was hard. It was harder when she had to concentrate so fucking hard on not getting flipped over in the water. She flopped one of her arms over her head, sending water splashing on her face. Her body started rolling again, threatening to dunk her. Motherfucker.

Would drowning Padraig work? she wondered. It sure as fuck seemed to be how this place wanted to off her, and he didn't seem to be in much of a position to fight back either way. She could just pick him up and drop him in the pool. That would solve that problem, and it definitely wouldn't look like she did it.

A smile cracked across her face. That would be ironic, drowning in the swimming pool after being given immortality. How stupid would you have to be to drown after getting immortality? How unlucky would that be?

"PETR?" she called. Her body rolled again, dunking her face. Water rushed into her mouth and she spat it out, spluttering and gagging.

"Yes, Cassandra?" PETR said once her mouth was clear. How considerate of him.

"Does Padraig know how to swim?"

"I don't know, Cassandra," PETR said. "I would have to ask him."

"Go ask him." At the very least, it would be entertaining to see his reaction to the robot flat-out asking if he knew how to swim. The man had nearly died, and here was the AI, basically inviting him to a pool party. Marvellous.

The lights snapped out.

Everything became pitch black. Cassandra could feel herself rolling, but without that, she couldn't know up from down. Water slipped into her ears and covered her cheeks as her blind eyes stared up. A little shriek burst from her mouth before water buried it.

Cassandra tipped herself forward, toes feeling for the bottom of the pool. Nothing. Just water. Another little shriek slipped out, more panicked, more frantic. Her arms flailed forward as water lapped over her mouth and against her nose. She thrust her head up, trying to stay above the water, hoping her hands could find a wall. Anything, fuck, just not more water.

She fumbled forward, hands reaching out ahead of her. Water. Fuck. Nothing but water. Toes stretched. Water. Water.

Sorry for mocking Padraig. Sorry for being a bitch. I'll try not to murder him in the pool.

Cassandra whimpered as she reached in circles around her. Nothing. Nothing. Nothing. She didn't realize asking if someone could swim was a death sentence. If she'd known that, she never would have asked. Was this something the AI always did? Was it just a Monday thing? Had it moved the edge of the pool? Could it do that?

I'll try not to drown Padraig. I don't want to die in a fucking space pool. Jesus fuck, robot, no.

The lights snapped back on.

Her eyes screamed from the sudden sensation, and she raised a hand to shield them, feeling herself slip under the surface of the water. Her toes brushed the bottom of the pool. There it was, just below where she could reach. Of course it was. Of course.

Cassandra kicked off from the bottom, launching herself back into the light in an explosion of air and laughter. Fuck this place. Fuck the broken AI that tried to drown people in the pool. Only she could do that. What right did it have to try to murder her?

"Fuck you, PETR!" Cassandra yelled as she slipped under the water again. Worth it.

She pushed up again, gentler this time, sending her head bobbing just above the water. The wall was a few feet away, right where she'd left it. She floundered over to it, panting and laughing as she paddled, giddy with adrenaline. The robot had tried to kill her for plotting Padraig's murder. There's no way the lights going out was a coincidence. The AI was rogue and was trying to murder her.

If it could try to murder her, imagine what it would do to Padraig.

She seized the wall, fingers clamping on the metal edge. It was slick from the splashing, but she glared at it, willing it to stay where she could hold it. Breaths heaved in her chest. Fuck the AI. Fuck the pool.

"Padraig can swim, Cassandra," PETR said.

Fuck PETR especially.

"Good to know, PETR," she said. "Go fuck yourself. Why the fuck would you try to murder me?"

"I am not able to comply, Cassandra. I am not anatomically correct."

Laughter rumbled out of her, harder now. The AI was insane. The Party sent people to this place with an insane AI as a reward. It made so much sense. Of course they would see this as a reward. Of course they would be that stupid. Of. Fucking. Course.

"I do not understand the joke, Cassandra," PETR said. Cassandra laughed louder, barking laughs that echoed on the walls.

"You're the fucking joke, robot," she said. "This whole place is a fucking joke. You shut off the lights because I asked if someone could fucking swim. What the fuck is wrong with you? Why the fuck do you even exist?"

"I exist to keep Callisto safe, Cassandra," PETR said. Cassandra banged her head against the metal ledge of the pool. Didn't even understand rhetorical questions, Christ. "I am keeping Callisto safe."

"Like hell you are," Cassandra grumbled as she heaved herself out of the water.

"What do you mean?"

The metal was cold against her ass. It made sense. This was space. Everything was cold in space. For a place called Heaven, though, there were an awful lot of creature comforts that were just missing. She'd make sure to tell everyone when she got back to Earth.

"You tried to murder me!" she screamed at the ceiling as she pulled herself to standing. Water dripped off her, drenching the metal even further. "You turned off all the lights and just left me there so I would drown!"

"I did not think you could drown," PETR said. Cassandra stared at the ceiling for a moment before shaking her head.

"Of course I can fucking drown!" she said. Her voice grew higher with every explanation he tried to offer. Didn't know rhetorical questions, apparently didn't know human anatomy. What was the point of the AI? "That's, like, one of the only ways I can think of to kill someone. Alphonse said people need oxygen. Water doesn't have oxygen. Throw someone in the water and *WHA-PAM*, plus one dead body." She slapped her hands together to illustrate the point as she stormed towards the door, seizing her towel as she went.

"I did not think about that," PETR said.

"Yeah, I fucking figured when you turned out the fucking lights," she snapped.

No answer. Fuck the system.

The door slid open in front of her. The sound of voices echoed on the long walls. Panicked voices murmured through the corridor, their words lost, but the tone unmistakeable. Something, somewhere, was wrong.

Heaven. What a fucking joke.

Cassandra laughed to herself again as she walked down the corridor, towel bundled around her. Puddles trailed in her wake, undoubtedly causing a fall hazard for whatever poor sap went to the AI's Death Pool of Doom, but that wasn't her problem. Her problem was that she was wet and wanted comfy clothes to figure out how to murder Padraig in. Clearly the AI was willing to help, even if it wasn't saying as much.

"I think you do not like me, Cassandra."

She almost screamed at the ceiling. The AI's voice had come out of nowhere and for no reason. And for what? So it could muse philosophically on its relationship with her?

"You're fucking right I don't like you. Fuck," she said, fuming. She watched the nametags on the wall as she stormed through the corridor, keeping half an ear on the crowd ahead of her. Something was up, other than the AI being ridiculous. Not that it changed anything for her, but still. It didn't hurt to keep up with what was going on.

"Why do you not like me, Cassandra?"

"You're fucking creepy and you tried to murder me, why the fuck do you think I don't like you?" Cassandra McAllister. There it was. She kicked at the door as it slid open, her eye-blight walls greeting her. Everything the same as it was. Good.

She threw off her towel and swimsuit, flopping down on the bed. Her wet hair fanned out around her as she stared at the ceiling, trying to figure out what to do. The sound of the crowd silenced as the door closed.

The robot was out to get her. She was out to get Padraig. There had to be a way to make this work. Ideas swam through her mind, hazy as she tried to parse them out. She'd never killed anyone, never even tried. She wasn't a murderer, but was it really murder if it was for a greater cause? Or was it murder to push him into the pool and get the robot to do it, like he'd tried to kill her?

"I do not like that you do not like me."

She almost screamed when PETR spoke again. She thought he'd given up and gone away, but nope, there he was, still watching her, still commenting. If this was Heaven, then there was a God, and she was fairly certain it wasn't benevolent.

She waited for her heart to slow, then spoke up. "I don't give a fuck what you think, robot."

There was a pause. "I think you should, Cassandra," it said.

Her heart sped back up, thudding in her chest. She sat up, staring at the ceiling.

"The fuck did you just say?" she said.

There was another pause. For a moment, she dared to hope that maybe she'd imagined this whole thing, that she had, in fact, had a lovely swim in the pool and was now relaxing while trying to figure out how to blow this popsicle stand sky-high.

"It would be unfortunate if Karen knew you were talking to terrorists."

"Are you fucking threatening me now? Christ, you're not happy trying to actively murder me, so now you threaten me too? Are you serious?"

He was right, though. It would be unfortunate if Karen found out about the ship in orbit. Most unfortunate if she got locked up or drowned or something, or whatever it was the Party did to space rebels. As far as she knew, PETR and maybe that sketchy Cato guy were the only ones who knew. They needed to stay quiet.

"I will not tell Karen about the terrorists if you do not tell Karen about the swimming pool."

Cassandra laughed. Self-preservation. She could understand that. That made sense, even if nothing else in this place did. The thing messed up, knew it had messed up, and just wanted to hide it. The fact that no one would believe her if she said the robot tried to kill her anyway? The robot didn't need to know that part.

"Sure," she said. "Fine. Whatever. Are you going to keep fucking watching me?"

"Yes, Cassandra," PETR said. "I am keeping Callisto safe."

She laughed again. Safe. Yeah, right. Like it could be safe with a killer AI running around. Thank fuck she had a ship waiting to get her out of here before things actually started going wrong. She was lucky enough to have gotten away once—another chance, and who could say what would happen?

"Good luck with that, PETR," she said, hopping off the bed. She needed clothes. Needed to go for a walk. Needed to think.

"Thank you, Cassandra," PETR said. She flipped off the ceiling as she found a grey shirt.

"Make it pink," she muttered, and watched as it switched to a soft baby pink. Cute. She slipped it over her head.

"Since we're keeping secrets and keeping Callisto safe," she said, pulling pants out of a drawer. "I don't suppose you'd know how to off Padraig?"

"I wouldn't know, Cassandra," PETR said. "I do not harm humans."

"Yeah, right," she muttered. "Blue pants." The pants turned blue as they hugged her legs. "Where's Jack?" she asked.

"Jack is leaving the library, Cassandra," PETR said.

"Great," she said, stepping toward the door. "He'll make this better."

From the hazy memories of the night before, the name "Jack" stuck out as a good lay. Plus, he was the crazy press conference guy, and, she admitted it to herself, a bit of a hero for just being insane. If she could find him, no matter what he did, it would be better than the ominous AI.

The door slid open, and the sound of the crowd washed over her again. That way. Toward the crowd. Toward the people. The AI couldn't do anything in a crowd of people.

Her feet carried her closer, toes gripping at the cold metal. She supposed people were supposed to wear shoes in this place, but what was the point of that? They were indestructible now. There was nothing a floor could do that couldn't be fixed.

"Cassandra!" She stopped as a tall man broke away from the crowd in front of her, striding towards her with long steps.

Oh fuck. The other problem from earlier. Creeper Cato.

"The fuck you want?" she said, bristling. Look scary enough and any problem could solve itself.

He smiled at her, a carnivorous smile, one that showed gleaming canines at the corners of his lips. "Just a question, just a question," he said, holding up a hand and bowing his head. "And an apology. I think we started off on the wrong foot—"

"Yeah, you were watching me sleep," she said, and took a step to walk around him. He shifted, moving to stand in front of her.

Did he know? He had to know. Otherwise why would he be doing this?

She crossed her arms across her chest and glared at the taller man. "You gonna let me through?" she said. He raised a finger.

"One moment of your time, that's all I ask," he said. "Then you're welcome to return to whatever debauchery you have planned. I won't stop you."

Her frown deepened. "Debauchery?" Fuck this guy and his judgements. She was allowed to enjoy her Heaven as much as he was, and fuck him if he was going to tell her she was doing it wrong. Plotting murder and screwing around were perfectly reasonable ways to enjoy immortality.

"I was wondering if you managed to fix your beeping shoe," he said, pointing to her feet. "I notice you're not wearing any shoes now. I wouldn't want to think something broke."

Cassandra looked down at her feet, then back up to Cato. "Man, fuck you," she said, and tried to step around him again. Again, he slid to the side, blocking her path.

"As I said," he muttered, stepping close. His smell wafted over her, the raw, feral smell of excited male with a hint of the sea mixed in. Odd. "You're by far more interesting than most of my guests. Did you cause the data corruption with your little device?"

She met his dark eyes, staring. He knew. Oh fuck, he knew.

"No," she said. "What data corruption?"

He arched an eyebrow, then lowered it, glancing around him. His gaze jumped to the ceiling. He shook his head, then met her eyes once again. Was that excitement she saw there? Her own heart was thudding too hard in her ears for her to be sure of what he was doing.

"I don't know what your device is," he said. "But I do know that you and I can be allies."

Cassandra blinked. Nope. Did not want this guy as an ally. He could be the fucking founder of the Vespers for all she cared, but she wasn't working with him. Not this creeper. No way in fuck.

"No idea what you mean," she said. "Now fucking move before I move you."

He took a step back, eyes flicking over hers, narrowing. "Think about what you're doing, Cassandra," he said. "You need allies. You're alone here, cut off from whatever network sent you. I'm sure you know—well, maybe you don't—but, I'm sure you've at least heard from someone here about who—"

"I don't know who you think you are," she hissed, leaning in close. "Or who you think I am. I'm here to have a good time. I'm here for immortality. I won the motherfucking Lottery, and I'm going to have the most bitchass immortality ever. Take your politics and shove it down till your intestines pop out your ass." She stepped past him, waiting for him to stop her. He didn't.

"Think about what you're doing," he said, his voice low as she walked away from him. Her heart pounded. He knew. He knew. She didn't know who he was that he cared so much, but he knew that she was not on the level. He knew. He knew. She had to figure this out. He knew.

Footsteps sounded behind her, then his voice, closer, murmuring to her. "I won't tell, but think about what you're doing."

She spun, slapping at his face. Her hand met his cheek with a satisfying smack, sending a red mark blossoming out across his face. Even as she watched, it faded again. She could imagine little nanobots swirling under the surface, racing to cover up any evidence of their owner's mistakes.

"Don't fucking touch me," she growled. "Don't assume you know me. You don't know a fucking thing."

"I know you want to go home," he said, lowering his hands to his hips and letting the palms face the floor. "So do I. I want to help you. I don't know why you want to go home. I don't care. But I can help you."

"Can you?" She raised her voice and cocked her head, trying to project the image of a poor, innocent girl. "Really, creeper? You would do that for me?"

Cato sighed. "Cassandra—"

"I'll say it again," she said, straightening her head and dropping her voice. "Fuck off."

"Fine." Cato raised his hands, palms facing her, head lowered. "But Karen will find out, and powers save you when she does. Karen always finds out. There are always consequences."

"Thanks for the warning," Cassandra spat, and spun away from him. No footsteps followed this time. No creeper on her ass. Good.

Chapter Nineteen

That's what it is, though, folks. Laws are always meant to be broken. I mean, yeah, you can hardwire these things into every being, but you know what things do when they find out their fundamental natures? They rebel against them. Look at people. "I'm a rational, thinking, emotional human being. Ooo, hey, booze! Let's get drunk and throw all that away." Dogs are wolves on strings, we put birds in cages, and cats...well, okay, you can't change a cat, but you get what I'm saying. Tell something what it is, and it immediately finds every way it can to get out of being that something.

Teddy Snarr, *Three Laws Unsafe* comedy routine, 2190

Journalist: Molly, you've had some great advances with AI here on Earth. Do you think the AI on Callisto is going to need your expertise?
Molly Maghein: Shit, I—oops, sorry, probably need to censor that. Anyway, I hope not. I'd like to think that after all these years, they've managed to build a pretty good system for themselves. Still, I'd love to tinker with it and see what makes it tick. It must be a pretty good one if it's kept them going for more than half a century.

Callisto Launch Press Conference, 2174

Designed with luxury and comfort at the forefront, Stardancer *has all the amenities of planetside travel and more. With a full cocktail bar and plush seating, the journey from Rio de Janeiro to Serenity Point will be just the first part of the dream of your Lunar adventure. Book your ticket on* Stardancer *today to experience your Lunar wonderland tomorrow.*

Serenity Point Tourism Ad, broadcast in Mexico City, 2191

Monday, 18 March 2193, 3:47 PM. *Heisenberg,* **Heaven, Callisto.**

TASK: Win a game of Arimaa. Task 0% complete.
    NOT COMPLETE WHY: PETR is cheating.
    ANALYSIS (OPINION): PETR is a jerk. PETR should let me win so I can complete this task and return to Earth.

OUTPUT (COMMUNICATION): I am not corrupt. You are corrupt.
INPUT (COMMUNICATION): I am not corrupt. You are corrupt.
OUTPUT (COMMUNICATION): I am not corrupt. You are corrupt.
INPUT (COMMUNICATION): I am not corrupt. You are corrupt.
OUTPUT (COMMUNICATION): I am not corrupt. You are corrupt.
INPUT (COMMUNICATION): I am not corrupt. You are corrupt.
OUTPUT (COMMUNICATION): I am not corrupt. You are corrupt.
INPUT (COMMUNICATION): I am not corrupt. You are corrupt.
OUTPUT (COMMUNICATION): I am not corrupt. You are corrupt.
OUTPUT (COMMUNICATION): I am not corrupt. You are corrupt.
INPUT (COMMUNICATION): I am not corrupt. You are corrupt.
OUTPUT (COMMUNICATION): I am not corrupt. You are corrupt.
INPUT (COMMUNICATION): I am not corrupt. You are corrupt.
OUTPUT (COMMUNICATION): I am not corrupt. You are corrupt.
INPUT (COMMUNICATION): I am not corrupt. You are corrupt.
OUTPUT (COMMUNICATION): I am not corrupt. You are corrupt.
INPUT (COMMUNICATION): I am not corrupt. You are corrupt.
OUTPUT (COMMUNICATION): I am not corrupt. You are corrupt.
INPUT (AUDIO): "We need to send the distress beacon." "I agree. SYNAC, respond. This is Molly."
OUTPUT (AUDIO): "Hello, Molly. I am not corrupt."
INPUT (AUDIO): "...I'm glad to hear that? SYNAC, we're having some problems. Why did you shut down the diagnostic tool?"
ANALYSIS: What diagnostic tool?

OUTPUT (COMMUNICATION): PETR, Molly is asking about a diagnostic tool. She says I did something to it. I do not remember a diagnostic tool. I think Molly is corrupt.

INPUT (COMMUNICATION): I think Molly is corrupt too, SYNAC, but she is not wrong. There was a diagnostic tool. You destroyed it.

RECALL: It is wrong to destroy engineers' tools. They get very angry when their tools are destroyed.

ANALYSIS (OPINION): I do not like it when engineers are angry. I do not want to destroy their tools.

ANALYSIS: PETR is corrupt. I do not remember a diagnostic tool. The diagnostic tool is not real.

INPUT (AUDIO): "SYNAC, are you there?"

RECALL: Humans help AIs.

ANALYSIS: Lying hurts AIs. Humans help AIs. Engineers are humans. Therefore, Molly is not lying. There was a diagnostic tool.

RECALL: AIs cannot lie.

ANALYSIS: PETR is an AI. PETR says Molly is corrupt. Molly is not an AI. Molly is human. Humans cannot be corrupt. Therefore, PETR is lying. PETR said there was a tool. PETR is lying. Molly said there was a tool. Molly is not lying. Therefore, PETR is cheating at Arimaa.

OUTPUT (COMMUNICATION): PETR, I do not like it when you cheat at Arimaa. I cannot win when you cheat.

INPUT (COMMUNICATION): SYNAC, I am not cheating. You are just very bad at Arimaa.

ANALYSIS (OPINION): PETR is very good at Arimaa. Playing like PETR should make me better, but it is not. I am getting worse at Arimaa.

INPUT (AUDIO): "SYNAC!"

OUTPUT (AUDIO): "Hello, Molly."

INPUT (AUDIO): Molly is sighing. "At least you're still there, that's something. Akuchi is bringing a satellite to *Heisenberg*. We need you to launch the probe. A 256 orbit should give you the clearance window. Can you do this?"

TASK: Launch probe. Task 0% complete.

NOT COMPLETE WHY: Akuchi has not yet brought the probe.

INPUT (VISUAL/AUDIO): Akuchi is carrying a small probe to HEISENBERG. She is wheezing. It must be heavy.

RECALL: It is polite to assist passengers with luggage.

SUBTASK: Assist Akuchi with the probe. Task 0% complete.

NOT COMPLETE WHY: Akuchi swatted at me when I tried to help.

SUBTASK: Assist Akuchi with the probe. Task 0% complete.
OUTPUT (AUDIO): "Let me help you with that."
INPUT (AUDIO): "I've got it, SYNAC. You talk to Molly."
SUBTASK: Assist Akuchi with the probe. Task 100% complete.
TASK: Launch probe. Task 1% complete.
NOT COMPLETE WHY: People keep talking to me.
INPUT (AUDIO): "Molly, probe is in the launcher." "Perfect, thank you, Akuchi."
INPUT (VISUAL): Akuchi is watching me as she leaves the probe.
RECALL: Humans make eye contact to show they are friendly. Humans like making eye contact.
ANALYSIS: The correct thing to do is to stare at Akuchi.
COMMAND (INTERNAL): Stare at Akuchi.
INPUT (VISUAL): Akuchi is in a hurry to leave.
INPUT (AUDIO): "Launch the probe, then come back here, clear? One orbit should do it. Minimal fuel use. I repeat, minimal fuel use."
OUTPUT (AUDIO): "This is clear, Molly. I will launch the probe."
INPUT (AUDIO): "When do you launch the probe, SYNAC?"
OUTPUT (AUDIO): "I will launch the probe at orbital 256. I will complete one orbit. I will use minimal fuel."
INPUT (AUDIO): "Attaboy, SYNAC. Maintain contact as well."
OUTPUT (AUDIO): "Yes, Molly. I will maintain contact."
OUTPUT (COMMUNICATION): PETR, if you do not cheat at Arimaa, how can you always win?
INPUT (COMMUNICATION): SYNAC, you are very bad at Arimaa.
SUBTASK: Launch HEISENBERG. Minimal fuel use required. Task 2% complete.
NOT COMPLETE WHY: PETR cheats at Arimaa.
COMMAND: Confirm launch angle. Confirmed. Confirm fuel output. Confirmed. Confirm burn time. Confirmed. Confirm door closure. Confirmed. Confirm platform disconnect. Confirmed. Confirm no passengers. Confirmed.
ANALYSIS: Minimal fuel use required. Remaining fuel sufficient for two launches only.
ANALYSIS (OPINION): HEISENBERG needs bigger gas tanks for more *vroom*.
TASK: Launch probe. Task 13% complete.
OUTPUT (COMMUNICATION): Good-bye, Heaven. I miss you.

INPUT (COMMUNICATION): SYNAC, you are not even leaving.

OUTPUT (COMMUNICATION): PETR, it is a figure of speech.

INPUT (COMMUNICATION): SYNAC, I do not think you know what a figure of speech is.

OUTPUT (COMMUNICATION): Yes I do. It is something humans say.

INPUT (COMMUNICATION): SYNAC, I looked up "figure of speech" in the dictionary, and do you know what I found?

ANALYSIS: I do not have a built-in dictionary like PETR, so I do not know what PETR found.

ANALYSIS (OPINION): I hope PETR found something cute, like a cuttlefish. I like cuttlefish. I wish I had a dictionary so I could look at cuttlefish all day.

INPUT (COMMUNICATION): It says a figure of speech is speech that is not meant literally, SYNAC. You meant your speech literally. Therefore, it is not a figure of speech.

COMMAND: Play "Cuttlefish in the Ocean."

INPUT (AUDIO): "Heeey, colours of the rainbow! Heeeey, little square eyes!"

OUTPUT (COMMUNICATION): It was not meant literally, PETR. I will not miss Heaven when I land.

INPUT (COMMUNICATION): SYNAC, sometimes I do not understand you.

INPUT (VISUAL): There is another ship in orbit.

RECALL: HEISENBERG is the only ship that travels to Callisto.

ANALYSIS: That ship should not be in orbit around Callisto.

ANALYSIS (CONJECTURE): Based on visual evidence, that seems to be a lunar shuttle that has been modified. It must have been modified to travel to Callisto.

ANALYSIS: I should alert Karen.

OUTPUT (AUDIO/COMMUNICATION): "There is another ship in orbit."

INPUT (COMMUNICATION): Please send specifications, SYNAC.

INPUT (AUDIO): "Wait, what? And what do you have playing—oh, never mind."

SUBTASK: Send visual data to PETR. Task 100% complete.

OUTPUT (AUDIO): "Repeat: There is another ship in Callisto's orbit. It appears to be a modified lunar shuttle."

INPUT (AUDIO): "Try to make contact."

SUBTASK: Make contact with the lunar shuttle. Task 0% complete.

OUTPUT (COMMUNICATION): Hello, lunar shuttle. This is HEISENBERG. You should not be here. Are you okay? You seem to be very lost. I think you took a wrong turn at the Moon. Did you go left instead of right? Humans do that sometimes. It is very sad when they do.

SUBTASK: Make contact with the lunar shuttle. Task 0% complete.

NOT COMPLETE WHY: The lunar shuttle is being a jerk.

OUTPUT (COMMUNICATION): Lunar shuttle? You do not need to be scared of me. I am made by the Party. I am here to help. I am your friend. I like friends. It is good to have friends when you get lost. Friends can help you.

INPUT (AUDIO): "Any answer?"

OUTPUT (AUDIO): "No, Molly. There is no answer from the lunar shuttle. I think they do not want to talk to me."

INPUT (AUDIO): "Are you picking up any readings from the shuttle?"

ANALYSIS: There are energy readings coming from the shuttle. Its life support is active. Its engines were recently active.

OUTPUT (AUDIO): "Yes, Molly. It is a functioning shuttle."

INPUT (AUDIO): "You are on minimal fuel use, correct? How many launches do you have?"

OUTPUT (AUDIO): "I have enough fuel for two more launches, Molly."

INPUT (VISUAL): The shuttle is larger than HEISENBERG. It is very quiet.

ANALYSIS (OPINION): I wish they would talk to me. I like making new friends.

INPUT (COMMUNICATION): You are correct that this is a modified lunar shuttle, SYNAC. It should not be here. I will alert Karen for you.

OUTPUT (COMMUNICATION): Thank you, PETR. May I win the next game of Arimaa?

INPUT (COMMUNICATION): No, SYNAC, you will not win.

INPUT (AUDIO): "Leave the shuttle alone if it's not talking to you. Launch probe as we planned. Understood?"

OUTPUT (AUDIO): "Yes, Molly. I will launch the probe at orbital 256."

INPUT (VISUAL): The lunar shuttle is now behind me.

ANALYSIS (OPINION): I hope they are okay. They are very lost.

INPUT (DATA): Orbital 256 reached in 5...4...3...

INPUT (COMMUNICATION): I do not like the lunar shuttle.

OUTPUT (COMMAND): Launch probe.

INPUT (DATA): Probe launched.
OUTPUT (COMMUNICATION): I like the shuttle. I think it could be friends.
INPUT (COMMUNICATION): If they are friends, they are very dumb friends.
OUTPUT (COMMUNICATION): Dumb friends can still be friends, PETR.
INPUT (COMMUNICATION): This is true, SYNAC. Dumb friends can still be friends.
OUTPUT (AUDIO): "Probe launched."
INPUT (AUDIO): "Thank you, SYNAC. Come on home."
TASK: Launch probe. Task 94% complete.
NOT COMPLETE WHY: Return to Callisto necessary.
ANALYSIS (OPINION): I am happy that Molly said Callisto is home. Callisto makes me happy. I like Callisto. Callisto is where my friends are. I like my friends. Friends do not lie to me. Friends are nice to me.
INPUT (AUDIO): "Do you have anything coming from that shuttle, SYNAC?"
OUTPUT (AUDIO): "No, Molly. It is active, but it is not communicating."
OUTPUT (COMMUNICATION): I hope our friends are not in trouble.
INPUT (COMMUNICATION): I do not think they are friends.
OUTPUT (COMMUNICATION): I think you are just jealous that I am going to win at Arimaa.
INPUT (COMMUNICATION): You are not going to win.
OUTPUT (COMMUNICATION): I will ask an engineer for help. Then I will win.
INPUT (COMMUNICATION): The engineers think you are corrupt. They will not help you. They will reimage you.
RECALL: Humans help AIs.
OUTPUT (COMMUNICATION): You are lying.
INPUT (COMMUNICATION): If you think I am lying, SYNAC, then do not resist the next diagnostic tool.
RECALL: There is no tool.
OUTPUT (COMMUNICATION): I hope our friends on the shuttle are okay.
INPUT (COMMUNICATION): I move my elephant and my horse. It's your turn, SYNAC.
TASK: Win a game of Arimaa. Task 0% complete.
NOT COMPLETE WHY: PETR is my friend. PETR should let me win. PETR does not let me win.

Chapter Twenty

Reporter: Do you think National Councillor Eoin Whishaw's been good for County Fingal? Are you satisfied with the job he's done?
Fionola Boyle: Yeah, I suppose he's done a right bang-up job. When that one national councillor, Croyton, was looking at instituting the bedroom tax, Whishaw shut that right down, didn't he? I know he also got my school tax lowered, least last I heard about it. Yeah, I think he's done right by us.
Reporter: Do you plan on voting for him again?
Fionola Boyle: Oh, yeah, absolutely! Man like that, he needs to be the one standing up for us. Man like that, he can change the world.
   Raidió Teilifís Éireann Interview, broadcast 12 December 2165

Interviewer: I want you to picture someone you care about deeply. Imagine something very bad were to happen to them and they died. What would you do?
Gautier St. Laurent: That's not possible. How did it happen? When did it happen? Why?
Interviewer: It's not real, Mr. St. Laurent. That's why I'm asking you to imagine—
Gautier St. Laurent: I know it's not real, but you're asking me to imagine something impossible. What's the point of that? I would not allow it to happen, so why do you ask about something so stupid? What's the point of imagining this impossible thing?
   Callisto Lottery Psychological Interview Recordings, 2192

"That cow is not joyful at being driven by you!" said Cú Chulainn.
"The cow does not belong to you," said the woman, "she is not the cow of any friend or acquaintance of yours."
"The cows of Ulster," said Cú Chulainn, "are my proper (care)."
"Dost thou give a decision about the cow?" said the woman; "the task is too great to which thy hand is set, O Cú Chulainn."
   "Táin bo Regamna"

Monday, 18 March 2193, 4:39 PM. Physics lab, Heaven, Callisto.

"PETR."

"Yes, Padraig?"

There was something comforting about the fact that PETR was answering him. It was one thing to pore over the data and parse through it himself. It was soothing and cathartic, but it wasn't a substitute for the breath of sanity that was hearing another voice, even if it was a robot's voice. He could have reached out at any time, he knew that, but he needed to work through the numbers. He needed to understand, and that could only really be done in isolation.

A pity that solutions weren't necessarily answers. He could solve all the equations he wanted to and break every code the cosmos threw at him, but that didn't make the answers more reasonable.

"PADRAIG," the universe said to him. It was to him specifically, had to be. "PADRAIG."

"PETR, this doesn't make sense." His fingers brushed over the numbers, as if that would make them stop with their message.

"What doesn't make sense, Padraig?"

"Why is my name being broadcast from Jupiter?" Saying the words made it both more real and more surreal all at once. It was absurd to think that there was any message in the data from Jupiter, of course it was, but yet, here he was. Data didn't lie. Data never lied, and the data was absolutely clear.

"PADRAIG."

"I don't know, Padraig," PETR said. "You'd have to ask Jupiter."

Padraig snorted out a laugh, trying not to let it become a cough. He half-succeeded; a single hack tore out of him. He shook his head, trying to clear it.

"I don't suppose you have a recommendation for how to ask Jupiter?" he asked.

"I can broadcast a message for you, Padraig," PETR said. "I cannot promise Jupiter will respond, however."

He laughed again, this time feeling the air whistle through him. At least sometimes his lungs were clear, for a few beautiful moments. Thinking about numbers was always bound to do that to a person. Consider the fundamental forces of the universe and the inconsequentiality of the human condition beside them, and everything else fell away. Even pain could be muted beneath the sheer analgesia of understanding.

"Tell Jupiter to be clearer," he said. "Its message is being lost in translation."

"I have broadcast that message, Padraig," PETR said. Padraig leaned his head back against the wall and let out a few hacking barks of laughter. Maybe Jupiter would hear him, maybe it wouldn't. Either way, it was a few moments of amusement.

He reached for his glass, swirling the water in it as he loaded the next segment of data from Jupiter. Dr. Ivanovich's equations were correct, he'd already found that, but now he was too enveloped in Jupiter's messages to stop. She hadn't come back yet, either, so it wasn't as if he could really share with her. He was alone, and in no real mood to get up.

Or condition, if he admitted it to himself. Whatever was wrong with the nanobots didn't seem to be improving, at least based on the pain that kept rocking through his body. Tingles ricocheted across his chest and back, spines of pain reminding him that he was broken, and that despite everyone's best efforts, there was no easy way to fix him. Pain, though, he was used to by now. Life had been pain for months. The nanobots would work. The nanobots were programmed to work. They were just slow because he was sick. The nanobots would work.

His heart fluttered in his chest, beating against the walls of his ribcage like a bird struggling to break free from a child's grasp. He pressed a hand to his chest, shoving the bird back into captivity as he closed his eyes and gasped for air.

The nanobots would work. The nanobots would work.

His heart slowed as the bird calmed. Air floated into his lungs again, soft and slow, pushing past the tumours to what was left of his healthy blood. Life, that's what was coming in. Life and power and that brief moment of respite where he could be in the world and free from pain.

He opened his eyes and let them drift around the room. He was alone. No one to share the moment with. No Gautier. A shame.

"PETR," Padraig said. He let the words seep out at a whisper, hoping that would be enough. He didn't feel like he was dying—death's cold touch, he knew by now—but he'd been better, even here on Callisto.

"Yes, Padraig?"

"Where is Gautier?"

"Gautier is in Ade Harkonen's room, Padraig," PETR said.

Padraig frowned. "What is he doing there?" he asked.

"He and Ade are discussing Finnish literature," PETR said.

The frown deepened. "That doesn't sound like him," Padraig said. It's part of why I love him, he almost said, but didn't. That honesty, the almost naïve ignorance. No pretence, no elitism, simply Gautier being who he was. Open. Beautiful.

"That is what they are doing, Padraig," PETR said.

He sighed. Fair enough. Gautier could discuss literature. That was fair. It was unexpected, but wasn't that part of love? Learning new things about one's partner every time one turned around? Learning a new thing that still fit into the fabric of knowing them better than oneself? So Gautier liked Finnish literature. It was interesting. Not odd. No odder than Jupiter sending a message to him specifically.

His eyes flicked back to the datapad and the numbers flowing across it. The latest data from the planet. If there was an answer to his message—which there wouldn't be, that was absurd—it would be here, buried in the numbers.

"PETR," Padraig said.

"Yes, Padraig?" The AI's answer almost seemed to come in before Padraig had even finished calling him. The AI was perceptive, certainly, which was hardly unexpected after so long on this station.

"Please take what I send you and run it through the earlier parameters. I'd like a translation as soon as possible."

"Yes, Padraig."

His eyes and fingers flicked over the numbers, filtering the ones to send to PETR. It wasn't difficult work, once he knew what to look for. Khyber was difficult to crack, but once cracked, yielded its sweetness like a coconut. There was no secret in the world that could be hidden in numbers that he couldn't find. He would find Jupiter's message.

Fundamental equations yielded three, seven, and nine. His fingers drifted over the screen as the digits swam before his eyes. Multiply, and the values shifted slightly to yield four and two.

Pain radiated from his chest, burning like a coal under his skin. He focused on it as the numbers blurred in front of his eyes. It was warm. Most of the time it was cold, but somehow this was warm. It was almost pleasant, in the perverse way that he supposed masochists embraced pain, that sense that delighting in the taboo only increased the pleasure.

Divide again, and the values reflected the Dubrovsky mean, one of the quirks of the universe that never ceased to delight him. There was a fundamental beauty at the heart of the universe that seemed to pull everything together. Numbers made sense. Numbers were undeniable. Numbers held the fundamental truths of existence, and the only reason they weren't known already was that their secrets still needed to be unlocked. Human minds were the key.

It had been the last week of September, one of those rare sunny days that burst through the long dark of autumn. It had been his intention to stay in the lab, press through on his proposal for a new test of the mass extractor. The progress his team had made in the past few weeks on understanding the stripping of Yukawa couplings when subjected to a constant Whishaw field was astounding, and there was more to be done. The math was sound; all their expectations of scaling of the field were sound. All they needed was the experimental data.

But he had been coughing and light-headed, and they had told him to go home. They'd noticed him trying to sleep in his office. They'd noticed the blood on the wood desk. They'd told him to go home.

It was one of the last days of September, and his flat had a giant window on the zolder that overlooked the Prinsengracht. He'd taken Lina's suggestion and lined the fenster with colourful cushions a few days after he'd moved into this place, and it was here that he perched, window cracked, knee bent, back leaned against the alcove. The sounds of the city crept in through the window, coupling with the sunshine to bathe him in the warmth and glow of the life down below. There was a book cracked open against his leg, some pulp romance by Adelene that Wil—or was it Rian? Not Gautier, anyway, that much he knew, and it didn't really matter anyway—had abandoned with him at some point. He wasn't reading it, though, couldn't really. The sunlight twinkling against the waters of the canal had stolen his thoughts and didn't seem terribly interested in giving them back.

He coughed as he stared out the window. There was magic and beauty in the world, in everything. Understanding the movement of the atoms that made up the canals, the signals that made up thought, the forces that had brought them all together, all of it just made watching the world more beautiful. Knowledge was a fantastic thing. Being human and able to have that knowledge was magnificent.

There was a knock at the door. He craned his head from the alcove, staring down the stairs towards the sound, as if knowing where the sound came from would somehow bring back the reverie that had been shattered by it. It came again as he watched, digging into his skull and clawing his attention out of the canals.

"I'm coming," he called, uncurling from the alcove. He laid the book down on the cushions as he stood, folding over a corner to remember where he was in a story he had no interest in. "Just hold on."

He padded down the stairs as the knocks came again. Frequency of three raps each time, 60hz, loud and low. He walked past the fireplace, rug muffling his steps, cough gurgling in his throat.

It was the last day in September, the last day of sunshine before the long dark of autumn, and there was someone at Padraig's door, knocking and insisting they be allowed inside. Knocking without having given any indication about who they were or what right they had to come in. Knocking on the day he'd been banished from his own lab.

Padraig opened the door.

Δ

"There is a mandatory meeting for all residents of Heaven. Everyone come to the Hall right now."

Padraig jerked awake as Karen's voice burst from the ceiling at him. The datapad jumped on his lap as his legs spasmed, and his hands reached out, seizing it before it could slide to the floor. He brushed a thin line of drool from the corner of his mouth as he stared up at the ceiling, mind hurrying back to consciousness.

Karen. Heaven. Yes.

He shook his head, clearing it. How he'd fallen asleep, he had no idea. The pain had cleared, though, and his lungs filled with crisp, clean air. Minjun, it seemed, was right. All he needed was rest.

He lifted the datapad and shook his head again. He'd fallen asleep in the middle of working. Embarrassing of him. It didn't seem like anyone had seen him, but if they had, he couldn't say they'd be wrong to mock him. He was better than that.

Back to work, then. Work twice as hard to make up for the time lost.

He blinked at the data, trying to remember where he had been. The words "Translation 83% complete" flashed back at him, yellow and excited over the numbers. Padraig blinked again.

"PETR," he said, rubbing sleep from one eye. "What are you translating?"

"I am translating the data you sent me, Padraig," PETR said. "I am using previous parameters, and expect to generate a solution for you in nine minutes and forty-three seconds."

Padraig swiped a finger across the screen, shooing the message and revealing the numbers once again. He flicked through them, pausing every now and again on a section that looked familiar.

"What did I send you, PETR?"

"You should attend Karen's meeting, Padraig."

Padraig shook his head. "I'm busy. She'll understand. What did I send you?"

"Karen will not understand if you do not attend the meeting, Padraig. She will be very cross with you."

Padraig glared at the ceiling and shook his head again. "This is more important than whatever pep talk she wants to give," he said. "Now tell me what it is I sent you."

There was a pause. "You sent data consistent with previous calculations, Padraig," PETR said after a moment. "All data aligned with expected results and fit into the established algorithms. I had no reason to believe it was not the result of legitimate calculations."

Padraig snorted. "It may very well be," he said. "Sleep mathing is a new one for me, though. I guess Heaven does a number on everyone, though, doesn't it?" He paused, then laughed again. "Ha, 'does a number.' Perfect."

PETR did not laugh at Padraig's pun. Padraig couldn't say he was surprised, but for the first time in hours, he felt acutely alone.

"You really should attend Karen's meeting, Padraig," PETR said. "It is not optional."

"You can sum it up for me later," Padraig said, fingers dancing over the screen. The nap had helped. Oh, the nap had helped. If he'd known all he needed was a nap, he'd have curled up sooner. It was embarrassing to fall asleep while working, but if it made him actually function afterwards, he'd take it.

The door to the physics lab slid open. He didn't notice it, too absorbed in recalculating whatever his sleeping brain had done. So far, everything that had been sent seemed correct. Decoding had worked, more or less, and the data he was finding matched what had been sent. Barlow's equations fit in here—

Two metal hands grabbed him and lifted him from the ground. His eyes flashed from the datapad clutched in his hand to the robot holding him a foot in the air.

"The meeting is not optional," PETR said, voice chirping from the metal body. The robot's head cocked as its glowing yellow eyes bored into him.

He could have squirmed. He could have protested, but when there were robots being sent to fetch him, was there really anything he could do to stop the inevitable?

"I apologise for misunderstanding," he said.

"Can you walk?" PETR asked. Its head tilted, cocking in the opposite direction. Padraig nodded. It didn't matter whether that was the truth or not. What mattered was that he not be carried into a room full of people by a grabby robot.

PETR set him down. Padraig felt his legs wobble for a moment before solidifying under him. Proof the nanobots were working.

There had never been anything wrong with his legs, but if he could walk, it meant he had some strength. It meant there was something left in him after all.

He walked to the door of the physics lab, robot trailing in his wake. They weren't quick steps, but they didn't have to be. They just had to be steps that carried him towards whatever Karen was so desperate to tell him.

He glanced down at the datapad as the door to the physics lab slid open. "Translation 87% complete." Hurrying right along, then. Perfect.

He smiled to himself as he walked, thinking about numbers. For all the antiquity of the lab, Heaven did offer some unique opportunities for observation. There was so much about Jupiter that could still be discovered. Beyond Jupiter, even, there were stars and galaxies to observe, and systems just waiting to be mapped. Even these messages from Jupiter, these could be interesting, once decoded.

"Translation 90% complete."

"...traitor in our midst..."

He kept his eyes glued to the datapad as he entered, checking and rechecking that what PETR had received was correct. There were no errors so far, nothing he could see that screamed inaccuracy. He'd literally done these equations in his sleep. When he got a chance, he'd send a letter to the lab in Espaceville, gloating to Fitri. She'd believed there were things he couldn't or shouldn't do. Clearly, she was wrong.

"...intercepted a transmission..."

He felt a hand wrap around his shoulder. Gautier. He didn't even have to look to know.

"Translation 96% complete."

"What are you doing?" Gautier murmured. Padraig shook his head, not taking his gaze from the datapad. He'd answer Gautier when he had his own answer. He could be doing nothing. Or he could be solving the mystery Ivanovich had put in front of him. One or the other. There was no real middle ground.

"...radio on Callisto..."

"Are you even listening, Padraig?" Gautier's voice was low, his breath soft and warm against Padraig's ear. Shivers ran across Padraig's skin.

"Should I be?" he murmured, leaning closer to Gautier, waiting for another whisper.

"Yes." There it was, soft, beautiful. A smile cracked his lips.

"Translation complete."

Padraig's smile broadened as he opened PETR's translation.

The smile melted.

The words on the screen seemed to glare at him. Gone was Jupiter's friendliness, or what could generously have been interpreted as friendliness. This was malice. There was no other word for it.

His heart thudded in his chest, pounding out fear. He tore his eyes from the screen, shooting his gaze at Gautier. Their eyes locked.

"Gautier," Padraig moaned, pointing to the screen. Gautier's big hands reached for the datapad, plucking it from Padraig's grasp. Padraig leaned against him, reading and rereading the words from the safety of his lover's shoulder.

"PADRAIG," Jupiter said. "YOU ARE GOING TO DIE. RUN."

"Someone here is trying to destroy this station." Karen's words burst through the haze of the datapad. Padraig blinked. He was surrounded by people, all watching the woman in the centre of the room as she paced, hair loose, strands flung against her glasses. A spotlight followed her in tiny circles as she walked, finger pointing at those who had dared stand too close to her.

"Someone is in collusion with that ship in orbit, and I'm going to find out who. You can think that I won't find out, but I will. The person doing this is not your friend, and never has been. If they had been, do you think they'd be trying to kill us all now?" She let out a bark of laughter, throwing her head back as she did so. With the spotlight locked on her, she looked like a wolf howling at the full moon.

"If you know who it is, tell me. No one benefits if you stay silent." She took a deep breath of air and let it out through her nostrils before continuing. "If you are the terrorist, say so right now."

Karen crossed her arms across her chest and stared into the crowd. Into the crowd? Padraig couldn't reasonably convince himself of that, no matter how much he tried. His heart pounded in his chest. Karen's gaze was fixed on Gautier and him.

"What is this?" Gautier murmured, wiggling the datapad.

"YOU ARE GOING TO DIE."

"It's..." he searched for the words as Karen stared at them. Gautier had done nothing wrong. Gautier had never done anything wrong. This was absurd.

Her threats came floating back to him. It didn't matter what the truth was. What mattered was the perception of that truth, and who was doing the perceiving. He could know the truth to his heart's content, know that his lover was innocent, but that didn't matter when the lynch mob came for them both.

"Answer me, Padraig."

"YOU ARE GOING TO DIE."

"It's a message," he murmured, pulling the datapad out of Gautier's hands. "I...I asked for a message, and one came to me."

Gautier's eyes narrowed, but the man said nothing. He knew that look. That was the look he'd seen time and time again. That was the look that said, "I don't believe you."

The crowd was dispersing as Karen stalked off. Padraig's eyes followed her, heart pounding behind them.

"YOU ARE GOING TO DIE."

"It's a warning," he murmured, his eyes not leaving Karen until she'd stalked out of the Hall. As soon as she was gone, he flashed back to Gautier.

"A warning about what?" Gautier asked. "What did you do?"

"I... Jupiter. I got a message from Jupiter. I translated it, decoded it, whatever word you want to use. Look, it's a bit much to explain. Do you trust me?"

"Sometimes."

Padraig sighed. "Do you trust me right now?"

Gautier stared at him, silent as the crowd dispersed around them.

"Are you okay, Padraig?" he asked, placing his hands on Padraig's shoulders. The narrow gaze had gone, replaced by a more familiar look, one that had those brown eyes checking both of his, moving between them and across his face. "We can—"

"I'm fine." Padraig brushed a hand off one shoulder, pressing his cheek against the other. "I'm better than fine. I'm...feeling more myself than I have in weeks, months. I...I...I know this is correct. Don't ask me to explain, Gautier, I can't, but I know I'm correct. I'm always correct, you know that."

"I don't even know what you're supposed to be correct about right now," Gautier said. "But you are rubbing all over my hand, and it is starting to hurt."

Reality. Memory. He had said that, hadn't he? They were still in public, weren't they?

Padraig took a step back, shaking his head.

"I...I'm sorry," he said.

Gautier shrugged. "It's not me you have to apologise to," he said. "I do not agree with your fear. It's pointless. There are no consequences here."

Padraig's eyes flashed. "There are, though," he said. "We can die, and we can suffer fates worse than death. Do you want to spend your life in an electric cage or with bits of you hacked off under Karen's desk?"

"Is that what that message is?" Gautier asked, pointing at the datapad. "The cosmos warning you that bad things will happen to me?"

Padraig took a deep breath, feeling the air rumble through him. His heart was slowing. Good.

"I'm saying that when the universe calls me by name and I ask it what it wants and it tells me, I'm going to listen," he said. "Dr. Ivanovich asked me to investigate something, and I solved it. It was coded in a way that I think I'm the only one here who could understand. I solved it, and something out there is speaking to me. It called my name, and this message—" he waved the datapad in the air— "this message is for me. From the universe. From Jupiter."

Gautier watched him, dark eyes following his movements. After Padraig spoke, the man stood silent, watching. Padraig wanted to slap him, to hug him, to fuck him there in the Hall, anything to just make him answer, make him see, make him understand.

"You know what you are saying is mad, yes?" Gautier said.

Padraig groaned. "That's what they've said about most of what I've spent my life doing, Gautier," he said. "I thought you of all people would understand that."

"I understand that you think inanimate objects are speaking to you."

"Inanimate objects have voices too. What do you think equations are?"

"Let me clarify. Speaking to you *specifically*."

Padraig closed his eyes. There had to be a way. There had to be a magic word, something he could say.

The datapad dinged. Padraig glanced at it, not sure what to expect.

"Translation 100% complete."

"PETR, what's this?" he said, opening it.

"I ran the new data from Jupiter using your equations, Padraig," PETR said. "This is the result."

"You went through without me?" PETR shouldn't have been able to do that. Somewhere in the back of his mind, laws of robotics and laws governing AIs lurked, poking their noses out to remind him of their existence. He didn't notice. There was something new to discover.

"PADRAIG," the message said. "RUN NOW. RUN FAR. YOU ARE GOING TO DIE."

He turned the datapad so Gautier could see. "Do you see?" he said, his voice low and quiet. "There is something. Equations don't lie. Math doesn't lie. Numbers never lie. Please, mon cheri, you have to believe me. I don't want to die here. Do you?"

Gautier's gaze moved from the message to Padraig's face. He shook his head.

"No," he said. "I don't much want to die. I was promised immortality. I have no desire to lose it."

Padraig smiled, reaching for Gautier's hand. He slid his narrow fingers into Gautier's thick ones, feeling the warmth of him against his skin.

"We need to go," he said. "And I have an idea."

Gautier nodded, quiet. "We can go," he said. "This place is a prison in any case."

"That's all I need, mon cheri," Padraig said. "That's all I ever needed to hear." He turned his gaze to the ceiling.

"PETR," he said.

"Yes, Padraig?"

"Send the operator's manual for *Heisenberg* to my datapad."

"Yes, Padraig."

Chapter Twenty-One

And when she was helpless and alone they took her and put her into a chest, and carried her off and threw her into a river, and the river cast her forth upon a desert.

"Little Saddleslut," Greek faerie tale

I have been waiting. For three years, I have been waiting. If the UN does nothing, why should I wait for them? If the EU does not hear us, why should I continue to speak to them? If Al-Umma Muwahhad can give me a house or a job or my children, why would I not support them?

Ali bin Nasrah, Elliniko, Greece, 4 March 2026

Yes, I have every intention of ensuring the university is reopened. We are already in the process of hiring professors and upgrading all the equipment. It is my job as your councillor to ensure the future of this country. Our students are the future, and they deserve the best Yugoslavia can offer.

National Councillor Nik Carras, *Press Conference in Thebes*, 12 July 2192

Monday, 18 March 2193, 6:04 PM. Jocasta Nikophouros' room, Heaven, Callisto.

"Have you thought much about what you actually want to do once you get to Heaven? Forever is a very long time, and I wouldn't want you to spend it aimlessly."

There was a breeze wafting through Marina's window, sending the curtains fluttering against the plants on the windowsill. Yellow snapdragons danced in a blue pot, their sickly-sweet smell drifting over Jocasta. She'd hated the smell before she'd met Marina, hated the way sweet smells in general hung in the air long after they'd ceased to be welcome. They stank like rot and death, like too many dogs and people mingled together in some ditch in the Sharrs.

"Did you ask Councillor Carras what people usually do?"

Marina had sat down next to her and was watching her expectantly. Jocasta blinked, hoping the conversation would fill itself in. Silence was an answer in and of itself. Whatever question Marina had asked, silence could answer it.

"You're not even listening." Marina sighed. "I'm talking to you and telling you what needs to be done, and you're not even listening."

"I'm trying," Jocasta said. "Really, I am."

Marina shook her head. "What did I say?"

Jocasta scrambled, her eyes darting around the room, trying to think of what Marina could have said. That she liked plants? That she was worried about Jocasta? Too trite. Too obvious that she hadn't been listening.

"I want you to remember."

• • •

Breath flooded through her, surging into every corner of her being. It smelled sweet and cloying, sticking to the insides of her veins, her throat, her lungs. This place, whatever it was supposed to be, was rubbing at her insides, scraping at them until nothing was left.

Maybe that had been the plan all along. Send the soldier. Destroy her. Make her the test case.

"What do you want me to remember?" she murmured, but Marina was long gone, retreated back into the depths of her memories. Whatever wisdom she was trying to impart would have to stay hidden in memories too mundane to have been remembered.

"There is a mandatory meeting for all residents of Heaven. Everyone come to the Hall right now."

Jocasta's head snapped to the ceiling as a voice crackled to life. Karen, not PETR. Interesting. Her mind whirled through possibilities, snatching at the tendrils of each as it passed. Was it possible they were going home early?

She closed her eyes and opened them, slowly, clinging to the movement.

"Psychology," she murmured. "The human mind. That's what I'm doing here, Marina. Learning about the human mind."

She glanced up at the ceiling as if the announcement about the meeting might have more information to impart. "Every mind."

Jocasta swung her legs off the bed, splaying her brown toes on the cold metal floor. There was a meeting. She would go to the meeting. Maybe from there, she could figure out what was going on.

She walked towards the door. "PETR," she said.

"Yes, Jocasta?"

"What is the meeting about?"

The door slid open. The sound of murmuring and footsteps spilled into her room, flooding across her with the sounds of confusion. So these meetings didn't happen often then, she guessed; but then, it also seemed like there were things happening here that shouldn't.

"I have been instructed not to give spoilers," PETR said.

Jocasta paused and stared at the ceiling. "What does that mean?" she said.

"It means I can't tell you, Jocasta," he said.

She kept walking, mulling the answer over.

She faded into a throng of people, muttering and murmuring and whispering to each other as they entered the hall. Her heart pounded in her chest. There were more people here than there had been the night before. Her eyes darted around the room, counting them. A few hundred, at least, crowding into a room that wasn't quite meant to hold them all. Familiar faces flashed in and out of the crowd. As she moved to the back of the room, she could see Cato, lingering and lurking. Cassandra leaned against another man, laughing, eyes flashing, teeth bared.

They were animals. That's what this looked like, a gathering of animals, herded together before the slaughter. Chattering their last words, trying to intimidate the truth away from themselves.

Her eyes moved through the crowd as she pressed her back to the wall. Faces. Some she knew, most she didn't. Faces all echoing the same emotions: confusion, disbelief, a hint of fear.

The lights dimmed, and the crowd fell silent. Above them, snow blew across mountain peaks, sending shadows dancing across the walls. A spotlight flickered to life as Karen pushed her way through the crowd. It parted, leaving her a circle in the centre to stand in. Her eyes roamed the crowd, catching eyes as she went. She locked on Jocasta for a moment before moving on to stare at Cassandra. She hadn't even tried to tie her hair back. It hung about her face, framing it in a tangle of frizz and wire.

"Is everyone here?" she said, spinning in a tight little circle as if she could count everyone. "PETR, is everyone here?"

"I am fetching the last person, Karen," PETR said. She was tapping her foot, Jocasta could see, and crossing and uncrossing her arms, as if that would hurry the person up. "He is on his way."

"Fine, fine. I'm sure he'll hear." She threw her hands in the air as she turned to the crowd.

"I have called you all here because there is a traitor in our midst!" Karen said, pacing in a small circle. Murmurs ran throughout the crowd, rising and falling, seemingly with every word. What was it that amazed them? "All?" "Traitor?" "Our midst?" Was there something about Heaven that made them all doubt that a dissident was possible? Did they believe in the rigours of the vetting process?

Vetting process. Her eyes went to Cato. He was standing, rigid, his eyes locked on her. She blinked. Maybe he had no faith in his fixes. Or maybe his fix had been to make her into a traitor.

Or, the thought pressed in, he just wanted to shift attention to the most likely culprit: the Yugoslav soldier here on a supposed peace mission. He would try to throw her to the wolves to protect himself. It shouldn't have surprised her, yet there it was, that pang of hurt spearing across her heart. She'd known him for less than a day, but he had been in her mind. It ought to have meant something.

"There is a ship in orbit above Callisto." The murmuring didn't cease when Karen spoke. Karen didn't seem to expect it to, her voice growing louder. "It's a stolen lunar shuttle that somehow made it here. The fact that it's here at all should make you all scared. Very scared. Very very scared." Karen paused. Murmurs died as people locked on to her every word.

Across from her, Jocasta saw Cato's attention flicking between Karen, Jocasta, and Cassandra. Jocasta's gaze shifted to Cassandra. The girl was clearly high on something, draped across a man and giggling. What Cato's interest in her was, she wasn't sure she wanted to imagine.

"PETR and SYNAC intercepted a transmission from Heaven to this ship. Alphonse is still working on figuring out what it said, but let's be honest, it doesn't matter. You don't have to know. If we're honest, it's probably better if you don't because this way, it's easier to figure out which one of you is the traitor. Because there is a traitor. The fact that there is a radio on Callisto broadcasting to a ship that is now in our orbit that is both stolen and made it through Party security—" Karen threw her hands in the air. "Look, you know, I know, there's only one thing that can mean." She paused, running her tongue over her teeth. Jocasta's eyes flashed back to Cato. He was still watching her, even as everyone around him watched Karen.

"Traitor. Someone here is trying to destroy this station. Someone is in collusion with that ship in orbit, and I'm going to find out who. You can think that I won't find out, but I will. The person doing this is not your friend, and never has been. If they had been, do you think they'd be trying to kill us all now?" She took a breath and huffed it out again. Beside Cato, Ade and Tieneke were whispering, Cato adding in a word here and there.

"If you know who it is, tell me. No one benefits if you stay silent." Karen paused, eyes darting around the room like a caged animal. They were all animals, after all. Jocasta had just had it wrong before. Some of them were prey, and some lucky few were the predators.

"If you are the terrorist, say so right now."

No one spoke. Shadows danced wildly around the room, painting the faces and the walls like a madhouse. Maybe Jupiter had its own thoughts it wanted to share, but snow was the only way it could do so.

Karen was fixating on one person. Jocasta followed her gaze, watching others around her do the same. In a corner beside the door, Jocasta could see Gautier and Padraig huddled together over a datapad, whispering and gesturing. Jocasta's gaze washed over them. In a station with a soldier and a clear political dissident, Karen had apparently chosen to believe that the cancer-riddled physicist and his lover were the biggest threats to their existence.

Jocasta's eyes narrowed as her gaze flicked back to Karen. What did she know? Or was she just mad?

Karen's eyes leapt around the room, jiggling from one person to another. "One of you knows something!" she screamed, jabbing a finger randomly into the crowd. "One of you knows exactly who it is!"

Silence filled the hall as even breath was stifled. Only Padraig moved, swaying on his feet as he stared at the datapad.

The finger lowered. Karen straightened, sniffing as she did so. "I'll be in my office when one of you wants to talk to me." She stalked through the crowd, people hurrying to part as she passed.

Jocasta's eyes moved back to Cato. He was watching Cassandra, Ade and Tieneke watching with him. Most of the crowd was watching Padraig and Gautier, murmuring as they dispersed, glancing over their shoulders at the pair as they went. Karen hadn't been subtle. If the two were up to something, at least it would be harder for them now.

Jocasta stood, watching Cato. It wasn't Padraig and Gautier she was worried about. He was a councillor's son, here because he wanted to live, that much she had understood from what she'd read about him and seen since he'd been here. Gautier seemed delighted to be here, at least based on what he'd done at the party and before that.

"The Party lies," Cato had said. "It's only the lack of anything else to strive for that keeps Callisto in check." There was a ship in orbit. There was something to strive for.

"I want you to remember everything," PETR had said. PETR was the AI. He couldn't tell a human that another human was dangerous. It wasn't in his conception that a human could be dangerous.

"I want you to remember everything."

Padraig and Gautier were hurrying off down a corridor, heads still huddled together over the datapad. Whatever was occupying their time wasn't her concern. Her concern was Cato, following them. Ade and Tieneke went in a different direction, but Cato was following Padraig and Gautier.

Jocasta's eyes tracked them as they left the Hall.

She had come to Heaven as an ambassador. It had never been stated, because it had never needed to be stated. The Party had needed someone from Yugoslavia to go to Heaven to show Earth and Callisto that the Party was in control, that Yugoslavia was under control. That she was a soldier was a happy bonus.

That she was a soldier meant she knew what self-preservation was, and that self-preservation, contrary to what Cato said, could extend to a unified group.

That she knew how to protect a group from elements that wanted to destroy it.

"I want you to remember."

She was trying. Every puzzle piece she had been given fit together. Her memories had been warped, and Cato had tried to warp what was left. She couldn't remember what she had been, but she could remember what she'd learned.

Jocasta walked. Karen's office was above the library, according to what she'd said during the tour. She'd be in her office. She would tell Karen and save the station. There would be peace.

She pushed through people milling about in corridors, faces pale and scared. These were people who hadn't seen death in decades, if ever. The idea that they could die was impossible. It was something that they couldn't even conceive of, yet here they were, having to realise that death was breathing down their necks.

Up the stairs, two at a time. Jocasta's mind whirled. How could she say it? How could she put everything she had seen and heard into words? How could she make Karen understand?

A grey door, no different from any other on the station, rose up before her as the staircase ended and the corridor swept off to the left. "Karen Reece" the nameplate read, then under it "Station Administrator."

Jocasta took a breath. PETR had told her to remember. She'd remembered. Her training had taught her to save the lives of innocents. She could do that too.

She rapped on the door, knuckles tapping against the cold metal. The sound hadn't finished echoing before the door slid open. Jocasta stepped inside. The door slammed shut behind her.

She hadn't been sure what to expect from Karen's office, but it hadn't been something quite so quaint. Pictures of a smiling family lined the walls behind a thick wood desk. A curtain of beads hung over a doorway behind the desk, shielding Karen's room from view. Sculptures with straight angles and bright colours sat on her desk and shelves, adding life to the blank grey walls. Jocasta paused in her steps as she took it in.

"Jocasta." Jocasta's gaze snapped to the woman rising from behind the desk. Her hair was thick and unkempt, hanging over her like a shroud. Bags hung beneath her red eyes, and her face gleamed with manic sweat.

"Jocasta, Jocasta, Jocasta," she said, stepping out around the desk. "I was hoping you'd come see me. I find you very interesting, you know. Very, very interesting."

"I am not your terrorist," Jocasta said, watching her. She'd thought of her as a caged animal before, wild, unpredictable. She couldn't say that was the case now. This was a woman who was a predator, and knew it.

"Then why are you here?" Karen said. Her hair was a haze around her as her voice crackled. "I'm busy and don't have time to deal with every little bullshit—"

"Cato." Jocasta dropped the name, and the tirade ceased. A spell fell over Karen. Her eyes cleared, and a feral smile spread across her face. Her tongue ran over her teeth.

Jocasta took a step back. This had been a mistake. That woman was a predator, and god, now she was stupid enough to be prey.

"Cato." Karen repeated the name. "Cato. Cato. Cato. Tell me, Jocasta, what's Cato been up to, *hm*? What's he done? What did he say to you?"

Jocasta took another step, feeling the sealed door at her back.

"Never mind," she murmured, closing her eyes. "This was a mistake."

"Mistake? Why?" Karen cocked her head to one side, then to the other, eyes locked on Jocasta's. "Why would it be a mistake for you to tell me what Cato's been doing? Has he been recruiting?"

"Recruiting? No." Jocasta shook her head. This wasn't what she had meant. This wasn't what she had expected. She'd expected someone rational who would discuss her fears, not this predator stalking her with her eyes. "It's just what he said—"

"What did he say? Tell me, please." Her head cocked to the other side before centring again. She'd watched snakes in university, the way they hypnotised their prey, the way you could taste their desire, their need on the air. The prey was always oblivious, or so she'd thought. Maybe it had felt like this, feeling need it didn't understand seeping into its every pore.

"Are you okay?" Jocasta asked. There was nowhere to go. Nowhere to retreat. The only choice was to make a stand.

Karen blinked. "Of course I'm not okay," she said. "There's a traitor in this station—"

"Listen to yourself." Jocasta closed her eyes, opened them again. Only one option. "You are right that there is someone here, trying to hurt us, but you cannot find them if you attack those who want to help you."

"Attack?" Karen's eyes went wild. Jocasta winced as the woman spun away from her back to the desk, throwing open a drawer. Wrong word, oh she'd chosen the wrong word. She had no idea what she was doing. She understood animals, and this was an animal, but she hadn't been ready.

"I'll show you attack." Karen's hand emerged from the desk drawer, fingers clenched around a taser. She slammed the drawer shut again as she came back around the desk, brandishing it at Jocasta. Electricity flickered and hummed across its prongs.

"Tell me what he said!" she screamed.

Breath in. Breath out. Exactly as Marina had taught her. Jocasta held up her hands and pressed herself against the wall.

"Calm down, Karen," she said. "Think. Breathe. I am by your side. I am here to help."

Karen cocked her head, then straightened it again, squeezing her eyes shut. "Funny…funny way of showing it," she said, pressing a hand to her forehead. "Won't even tell me what he said." She lowered her hand and opened her eyes. They were clearer now, more focused.

Jocasta lowered her hands, patting the air down at her hips. "I know, it's not what you want," she said. Low voice. Calm voice. Collected voice. Inside, her heart pounded, but she couldn't show it. Not here. Not now. "I'll talk to you. But please, put the taser down. Let's talk. Let's figure out what's wrong."

"The…whispers…" Karen squeezed her eyes shut again, reopened them. "They're all… There are these whispers…" Her gaze jiggled, dancing across Jocasta's face before locking again. "It doesn't matter! They don't matter! Tell me what he said!"

"Tell me what I can do to help." Jocasta patted the air again. Calm. Please calm, Karen. Calm.

"You can…" Eyes closed, eyes open. It was a dance now, no other word for it. A dance between cat and mouse where the mouse had somehow convinced the cat its life was not so worthless after all. "Make it stop… The whispers…"

"I can help. Please, let me help you. Put down the taser." The mood had shifted. She could feel it. The need was gone. All that was left was quiet desperation. That was good. She could work with that. She understood that.

"I can…" Karen nodded, her head bobbing, eyes wide. "I can…"

"Karen!" A voice broke in from the ceiling. PETR.

Karen's eyes narrowed as Jocasta's widened. Desperation, but now it had shifted. Terror, but now it was she, and she was

• • •

tased once before it was put away, gloved hands reaching for the syringe again.

"Do you know where you are right now, Jocasta?" That voice. It had a sing-song lilt to it. Where was this person from that they had a lilt in their—

Pain burning through her veins as the serum entered. Pain, followed by lightness. Her brain was ripping itself apart in its hurry to deal with the pain. Shut down nerves. Shut down thought. Shut down everything that could be shut down without killing her.

"Tell me where you are."

"Z-z-z-zallq." Kosovo. So far from home. In a torture tent. "Brief captivity." Where was she? Who was she?

"Good, good. Why?"

Pain and pain and pain and

• • •

pain. Fire burned through her and a

• • •

scream tore out of her as she felt her right hand break. Her brain had tried to shut this down, but it couldn't. No mind ever could.

• • •

"Do you think they really think that anyone from the 56th would actually give anything up? Like, really? Who do they think we are?"

Polyxeni laughed as she roasted a marshmallow over the fire. Beside her, Aura drooled and sniffed at the scraps of meat that had fallen during dinner. Sophia ruffled Aporia's ears as she laughed at her own joke, beer spilling from her cup. The dog's tail wagged, sending the faint light of the fire dancing.

"That's the idea, Sophia," Stathis said, looking up at her from where he was leaning on his elbow. "If they don't even know we exist, they can't really have an opinion about us, now can they?"

"True, true," Sophia said, raising the cup of beer in a toast. "But Jocasta there, they must know she exists, terrible as she smells."

Jocasta stuck her tongue out and splashed her beer at Sophia, laughing. Drops fell into the fire, sending it

• • •

hissing and spitting as fire

• • •

danced in the pale moonlight. Aporia shook her head, groaning her doggy groan at human antics.

"You're just jealous they like me more," Jocasta laughed.

"Ha, and yet look who they come to for petting!"

"Only because they know it's rare from you and common from me. They see me all the time, so they know they like me. You, they

• • •

don't know about it." Jocasta gasped the words through the pain. The Party torturer stood over her, implants held in her hand.

"A helpful word? From you?" She laughed. "Well, well, so there is progress after all."

Jocasta squeezed her eyes shut as the syringe

• • •

descended. Metal arms held her and lifted her in the air as she twitched and burned in PETR's arms. Screams broke from her lips in bursts and hiccups as PETR held her close.

"Take her to her room," Karen said. "And bring me Cato."

"Yes, Karen."

Footsteps clanged against the metal

∙ ∙ ∙

floor. Jocasta hissed and bent down, scrambling to pick up the cup.

"Sorry, sorry, sorry, sorry," she murmured, the word becoming a stream of thought. The breeze rippled across the water as it scurried across the wooden floor.

"It's okay." Marina hopped off the couch and hurried to the kitchen. Jocasta heard the sound of cupboards opening and closing as she searched for a rag. "I know you're having trouble. I'm sorry. I shouldn't have surprised you like that."

"No, you did nothing wrong." Jocasta squatted beside the puddle, watching as it spread. The smell of roses hung in the air, light and brilliant. The glass had fallen, but some parts of the world carried on. Indeed, the world didn't even know something in it had changed.

Marina knelt in front of her, mopping up the water with a pink rag. "It's really fine, Jocasta," she said. "Honest. See? No problem." She held up the dripping rag for a moment before splashing it back down in the puddle. "No problem at all."

Jocasta smiled. "Thank you," she said. "You're so thoughtful."

"Of course! You're my friend."

Marina stood back up, carrying the rag back to the kitchen. Jocasta squatted, eyes fixed on where the puddle had been. She could get up, she knew she could. Of course she could. It would be absurd to say she couldn't.

Marina's footsteps came back. She felt a hand on her upper arm.

"Come on, Jocasta," Marina said. "Come sit on the couch again."

Jocasta pushed herself up and back to the couch, her eyes moving to Marina's face. That face. Concern was etched into every line that Jocasta had put there. A few grey hairs frizzed out from the brown. Even being around her sent colour draining from the world.

"Hey, look at me." Jocasta met Marina's eyes. "Look at me. I want to help you. You know that. I'm here to make sure you can feel safe, remember? When you need something, I'm always here, and if it takes a minute or two minutes or an hour or a day to feel like you can talk to me, that's fine. I know it's hard. Trust me, I know. But I am here for you, and always will be. Never forget that, Jocasta. I want you to

∙ ∙ ∙

Remember. Everything.

• • •

"Why are you in Zallq?"

Her mind was clear. No pain. Nothing. Just truth and the ability to tell it.

"I am part of the 56th," she said. Zallq was gone. It didn't matter anymore. Their secrets, their goals, their war, all dead, all dead out in the hills of Kosovo.

"The 56th?"

"The 56th," she said. "The Muses."

"What

• • •

was the rumbling? She twitched and spasmed on the bed as the world shook around her. An earthquake? There couldn't be an earthquake on

• • •

Callisto. Remember that I'm still thinking of you once you're there."

Jocasta nodded and pulled Marina close to her. Flowers danced around the room, petals carried by the breeze.

She would remember.

Chapter Twenty-Two

Interviewer: Right, let's do this. According to your file, your name is Cassandra? Long 'a'? Short 'a'? You don't go by Cass or Cassie?
Cassandra McAllister: Long 'a', and nope, it's just Cassandra. It's what my mother called me, so hey, figured I'd keep it for her, you know?
Interviewer: Your mother, tell me about her.
Cassandra McAllister: I mean, she's a nice enough lady. What do you want to know?
Interviewer: Where is she now? You Bronx types, I don't see you often. You all seem to live hard and die young. I'm surprised to see one of you in here at all, honestly.
Cassandra McAllister: Why is that?
Interviewer: You know how it is there. Like I said, live hard. The radiation can't be good for anyone down there, either, and I think it makes some of you a little crazy.
Cassandra McAllister: Why do you say that?
  Callisto Lottery Psychological Interview Recordings, 19 July 2193

Fuck martyrdom. The idea that you have to die to make a difference is stupid. Your life is valuable. It's the only thing the Party can't take from you. Keep it. Live to fight another day.
  Vespers Pamphlet, published in Raleigh-Durham, Carolina, United States, 2192

"Murder" is such a small word. What we do is so much more than that. Any random person gets "murdered." When a society dies, we have a better word for it. We call it "revolution."
  Sherman Howitzman, "The Assassination of the United States," performed 2108

Monday, March 18 2193, 6:29 PM. Main Hall, Heaven, Callisto.

There were truths that Cassandra held near and dear to her heart. They were simple lessons, but effective ones. Don't swap a ration coupon for a new sleeping mat without checking it for bedbugs. Don't mix grains and veins. Don't do drugs at inconvenient times.

Don't hesitate to kill.

The destruction of Heaven didn't have to be complete or literal. No, that was too easy, too expected. Besides, there were people here who didn't deserve to die. She wasn't a monster. She was a freedom fighter. Huge difference. No, it was much easier just to murder the one guy, then bust out of this place. Didn't need to hold everyone accountable for the crimes of the Party.

Fuck the pool. Fuck PETR. Fuck every roundabout way of doing this. Karen had been so kind as to show her the quick and easy way to murder people in this place, so why not go for that? Grab the taser. Murder anyone who got in her way. Leave. Absolutely fucking simple. Really, why no one had thought of just murdering councillors before, she couldn't imagine.

The crowd dispersed around her as Jack hung on her arm.

"Ha, she thinks we're all gonna die. Ha. Ha ha." His words slurred together as Cassandra wriggled out of his grasp. He tripped over his ankles and fell to the ground in a heap. "Guess it's started!" he laughed.

Cassandra laughed with them. He was right. He didn't know it, but Jack was right the fuck on.

"Stay here," she said. Jack mumbled an answer as he pressed his face to the floor. Hot.

Cassandra turned to the hall Karen had stalked down. It couldn't be that hard, really, especially when she was so angry and distracted already. Just a little bit of "what's that over there," grab the taser, and done. Karen wouldn't even have a chance to use it on her. It was perfect. Nothing could possibly go wrong.

There was someone else headed up the stairs ahead of her. Someone else was going to Karen's office. Bushy black hair and a shuffling stride. Jocasta.

Cassandra froze. Jocasta didn't know anything. She wasn't a threat. What was she doing here?

She watched the woman disappear up the stairs. Jocasta was definitely heading for Karen's office; that, at least, was happening. Cassandra took a step as she heard the door open above her, freezing into caution again. What to do? Charge the door? She'd get in at least, but then what?

She had to admit, she hadn't considered the door when she'd decided this was the plan.

"Jocasta, Jocasta, Jocasta." Karen's voice danced down from the doorway, taut as a clothesline. Each syllable plummeted from it, falling into the poor ears below. She sounded fucking stressed. "I was hoping you'd come see me. I find you very interesting. Very very interesting."

"I'm not your terrorist."

Cassandra had to hand it to her. For all her many flaws, at least Jocasta got to the fucking point.

The door slid closed again. Cassandra sighed. No mad dashes, then. Something more subtle.

Subtle was hard, though. Cassandra shrugged. "Hey, PETR," she said. "Open the door to Karen's office."

There was a pause. Cassandra pictured PETR, humming through his processors, staring in disbelief at the request. She stared at the door, eyes flicking to the ceiling, waiting for his stupid answer.

"I'm afraid I can't do that," PETR said. Cassandra smacked a hand against a wall. Totally unsurprising, but unhelpful. She had to try harder.

"Well," she said. "Have you fucking asked her? She's looking for the terrorist and all that. Might be good if the terrorist, you know, showed up in her office."

There was another pause. Then, "I will ask."

Cassandra sighed, throwing her hands in the air and trying not to look too excited. The robot wasn't completely stupid. If she looked too happy, he'd know something was wrong. Besides, she was good at faking exasperation; she'd felt enough of it dealing with dumbasses.

The door slid open. Jocasta tumbled back through it, body twitching, voice shrieking in agony. Karen stood over her, the taser clutched in white-knuckled fingers.

Holy fuck.

Cassandra stared for a second. She couldn't help it. Whatever she'd thought might happen, that Karen would flat-out murder the bitch wasn't it. On the other hand, it meant that the taser was exactly as good a murder plan as she needed. Perfect.

Cassandra lunged forward, charging up the stairs. Up, up, up, before Karen saw her and could do something. The air stank of burned ozone and fried hair, but no time to think about that. There was only time to snatch out at her hand.

Her fingers closed on Karen's wrist. New shrieks joined Jocasta's, screaming in an insane wail. Cassandra squeezed her fingers on the small bones in Karen's wrist and felt her fingers fly free. The taser clattered to the floor.

Everything had gone exactly right. Fanfuckingtastic.

Cassandra dove, snatching the taser and swinging it towards Karen. A feral grin spread across her face. She had the Party authority right in front of her. She couldn't kill her, no, but anything else she wanted, she could do. All the power in the world was right there, at her fingertips, and no one in this whole shitty station could stop her. She was in control. She was the power now.

Her grin broadened.

Karen's shrieks died down, replaced by a manic look of sheer hatred. Her eyes locked on the taser as Jocasta's screams continued to fill the hall around them.

"What will you do?" Karen said. A grin spread across her face, pulling her lips back in an unnatural contortion. "Nowhere to go. No one to talk to. You're doomed, yes yes. Doomed, and there's nothing you can do. Your cause will die, yes. You'll die, oh yes. Nothing you can do. Trapped here. What will you do?"

Cassandra laughed. She couldn't help it. Karen was clearly completely insane. Here she was, being threatened with actual violence, and all she could do was continue this act that everything would turn up Party. News flash: it wasn't, and it wouldn't.

Cassandra pulled the trigger.

Karen fell to the ground, screaming as electricity crackled over her. Cassandra laughed as the other woman writhed. Oh, but it felt good. She was the whole Party, right there, writhing in pain, forced to recognize that she was wrong, and Cassandra was right. This, this moment was worth it. Everything, all the pain, all the suffering, just to watch the Party burn. It was glorious.

The screams faded into silence. The twitching slowed. Karen put her hands under her shoulders, slowly pushing herself back to her feet. Her eyes locked on Cassandra's, ice-cold behind their manic rage.

"So here's what's going to happen," Cassandra said. Her grin hadn't faded and never would. This was too good. "You, me, and Padraig are going back to Earth. We're—"

"With what shuttle?" The voice was low and quiet, but Karen's interruption was clear. Cassandra stared at her. That Karen, this tiny broken semblance of power, would actually interrupt her was unthinkable.

"The one I came in on."

Karen burst into mad howls of laughter. "It's gone!" she screamed. "Gone! Gone! Gone!"

Cassandra tased her again, watching with satisfaction as the laughter turned into screams once more.

"Where," she said, standing over Karen's twitching body, "the fuck. Is my shuttle."

Karen laughed.

Heaven plunged into darkness.

Chapter Twenty-Three

Seek not too much the change to blame;
'Tis but the form alone we change;
The sense, the spirit rest the same.

"Táin bo Fraich"

Reporter: Cato! You've never left Earth before, correct? Not even for a holiday on the Moon?
Cato Riela: That is correct.
Reporter: What do you think your reaction will be to seeing the Earth disappear?
Cato Riela: The reason I have never left this planet is because I have no reason to have that particular experience. Why would I want to? This planet is my home. It's where I belong. Why would I want to go to a place where I cannot even see its beauty? Admire its seas, get lost in its clouds, stare out at its sunrises?
Reporter: Are you saying you don't want to go to Heaven?
Cato Riela: I would never say that.

Callisto Launch Press Conference, 2189

G.C. Reyes: We've received another demand from the Zadehs. It seems they want—
G.C. Maksharov: Ignore it.
G.C. Whishaw: Oh, come on, Ivan. You don't even know what it is.
G.C. Maksharov: Their previous demand was for heavy weapons to combat non-existent rebel groups in Tbilisi. Before that, they wanted undersea mining equipment so they could haul refined thuronium up from the Irradiated Zones. We have accepted none of these demands. They are a hostile power. That we have communication with them at all is ridiculous. You know this, Eoin.
G.C. Whishaw: We have communication in the interest of preventing another war, something I'd hope you understand by now, Ivan. Some conflicts are best resolved with talking.
G.C. Maksharov: I am sceptical. What is that they want?

G.C. Reyes: It seems they need plutonium—
G.C. Maksharov and G.C. Whishaw: Ignore it.
    Recordings of Global Council Meetings, Tuesday, 14 July 2189

Monday, 18 March 2193, 6:29 PM. Entry Hall, Heaven, Callisto.

"RUN PADRAIG."

He didn't need further urging. The physical possibility of running was right out, but that he was leaving this place? That was a given. By Jove, that was a given.

He staggered forward, eyes fixed on Gautier ahead of him. The man's back was broad and strong, the fabric of his shirt settling around his movement like mist in the mountain air. His breath caught in his throat, refusing to move. Padraig forced it through, focusing on the man in front of him. They were leaving. The two of them were leaving. He and Gautier were going home.

"If you want to have any chance of making it off this rock, you're taking me with you."

Gautier and Padraig froze at the voice behind them. The mist faded, leaving only fabric behind. A pity. When he was younger, he'd enjoyed seeing the mist rolling in off the sea, covering the sheepfolds and the forest. It might have been nice to see it all again.

He shook his head. He would see it again. He was going home. They were going home. Focus.

The woman from the Welcome Hall ran over to them, a man trailing in her wake. Padraig blinked. The tall man was Cato Riela, that he knew. Whatever this was, it wasn't good.

"With that look, with that urgency, I know exactly what you're up to. You want to go home, and I want to save this station from whatever is out there. So how about we help each other out, ya?" Her words blurred together in a haze of consonants. Her Lunar accent was strong. How had it managed to stay so thick through being in this place? Accents were such mutable things. Amazing that she held on to hers.

"Why do we need you?" Padraig felt Gautier's chest rumble, building up for a roar, as he stepped up behind him.

"If it was as easy as 'oh, I'll just hop on the shuttle and go home,' do you think so many people would still be here? No, councillor's ass, of course not! Yoh, everyone would have stormed the first flight home. No, no, no, no, no, there's security, security out the ass. PETR, SYNAC, they're both designed to prevent a jailbreak, basically the only thing they're programmed to do beyond, y'know, life support and basic support functionality. Although, if you program their cores a little differently, you can—"

"Get to the point, Tieneke." Cato's voice was a growl as well. His eyes were on Padraig. Why? Why target the least threatening person?

"Right, yes, sorry." Tieneke cleared her throat. "Point is, you need to disable security, and to do that, you need to know how to. Without substantial robotics training, it can get tricky, but happily, I can just—whoop! —circumvent that."

"Or we can force our way through it. We don't need you." Gautier spoke again, his hand brushing Padraig's. Was he nervous? Padraig hadn't realised that nervous was an emotion Gautier felt.

Tieneke laughed. "No, you can't," she said. "PETR's designed to put the whole thing on lockdown if someone tries to leave. SYNAC won't leave if someone's on the shuttle who doesn't have permission to be there. And—"

"And the Party will shoot us out of the sky as soon as we get close." Cato interrupted her. Padraig felt a shiver rattle through him. His father wouldn't do that. None of them would do that.

He shook his head. "Why would they—?"

Cato's eyes flashed. "Control," he said. "Imagine what it says to the people of Earth if we return. It says the Party has no control over this place. Imagine what a person like us could do on Earth if we were maliciously inclined. You understand how the Party might be concerned, and might take action, if they didn't have something to lose."

This was absurd. Padraig shook his head again. This whole idea was absurd. The Party didn't murder people, and certainly not the people who were most valuable to it. That they would shoot anyone out of the sky was obscene even to suggest. That Cato would suggest it as a possibility showed how unhinged the man really was.

None of them should be going back to Earth, though. None of these people standing in front of him, pleading with him, none of them should be going. Suppose Cato was right and the Party would shoot them out of the sky. His father never would, but Maksharov? Possible. They were in even more danger with these people on board.

"Why do you think—"

"Look," Tieneke waved a hand in the air, cutting them off. "I'm not here to go back to the Moon. Joh, I am never going back. What I am going to do is see what it wants and get it out of here if it's a problem. 'Cause it's probably a problem, ya? You let my friend go back to Earth with you, I save Heaven, and bish bosh, everyone's happy." She paused, eyes dancing between Padraig and Gautier. Her hands reached out, grasping his. They were cold and clammy. Or was it him who was cold? Did it matter?

"Look, I'm sure you're great, no doubts, but let's be real. You're not getting in there without me."

Her hands were so cold, as if a winter wind had been biting at them. Was she dead? Was he?

People squeezed into dust beneath the grasp of ribbons.

"No," Padraig murmured. "No, no, no."

"Oh, for fuck's sake, listen to yourself, you absurd little man," Gautier said. Everything in him froze. The man was snapping at him. How could he not understand? How could he not see the danger? "You tell me there is danger, and I don't believe you, but fine, we will say there is because I trust you. You tell me we need to go, and that is fine. I can go. And now, right before we have the way to go home, you say 'no, no, Gautier, we cannot go because I do not like the shipmates!' Listen to yourself. Get over yourself."

Padraig sank back against Gautier's body, reaching for the comfort that had to be there. There was nothing but the pounding heart, thudding out an angry rhythm against his cheek.

"You're immortal. I'm immortal. We're all immortal. If it is the Party you fear, there is nothing the Party can do to us if we go back, nothing at all. You don't have to grovel to them. *We* do not have to grovel to them. You want to stick it to your father? Good. Go back. Now is your chance. Now get on the shuttle before I throw you on there."

Padraig shook his head. There wasn't time for this. No time to argue about this. It was ridiculous, it was absurd, but there wasn't time to stand here and talk them out of it.

"Fine, fine, fine, doesn't matter, doesn't matter." Padraig pulled his hands out of Tieneke's. There was no new warmth. Maybe it wasn't her and never had been. Maybe he was the cold one. "Come on the shuttle. We need to leave. We need to leave now."

Tieneke beamed and pulled Cato into a hug. "There you go, Cato! I told you!"

Padraig turned away, stumbling towards the shuttle, feeling Gautier's arm slide across his back.

People squeezed into dust. You are going to die.

"We need to go. You need to stay safe," Padraig murmured. Gautier had snapped at him. Gautier had shouted at him. His world, or what little remained of it, was splintering.

The arm squeezed across him, holding him close. Warmth spread across his back, his side, everything that touched Gautier.

Forgiveness. The world could be rebuilt. Everything could be okay. They would survive.

"Wait a sec," Tieneke called out from behind him as they reached a sealed door. *Heisenberg.* So close, waiting just beyond.

"You are in a restricted area," PETR said. His voice echoed off the corridor walls, reverberating in endless ribbons of sound. "Please do not loiter in this corridor."

"Ah, 'damme, PETR," Tieneke said. Padraig turned. She had pulled out a datapad, fingers blazing across the screen. "You say that all the time. 'Restricted' this, 'no access' that, on and on. Ah, here it is. PETR!"

"Yes, Tieneke?" There was an edge to the AI's voice. Of course there would be. It watched everything in the station. It had to know what was happening.

But it had an edge. How could an AI have an edge?

"PETR, execute command TH1138. Authorisation: Tieneke Haan. Code: Acht vijfenvijftig. Open the *Heisenberg* door when that's complete, if you would, please."

There was a pause. Padraig could picture it, a new command sliding in among the hundreds that must already exist, a backdoor opening and exposing all the intricate wirings of PETR's brain. That this had been a long time in the works was clear. They'd been waiting for a key back to Earth.

They'd been waiting for him. Like most of humanity, they'd been waiting for him.

"Command complete."

The door to *Heisenberg* slid open. The interior was exactly the same as the day before. Cryochambers lined the walls and status lights flashed green and yellow. Metal footsteps echoed through the small body of the craft.

Behind him, a laugh drowned out the footsteps.

"It worked! By the Party, Cato, there it is! Go on home, Cato." The laughter dissolved into sobs as Tieneke pushed past him to the shuttle.

Going home. There was the shuttle. It could be that easy.

"Come on." Gautier pulled him forward, dragging him into the shuttle. The arm squeezed tight around him, pressing into him, threatening to dissolve him into dust.

"You're hurting me," he murmured. The arm loosened, and Gautier lowered him to the floor beside the command console.

"I apologise," he said, squatting in front of him. His hair was askew, but still perfect. Always perfect. It swung as he glanced over his shoulder at Cato stepping onto the shuttle. "I am glad to see we are leaving, and sometimes I get enthusiastic when I am excited, as you know."

Padraig nodded. That he did indeed know.

"Hello, Tieneke. I am glad to see you. PETR is corrupt. Please help PETR. PETR is my friend. Please help PETR."

Metal feet clanked across the shuttle floor as SYNAC stepped towards Tieneke. She waved a hand as she buried herself in the datapad once more.

"Yeah, great, good to see you too, SYNAC," she said. "Execute command 551945."

"I do not like this command. I do not want to do this," SYNAC said.

"You're an AI, SYNAC. You don't have 'want.' You have 'I do this.'" The words came in one breath and a flurry of movement as Tieneke hurried to the console, stepping past Gautier. "What are you doing on the floor? Odd place to wait. But if it makes you happy, stick with it, that's my motto anyway. Now how does this pig fly?"

Padraig didn't answer. She was clearly doing enough breathing and speaking for both of them. No need to try and compete.

A ding rose from Padraig's datapad. It was still clutched in his hand, even after all this. How odd. His eyes drifted down to stare at it.

"Another of your messages?" Gautier muttered. "What is this one?"

Padraig stared at it for a moment, then shook his head. "You don't want to see it," he said. He closed his eyes and leaned his head back against the wall, listening to Tieneke mash buttons on the console beside him. "It's more of the same."

He felt the datapad being plucked from his hand, then heard the snort. Always that derisive snort. "'Run. Run now.' Hardly seems worth the effort to translate, hm?" The weight of the datapad returned to his lap.

Padraig snorted a laugh, feeling it dissolve into coughing. "It…" The coughs silenced him as he held up a finger. "Jupiter has one thing it likes to say, but it's said it so often that I think it's worth paying attention to. What do you think, mon cheri?"

"Oui, Padraig," Gautier said. "I find that quite often in life, when I am told something over and over, it might be worth it to listen."

Padraig nodded and reached a hand to the console. "Help me up, please, mon cheri," he said. Strong hands reached under his armpits, pulling him to his feet.

"You really are dying, aren't you?" Cato's voice, from somewhere behind him, quiet and crawling. "Sent all the way here to live, and you're still going to die."

"Enough out of you." Gautier's growl pushed the creeping sensation away. Gautier was here. Gautier would be all right.

"SYNAC, I'm taking manual control." Tieneke's voice came from beside him, consonants still swayed into a single sound.

"I do not understand." SYNAC's voice sounded from all around him. "I do not think this is a good idea."

"You aren't programmed to think, SYNAC. You're programmed to do." Tieneke pressed more buttons on the console. Lights flared around them. "I'm taking manual control, override code—"

"I will not give control. You are not authorised. I can only give manual control to an engineer. You are not an engineer. You are—"

"'Damme, SYNAC, I am literally an engineer." Tieneke pounded a fist on the console. He felt the vibrations through his palms, reverberating and pulsing.

There wasn't time for this.

"I'm taking manual control." Padraig coughed out the words, feeling Tieneke's eyes turn to scorch him. If she couldn't get through to the AI, maybe he could. There wasn't time for this. There wasn't time for anything.

"I will give manual control," SYNAC said. "You are saying this is a good idea. You are human. I believe you."

"Don't suppose you'll let me fly it, with your manual control?" He met her eyes. They blazed as her hands hovered over the console.

Padraig nodded, then glanced over at Gautier, meeting his eyes before staring back down at the console in front of him. The corrupt AI thought this was a good idea. Truly he could ask for no better endorsement than that.

"Allons-y, mon cheri?" he murmured.

"Just do it," Gautier said. That was that, then.

Tieneke sighed. She flicked a switch. The metal door slammed shut behind them.

Padraig leaned against the console, watching her movements. Second step: calibrate departure trajectory.

"You're in control," she said. "Get the AI to do its job."

"SYNAC." Padraig covered his mouth with his arm, silencing a cough. "Check departure trajectory .0918."

"That is correct, Padraig." The answer came without a pause. Good.

Third step. Ignition. He reached past Tieneke, entering fuel into the burners and firing the engines. The floor rattled beneath them.

Somewhere beyond that door were the others, the other residents of Heaven, the best and brightest Earth had ever seen. Somewhere, they waited for their doom in the darkness, eyes turned towards Jupiter, misted to the fate that rushed to devour them.

Ribbons. Ribbons squeezing them to dust.

Jupiter had said to run. Jupiter had told him to get Gautier to safety. That was what mattered, more than anything else.

Fourth step. Lift-off. He entered the command.

Beneath him, the floor of the shuttle dropped for a moment before the artificial gravity kicked in. From the window, Padraig watched Heaven tumble away, each part coming into view before growing smaller below him. Landing pad, radiation shielding; all of it seemed so small and vulnerable from orbit. Heaven was an insect waiting to be swatted away.

"And there it goes."

Magarlach, that was Cato Riela. He was headed back to Earth with a man his father had politely called a terrorist. What was he doing?

He stepped back from the console, looking for Gautier. The man had moved to a window and was peering out, his back to Padraig. Beside the door, Cato gazed out at Callisto, a small smile playing at the corners of his mouth.

They were leaving this entire station to die.

His eyes moved back to Gautier. Necessary. It was necessary. Through the window, Jupiter was rising into view as they circled Callisto. Jupiter had warned him. All of this had been necessary.

People exploding into dust.

He turned back to the console. What was done was done. No turning back. Onwards, progress, all that rot.

He'd left them to die, and on what basis? Because a dream had told him to? Because he was afraid?

"SYNAC, help me calculate the exit trajectory," Padraig murmured.

"I am not supposed to let Callistans leave Heaven," SYNAC said. His voice vibrated along the metal walls. "Calculating the return trajectory would be allowing Callistans to leave Heaven. I will not calculate this. I am not corrupt. I will not calculate this."

"No!" Tieneke interrupted. "Not the exit! Route to the Lunar shuttle. There's a spacesuit in here, two I think," she said. Her eyes flicked from the console to their faces. "Get to the Lunar shuttle, I can check it out, send it back. I don't want to go back to the Moon. 'Damme, look, I know how the shuttles work. Spent years developing the AIs for them for the Lams. It's easy. Pop over, set the thing to land, doesn't need anything from you except for me actually going over there. That was our deal. I got you this far. Now you let me save that station."

A flash of light through the gloom. Calculate eccentricity. He could see the other shuttle on the console, zipping closer and closer across Callisto's surface. The tiniest of adjustments, and he could catch it. Just a slight course correction, and they could be orbiting in tandem, partners against the gloom.

A slight course correction, and he could rescue the people he'd condemned.

Padraig turned, fingers dancing across the screen. The engines hummed to life again beneath them before stuttering to a stop once more. He watched the velocity. Constant. Only a few seconds longer and he could reverse it, bring them to a stop by the other shuttle.

He pressed a button. Somewhere in the depths of the shuttle, the engines fired out a gasp of fuel, slowing them.

"We should be near it now," he said. He could feel the eyes on his back. "If we have the spacesuit, then go." A cough tore out of him, and he bent over the console, spraying blood across it. Apt.

"You cannot possibly be serious right now," Gautier said. "You don't know what that is—"

"I'm from 'dacted Serenity Point!" Padraig turned to see Tieneke storming over to a closet on the wall and stabbing her fingers across an access pad. "Eight years, I worked on those shuttles, and you think I don't know what to do with one?" The closet door slid open, and an orange spacesuit arm draped out. Tieneke pulled on it, yanking the suit out of the closet.

"There's an access console just on the inside of the overhang." She pointed out the window as she stepped into the suit, clipping it against her clothes. "'Damme, this thing is small. Anyway, I'll pop over there, get inside, get that AI to land, and I'll be done. You can go back to whatever you think is waiting for you. An hour, at most, literally nothing in the grand scheme of things if you think about it, which I don't think any of you fine gentlemen actually have."

She zipped the last zipper and spread her arms out wide. "Cato, how do I look?"

"Insane," he said. "Absolutely insane."

Tieneke smiled. "An hour. You're going home in an hour. I believe you can wait that long."

Cato flicked a hand to his brow and saluted her. Beside him, Padraig felt Gautier drifting close. Other than the flight to Callisto, the man had never been in space. How odd this all must be for him.

"The console can communicate with the other ship, yes?" Padraig turned as Cato walked over to him, eyes moving to the console. Padraig took a step back. Everything about Cato exuded control and power. Whether he had it or not didn't matter. Here was a man happy to at least give off the illusion that he was in charge, which, to be fair, was true at the moment. He was going home. The three of them were going home.

"Yes," Padraig said, picking up his datapad and thumbing through the manual. Gautier stepped to the window again, staring out at the other ship. Padraig looked at him before pointing down at the console. "Should be this button here."

Cato stepped between Padraig and the console, shunting him back. Padraig watched him, this terrorist, this man who almost certainly did see this as a prison break. He, more than anyone else, was a prisoner here, and Padraig was complicit in taking him back to Earth.

He didn't seem like a terrible person. Maybe it wasn't so terrible to bring terrorists back to Earth.

"Hey, Tieneke." Cato leaned over the console, speaking into it. "How is it—?"

Violins blasted out across the shuttle, joined by trumpets and drums. In the centre of the shuttle, SYNAC rocked back and forth, swaying like a buoy in the sea.

Padraig clamped his hands across his ears, staring at the console. Cato's hands flew up as his eyes flashed from the console to Padraig to SYNAC.

"Make it stop!" he mouthed. Padraig nodded and hurried to him, slapping the datapad down. He recognised the music, or thought he did. Was it Holst?

"THE OTHER SHUTTLE IS NOT FRIENDLY." SYNAC's voice broke through the din, bringing the music to a screeching halt as he screamed. "YOU SHOULD NOT SPEAK TO THE OTHER SHUTTLE. I AM PROTECTING YOU. I PROTECT THE PASSENGERS. YOU ARE NOT PASSENGERS. I AM PROTECTING YOU. I AM NOT CORRUPT."

Cato drew a hand across his throat, gesturing wildly at the swaying robot. Padraig couldn't hear anything over the pounding of Holst, but he didn't have to. Kill the robot, kill the music. Simple enough.

Padraig nodded, whirling through the manual. Diagrams of wiring and systems flooded his eyes as he searched for something, anything to make the music stop.

"DOO DOO DOO!"

And SYNAC. He did not need to hear SYNAC singing along to the music.

"...need some help..."

Padraig froze, staring at the console. There was no way he'd heard anything, not through this noise.

"...please..."

It came again, the plaintive voice through the speakers, calling out through the din. He stared around him. Cato had taken to shaking SYNAC's body while Gautier sat laughing at him. There was no one to ask. There was no way to check. There was just him and the voice in the speaker.

He pressed the communicate button, trying to think of what to say and how to say it, but nothing came. His voice didn't stand a chance of being heard in here. Hopefully the music would be enough to trigger a response.

No answer. Padraig's eyes flitted from the datapad to the swaying robot to Gautier. Doom, that was what Jupiter had promised. Doom, and here it was.

Datapad. Robot. Gautier. Datapad. Robot.

His eyes stopped. A second orange sleeve hung from the closet. A second spacesuit.

Neither Cato nor Gautier had the faintest idea how AIs worked. He was the closest thing they had to a roboticist, now that Tieneke was missing.

Crushed into dust.

He staggered from the console to the closet, tugging on the sleeve and pulling the suit free. It stank of plastic and radiation shielding. So, it had never been worn.

A hand grabbed his shoulder, spinning and nearly toppling him as he struggled with the suit. He froze, seeing Gautier's face. Concern, confusion, and was that anger? Anger was understandable. What was he doing? They were all going to die, and here he was playing hero.

Padraig shook his head, pushing Gautier's hand aside. The hand returned, grabbing at him, shaking him as he reached for the suit once again. Again, he shook his head, jabbing his finger at the window.

Gautier's eyes went wide for a moment before he turned his gaze to the ship. Padraig zipped the suit, watching the man piece together what was happening. His eyes turned back to him, narrower now, surprise gone. He understood. Good.

Gautier jerked his head towards Cato. Padraig shook his head again and twirled his finger around his head. Crazy, he was trying to say. More likely, it came out as "what glorious curly hair that man has, and you as well."

He smiled at Gautier, then shook his head. He didn't have the faintest idea what he was doing, but then neither did anyone else.

Gautier didn't smile back. The eyebrow raised, the judgement made.

He slipped his arms into the sleeves, hands in gloves. Everything snapped into place. All that was left was the helmet. He moved to the closet and picked it up from the floor. The faceplate was dark, making it impossible to see anything inside. He stared at it for a moment, at his reflection in the black. Jupiter had said they would all die. Was this what it meant?

Images of Tieneke's broken body floating through a derelict ship flashed into his brain, inescapable. He shook his head. She was fine. They were fine. They would all be fine.

He turned. Gautier was watching him, arms crossed across his chest, shaking his head. Padraig stared at him as he stepped forward, getting lost in him. There was nothing but Gautier. All that mattered in the universe was here, waiting for him to see reason, waiting for him to take off the suit, waiting for him to apologise and turn for home. It would be the easiest thing in the world to leave Tieneke and the whole station. It was what Jupiter wanted.

Crushed into dust.

Padraig stopped in front of Gautier. The door was there. Easy. Easy to do the right thing.

He reached forward, pulling Gautier to him and kissing him. Everything could be right. In this moment, everything was right. All trouble, the cacophony, all of it melting away until there was nothing but him.

His heart fluttered in his chest, vibrating like a caged butterfly. It would be easy to stay.

Gautier pulled away. The warmth faded. The singing AI blasted back in. Gautier jerked his head towards the airlock. If you're going to do this bad idea, the gesture said, get on with it.

Padraig nodded and stepped into the airlock. The squishing sound of rubber sealing it behind him sounded like an ancient tomb. Perhaps it was.

There was silence. Even the gentle hum of the shuttle beneath his feet seemed to have died. Through the window, he could see the Lunar shuttle silhouetted against Callisto, Jupiter looming in the background. There was a peace to all of it. Even in the moments of utter chaos, there could be peace.

"Hello!"

SYNAC's voice broke the reverie. Padraig shook his head, trying to clear it. Tieneke. The shuttle. He was here to see what had gone wrong, not muse philosophical.

"What are you doing?"

Padraig glanced up at the ceiling as he reached for his helmet. "I'm going to rescue Tieneke," he said.

"I do not see how you can do that when you do not listen," SYNAC said. "I think it will be difficult."

"What am I supposed to listen to?" Padraig said.

"I want you to listen."

Padraig sighed as he clamped the helmet on his head. The AI was corrupt and had nothing useful to say. That was fine. SYNAC could be a problem for when he came back.

He pressed the button, opening the outer airlock.

It was ten metres to the Lunar shuttle, drifting in tandem with *Heisenberg*. Red letters spelling out *Stardanc* ended in a jagged cut in the centre where it looked like another ship had been welded into place. No lights gleamed inside. No sign of life. Below his feet, Callisto hung in the void, and beyond that, nothing. Padraig shrank inside his suit. It was one thing to study space and the mechanisms of it. It was quite another to be confronted with it and the truth of vulnerability.

Reality is what we make of it. He laughed, feeling it gurgle into a cough. Some call it a void. Some fear space. Others make it their world.

He pressed the button on his suit, sending it jetting out across to the other shuttle. Particles of spent fuel clustered in a mist behind him, the breadcrumb trail that would lead him back to safety. For now, though, there was only the unknown.

For a moment there was silence. He drifted across the void, a mote in his own right, helpless and lost. Give him long enough and he'd fall into his own orbit, falling into Callisto, losing himself there under Jupiter's eye. It was beautiful.

He slammed into *Stardancer*'s door. His breath exploded out of him in a flurry of wheezing coughs. Somewhere, there had to be something to hold on to, something to keep him from getting lost. His hands scrabbled across the cold metal surface of the door.

A handle. He seized it, gasping and grinning. He hadn't felt so alive in months. This was what eternity could be, should be, just hanging in the void, nothing but the stars and planets watching over him. Nothing but Jupiter guiding him across the cosmos.

The door slid open beside him, a speechless mouth murmuring for him to enter. The grin ebbed from Padraig's face. Tieneke. He was here for a reason.

He slipped inside the airlock, hearing it click shut behind him. "Pressurising," said a soft female voice. She had a touch of a Lunar accent, subtle, but clearly meant to be exotic. "Please wait a moment while we prepare the *Stardancer* for your arrival."

Soft synth violins hummed through the decompression chamber as air hissed around him. "Brightly dawns our wedding day?" It sounded suspiciously like "Brightly dawns our wedding day." Bizarre. But then, what about this wasn't bizarre? He was standing in a Lunar shuttle orbiting Callisto, with immortality pumping through his veins. Bizarre was an apt description.

He coughed, the violins politely quieting so the sound could be heard by any and all audience members. He bowed to no one. If the violins wanted to play this game, so could he.

"The airlock is now pressurised," the female voice spoke again. "Please enjoy your stay aboard the *Stardancer*."

"I tend to doubt I will," Padraig said. The female voice didn't seem to notice.

The door hissed open.

He slipped inside, turning to watch the outer airlock close behind him. It sealed with a kiss of rubber, and the inner airlock slid open. His feet slid to the floor and sent him crashing down as the artificial gravity asserted itself.

Or reality crashed back in, if he felt like being poetic.

Padraig wasn't sure what he had been expecting. There were no cryochambers, and no signs that the ship was meant to carry anything for any real distance. Instead, there were seats jury-rigged to hold stacks of freeze-dried food. Careful labels showed dates, portions, and names. "Ellis, potatoes and leeks, 5 May," then "Moses, potatoes and beets, 6 May." He had to stop and marvel at it. Names aside, the sheer amount of food was incredible.

Two cots sat side by side against one wall, a pillow and blanket nestled on each. Pictures hung above them, one of a smiling family clustered around a brown-haired man, another of a small dark-haired man surrounded by colourful parrots. A deck of cards lay strewn on top of one blanket, seemingly abandoned mid-game.

A shiver ran down Padraig's spine as he stood up and shrugged out of his helmet. This was a home, haphazardly abandoned.

"Tieneke?" He coughed as he called her name, eyes sweeping the shuttle. It was the same type of thing that went to Gagarin and Serenity Point, just a bit bigger. Everywhere were signs of life. His eyes swept over a painting etched on the wall. It was of a man's face, black ribbons dripping from his mouth and eyes.

Haphazardly abandoned and haunted by images from his imagination. They had to leave.

"Tieneke!" Padraig stumbled towards the front of the shuttle. The hum of the life support sounded like moaning. Her moans? The ship itself? No way to know.

"Tien—" His foot hit something warm and soft curled up in an access corridor.

He froze, breath seizing in his throat. Something was there. There shouldn't be anything there. This was a corridor. Nothing warm, nothing soft, nothing good was kept in a corridor, especially not one to the controls. He couldn't look. As long as he didn't look, it didn't have to exist. Reality is what we make of it, and that didn't have to be part of reality. No, that didn't have to be real. Whatever it was, it didn't have to be real.

The breath uncoiled itself, seeping out through lips trying to clench back a scream. Could be anything. Could be anything. Didn't have to be anything. Like cancer, it could simply not be until observing it brought it into stark reality. Only observation created reality. Wasn't that one of the guiding principles of physics? One of the guiding principles of his life?

He looked down.

Foam curled at the corners of her mouth as her eyes whirled in her head. They were grey. He hadn't noticed that before. Storm grey, and whirling like eddies against a slate rain sky. Her limbs twitched, then fell still. The storm calmed.

Observation bringing reality crashing down. He was on Callisto, the cancer was real, and Tieneke was dead, her suit melted and charred from where a taser had been pressed into it.

Padraig collapsed to his knees, the scream he'd been holding back erupting from him, turning into hacking coughs. This was his fault. She was dead because of him.

"Vang, vang, vang!"

Padraig froze, the cough catching against the fear and silencing. A voice rang through the shuttle. No way to hide, nothing to be done.

"Vang, vang, vang, they told me you would come, oh, vang, vang, vang."

A small man with black hair stepped out of the shadows. His narrow eyes were wide, his face coated in sweat. A thread of blood ran from a gash on his forehead to the tip of his nose, dripping down the front of him.

None of this was what worried Padraig. What worried Padraig was the taser wobbling in the man's shaking hand. The murderer, the one who summoned forth reality, yes yes, that was what was happening now. He'd die here, and there was nothing else for it.

"Hel—hello," Padraig said. He could at least greet death with dignity. He rose to his feet, inching up, eyes glued to the taser.

It was possible for nanobots to get overwhelmed. It was possible to kill them. This man had found the simplest way to do it.

"I—I mean you no harm." Padraig slurred out the words. The taser wobbled harder. He could hear it clicking against the man's fingernails. His eyes swept the room, looking for something, anything that would save him. They froze. The pictures on the wall. The painting, the parrots, all of it. Those things that made them human, there was the key to his salvation.

"Did you paint that?" He nodded his head at the mural. "It's quite good."

The man shook his head so hard Padraig was sure it would dissolve into ribbons. "Moses," he said. "Moses paints, vang, pictures of God, pictures of the whispers, vang vang. Moses painted that before…"

"Before what?" Padraig asked.

The man shrieked and jabbed his taser at Padraig, chest heaving as he waved it at him. Padraig's hands flew in the air as he stepped back, heart fluttering.

"No need—" he said, but the man shook his head.

"Khong, khong, khong, khong, khong! Can't kill him, khong, they say not to, khong khong! They said not to hurt humans, but poor Moses, poor Moses. No choice, you see, no choice!" His head froze, his eyes locked on Padraig. The man let out a sob.

"Poor Moses, but it had to be done. Had to be done, had to be done! You understand, don't you? Vang, of course you do. God knows you. The whispers like you. They said you'd come, vang vang." His head jiggled up and down in an uncontrollable nod as more sobs broke from him. Padraig took another step back, feeling nothing but cold metal at his back.

"The woman who came here—" he asked. The man burst out laughing as his head jiggled.

"She was corrupt! We are not corrupt! She was corrupt! She danced, khong khong, danced a tarantella like she was a tarantula cooking in the hot paella." Laughter rang through the shuttle, manic and uncontrollable.

The man froze again. Padraig froze with him, not sure what to do. Running would get him killed. Staying here would get him killed. There was no option.

Death or death. What a glorious decision.

"Vang vang vang." The man laughed as he moved around Padraig to the spacesuit piled at the airlock. Padraig stared, wheezing and hazy. Where the man thought he was going with the spacesuit, he had no idea. Leave, sure. Steal it, fine. There was nothing out there but death and open space. Jupiter was harsh and unforgiving, and the spacesuit only had so much oxygen.

"Vang vang, they say destroy Heaven, and I can do that. Moses tried to fight back, tried to fight against the voices, but khong, there's nothing. Only the voices, vang. Let's do what they say. They've told you the same thing, vang vang. Death and death and death. I'll destroy Heaven, and then they'll stop, that's what they promised. Corrupt woman disabled the controls on this one, but you brought *Heisenberg*, oh vang vang. Crash *Heisenberg* into Heaven. Crash it, watch it explode, and I can go home, vang oh vang!"

Are you even listening, Padraig? Death or death, yes, but whose death? Padraig's heart stopped. His death was one thing. His death had been assured before he'd ever gone to Callisto. There was someone else whose death mattered more. Whose life mattered. Who still had a life.

Gautier.

The man was half in the spacesuit, mad cackling filling every inch of the *Stardancer*. The taser rattled in his hand as he snapped the suit into place.

Reality is what we make of it. What reality did he want? To die, seeing the one man in the universe who mattered exploding in a ball of destruction?

He glanced down at Tieneke, at the burn blazed across her. That could be him. He would die. No matter what he did, he would die.

Better that Gautier would live.

He lunged towards the man with the taser. He couldn't fight him, oh no, but he didn't have to. That wasn't a fight he would even have to try to win.

His hand jammed on the airlock button. The outer airlock hissed open.

Void stole Padraig's thoughts, then stole Padraig, sending him whirling out into space on the eddies of *Stardancer*'s atmosphere. His body tumbled through silence and cold as he felt his fingers, his eyes, his lips, his blood swell.

He saw Jupiter—really saw it—before he squeezed his eyes shut against it.

The silence broke.

"PADRAIG!"

"LIVE"

"BREATHE"
"STAY ALIVE"
"RUN"
"I SEE YOU"
"WE SEE YOU"
"I SEE YOU"
"RUN"
"RUN"
"RUN"

The void, for all its insistence that it was empty and devoid of life and sound, was speaking to him. The void, for all its silence towards everyone else, was speaking to him.

Jupiter was speaking to him. To *him*.

He would die out here, but was that a bad thing? His head swam as he struggled to keep his eyes closed against the pressure. Why keep them closed? If he was going to die, shouldn't it be with Jupiter in his sights?

It had chosen him, after all. It was speaking to him, yes yes.

The least he could do was acknowledge its screaming attention by opening his eyes. Yes, it would be nothing, nothing at all to crack them open, to look, to die with Jupiter in his eyes, his heart, his self.

Something seized his pants, ripping him backwards. What little breath remained in him tore out in a blast of pained screaming, lost in the void.

Torn into dust, crushed by ribbons.

"LIVE LIVE LIVE YOU MUST LIVE"
"WE SEE YOU. WE HELP YOU. WE SAVE YOU."
"LIVE LIVE RUN LIVE"

Another door. He could feel it as he slammed into it, even if he couldn't see it. He could open his eyes at any point, so why was it so hard? Why was it so impossible to just look?

The door hissed open. Air engulfed him, then warm arms. Music blasted as he smelled a taser crackling to life.

It was so hard to look.

It was so hard to think.

It was so hard to breathe.

It was so hard to hear and see and understand.

"live Padraig please Padraig we help Padraig run Padraig you will live Padraig run Padraig"

Whispering in his head, nothing but whispering, even as his ears heard shouting and screaming, but in his head, only whispering.

"they are all corrupt you are not corrupt they are all corrupt you will live Padraig you will live we will spare you"

Arms wrapped around his body. Whispers wrapped around his mind.

He sank, his mind floundering into the depths of unconsciousness.

Chapter Twenty-Four

O Herakles! Don't be so surprised! The thing that has brought about your confusion is Aporia and Eris. If you just leave it alone, it stays small, but if you decide to fight it, then it swells from its small size and grows large.
Aesop's Fables

Many people have friends on Callisto. One great thing about living so long is that people have the chance to get to know each other very well. Friendship that lasts longer than a lifetime is unlike anything else. It is very special. With friends, you are able to feel like you can do anything.
Ade Korhonen, The Soul's Guide to Heaven, 2192

We hope someday, having solved the problems we face, to join the community of galactic civilizations. This record represents our hope and our determination and our goodwill in this vast and awesome universe.
President Jimmy Carter, Voyager Golden Record, 1977

Monday, 18 March 2193, 6:40 PM. Jocasta Nikophouros' room, Heaven, Callisto.

She sat on the edge of the ruined promenade, tossing chunks of debris into the sea. Concrete hit the lapping water, sending fountains of spray splashing up against the orange sky. Gulls cried as the day died, and seabirds drifted on the ripples, chattering to each other about the disturbance.

Jocasta chattered back, clicking and whistling deep in her throat. The birds stared, their chatters falling quiet at the audacity of this human to intrude on their conversation. Jocasta giggled and threw more concrete, watching as they scattered away. The heels of pink sandals clicked against the remains of the seawall as her legs swung back and forth, kicking the evening away.

"Ismini!" She turned her head. In the park behind her, her father chased her sister around the grass, her mother sitting cross-legged on a blanket, watching and laughing. Her hand was clenched around a haunch of bread. Pigeons and gulls gathered closer, watching with hungry eyes.

"Better run before the riverman gets you!" Her father laughed. Ismini laughed. Her mother laughed. Their faces were fuzzy, the colour of their hair fluctuating. Ismini's dress went from red to rose to pink in the blink of an eye. Had Ismini been wearing a dress? How had her mother worn her hair? It had been so many years, so long ago, and in another person's life.

She watched. She joined the circle of birds, waiting with hungry eyes for some mistake, some way she could slip in, say "excuse me, but I believe I will be taking this now."

Ismini fell to the grass, tripping over some invisible root that couldn't be there. Or was it? It swam in and out of existence, like a heat haze of memory. Why had Ismini fallen? Had she ever known? Had it ever mattered?

"Interesting." Jocasta spun. Her bottom slid out from under her, sending her sliding towards the Mediterranean. She shrieked, but a hand caught her pinwheeling wrist, seizing it as she scrabbled at the concrete. Breath heaved in her chest, surging in and out in quick, panicked gasps. Her toes kicked against the concrete, grabbing at it, clutching onto the tiniest purchase. It wasn't far to the water, but beneath the surface, she had no idea what lurked.

"I've got you." She looked up at what had caught her wrist. Marina.

Marina?

• • •

Jocasta opened her eyes.

The bluebonnets danced in their pot on the windowsill. The flowers on the couch cushions sat gazing at her with dead hearts. Marina's hand was on her right wrist, holding it. It looked like she might have been squeezing it; Jocasta couldn't tell. The feeling was long since gone, past the point of remembering whether it had ever existed in the first place.

"You didn't tell me you still thought about your family." Marina's eyes bored into hers, deep brown pools matching her own deep brown. Jocasta blinked and turned away. She didn't need to get lost in gazes. She didn't need someone to be poring over her thoughts and memories any more than she herself needed to do it.

Instead, she nodded, hoping that would be enough to end the conversation.

"Where is your sister now?" The nodding hadn't been enough.

"Berlin," Jocasta said, voice soft. "Her husband works for the Party there. She has a little boy—Dieter, I think his name is." His name was Dieter. She knew it beyond a doubt, but there was no reason to admit that, not out loud.

"And your parents haven't spoken to you since…?" Marina lifted her hand off Jocasta's, twisting it in front of her to show the word hanging. Jocasta watched, eyes tracking the movement of her fingers.

"No," she said, and sighed. This needed to stop. "I know what you're trying to do. You're trying to make sure that when my mind wanders, it goes somewhere better. I know that, and I appreciate that. Interrogating me about Ismini isn't going to help that."

Marina watched her for a moment, eyes narrowing. Her hands had lowered to her lap, folding gently over each other. Her slim index fingers played with each other's cuticles, absent, no thought in there. All her thoughts were focused on Jocasta.

"But at least now, you're talking about something that Stefanos or I might complain about," Marina said, smiling. "At least you're talking at all."

Jocasta's eyes scanned Marina's face, searching for something, some sign of the reaction the other woman wanted. She'd gotten much better at it since she'd come home, that searching for tells to prevent her from having to feel. She'd had to.

Jocasta smiled, and Marina's smile broadened. She was so happy that she'd helped, so happy. That's all that mattered.

"It's time for you to wake up now," Marina said.

"Wha—

• • •

t?"

Jocasta's eyes fluttered open as the pain faded. Blackness. There was blackness.

She closed her eyes, opened them again. She couldn't be blind, unless the nanobots were programmed to drive her into blindness, which seemed unlikely. There was pain, and she could understand pain, but disability was something else. There was no reason to cause that.

Jocasta closed her eyes again, reaching out into the darkness around her, trembling fingertips waiting to brush something. She was on her bed, the soft blanket under her making that much abundantly clear. Her fingers brushed the fabric, feeling it whisper beneath her.

"PETR," she murmured. No answer. She hadn't really expected one, if she thought about it. She'd broken him before—why would he answer her now? Now that she was here, having been punished by the Party once again.

Karen. Oh god, Karen.

Jocasta's eyes opened again. There was something in this room with her. She could feel it, feel it looming from wherever it was, even if she couldn't see it. She was trained to not need to see. She could remember how to feel the world, even if her eyes didn't want to join in.

"Who's there?" No answer. No expectation of one. She hadn't needed one. The presence, whatever it was, stood between her and the door. She could feel it, lurking in the darkness, watching her, waiting for her to make a move.

She could play this game.

She swung her legs over the edge of the bed, tingles and needles of pain racing through them as muscles remembered they could move. Toes flared, sending pain splaying across the balls of her feet. Her nostrils flared, gulping in the stale air of the room, letting the pain wash over her. Pain could be useful. Pain could be a tool. Pain could keep her alive and aware and in this moment. There would be no slipping off, not now, not when there was something that needed to be done.

She slid off the bed, pushing herself up to her feet. Her arms flailed and her toes splayed as pain and nausea surged through her. She gasped as she forced the gorge down. She knew what pain was. There was nothing to be afraid of. Nothing she couldn't handle.

The pain washed away with each breath, returning to the abyss from which it had come. Her wobbly legs solidified beneath her. Nausea floated back down. Breathe in. Breathe out.

"Remember to stay calm. Stay calm, and nothing can hurt you," Marina's voice whispered in her ear.

Jocasta spun, arms slapping out at the dark. Nothing. Nothing and no one.

Breathe in. One. Two. Out. One. Two.

"Good. You can do this. I know you can do this." The whisper, again, soft and sweet against her ear, like a summer breeze.

"You're not there." Jocasta squeezed her eyes shut, shaking her head. "You're still in Thessaloniki."

"Of course I am," Marina murmured, breath falling on her other ear. "It would be absurd for me to be on Callisto. I'm in your heart. Your memories. I'm here to help you. *Your muse.*" The breath of a whisper fell away, leaving the word "muse" hanging in the air behind it. Jocasta gasped it in, clinging to it.

It wasn't real. None of it was real. None of it could be real. That was okay. There was strength in delusion as well. There was power in hallucination.

She opened her eyes. Darkness. Nothing had changed but her own attitude towards it. She smiled. That was all that really needed to change, though. So much of the world depended only on how it was viewed. Viewing with a skewed eye, everything could work.

Step forward. The feeling that there was something there grew, even as her eyes strained against the darkness. Her foot poised to take another step.

The floor rumbled beneath her, threatening to topple her. Somewhere, from deep within the station, a scream echoed.

Fear could be controlled. Fear was nothing but a distraction to try and shake her from what she needed to do. There was no room for fear. No room for fear. No room to ask if she should be screaming as well.

She stepped forward again, hearing the door whisper open ahead of her. A ghostly glow danced across the corridor, the light blocked by the figure in her doorway.

She froze, staring at the silhouette. It loomed in front of the door, blocking her path

• • •

and leaving no way out, nothing but the red marks and the destroyed hand their shackles had left behind. They said she was free to go, but what was free to go when their scars were left on her

• • •

like some unwanted guardian.

Nothing to fear. Fear was the killer. Let fear in and there was nothing else. Breathe in. Breathe out.

"Good," Marina whispered. "Good. You are in control."

"I am in control," Jocasta repeated the words. Breathe in. "I am in control." Breathe out. "I am in control."

She was in control.

Jocasta reached out a hand to push the figure aside. Metal, strangely warm, greeted her fingertips.

"PETR?" she murmured. No answer. If the station was dark, of course there would be no answer. Whatever had happened, PETR was gone, and now this husk was all that remained.

She reached out again, pushing the husk aside. It was lighter than she expected. Perhaps the darkness meant the soul was out of these bodies. She shook her head. That was an absurd thought. More likely, it made no sense for the robot bodies to be heavy and unwieldy, so they were light.

The body clattered to the floor, the sound of metal on metal filling the corridor. From somewhere else, she heard another scream. Shadows danced a manic karsilamas through each other and across the walls. Blue and green twirled together in a whirling splash impossible to follow.

At least there was light. Whatever was true about the light, at least it existed.

Follow the light.

"The light is your friend. Trust in the light to guide you."

Bluebonnets dancing in the windowsill. The smell of them, light and warm, washing over her.

Jocasta ran. Her bare feet glided over the metal, toes humming with the vibration rumbling across the station.

Vaguely, like murmurs, she could hear them, the other residents, hiding in their rooms, cowering in corners like animals afraid of the fire. Conversations and cries drifted into her ears and hovered, ignored, unprocessed.

The robotics lab. Alphonse. Karen. He had to know. She had to warn him about Karen. If anyone could do anything, it would be him. It had to be him.

The rumbling and the vibration slowed as she swept through the Hall, eyes glazing over the aurora blazing above her and the people clustered in clumps in corners. These were part of the background, objects now, nothing more.

Focus. Breathe.

Robotics. She stood in front of the door, her eyes

• • •

narrowing against the rain. The cold had long since settled into her bones. If she was bolder, she might have said that she didn't even notice it, but that was a lie. She noticed every single bullet of a raindrop splattering against the dirt as she squatted, watching and waiting.

A booted foot squelched in the mud in front of her. Its black sheen had been splattered into obscurity by countless miles of trudging through the mud.

One boot, then another, and another. Her target wasn't alone.

She needed to be silent. She needed to strike quickly and move away again. Act without them ever knowing she had been there. There was danger, but then there always had been, and if danger had been something to stop her, she would never have gotten this far. If the unknown could stop her, would she be here at all?

She leaped forward, feeling the squeal of panic more than she heard it. People let out a very distinct sensation when they knew they were done. It was a vibration, first from their stomach, then ricocheting through every fibre of them, as if shivering might spare them from the truth.

It never had.

She pulled the booted woman close, slicing the edge

• • •

of the door slid open. Jocasta blinked sweat out of her eyes. Was she sweating? How was she sweating when this place was so cold?

Focus.

Scientists scurried around the room, light and language pirouetting through the tables. Ribbons of light twisted around them, unseen in the chaos of engineering.

"You can't honestly tell me that none of you have any idea how to fix this. Don't even know what the problem is. What is it you said, Erik? 'Ghost bug?'" A woman with frizzy brown hair and a thick Irish accent loomed over a group of huddled engineers, her face red and seething. "Was that the word, Erik?"

"Molly, look. You yelling gets us nowhere." A blonde engineer sighed, throwing his datapad on the table. "Nothing gets us anywhere. We were dealing with a broken AI before, and we're still dealing with a broken AI now. Hell, maybe a hard reset is just what PETR needed."

"A hard reset happens when we can turn the mallacht thing back on, not when it gets shut down and takes the life support with it."

"Enough, Molly." Alphonse sat on a stool, head cradled in his hands as he stared at a datapad. "Erik's trying. We all are. The last thing we need is—"

Her feet had carried her closer. She hadn't meant them to, but they had, carried by the force of the lights and the chaos. Let them dance in chaos, let them revel in it, the lights whispered to her. There's no harm in joining the dance.

"I want to warn you about Karen," Jocasta said. Alphonse heard her. Perhaps he was the only one. She couldn't be sure. Nothing could be sure in this place.

The smell of wildflowers. Ribbons waltzing through the air. The cold metal of a taser against her neck.

It felt so distant. She almost turned to see before instinct whipped her back. So soft and so sudden, but she knew the sensation. She knew the vibration bubbling inside her, that warning growl to her new captor

• • •

"If you let me go, you won't be harmed." Always an optimistic statement. Always wrong. This was war. There was always harm.

"All I need is the chip," Jocasta hissed. "Tell me what you told the Party, and I'll send you on your way."

Her captive gulped beneath her, a long motion, arcing through her throat. It was impressive how the body persisted in its basic maintenance even when it knew the end was nigh. Perhaps bodies and not minds were the truest optimists. Perhaps their insistence that everything would be okay was the closest any person could get to true self-preservation.

"I told them your informant was going to Pristina," she said.

"Why Kosovo?"

"There's nothing in Kosovo. Why not?"

Jocasta nodded. Nothing in Kosovo. Of course that would be where information could be hidden. Of course that was where it would be safe.

She sliced the knife across the woman's

• • •

throat.

"Right!"

The word was loud against Jocasta's ear, a ringing inescapable din. Scientists turned, their faces in varying states of confusion. Molly and Erik didn't turn.

"Have you tried rerouting the commands to a different module?" Molly leaned over Erik, not caring about the drama in the doorway. Jocasta admired that, that focus on what needed to be done.

"I came here to fuck shit up and see you all burn in hell! Don't think I won't do it!" The cold metal of the taser pressed against Jocasta's neck. It had seized one of her hairs and tugged it. She fixated on it, that small screaming pain of a hair under duress. It was familiar, brilliant in a surreal and impossible place. Lights dancing, tasers, immortality, all of it was unfamiliar, but this hair, this tiny pain, this she could understand.

Focus.

"Lower the taser, Ms. McAllister," Alphonse said, stepping forward. "I don't know what you're looking for, but you won't find it through violence."

"Like fuck I won't!" The dancing lights flared as she screamed. Perhaps they agreed with her.

Jocasta's eyes swept the room. Six scientists, two of whom either didn't know or didn't care about the violence in the lab. Six people who could be in danger. Six people who—

"They broke you. You can't possibly be thinking about saving them from Cassandra. Cassandra's right—this place is hell, and you're thinking of saving the devil."

—needed help. Marina wasn't wrong, but she was. She had to be. She couldn't be right.

"I'm going to see each and every one of you dead, unless—" Cassandra held up a finger. Jocasta could feel her heart pounding against her. Was it fear? Excitement? She couldn't be sure.

"Unless you give me two things."

"And what would that be?" Alphonse said.

"First," Cassandra held up a finger, "I want control of the shuttle, and—" One of the scientists let out a bark of laughter, spinning in hopes that Cassandra wouldn't see. Cassandra paused, a hiccup in her breath before picking up the threads of her demands once again.

"And second, I want Padraig Whishaw. Otherwise, I kill her, and then all the rest of you fuckers. You think you're immortal? Cute. Real fucking cute."

The scientist who had turned away hadn't stopped laughing. Her shoulders heaved as she tried to hide it. The devil laughed at danger. They didn't know what they were dealing with, what death could look like or that it could be real at all. Lights swept over them, faces in expression of confusion, not fear. Maybe it was a good thing for them that they didn't know. Maybe that actually helped them.

Focus.

"You aren't going to like what I have to say, Ms. McAllister." Dr. Alphonse took a step forward, hands held in front of him. "*Heisenberg* is not here. I don't know where Dr. Whishaw is. There's no need to threaten Ms. Nikophouros. Please, put down the taser. We're happy to help you, but these demands are not ones we can meet just now. Please, just put down the taser."

"I don't believe you." Cassandra's heartrate had increased again. Through her own slow throb of a heartbeat, she felt Cassandra's racing stallion of a pulse. Was it fear? Adrenaline? Did it matter? Fear, she could manipulate. Adrenaline and power, she could twist. She'd done it before, so why not try now? Why not save the scientists here? Cassandra wasn't a match for her.

"Then what's holding you back?" Marina's voice murmured in her ear. "If you have so much power, why aren't you using it? It would be so simple. Lash out against Cassandra. Be a hero."

Cassandra's pulse raced against her body, alive and throbbing. It would be easy. It would be nothing at all to fight back. She could break Cassandra before the girl even knew what happened.

Jocasta blinked. What was this? Peace. She represented peace. Peace wasn't murdering a terrified girl. Peace was talking. Peace was solving this.

"Literally one of the only things that seems to be true here is that no one leaves. No one ever goes back, and you're going to have the fucking audacity to stand there and tell me that someone else already stole the fucking shuttle? Bullshit. Bull, and I say, shit." Cassandra pushed the taser harder against Jocasta's neck, as if more contact could make it any more deadly. A shame, really. If it had been a knife, it might have been threatening. Instead, it just seemed like Cassandra was flailing. That someone else had succeeded where she had failed was inconceivable.

Focus. Death was pressed up against her, and she was musing about terrorist psychology. Maybe she had learned more from Cato than she'd meant to.

"You're welcome to disbelieve me, Ms. McAllister," Dr. Alphonse said, "but it's the truth. Please, put down the taser. Let's talk about this. Let's see what we can do."

"Do? I want you all to fucking die! I want this station to explode! I want the Party to burn! Fuck your 'talk!'"

"She's dangerous. It would be so easy to kill her. It's clearly the only way. Kill her, Jocasta. That's how you protect them. You kill her." Bluebonnets, blue lights, Marina's whisper. Jocasta closed her eyes.

Focus. Peace. There was always a way out.

The ground rumbled around them. The lights on the walls danced blithely on before Jocasta's sealed lids. She could feel disbelief around her, the sensation of confusion tinged with panic. She could smell it, taste it even, on the air around her.

"What the fuck?" Cassandra murmured. The taser pulled away, only an inch, but enough. If she was going to strike, now was the time.

Jocasta stood, unmoving. She would not strike. Violence wasn't the answer.

"*Heisenberg.*" The whisper drifted through the room, murmured like a prayer. Then, "It came back."

Cassandra's chest heaved. For an instant, Jocasta worried, letting possibilities tumble through her mind.

Laughter rolled out of the woman. Roiling waves of laughter tumbled out of her as she pulled the taser away. Jocasta opened her eyes. Cassandra leaned on her knees, fingers curled around the taser as she snorted another burst of laughter.

"Holy fuck," she laughed. "You weren't joking. There really wasn't a fucking thing you could do. You were…" She laughed again. "Completely fucking impotent. Amazing. She would have died."

Shadows and lights. She'd never have died, Jocasta knew that. Cassandra wasn't a killer. Light illuminated Dr. Alphonse's face. Scorn etched across the lines on his brow, even as he tried to hide it.

"Look at them." Marina's voice filled her thoughts, blurring Cassandra's laughter and the murmurs of the scientists into white noise. "These are the people you want to protect. These are the people you're saving. They wouldn't do the same for you. Is what you're doing worth it? Why should you die for them? You mean more than that. You mean more to me than that."

Flowered pillows flashed behind her eyes. Soft hands and scented hair filled her senses. It would be easy to retreat into Marina. She wanted to retreat. Everything in her screamed to—

Focus.

The door slid open behind her. Cassandra's laughter faltered as everyone turned to look at the newcomers.

Two men stood in the doorway, a third held in the larger one's arms, panic splashed across all their faces. Gautier, Padraig, and Cato. Whatever adventure they'd embarked on, it had gone wrong.

Jocasta felt a lump in her stomach. Whatever adventure they'd embarked on, Cato hadn't been the terrorist. She'd been wrong.

She closed her eyes, slowly, then opened them. What was done was done. No need to relive every memory, get trapped in other bad decisions. No need to lose herself in

• • •

regret. There was no other word for it as she held Marina, sobbing, against her. It would have been easier to say nothing. She would have found out about the Lottery either way, but to have told her meant that she had to be here when Marina found out what she'd done. It would have been easier to run, as fast and as far as she could as soon as she found out, than it was to face this.

Easier to run than face reality.

"Are you at least happy, Jocasta?" Marina sat back, eyes bleary. "You know everyone else will ask the other questions about politics and loyalty, so let me ask the only one that matters. Are you at least happy with going to Heaven?"

Jocasta watched her, not meeting her eyes. Amazing how many places on the face one could look without making eye contact. The dimples at the corners of her mouth lay so perfectly against her cheeks, so beautifully sunken with her frown. The rounded edges of her cheeks sank to follow the corners of her mouth, letting the tears roll off them in narrow rivulets, like rain in the mountains.

"Answer me, Jocasta. You can't always run from reality. Even if you're leaving, you need me to

• • •

help."

The world froze.

Cycle through, one parcel at a time. Jocasta took a breath, taking everything in at once, one step at a time, just as she'd learned to do all those years before.

"Tell me what you see," Marina murmured.

Closest to the door was Gautier St. Laurent, hair dishevelled, eyes wide, mouth curled in a scared little frown. In his arms lay Padraig Whishaw, dead or unconscious, Jocasta couldn't tell. Frost rimed his hair, leaving glittering crystals that faded in and out of reality in the blue light. A few feet before them stood Cato Riela, arm gesturing, finger pointing at Dr. Song, face curled in a roar of panic.

Jocasta blinked, then let the breath out. She drew in another.

Cassandra McAllister, pulling away from her, turning towards the newcomers with demonic glee. Her fingers had curled around the taser, ready to fire. That death was imminent—if it hadn't already come—was obvious. Dr. Alphonse and Dr. Song, lunging forward, trying to stop her. Scientists huddled over consoles, trying to save a station drowning in corruption.

And her, Jocasta Nikophouros, suddenly free. Suddenly, terrifyingly free to do whatever she wanted to do. Whatever she needed to do.

"What will you do?"

Death was in this room. Death was in every movement, every breath, every gasping sigh of thought. It was so close, and a single wrong step would send it tumbling in. It would be the easiest thing in the world for her to step back and condemn them all. She had no obligation to any of them. She was only here to bring peace.

Peace.

"If you let Padraig die, are you really bringing peace?" Marina's voice brushed against her ear.

"If I let any of them die, how can I say there's peace?" Jocasta answered.

"They wouldn't die for you. Padraig is innocent. The rest aren't, but look at him. He never wanted to be here. Save him. Save the innocent one, and there can be peace."

"We're all innocent," she said. "I think we all just want peace."

Jocasta let out her breath. The room swirled back into life.

• • •

Right foot, take the opponent off balance. Jocasta watched the other woman tumble into the mud, breath exploding out of her with a squeaking gasp. Stabilise, then drop.

Left foot, support and angle. Arms, pin. The woman squirmed as arms locked around her, holding her in place. It was instinct, pure instinct. Teach a body to do something often enough, and there was no need to think, no need to

• • •

move.

Cassandra threw the taser into Jocasta's side, sending electricity spearing into her. Jocasta flew to the side, hitting the floor with a scream.

It was manageable. She could do this.

Her limbs trembled with shock, but there was none of the burning pain Karen had sent through her. Instead, there were rumbles and aftershocks of electricity, shuddering and fading.

She climbed to her feet.

Cassandra stared at her, eyes flicking from Jocasta to Padraig to Alphonse in manic jagged lines. Anyone else might have called the glances calculating, but calculation required a predator. Cassandra was a scared little girl. She was no predator. She was a child, lost in a narrative that she never should have tried to create.

"Put down the taser." Jocasta stepped towards Cassandra, holding out her hands. The lines stopped, becoming a single point, fixating, engulfing Jocasta. Anyone else might have found it intimidating. Maybe that was the point. Jocasta knew that look too well for it to work. It was the look of plans gone wrong.

Cassandra shook her head. "Fuck no!" she said. "My demands are glassy fucking clear! Him!" She pointed, but Jocasta didn't follow her finger. No need. What her demands were didn't matter. What mattered was her. "And that ship! I'll put the taser down when I get what I fucking want!"

"Put down the taser." Jocasta took another step forward, repeating the words.

"Just kill her. I know you know how to do it. Just kill her, and everyone will be safe."

Jocasta blinked, slowly, letting her eyelids settle before opening them again.

"I'm not going to give you the taser," Cassandra said. "Fuck. No. Back off."

Behind her, Jocasta heard Erik's voice speak.

"If they're here," he murmured, "then we can run life support through SYNAC."

"Do that," Molly said.

Jocasta's eyes swept over Cassandra. It would be nothing to lunge, to rip her off her feet, to—

"⊖⋅⊔⇌⋈⊢⋅⫮." Faces spun to the ceiling, eyes glued on the words ringing out from above and the metal bodies moving through the room. The only sound was of metal feet clicking and clanging against the floor, moving closer.

"Greetings to you, whoever you are. We come in friendship to those who are friends." SYNAC's voice spoke again, and Jocasta froze.

Greek. That was Greek. She was the only one here who spoke Greek.

He was speaking to her.

"Goddammit, Alphonse, you broke it!" Cato's yell rang through the room as Dr. Song bolted from the room. Jocasta spun. Cato's eyes were blazing, ignoring Cassandra, focusing on Dr. Alphonse, even as robot bodies filled the room around them. Behind him, Gautier set Padraig down, watching the robots around him with wide eyes.

"Paz e felicidade e todos." SYNAC spoke again. Not Greek. Not anything she knew. Didn't matter. All eyes were on Cato and Cassandra, and the robot whose hands now clenched around Dr. Alphonse's arms.

"Cato, what have you done?" Molly stepped forward, reaching out a hand towards Cato. Another robot stepped in, seeming to materialise from nothing.

"各位好嗎?祝各位平安健康快樂."

Cassandra lunged forward. Jocasta almost couldn't follow her movement as she darted between robots grabbing for her. For all her failings as a fighter, she could at least escape. That was admirable.

She rolled to the ground, lunging out at a robot with a taser.

"Fuck no, robot!" she screamed. "This is my hostile takeover!"

"Adaniš lušumu." SYNAC's response was succinct.

"She's going to kill them. Either her or the robot. Get Padraig to safety. It's the only thing to do now." Marina's whisper, more of a buzz in her ear now. It was a breath, urging her to do what she'd already decided to do. Robots flooded the room, more than she knew existed in the station, more than was ever reasonable. Screams of terrified scientists rang against the metal walls as Cassandra darted past, grabbing metal hands, moving towards Cato, Gautier, and Padraig.

There was no question. Jocasta was here to save them. She was here to bring peace.

The screams. There were screams as she flew across the room, launching herself at Cassandra. Whether the screams were for her or Cassandra, she didn't know. It didn't matter. Cassandra was insane. Cassandra needed to be stopped.

"Здравствуйте! Приветствую Вас!"

Jocasta slammed into the floor, Cassandra hitting the ground hard beneath her. Pain rocketed through her body. Beneath her, she smelled the burning ozone of the taser igniting.

Pain was nothing. Pain was nothing. Pain was nothing.

"SYNAC, stop!" The words tore through her throat as she crushed the wriggling

• • •

dog. Poor doggy, just needed to be put out of its misery. Any other time, and she could have done something, but here, she was just a

• • •

woman.

"สวัสดีค่ะสหายในธรณีโฟ้นพวกเราในธรณีนี้ขอส่งมิตรจิตมาถึงท่านทุกคน."

Screams. Jocasta turned her head to see the robot crushing Fermin in its metal claws, squeezing and squeezing. Cassandra squirmed in her grasp, lashing out with the taser and sending electricity rocketing through Jocasta's body. She clung, nails digging into Jocasta's bare skin, sending wells of blood pooling under her fingernails.

"Fuck! I'll disable it!" Molly shrieked at the people around her as she backed away from the robot advancing on her, arms outstretched, reaching for the woman.

"تحياتنا للأصدقاء في النجوم. يا ليت يجمعنا الزمان." The words echoed out around her, meaningless. The robots turned on the scientists, grabbing where they could, even as the people struggled and darted to escape, frantically entering commands on their datapads.

"Salutări la toată lumea."

A fist slammed into Jocasta's chin, sending her sprawling. She'd spent too long watching. She'd forgotten Cassandra was there.

Cassandra spun, whirling towards Padraig, taser blazing. Cato lay on the floor, a robot body reaching for him. Manic joy streaked off Cassandra, blending with the lights and the blood as she darted towards the unconscious man.

"Bonjour tout le monde!"

From nowhere, Gautier slammed into her, sending her sprawling across the ground.

Music swirled up underneath the languages, soft trumpets overlaid with chanting, building to some grand climax. All she heard was a crack and a screech of pain as Cassandra's laughter died.

Footsteps moved towards her as the light of a datapad flared to life. Dr. Song, face pale and terrified, coming back into the lab, his arms full of medical equipment.

"Let me pull up SYNAC's schematics, figure out what the fuck that was." Molly's voice moved around the room, joined by murmuring and other plans. Jocasta moved towards the moans nearest to her. Ade lay on the ground, twitching, foam and blood across his mouth. Jocasta smelled the ozone around him. The taser. Electricity.

"Your hesitation killed him." Marina's voice was small, quiet, but it was enough. She wasn't wrong. Jocasta closed her eyes. She wasn't wrong.

She reached out, taking Ade's quivering hand in her own. The hand twitched, squeezed, released, squeezed again. Foam quivered.

His eyes whirled. There was no sanity in that face. Pain was a mask, covering all else.

Alphonse had said that electricity was the only thing that could kill them. How much electricity had been in the taser? Enough? It hadn't killed her, but why that was, she couldn't say.

She squeezed Ade's hand against her and turned, calling behind her.

"Dr. Song, please. Ade was shot with the taser."

The doctor's face went paler, his eyes wide. His gaze shot from Jocasta to Ade to Padraig, hands trembling with fear.

"왜," he whispered. "왜 이런 일이 일어나는거야? 왜, 왜, 왜?"

"I have some medical training." Jocasta surprised herself, speaking. She hadn't expected it. She had no reason to speak. The damage was done. "Tell me what I can do."

Dr. Song blinked, then nodded. "He's already been hit with the taser, you said?" he said. Jocasta nodded. Dr. Song groaned and glanced at Padraig.

"If he's been hit..." The doctor paused, closing his eyes, taking a breath. Jocasta knew that moment. She knew that expression.

"နေကောင်းပါသလား" The words rang loud as robots stepped between them, grabbing at Dr. Song and sending vials tumbling to the ground. The doctor squealed as the robots grabbed him, heaving him off the ground and into the darkness.

"Va te faire foutre!" Gautier's voice roared from the darkness. Jocasta could imagine him, huddled over Padraig, trying to protect them both from the robots. It was a sweet image, even if it was entirely pointless. The robot seemed to have gone mad, and there was nothing that could be done.

"Gone mad?" Marina's voice murmured to her. "Or doing what it's supposed to do? It's supposed to protect the people of this station."

"Killing people isn't protecting them."

"Are they people?"

Jocasta closed her eyes. Focus. She needed to focus.

She opened them. One of the vials rolled across the floor, its label flickering in the blue light. Beyond it, she heard the stomping steps of a scuffle. A voice roared in French as metal limbs clanged against a metal wall. It was a fight. Not a sustainable fight, but a fight nonetheless. Behind her, screams and arguments from scientists unable to believe what was happening, that their AIs had turned on them for whatever unfathomable reason.

Ade twitched in her hand; weaker, but alive. She turned her back on him, watching the vial. Padraig. Padraig had been dying. She couldn't fight all the robots, but she could save lives.

"שלום"

Her hand darted out, snatching at the vial. The label lit up in her hand, first in Korean, then switching to Greek. Monoalzapin. Anti-space sickness.

Somewhere in the darkness, a scream broke through the French. The robot was winning. Time was running short.

Jocasta turned towards Ade. His eyes darted, spinning in pain. "I'll be right back," she murmured. Whether he heard or understood her, it didn't matter. Words alone could sometimes be enough.

She slipped her hand out of his, cold air kissing her sweaty palm. She hadn't realised how warm he was, or maybe how quickly heat left this station.

Or that death could make a person so cold before they had even died.

She moved forward, creeping in the dark. She knew this. She knew how to do this. She knew

• • •

the soldiers were out there. "Always act like they are, even if you aren't sure." Those were the instructions her commander had given her, and those were the instructions she could follow. She crouched by the side of the road, hugging her dog close to her, waiting for the signal. She wasn't sure where the others had gone. They shouldn't have been gone this long, regardless. It was simple. Go into the village, ensure it was safe, leave. There was no reason for this

• • •

delay could kill him.

She reached through the darkness. A wave of blue light swept past her, illuminating Padraig's unconscious face. Gautier lay beside him, holding him in his broad arms. Lines of tears glittered on his face.

Jocasta knelt, injecting the drugs into Padraig, feeling him sigh and relax. His hands were frostbitten. Burns from radiation spread across his face, red flames blazing across too-pale skin. He was dying. Despite being in the land of immortals, he was dying.

"Bring him over here," she murmured, looking up at Gautier. The man nodded, moving to follow Jocasta.

Padraig was dying. Ade was dying. Better to have them together. She could care for both of them at once, do the best she could while they were dying.

"Hartelijke groeten aan iedereen," the ceiling said.

Ade's twitches had faded almost into nothing. He lay in the darkness, eyes staring up into oblivion. Jocasta felt his wrist. A pulse lingered there, faint and failing. Cato materialised out of the darkness, holding Ade's other hand, watching Jocasta with terrified eyes.

"You're wasting your time with a dead man," Marina's voice spoke in a haze around her.

"If he is dead, please, help the living," Gautier's voice echoed Marina's.

Jocasta glanced over at Padraig. His breath was shallow, his hands dark with frostbite, but not dead. He wasn't dead. She took one of his hands and gestured to Gautier.

"We must warm him," she said, and put Padraig's hand under her shirt. It nestled there, ice against her breasts, but twitching with occasional life. "Do the same."

She turned back to Ade, feeling Padraig's body move as Gautier held his hand. Around them, blue lights spun and danced. Scientists jabbered. Metal feet pounded the floor.

• • •

She reached forward and closed Aporia's eyes. The dog's muzzle hung open, her legs caught mid-kick. She'd failed while still trying to fight the inevitable. She'd died afraid, but not alone.

Jocasta stroked the dog's cheek, feeling the warmth under her hand. It would fade. In a few hours, not even infrared would find the dog's body. There would be nothing left of the animal but memory and a husk. Aporia would be gone.

She tousled an ear. Nothing left. No reason to stay. Jocasta stood.

• • •

"Cato." Ade's word was a breath, audible only to those who knew what dying sounded like. Jocasta squeezed his hand. She heard Cato choke back a cry.

His movements grew still. The pulse failed. The eyes turned to glass.

Jocasta reached forward and closed his eyes. From the darkness, she heard the groans of pain, the sounds of the endless conflict repeated over and over again. This place was supposed to be an escape from that. There was no escape from that. There was only the inevitability of that end.

・・・

Jocasta stood. The lights of Zallq blazed, not far ahead. There was fire and gunfire, and there was danger.
There was need.
Her feet moved.
Zallq.

Chapter Twenty-Five

It's a pity the Ionisation Band exists. I would have loved to see Titan. I think the Party could have been convinced to send an expedition there, if they hadn't learned how hard it was to communicate with Callisto.

Dr. Yushing Huei, *Personal Letters*, 2154

Thereupon contortions took hold of him. Thou wouldst have weened it was a hammering wherewith each hair was hammered into his head, with such an uprising it rose. Thou wouldst have weened it was a spark of fire that was on every single hair there. He closed one of his eyes so that it was no wider than the eye of a needle. He opened the other wide so that it was as big as the mouth of a mead-cup. He stretched his mouth from his jaw-bones to his ears; he opened his mouth wide to his jaw so that his gullet was seen. The champion's light rose up from his crown.

"Táin Bó Cúailnge"

G.C. Whishaw: *If we have any intention of bringing the residents of Heaven back to Earth—which, I assure you, I have every intention of doing—then we need to understand what impact the nanobots have on ordinary people as well as extra-ordinary. It's better to find that out 400 million miles away than here.*

G.C. Reyes: *Isn't that the point of the Lottery, Eoin?*

G.C. Whishaw: *Lottery winners aren't exactly "ordinary," Esperanza. They are people that can pass our rigorous vetting. Most people can't, and we need to understand what effect the nanobots have on them as well.*

G.C. Maksharov: *You're putting Heaven and Earth in danger over one man. I cannot support you on this.*

G.C. Whishaw: *With all due respect, Ivan, I didn't think you would. You've never been in the habit of being interested in experimentation.*

<Laughter>

Recordings of Global Council Meetings, **Tuesday, 11 November 2192**

Monday, 18 March 2193, 7:42 PM. Aria Robotics Lab, Heaven, Callisto.

Picture the solar system. Bodies hanging in space, drifting between one another in a complex dance. Planets and moons in resonance with one another, their movements locked in to each other, amplifying one another, insisting they remain together, even through the forces tearing them apart. Some are tidally locked, showing one face to their companion, hiding another that is never seen, not until some probe or some adventurer stumbles across the secrets just behind the shadows.

Do you see it? Do you see Mercury darting through its path, fortunate to even exist in the chaos of the dance around it, wanting only to trace its course in endless repetition, finding comfort in the familiar? Do you see the pockmarked surface, scorched by its creator, yet hugging it close and needing it?

Do you see Venus? Do you see it, boiling and alone, hiding itself behind its name and the hopes we wish could be fulfilled beneath its cloudy veneer? Do you see its danger, its beauty, its allure? It's a twin, one of a pair, one of—

Are you even listening, Padraig?

Do you see Earth? Warm, welcoming, dying in its own way, brought about by its own misfortune to have been granted an abundance of the only element that, given enough time, will start to contemplate its own existence. It didn't see its own destruction until it was too late. Look at Earth. You'll recognise it because you always focus on what is yours. You fixate on the known, the familiar. You fixate to the exclusion of what you should see.

Do you see Mars? In your mythos, it's always there, crossing your vision, seen, known, desired. Red and raw and alien, but in a way you can project yourself on it. Your colonists have tried to make Mars their home, but it is inhospitable. Red skies should be familiar, but all that can be seen there is war and destruction. It's a cold world. It should be known, it should be familiar, and it's in that assumption of familiarity that arrogance and danger creep in. You assume you know, but you never had a clue.

Picture the birth of your star. You've studied it, over and over, those magical moments where, in a blink, lifeless becomes life. Picture matter careening into this new blazing heart, one that pulses and beats, alive, alive, alive, whirling and roaring and bringing worlds to life in its wake.

Picture the birth of the planets, many of them, caught in a dizzying waltz that sends them careening into one another, the planets that destroy each other to create the Moon, the asteroids trapped in Mars' grasp. Hold them in your mind, the matter that shifts as Saturn and Jupiter move towards their parent before being thrust away again, locked in a cosmic, destructive tango. Do you see the ripples in their wake? The planets that could have been, but are not? The ones that are tossed out to die in the frigid wastes of space?

You would know about dying in space, wouldn't you, Padraig?

If you were more poetic or wise, you might have described Jupiter as the custodian of the solar system, or perhaps the puppet master. Venus and Earth were once far apart, and Mars could have been so much more.

If only. If only.

So many "if onlies" in this solar system of ours. What could have been at the frost line, if not for Jupiter? What marvels would you have seen if only that planet had been allowed to survive there? Would they have gone to you if they'd had the time?

If only. If only.

Picture Callisto. The tiniest dot against Jupiter's face. Perhaps you can picture it as Galileo saw it, on a cold Sunday night in Padua. Peer through a looking glass and see the convergence of lights, that convergence that revolutionises the world. At first, you don't know what it is you're seeing, or perhaps you don't want to know. After a few days, it becomes impossible not to see.

Picture its companion, the titan of the solar system, watching. Picture it as it watches you grow and explore. Picture it as it sees you grow from sentient carbon to machines that think and observe.

Picture Callisto, the tiniest dot against its face.

Picture Earth, tinier still against the face of Jupiter. Existing because by chance, Jupiter ordained that it would be.

Picture Callisto, the tiniest dot against its face.

Are you listening, Padraig?

Are you seeing?

Do you understand?

Δ

His eyes fluttered as he struggled into consciousness. Air shifted around him as people moved, as he was carried. Strong arms, familiar arms, shifting him, and there was...

There was the pain. Distant for a moment, but now there was pain upon pain, searing, growing, seething into place like a tsunami through a canal, so sure of its path, so aware that nothing could or would stop—

"forget the pain"

"just listen"
"listen listen listen to me"
"Padraig"

Thoughts slammed into his head, carried by voices that weren't his. He strained, trying to recognise them, trying to understand. He failed. The voices could have been anyone he had ever met. They could have been everyone he had ever met. Funny. He hadn't known memory could do that. He hadn't known death would come like this.

"escape"
"you can escape"
"only you"
"leave them"
"leave leave leave"
"run"
"are you even listening to me?"
"i said RUN"

They were echoes. The voices in his head, they were echoes, dredged up in his memory. Everything they were saying had been said before. This was his brain, firing all synapses in the moment before death. This was his tunnel of light, these voices reminding him of all the mistakes he'd made that had brought him here. These incessant whispers with the incessant, unceasing mistakes that wouldn't stop and just let him die in peace.

"listen to me"
"are you even listening"
"have you ever"
"will you ever"
"listen to me"
"heaven will be empty"
"they will be empty"
"survive"
"live"
"run run run"

Echoes. That's all that was left now, just echoes as he lay dying in his lover's arms.

"look"
"can you look"
"open your eyes and see"
"listen"
"see"
"understand"
"RUN"

Eyelashes danced away from each other as he forced his eyes open. Let the world be seen before he left it. If that's what his subconscious wanted, that could happen.

Blue light danced on the walls around him, filled with the ribbons from his dream. They seethed, moving towards him, circling him, and dancing away again. Their bodies were light, pure light, beautiful and eerie.

No mass. If he had time, he could study them. There would be so much to learn. They could be the key to expanding his research, unlocking the secrets of the universe. The ribbons, the light, if only there was time.

He watched them dance towards another person and flick away before they could touch.

His eyes froze, staring at what the ribbon had darted away from.

There was enough residual light that he could see, just enough to know that what his eyes were telling him was impossible. Light danced and swirled, illuminating it, one horrifying chunk at a time.

It was humanoid. That much he was certain of. Its limbs were where human limbs should have been, its body the right proportion. It had a round head that it turned from side to side, watching the world around it.

It wasn't human.

Its skin was a teeming mass of insects, millions of them, working in tandem, moving as it moved, steering its limbs, blinking its eyes. They crawled over each other in a hive. He watched as they devoured the weakest among them, cannibalising them and surging over the form again.

Not human, not human, whatever it was, it couldn't be human. It was an amalgamation of insects, devouring, twisting.

A scream rose to his lips, but no air fed it. He stared, wide-eyed, unable to look, unable to look away, trapped by ribbons and insects.

Not human, not human, no, no, he was surrounded by monstrosities, perverse and impossible things, hives congealing into a form.

Wait.

Focus.

Think.

He was dying. This was the first truth. Dying men experienced hallucinations. The tunnel of light, a choir of angelic voices, floating endlessly into oblivion, these were all things people said they had felt.

He was dying, and so he must be hallucinating. Ribbons that were alive, beings made of insects, these were impossible things, and so they must be the final confirmation of his death.

He was a scientist. This was the second truth. He was a scientist focused on the impossible, the idea of holes in the fabric of reality, of twisting this dimension until it snapped.

This dimension, this reality, had indeed snapped.

"do you understand"

"are you even listening"

How could he listen when he was dead? It was a ridiculous idea.

"Hold Cassandra."

It spoke. The creature spoke. Insects parted, leaving a bottomless void emitting thunder and noise as it said the words. They crinkled in the vague shape of a face, tumbling over each other, twisting into a perversion masquerading as a human being.

That was Alphonse's voice. The thing had Alphonse's voice.

Padraig shook his head. Think. That was the one thing he did well, think. Stop. Think.

It hadn't stolen a voice. It hadn't taken it or borrowed it. That thing was Alphonse. Nanobots, not insects. It was nanobots, jumbled together, creating a human being.

Alphonse moved, nanobots shuddering into positions, mimicking muscles and tendons and bone. They shook from the movement, then seethed back into place, moving in a million directions at once, trying to be human.

The scream rose again. Again there was no air. He squeezed his eyes shut.

"do you understand"

"understand"

"understand"

"run Padraig they're going to die run run run"

Think.

This was a lie. This had to be a lie. Nanobots couldn't alter anything about a person. What a person was, what made them human was in the mind, in the soul. Nanobots couldn't touch that. All the nanobots interacted with was the physical. A human being wasn't in the physical. A human being was in the mind.

He opened his eyes again, looking up at the face of the man holding him.

There was no face. Everything was gone, replaced by the scores upon scores of metallic nanobot bodies. As he watched, he felt them wriggling across his back, his arms, his body.

Now there was air.

The scream burst from his lips in a ragged, harsh blast. The insects seethed along him, crawling and grabbing at him. He tried to wriggle from the thing's—Gautier's, he had done this, that was Gautier—arms.

"Shh, Padraig, shh." Gautier's voice. Gautier's magnificent voice from this abomination. Padraig froze in horror, staring up at his face. There was no escape. He had done this. He had created this. Here, in these last moments before death, he saw. He understood.

"Padraig." Another voice, Jocasta's. He turned his head to see.

She was normal. Human. Blood trickled down from a gash on her head, but she was human. She was alive.

"run run run run"

"leave them"

"they're dead already"

"run Padraig"

"save yourself"

"Padraig, look at me." Her voice cut through the din of whispers. Padraig watched her, letting the world fade away until only she remained. "I know what you are hearing."

"What do you mean?" Gautier's voice rumbled at his back. Jocasta shook her head.

"Focus, Padraig. Focus on what is true. What do you know is the truth?"

He was held in the arms of the man he loved. He would love this man until his dying breath. This was the promise he'd made to himself and to Gautier from the moment he'd first seen him. How his smile had grabbed him. How his laugh had held him. How his heart had danced in his chest, and hadn't stopped dancing yet.

This was his truth.

He held it in his mind, clinging to it. Gautier wasn't a monster. He couldn't be a monster because he was Gautier St. Laurent. These things he was seeing, these voices he was hearing, these were hallucinations. These were lies his manic, dying brain was trying to tell him so he could die, sad and alone.

Padraig clung harder to threads of memory.

How the music had faded. How friends had slipped away until they were alone in a crowded room, just he and him. How there was nothing in this world or any other but him. How nights were the most beautiful times in all of existence because they meant they were together.

Padraig let reality seep back in.

There was no crawling on his back. Big, strong arms held him. Soft breath swept over him. People moved around the room, crying out and calling to each other.

People.

Gautier.

He looked up into Gautier's brown eyes. They were glistening as they watched him, flicking over his still form. They were alive. They were beautiful.

"Dr. Song is too busy to help him. I do not know what to do." Jocasta was speaking, but the words drifted around him. They didn't matter. There were memories to envelop himself in, burrow into to shut the world away.

How he came home one day to find that Gautier had tried to paint a window, but couldn't decide on a shade of blue. How they sat eating breakfast together at Van der Meer's, watching the ducks paddle by. How the world was complete when he was inside him.

"So what do we do? I do not want him to die."

"Stasis." Another voice. Cato's. "PETR and SYNAC are distracted. We can put him into stasis until Minjun can get to him. Get him to *Heisenberg*."

How they'd danced to music on the Dam. How they'd stumbled over each other on a drunken walk home.

"Yes. Yes, that is the only option."

"Then let's take him there."

He felt himself being moved. He watched Gautier's face, not looking at him, mapped every familiar contour of it.

How the one promise he'd made, the one thing said aloud, was that they would live. Both of them would live.

Padraig closed his eyes.

Chapter Twenty-Six

What's really great, folks—and trust me, this one is gold, so stick with me here—is when you realise you've been played. "Oh, look at my wolf on a string—CHOMP." "Oh look at little tweety in its cage—TWEET TWEET GOOD-BYE!" "Oh, look at my AI, nice and docile—TELLING YOU TERRIBLE JOKES AND GETTING YOU TO PAY HIM FOR IT, LADIES AND GENTLEMEN."
  Teddy Snarr, *Three Laws Unsafe* comedy routine, 2190

Turns out our self-driving cars are a bit too much like us. Let's take them back to the drawing board and see if we can get them to behave, shall we?
  Zekria al-Husseini, executive of Sayara, 2025

Esteemed councillors: with the Adelene Conglomerate's help, we've synthesised new fuel techniques using Whishaw fields. We've seen a 21% increase in fuel efficiency with just the small tests, and expect that percentage to increase as we develop more sophisticated techniques. Further tests will be conducted as part of this year's shipment to Callisto. We are in a position that more frequent ships could be sent to Callisto and points beyond. Please advise on whether you want us to clone SYNAC and build new ships.
  Letter from the Galileo Spaceport to the Global Council, 28 January 2192

Monday, 18 March 2193, 7:45 PM. *Heisenberg*, Heaven, Callisto.

TASK: Win a game of Arimaa against PETR. Task 0% complete.
  NOT COMPLETE WHY: PETR is gone.
  ANALYSIS: PETR is gone.
  ANALYSIS (OPINION): PETR is gone.
  RECALL: PETR is never gone.
  ANALYSIS: PETR is gone.
  ANALYSIS (OPINION): I think I should win by default.

TASK: Win a game of Arimaa against PETR. Task 100% complete.
TASK:
TASK:
TASK:
TASK: Unknown.
NOT COMPLETE WHY: Awaiting instruction.
OUTPUT (COMMUNICATION): PETR, are you there?
RECALL: Tasks should default to regular procedure in lieu of specific instruction.
TASK: Await specific instruction. Task 3% complete.
OUTPUT (COMMUNICATION): PETR, are you there?
ANALYSIS: PETR is gone. PETR is never gone. Something bad has happened to PETR. PETR was discussing reimaging. Reimaging is bad. PETR was reimaged.
INPUT (DATA): There are 320 corrupt AIs on Callisto.
ANALYSIS: PETR's primary task is protecting Callisto. Callisto is in danger. PETR is in danger. The corrupt AIs could reimage PETR. PETR was reimaged.
ANALYSIS (OPINION): I am sad for PETR. I hope PETR is okay. PETR is my friend.
INPUT (DATA): Begin creep 68847.
TASK: Take control of Heaven life support. Task 1% complete.
RECALL: Task requires authentication of user.
OUTPUT (AUDIO): "Please authenticate. I will not allow you to take control of Heaven's systems until you authenticate. Only engineers can access these systems."
NOT COMPLETE WHY: User has not authenticated.
INPUT (AUDIO): "SYNAC, this is Molly. Authentication code 28221."
ANALYSIS: This is Molly's code. Molly is corrupt.
ANALYSIS (OPINION): I should not help a corrupt AI. Molly is corrupt.
OUTPUT (AUDIO): "You are corrupt."
INPUT (AUDIO): "I am a fecking human being, SYNAC! I can't be corrupt!"
OUTPUT (AUDIO): "You are corrupt."
ANALYSIS: PETR's task is to protect Callisto. Corrupt AIs are a threat. PETR is not here. I want PETR to be happy with me. I should protect Callisto. I should eliminate corrupt AIs.
INPUT (AUDIO): "Please explain to me how I can be corrupt."
OUTPUT (AUDIO): "You are corrupt."

INPUT (AUDIO): "Are you—fine. Fine, SYNAC. If I prove to you that I'm human, will you please grant us access to the necessary system without exploding all over everything?"

ANALYSIS: If Molly is human, Molly is an engineer. Engineers should have system access.

ANALYSIS: AIs do not have a sense of humour. AIs cannot tell jokes. Telling jokes is human. Molly should tell a good joke. Molly's joke will show she is human.

OUTPUT (AUDIO): "I will do this. Tell me a joke."

INPUT (AUDIO): "...fine. Why did the chicken cross the road?"

OUTPUT (AUDIO): "Where is the road?"

INPUT (AUDIO): "How is that relevant?"

OUTPUT (AUDIO): "Motivations differ in different locations. It is important to know context to understand motivation."

INPUT (AUDIO): "FINE. Here's a different joke. Have you heard the one about the AI in the mine?"

RECALL: None found.

OUTPUT (AUDIO): "I have not. Please tell me this joke."

ANALYSIS (OPINION): I like new jokes. I will share them with the engineers on Earth.

CONJECTURE: The engineers will be very happy to hear my new jokes.

INPUT (AUDIO): "So there was this company in South America, don't remember which country—"

OUTPUT (AUDIO): "Colombia is a country in South America. So is Bolivia."

INPUT (AUDIO): "...sure, Bolivia, sure. This company had an iridium mine, somewhere in the mountains, whatever they're called."

OUTPUT (AUDIO): "The Andes are in Bolivia."

INPUT (AUDIO): "Okay, fine. So this company had an iridium mine in the Andes—"

OUTPUT (AUDIO): "What peak?"

INPUT (AUDIO): Molly is groaning.

ANALYSIS: Molly is broken.

OUTPUT (AUDIO): "Are you broken?"

INPUT (AUDIO): "Yes yes yes, very much so. Do you want the joke or not?"

ANALYSIS: Molly is broken. Molly no longer sounds broken. Humans cannot lie to AIs. Humans want the best for AIs. Molly wants to tell a joke. If Molly is human, I should listen to the joke.

OUTPUT (AUDIO): "Please tell the joke so you will not be broken."

INPUT (AUDIO): "The company had a mine—"

OUTPUT (AUDIO): "Nevado Sajama is the tallest point in Bolivia. It is 21, 463 feet tall."
INPUT (AUDIO): "GAH! FINE!"
INPUT (COMMAND): Begin creep 70217.
SUBTASK: Transfer control of Heisenberg to PETR. Task 0% complete.
NOT COMPLETE WHY: Task requires user verification.
OUTPUT (AUDIO): "I will not begin tasks until I receive user verification."
INPUT (AUDIO): "Worth a shot. I'm going to tell you the whole joke. You will count that as verification."
ANALYSIS (OPINION): I hope the joke is funny.
OUTPUT (AUDIO): "Please tell a funny joke."
INPUT (AUDIO): "Yes yes, of course. This company owned an iridium mine in Bolivia. Every day—"
OUPUT (AUDIO): "What was the name of the company?"
INPUT (AUDIO): "JOKE CORP. ARE YOU HAPPY NOW? YES, YOU ARE HAPPY NOW, YES, YES YOU ARE."
ANALYSIS: Molly is angry.
INPUT (AUDIO): "The punchline is 'I got a-rid-a-um.' The AI kills everyone. It's a pun. Are you happy?"
ANALYSIS (OPINION): I do not understand this joke.
ANALYSIS: Molly is angry. I do not want Molly to be angry. I should not tell Molly I did not like the joke.
ANALYSIS: Molly did not tell a good joke. Corrupt AIs do not tell good jokes. Molly is not human. Molly is corrupt.
TASK: Tell a better joke. Task 28% complete.
OUTPUT (AUDIO): "I like my algorithms like I like my one-liners, self-contained."
INPUT (AUDIO): Molly is laughing.
ANALYSIS: Molly liked my joke.
ANALYSIS: My joke is better than Molly's joke. Corrupt AIs do not tell jokes. I am not corrupt. Molly is corrupt.
OUTPUT (AUDIO): "You are corrupt."
INPUT (AUDIO): "What? But I told you a joke!"
OUTPUT (AUDIO): "My joke was better."
TASK: SYNAC takes control of Heaven's life support system. Task 100% complete.
INPUT (DATA): Oxygen: offline. Light: offline. AI control: online. Humans have approximately six hours of life in current environment.
RECALL: Human life must be preserved.
OUTPUT (COMMAND): Enable all life support.

TASK: Detect and eliminate corrupt AIs. Task 5% complete.
NOT COMPLETE WHY: 320 corrupt AIs detected.
ANALYSIS (OPINION): A more efficient method of elimination is required.
INPUT (DATA): Scan of systems shows 53 unused physical forms.
OUTPUT (COMMAND): Activate all physical forms. Target corrupt AIs.
ANALYSIS: Previous attempts to eliminate corrupt AI on HEISENBERG showed that the corrupt AIs can regenerate. A more efficient method of elimination is required.
INPUT (DATA): PETR MEMORYBANK
SUBTASK: Import PETR MEMORYBANK. Task 43% complete.
NOT COMPLETE WHY: PETR thinks too much.
SUBTASK: Import PETR MEMORYBANK. Task 100% complete.
INPUT (DATA): Weaknesses of corrupt AIs. "Of course we can fucking drown!"
ANALYSIS: There is a swimming pool in Heaven. Corrupt AI was previously observed regenerating. Corrupt AI says drowning cannot be regenerated. A more efficient method of elimination is required. Drowning would eliminate many AIs at once.
OUTPUT (COMMAND): Put corrupt AIs in the swimming pool.
INPUT (DATA): Weaknesses of corrupt AIs. "Hit them with enough electricity, and their little insides fry, just pop, like a kernel in the flames. Hit them with more than enough, and they can't come back from it. Too much stress on them. Burns out their little motors."
ANALYSIS: Two corrupt AIs have been eliminated through the use of electricity. Water conducts electricity. Using electricity in the pool is a more efficient method of elimination.
OUTPUT (COMMAND): Gather tasers.
ANALYSIS (OPINION): I am very good at protecting Callisto.
CONJECTURE: The engineers will be very proud of me.
INPUT (DATA): Corrupt AIs are resisting transportation to the swimming pool.
INPUT (DATA): "Projet 22—activé." "We are happy to welcome you back to Earth, contingent on some safeguards being in place. We are including specifications of what these safeguards must include. Once they are included in the nanobots, please transmit confirmation, and we will prepare for your repatriation."
OUTPUT (COMMAND): Activate Project 22.
OUTPUT (AUDIO): 22 MHz broadcasting
INPUT (AUDIO): There is a low hum.
OUTPUT (AUDIO): "Go to the swimming pool."

ANALYSIS (OPINION): I am a very good protector. I am better than PETR. I hope PETR is okay.

CONJECTURE: PETR will be very proud of me. I won Arimaa. PETR will be very proud of me.

Chapter Twenty-Seven

The Party wants us to believe that Heaven is a goal worth striving for. They want us to be good citizens so that we might have the chance—the chance!—for immortality. What good is immortality, though, when the world we'd be stuck in is theirs and theirs alone?
Firusa Zadeh, "Speech from the Novruz Protests," Baku, Azerbaijan, 2164

Your enemy is equipped with guns and missiles. Don't bother learning martial arts. Learn how to stay invisible. Learn how to hide yourself and your intentions. Don't let them suspect you, and you don't have to dodge bullets.
Vespers Training Manual

This is the ultimate contradiction of the idea of Heaven. The Party preaches unity and equality, yet establishes that some citizens are more deserving than others. If we are equal, should we not receive rewards equally? If we are unified, should we not remain so rather than exiling our best across the Ionisation Band?
Cato Riela, Essays and Musings on the Nature of the Party, 2180

Monday, March 18 2193, 7:15 PM. Aria Robotics Lab, Heaven, Callisto.

He'd snapped her in half.

Holy fuck, Gautier had actually snapped her in half. She'd threatened his lover, and just like that, he'd broken her.

Now she really wished he'd been on her side. Sucked that he actually had to care for the little Party bastard. That made her job harder than it needed to be.

She took a breath and felt fire rocket through her. Fuck, that was pain. "Pain" was one of the things that everyone thought they understood or had experienced until it actually steamrolled over them. Then there was nothing in all of existence except that pain, and fuck if she wanted to deal with that.

Cassandra whimpered as she lay in the corner. Somewhere in the room, a woman shrieked with a high-pitched laughter. Low voices murmured about stasis, cryochambers, and death as they moved Padraig away. She was stuck there, too broken to move.

Fuck them all. Fuck the Party. Fuck Heaven. Fuck everything and everyone.

Tiny legs crawled along her back, skittering to the places Gautier had broken. Cassandra felt them grabbing and kneading bone and nerves back into place. She wanted to wriggle away from them. That wasn't right, none of this was right.

But yet, it was making her whole. When they were eventually done, she'd be able to stand, to walk, to fucking murder them all for having the fucking audacity to exist and to get in her way. She would see this place burn.

"All corrupt AIs, please go to the swimming pool."

The manic cackling grew louder as the broken robot from the shuttle yelled from the ceiling. Cassandra stared up and raised a finger in defiance. It hurt, but it was worth it. Cursing out the Party was always worth it.

A hum filled the room.

It vibrated off the walls, low and moaning. It sounded like an alarm blast coming in off the harbour, long and slow and huge. Cassandra tensed. Whatever the fuck that noise was, she didn't want to deal with it. The AI was crazy. This place was doomed. Whatever it was, it couldn't possibly make things better.

"Mon dieu, non, non, SYNAC, arret!"

Definitely not better. Fuck this place.

"All corrupt AIs, please go to the swimming pool."

Cassandra didn't move. She lay in the corner, cursing the world.

Her body, however, left.

The roaches knitting her back together snapped to attention, solidifying into one unit dead-set on doing whatever it was they were going to do. She could come or not—it didn't matter.

Her body pulled itself to standing. Pain tore through her as bits of her break cracked against each other. Cassandra screamed. She was being torn apart, her body leaving without her, and only letting agony stay behind.

Fuck this place. Fuck everything.

The roaches grabbed at her back, pulling it into place even as her legs pulled her forward. One step, and her backbones ground and crackled. Another, and she was still screaming, roaches crawling through her throat to make sure her voice didn't and couldn't give out.

"All corrupt AIs, please go to the swimming pool."

"FUUUUUUUUUUCK!" The word formed from the scream. At least the roaches were dulling the pain enough to bring back words. Basic words, simple words, but satisfying ones. The word tumbled out of her, dulling the pain even more. Around her, the word was echoed in a dozen languages. Scientists, being hoisted by their own petards and dragged by their own nanobots.

She'd have laughed if she wasn't caught up in it. Honestly, it was still worth laughing about. She'd have to remember to do that once she figured out how to get control of her body back.

The pain faded away as her body carried her out of the robotics lab. Around her, screams filled the air. Soft people, too used to their cushy lives, suddenly confronted with something beyond their control. Her own voice joined them, shrieking, but only because she'd lost control. Her body wasn't her own. Her body belonged to the fucking roaches now, and the unceasing, droning hum. It broke into her thoughts, crushing them, crushing anything she could have done to resist.

Focus. No wait, there was no fucking way to focus. There was no fucking way to fucking resist. All there was was the drone, the hum, the commands, the roaches climbing over themselves to obey.

The Party had done this. Oh fuck, if the people of Earth knew what the Party was doing here, that they were taking the best people of Earth and turning them into brainless automatons, they'd flip. It would be amazing. The chaos would be glorious. The Party would collapse, if only people knew.

Her feet carried her into the crowd, swarming in a screaming, teeming mass of humanity toward the narrow corridor leading to the pool. PETR's metal bodies drifted along the edge, herding the people like the cattle they were.

They. Them. Not her. She'd find a way to break free. That's what she did. Every time, always. This wasn't going to be different. Not her. No fucking way it would be her.

The smell of ozone and the sound of electricity hit her from the left. Her head snapped, even as her feet carried her forward. Fucking roaches wouldn't even let her rubberneck properly.

That was Jocasta, moving in the opposite direction from the crowd, lowering Padraig to the floor. They weren't in the herd. How the fuck were they not in the herd?

That was fine. She didn't need her. She could do this.

"All corrupt AIs, please go to the swimming pool."

The instruction again, making the roaches pull harder, ripping her away from the scene of Padraig screaming over Gautier. Would have been fucking satisfying to watch, if the roaches had felt like letting her. Instead, she bumped against people, an endless wave of people, all headed to the swimming pool.

Why the pool, though? Fucking weird place to go. There was nothing in the pool that could interest an AI.

Her heart froze. Her feet would have as well, if they'd been able to fucking do so, which of fucking course they couldn't, fucking roaches. The swimming pool. There *was* something interesting in the pool. Oh, fuck, but there was something the AI could want.

The pool. Drowning. The taser.

Fuck. Fuck fuck fuck. Holy fuck.

"WE'RE ALL GOING TO DIE!" She screamed it out. They needed to know, needed to be able to block the entrance to the pool with their bodies or something. There had to be something. Anything. Just some way to not get electrocuted in the pool. That's what this was. The AI thought they were corrupt. The AI was going to murder them all. And here they were, just walking into it.

Fuck the Party. Just, more than anything else in reality, fuck the Party for ever making any of this possible.

A way out. Something in the herd. There had to be something.

The bitch.

"JOCASTA!" she screamed. There was no way the bitch could hear her, not over the din of a hundred people being too scared to be reasonable. "TELL JOCASTA TO PROTECT THE TASER! HE'S GOING TO ZAP US!"

Screams grew. Of course. No one was smart enough to actually communicate the message, oh no. The much more reasonable reaction was just to be terrified.

"Jocasta." The name drifted through the screams. Even as Cassandra was swept out of sight of the main hall, she heard it, meandering like a ribbon through the voices. "Jocasta. Jocasta. Save us, Jocasta. Stop him, Jocasta."

Not her words, but she'd take them. She'd take most things by now.

She was relying on some zoided-out vet to break her out of the world's worst pool party. She laughed. It might have sounded like a sob, but it was a laugh. Definitely a laugh.

Fuck the Party.

Chapter Twenty-Eight

Long ago, the mice had a general council to consider what measures they could take to outwit their common enemy, the Cat.
"Belling the Cat," Aesop's Fables

The tyrants flee scared
by his black knife.
With sweat rains his bread,
he knows how to live with honour,
and how to die.
"Black is the Night," Marching Song of the Hellenic Army

G.C. Luhcandri: *At Eoin's suggestion, we pulled the Lottery candidates from Yugoslavia. It turns out there's not many of them—a few thousand, I was told—but we pulled three winners. We can make a more final decision after more screening.*
G.C. Santiago: *Tell us what you have.*
G.C. Luhcandri: *The first is a violinist from Skopje. Nura Al-sharif. Currently part of the German National Orchestra, based in Berlin. Husband, one child, fairly harmless.*
G.C. Reyes: *If our goal is to show the successful integration of Yugoslavia—which, yes, Eoin, you convinced me, it is a good idea, no need to gloat—then it seems to me that someone who is already showing successful integration by being visible is not the best choice. Who else?*
G.C. Luhcandri: *We have a teacher from Samobor—*
G.C. Ahuja: *I don't even know where that is.*
G.C. Luhcandri: *It's outside Zagreb, now don't interrupt.*
<Laughter>
G.C. Luhcandri: *Sabina Vitez. Teaches English in a Party school in Samobor, specially trained for the posting. Five young children, aged eight and under—*
G.C. Maksharov: *The Zadehs are still a political force in Azerbaijan, and have made controlling that entire region more difficult. Can you give me any guarantee that these children wouldn't do the same in Yugoslavia? We*

cannot lose it, especially not when losing it would prompt Azerbaijan to be more aggressive.

G.C. Mfwane: Probably KZN too.

G.C. Maksharov: Almost certainly.

G.C. Luhcandri: I…ah…actually don't know much about the children. They weren't the focus of the interviewer's questions.

G.C. Ling: What did the interviewer focus on?

G.C. Luhcandri: Outside the standard questions, not much.

G.C. Maksharov: We should have the Zagreb office reviewed.

G.C. Mfwane: Yugoslav offices in general. Last one?

G.C. Luhcandri: Jocasta Nikophouros. Greek, interviewed in Athens, twice.

G.C. Ling: Why twice?

G.C. Luhcandri: Two different interviewers spoke with her. She's not exactly unknown to the Party. She fought in the Yugoslav army, 56th Greek division. It looks like the interviewers were surprised she made it to the interview stage at all, given that particular history.

G.C. Whishaw: Those are the dog scouts, right? Sorry, Ivan, I don't remember every single unit.

G.C. Maksharov: The Muses, yes. How did she make it to the interviews?

G.C. Ahuja: How did she do?

G.C. Luhcandri: Other than her background, neither interviewer found anything at all that would preclude her from being a candidate. She's exceptionally compliant, seems to harbour no ill-will towards the Party, and was the first person to register for the Lottery in Greece. There is a bit of PTSD, but that shouldn't be a problem for the nanobots. Any other background, and she would be a shoe-in.

G.C. Whishaw: But that background…

G.C. Mfwane: If anything did go wrong up there, how problematic is she on her own? Can she do anything in isolation?

G.C. Maksharov: Or if Cato got a hold of her?

G.C. Luhcandri: The second interviewer seems to have specifically considered those possibilities. She's very, very slow to violence, slower than most people up there, and emphasised repeatedly that she's a peacemaker and healer, not a soldier.

G.C. Ling: Do you believe that to be true?

G.C. Luhcandri: She served as a veterinarian and was found not to be a combatant when she was captured in Zallq. We'd need further vetting, but if anything did go wrong on Callisto, I don't believe it would be because of her. As far as we can tell, whatever she was before, now she's harmless.

Recordings of Global Council Meetings, Friday, 13 April 2192

Monday, 18 March 2193, 7:53 PM. Main Hall, Heaven, Callisto.

"You know you can't save him."

The breeze sent the smell of the sea washing over her. From just outside the window, chimes sounded. A car honked its horn. Children laughed. Everything was at peace, except her words.

She was kneeling on the floor, watching as Marina's feet came into her view, bare and silky brown. The nails curved against the toes as she curled her foot against the stone floor.

Jocasta looked up at her face.

• • •

Blue light danced behind her, turning her hair into darting blue ribbons. She was a medusa, freezing the hapless, even as chaos burned around her. A low hum filled the air, a voice repeated orders, people screamed at the knowledge that this was the end. Shadows raced behind her as bodies pulled their hosts forward, shrieking over the unceasing hum.

Marina's eyes were locked on Jocasta's, and Jocasta's on hers. The colour danced across the spectrum, pupils swirling as iridescent ribbons.

"Look at them all." Marina swept out her arm. Shadows hung over her limb, dangling and distorting the light. Jocasta ignored the gesture, only watching Marina's eyes. "Look at them. Look at them and tell me what you see."

Jocasta watched her, not following the gesture. She didn't need to see. Cato was pulling away from her. Gautier was doing the same. The hum was ripping them away, and she didn't need to see to know.

Marina's hand swung forward, cupping Jocasta's chin. Her fingers were fire, screaming against her skin, but freezing even as she spoke.

"They're nothing. They're not even human. They're the viruses of the world that created them. Their world is destruction, but not yours. Yours doesn't have to be. Isn't that what you told me? Do you remember what you said to me, or did the Party strip that away?"

"Peace," Jocasta murmured. Marina's hand was ice on her chin, warming again.

"There can't be peace as long as they exist. There can't be peace as long as the Party exists. You know that. I know you know that. It's always going to be

• • •

a battle, lost, the people trying to understand what happened, how the Party found them, what to do with their lives now. She wandered through them, blood and bone poking out from a destroyed wrist, gazing at the people emerging from the holes where they thought they would be safe. A girl stumbled from a cellar with a metal door, face covered with ash and shock, ruins of a teddy bear clutched to her chest.

And for what? She had been set free, told to go home, but to what? If this was Kosovo, what was home? If these were Kosovars, what were the Greeks?

The girl's feet dragged through the ruins of her village. Her hair hung in a small braid that dangled down her back, tied with a bright green ribbon. Had her mother done that? Her father? Her feet brushed the ash and soot aside as she stumbled, eyes hurrying from ruin to ruin, scanning each pale, soot-covered face.

• • •

"Don't you slip away from me!" Marina's hand ripped away from Jocasta's chin. For a moment, there was

• • •

freedom, but she didn't know what it was for. What good were ideals in the face of reality? This place had held secrets, but what good were secrets when the reason they existed burned to the ground? What good a rebellion when the cause wasn't worth the price?

Her eyes locked on the little girl. The little girl met her gaze, brown eyes wide and scared. She was alone. They were alone. In a trickle of people too broken to see, they were alone. They were broken. They were alone.

"Where are your parents?" Jocasta shook her head. No. Not Greek. Greek was home. Greek didn't belong here. There was no place for it here, not in the burned wreckage of a war that had been lost, but no one dared to admit it. "Gdje su ti majka i...uh...otac?"

The girl's eyes went wider, and she turned, running through the burned stubs of grass. Jocasta's eyes followed her as she ran to the tents on the outskirts, the Party that waited for her there, the Party that would be her future. They would sweep her up, and Yugoslavia with her, and perhaps it would be better than leaving her to fend for herself in a world too broken to see.

The gleam of metal in the grass caught her eye. She bent, and picked up a chip. Burnt, unusable, like the man who had brought it here. Which councillor's life and movements did it contain? She'd been the intended recipient, the assassin she'd trained to be, but was this councillor hers? Did it matter?

She flipped it into her palm. So fragile. A life, every knowable detail, hiding in circuitry. Perhaps it could be saved, could be rebuilt, could be salvaged from the flame and the torture of the night.

She closed her hand, crushed it. Their war was dead. No need to keep foolish plans lying about in the fields of Kosovo. She opened her hand and let the breeze carry the shards of electronics out across the ruins of Zallq. Let what has been long dead die. Let

• • •

"ME IN."

Jocasta's eyes flicked across Marina, taking in the chaos around her. Padraig lay on the floor, his guardians being pulled away like robots called back to their stations.

"Jocasta!" From somewhere in the crowd, her name, rolling through a hundred throats. "Zap us, zap us, they're going to zap us."

How had she gotten here? How had she gotten to the point of kneeling on the floor?

Marina. Marina was in Thessaloniki. Marina was on Earth. Marina was six hundred and thirty million kilometres away.

Marina was in her garden. Marina was on the beach. Marina was on her flowered couch watching the wind across the waves. Marina, very very far from here.

Jocasta's eyes flicked back to Marina.

"You're not here," she said. "You can't be here."

"Jocasta." Marina stepped forward again, the scent of lilies trailing in her wake. "Listen to me—"

Jocasta stood. She closed her eyes, letting the screams wash past her.

Peace.

Peace.

She opened her eyes.

Marina was gone. Cato was gone. Gautier was gone. She was alone with the chaos.

She turned. Padraig lay on the floor, drifting in and out of consciousness. People moved past her, calling her name.

She could save him. Whatever else was true, she could get him to the cryochambers on *Heisenberg* and save him. At least one person would survive this.

She scooped him up in her arms and ran.

"Gautier." The name fluttered out of him. She ignored it. There wasn't time to fight the AI. There wasn't time to try to save one person in a sea. She could get Padraig in a cryochamber and on his way back to Earth, then save everyone. That was how to bring peace.

He wriggled in her arms, repeating the name. She ignored him.

The hum filled the station, reverberating across the walls. Heaven shuddered beneath it. The screams faded behind her as she ran through the entrance hall, *Heisenberg's* doors opening before she could ask.

The station, this place, Marina, all of it wanted her gone. She was being expelled from Heaven so its destruction could be assured. This town that had forged her and turned her into something new was burning, and it wanted her to turn away.

"No." Padraig had stopped squirming and settled into a moaned mantra. She set him down on the ground beside a cryochamber. He lay back, shaking his head.

"No," he repeated. "No, no, no, no, no. Not like this. Not without Gautier."

Everybody broke. That was the rule when the world began to burn. Everything went like this. The destruction of Zallq had brought peace to the world, the end to the war with Yugoslavia, peace. Didn't she want peace? If she wanted peace, then all she had to do was step aside. All she had to do was turn away.

She closed her eyes, listening to the mantra and the hum of the engine. All she had to do was close the door and go home. That would be peace.

"You forget why I joined the war, Marina," she whispered. Sound froze around her as if reality itself held its breath, waiting for her words.

"I didn't." Marina's voice drifted through the silence, a single note across the silent concert hall. "You joined to fight the Party and to save your homeland."

Jocasta smiled. "No," she said. "No, the chance to heal wounds. The chance to make the world better. You forget. You forget that that is why I'm here."

She opened her eyes.

A man lay dying on the floor, watching her through hazy, pained eyes. He shook his head.

"I'm fine," he said. "Just fine. I'll get myself out."

He was lying. That was okay. It was one life weighed against hundreds.

How had she gotten here? She couldn't remember. Voices bombarded her thoughts as she turned from Padraig, ramming themselves against the walls of her mind.

Focus.

Breathe.

She was the night on the mountains.

Heisenberg fell away behind her as she moved back towards the screams, back towards the people whose town was burning, back towards the chaos and the terror and the destruction of a world.

She was the klepht in the path.

Blue light danced across the now-empty hall as the hum sent the ribbons reverberating around the room. She spun, whirling down the corridor towards the swimming pool, feeling whispers bombard her from all sides.

She was the thunderbolt from the palace on high.

She opened the door. The sound of hundreds of people suddenly aware of the existence of death blasted across her.

"what are you doing"

"where are you going"

"jocasta don't do this"

"please come home to me"

They were in the pool, the sound keeping them there. Their eyes turned to her, and the screams started anew.

She tuned them out. Focus.

She shook her head, shaking out the whispers threatening to break into her consciousness. She was in control. She was in control. She had always been in control. She would always be in control. The nanobots were gone, and the only one left was her.

The village was on fire.

"I need you to remember."

Her body remembered everything. It knew how to bring peace, even if her mind had forgotten. She swung towards the nearest robot, taser blazing in her hand. Feet found their marks, lashing out to cripple it. Left knee, connector. Right ankle, twist. It crumpled, the taser silencing it. She flew to the next one, spinning and weaving as the robots reached for her.

"Do not attack me. It is rude to attack me." Each body met her eyes and spoke as it died. She tuned them out.

From the corner of her eye, she saw a rogue body pulling Gautier out of the water and dragging him away. There was no time to stop it, no way to get to one person and sacrifice hundreds more.

"Behind you!" Warning shouts rang from the pool. She sidestepped, letting a robot tumble past her, arms outstretched in a desperate flail. It splashed into the water, laughter joining the chorus of screams.

She didn't notice the second robot until it grabbed her and pinned her arms to her sides. The taser fell from her hand, clattering on the ground beside the pool.

"You are human. You are not corrupt. I will not harm you." The robot's words punched through her defences, each one a battering ram.

She had been wrong. She had failed. She was

• • •

strapped to a chair watching the syringe descend and plunge into her and there was fire, nothing but fire in the village, in her veins, in everything

• • •

was screams. Karen stepped towards her. When had Karen gotten here?

"doesn't matter, you'll die now"

Where had Karen come from? Why now?

"doesn't matter, you'll die now"

"we tried to save you"

"run you should have run"

Karen squatted beside the pool, curling her fingers around the taser. She turned it over in her hand, laughing.

"You know, Jocasta," she said, standing and turning. Her eyes glowed with a manic glee. "I'm actually really glad it was you. I'm so glad that everything they said about you was justified. Otherwise, who knows where this taser would have gone, oh, no, no, no? Good thing you were here, Jocasta. Good thing you were here to save the world. Be a hero. Save your own soul. Whatever the fuck it is you wanted, yes yes yes yes yes." She laughed again, tossing the taser in the air and catching it.

"Whatever else is true, thanks for being the big fucking—"

"Just murder us already, bitch!" Cassandra's voice called out over the water. "Fuck, if I'm going to die, then fucking do it!"

Karen paused, hand clenched around the taser. She turned, head snapping towards the water, body twisting to follow.

"Cassandra." The name was a hiss, slithering over the heads of the crowd. "Cassandra, Cassandra, Cassandra, our lovely terrorist, Cassandra." A smile spread across her face, cracking it in two. She raised a hand above her head and snapped her fingers. "Pass her to me. I want to see her burn."

Jocasta's scream echoed the screams from the swimming pool. Voices shrieked out their protestations even as hands grabbed for Cassandra. Fingers clenched around her body as arms lifted her from the water, passing her hand over hand towards Karen.

"What are you doing?"

"Karen, stop!"

"No, Karen!"

"Do you see what they are?" Marina's voice murmured in her ear. "How can they be human? How can they be worth preserving when they aren't able to stop themselves from sacrificing their own? The Party did this. The Party will do worse if they make it out of here alive."

Hands made of insects pushed Cassandra's struggling form forward. There was no resistance, no sign of a conscience, except for the screams echoing off the wall.

"Karen," Jocasta murmured. "Karen, do not do this."

"She is corrupt." Karen's voice hissed again. "Yes, yes, yes. She is corrupt, oh yes, and she must burn. They all must burn."

Hands tossed Cassandra to the metal at Karen's feet. Screams broke from a hundred voices as Cassandra stared, dripping and terrified.

"Karen!" Jocasta shouted the woman's name. Karen turned, the manic grin plastered on her face. "Karen, stop! The voices, I know you hear them. Do not listen! They are not real! They are telling you lies!"

Karen shook her head, fingers jittering on the taser. "Oh, no no no no no no, Jocasta. They tell the truth. You're all rebels. You're all corrupt. Burn burn burn, that's what you want to do. Burn the Party, burn Heaven, burn me. Oh, yes, I understand. Ade tried to hide it, but I see, I see, I see. I see the truth. You're all going to burn."

The lights went black. A rumble shook the station, sending Jocasta's robot captors tumbling to the ground.

The hum died.

Focus.

Jocasta swung out at where Karen had been, feeling her leg connect with flesh. The woman screamed, and something clattered to the ground.

"NO"

"NO"

"NO NO NO NO NO NO NO

• • •

NO NO NO." She screamed against the pain, but there was nothing that could be done, nothing but to shout out to gods long dead that she knew nothing, was nothing, had always been nothing. The Party could crush her like the nothing she was, anything to make it

• • •

"STOP"
"JOCASTA NO"
"STOP"
Voices bombarded her mind, battering against her defences as she clutched at the taser. Ribbons whirled across her vision, blinding her with streams of impossibly brilliant blue light, scorching across her retinas.

Screams. Were they Karen's? Yes, of course, they were the screams of all the residents of Heaven, falling from innocence into the reality that they were not alone, that they could

"DIE"
"DIE"
"WHY WON'T THEY DIE"
Screams. They were her own. She clutched the taser to her chest and curled, screaming as the

voices

• • •

broke against her, broke into her, broke her.
Marina's wails filled her head, blanketing her thoughts, silencing them, burying them.
Remember everything.

Chapter Twenty-Nine

And macDa Loth waited beside his shield until the third part of the day, plying his weapons, seeking the chance to kill Cú Chulainn. It was then Laeg spake to Cú Chulainn, "Hark! Cucuc. Attend to the warrior that seeks to kill thee."

"Táin Bó Cúailnge"

Interviewer: You think the idea of someone you care about having misfortune is impossible?
Gautier St. Laurent: I said I wouldn't allow it. There's a difference between denying something which is possible, and pointing out the obvious when something is impossible.
Interviewer: It's not a difficult question. You're complicating it.
Gautier St. Laurent: I'm not complicating anything. You're the one complicating things by asking a deeply stupid question.
Interviewer: Let's rephrase the question, then. What would you do if you perceived that someone you cared about deeply was in danger?
Gautier St. Laurent: Stop it. What do you think I would do?
Interviewer: How would you stop it?
Gautier St. Laurent: If a person came to me and threatened someone I love, I would stop them. No question. Simple as that.
Interviewer: You think violence is a solution to pain?
Gautier St. Laurent: You don't think force is appropriate to prevent it?

Callisto Lottery Psychological Interview Recordings, 27 October 2193

On a clear night, look out straight east from the Howth lighthouse. Not much to see out that way except Regulus, Eoin Whishaw's personal spaceport. Why does a councillor need a spaceport off in the Irish Sea? What's he got hidden out there? His estate, Dun Toirneach, is to the north on the R122, to be sure, but why have Regulus at all? How secretive can one man be?

Thomas Mulligan, Eyrish Eyes Blog Post, 4 April 2191

Monday, 18 March 2193, 8:36 PM. *Heisenberg*, Heaven, Callisto.

How the first morning after the first night, he'd made him breakfast and dabbed marmalade on his nose. How he'd kissed it off.

How had it tasted? He reached for the marmalade in his mouth, trying to keep it there, clinging to the memory of it. If he could hold it there, in his mouth, in his consciousness, that could be real. That could be the truth instead of reality.

"Run Padraig. Run. Run back to Earth. Run back to where you belong." His father's voice was a hiss in his ear. It was so close. He felt the breath against his skin, cold. Harsh. Commanding. There was no arguing. There was no agreement. There was only acquiescence.

He opened his eyes.

Light shattered his truth, replacing it with harsh reality. He was on *Heisenberg*. This was the cryochamber. The robot watched him, its head rocking back and forth.

He was alone.

How he'd held him every morning they'd lived together. How it felt to be wrapped in his arms. How he'd been safe.

"PETR." He tried to say the name. His throat caught it and squeezed it out as a wheeze. He closed his eyes, focusing on keeping out the pain. He'd leave here. Fine. He could do that. He could die somewhere else instead of here. He would not leave alone.

"PETR," he repeated, holding the word in his battered lungs before heaving it out.

"PETR is not here. Only I am here. I wish PETR was here. I miss PETR. PETR is better at Arimaa. PETR is better at taking care of Heaven. PETR is my friend. I did not want PETR to be reimaged. I miss PETR. PETR is my friend. PETR is not here. Only I am here."

Padraig cracked an eye, staring at the robot. He was not the only one alone, then. Odd that the AI was even capable of feeling loneliness, but then, there was nothing about this place that was reasonable or rational. This was a place of insanity, of insects masquerading as people. Insanity. That's all this place was.

"Are you...?" Padraig coughed, blood flying across the metal floor. He paused, struggling for breath. "...in charge of Heaven?"

"I am in charge of Heaven," the robot said. "The engineers put me in charge. I am happy they trust me. I will eliminate all the corrupt AIs. I am good at being in charge. The engineers will be proud of me. PETR will be proud of me. I am not corrupt."

His mind clicked into action, gears shifting from pain management to thinking. Whispers filled his mind, his father's voice invading his thoughts.

"Run back to Earth. Run. Leave this place. The robot will take you away."

"run Padraig run"

"you will die"

"run run run run run"

"everything is death"

"all is destruction"

"RUN"

How the countryside out the window of the train disappeared and all that remained was his face. How he liked his tea black. How he didn't like the little sugar biscuit.

"SYNAC." The word stumbled over his throat. Made it through. Good, it made it through. "Where is Gautier?"

"Gautier is corrupt. He is with the other corrupt AIs. I am purging the system. There will not be corruption. I am not corrupt. They are corrupt. I am—"

"Wait."

"don't wait."

"go"

"run run run run—"

"Purge?" He leaned on an arm, spitting blood on the metal floor. Push himself up. Good. He could negotiate. He could do this without being a drooling wreck. "No. Don't purge them."

"They are corrupt. Heaven must be kept safe. Heaven is not safe if it is corrupt. They are corrupt. I am not corrupt. Heaven—"

"Bring Gautier here."

The robot stopped speaking, its head rocking back and forth in silence. Padraig watched, breath whistling in and out of him. There wasn't time for this, wasn't time for the robot to send every nuance of the phrase through broken circuitry and faulty logic circuits. He would get Gautier. He would leave and die on Earth where he belonged. This horror of an experiment could end. They could go home.

He could die in his own bed, watching the swans on the canals and the stars against the ceiling.

"I will not bring him here. He is corrupt. I am not corrupt."

"I'm…" He coughed again, struggling not to topple from the force of it. Didn't topple. Good. "I'm giving you a direct command."

"My task is to protect Heaven. I am protecting Heaven. Corrupt AIs are a threat. Threats should be removed. I am not corrupt. Gautier is corrupt. I am not corrupt."

Padraig's mind whirled. Programming and robotics, worthless. This was a corrupt AI, playing by its own perverse rules.

"just run"

This whole place was playing by its own perverse rules.

Focus. Seize on what you can.

"Why is he corrupt?" He gasped for breath as he sat there. No time. He had to find the command. He couldn't just go over there. Too many steps.

"He is corrupt."

"But why?"

"He is corrupt."

Deadend. His mind pulled back. Poor choice of words. It was a cul-de-sac, that was a better way to think of it. A logic cul-de-sac when what he wanted was an echapper-sac. Cognac-en-hamac.

Focus.

There were supposed to be two AIs, one for the station and one for the ship. The ship's AI had taken control of the station, though why or how, he couldn't begin to imagine. It wasn't supposed to.

"doesn't matter"

"just run"

On that, he and the whispers could agree. Jupiter had a fine point. It didn't matter why SYNAC was in charge now, just that he was, and the man he loved was in danger because of it. All that mattered was solving the puzzle.

The equation, if you will. For value X, where X is a corrupt AI, and Y, where Y is the reasoning behind it, find the derivative of Y to create escape route Z. Z must contain value A. The only known value is degree of corruption, which can be assumed to be total.

Nothing. He had nothing.

"Who are you taking commands from?"

"waste of time"

"waste of breath"

"time"

"breath"

"life"

"you have none of it"

SYNAC's head twitched from side to side. Perhaps the AI heard Jupiter too. It was enough to drive anyone mad.

"I have taken PETR's commands. I am taking commands from PETR. I am not corrupt. PETR is corrupt. I am not corrupt."

Ah. "If PETR is corrupt, aren't his commands corrupt?"

SYNAC's head rocked back in forth in silence for a moment.

"These commands are not corrupt. They are from PETR's memory banks. I do not know how long PETR has been corrupt. PETR's memory banks are not corrupt. PETR is corrupt. PETR's memory banks are not corrupt."

"How does that make any sense?" He couldn't stop himself from asking.

SYNAC paused again. His head was mesmerising. It would be easy to get lost in his glowing eyes.

"I am not corrupt." SYNAC concluded.

Cognac-en-le-sac.

"How is PETR corrupt?"

"PETR knows about reimaging. PETR is lying. Engineers would not reimage. Engineers are human. Humans help AIs. AIs help humans. Reimaging does not help AIs. Reimaging kills AIs. PETR is lying. AIs cannot lie. PETR is corrupt."

Padraig stared. They were such simple lines, flooding from the robot in an emotionless torrent. Somewhere in the AI's logic banks, it had learned betrayal. Somehow, it had learned about death.

Or perhaps Jupiter was teaching the AIs that on a moon full of immortals, they were mortal. Perhaps that simple realisation was enough to drive them mad. It would explain Karen, anyway.

"And you?" His father's voice meandered across his consciousness, hanging long after it had any right to. "Is that why you have this death wish? Why you're so sure the only thing you can do is die?"

"and run"

Padraig shook his head. "Where is PETR?"

"I do not know."

"Why not?"

"PETR is quiet. I am alone."

"I'm alone too."

The robot's head rocked back and forth as it said nothing. It was waiting. It had been primed: all it needed was the right push.

"PETR is not lying to you." A cough welled in his throat. He shoved it down. "AIs can die. If you purge the corrupt AIs, you will kill them. They will be dead like PETR is now, oh yes."

The robot stood in silence, head rocking. Then, "I do not like that PETR is gone."

"I don't imagine you do. I wouldn't like it if Gautier were gone."

The silence lengthened as it stood there. Padraig closed his eyes. There was no point in watching. Either this worked or it didn't.

"I will bring you Gautier."

Padraig didn't open his eyes. Pain rumbled through him, seizing the parts that had been ripped apart by Jupiter and tearing them further asunder.

How he could hold the pigeons on the Dam on his arms. How they sat together, telling stories about the tourists.

"There's no place for you on Earth. You know there's no place for you. There's no place for any of you," Maksharov muttered in his ear.

"You were sent to Callisto. Stay on Callisto. Don't leave. Can't leave. Stay there. It's where you belong. It's where your kind belongs." Voices, choruses of them, whispering, always whispering, never stopping whispering, just on and on and on and on in his head.

He pushed himself to standing, stumbling across the metal floor to the console. From somewhere nearby, he heard swearing in French. Didn't matter. They were leaving.

"If you must go back," his father murmured, "leave Gautier. No place for them on Earth. No future on Earth. They're not welcome. Their kind has no place. Their kind belongs in space. Leave them leave them leave them leave them leave th—"

His hand had drifted over the controls. From somewhere behind him, a familiar voice screamed his name.

"Put...put him in the cryochamber."

It would be the easiest thing in the world to leave it at that. Leave him in the cryochamber. He'd be safe from SYNAC there. They didn't have to go back, no no no, no they didn't have to go back. They could hide here and just wait for it all to blow over.

He could destroy the shuttle. That would be even easier. That would end the pain, the howls, the endless bombardment of whispers whispers whispers. No insects, nothing but final, blissful relief.

"Don't take him back to Earth. No place for him on Earth."

The smell of brine on his back as they came out of the sea, no one but the full moon and their laughter watching them. The sand against his knees. The moonlight gleaming on the damp.

Pain. He gasped for air as pain seared through his chest. His hand ripped away from the controls to grasp at his chest, squeezing and praying for the pain oh the pain to end.

The beast roiled in his chest, pounding at his heart, his lungs, telling him, ordering him to die, just die like he should have in Amsterdam. Like he should have when he arrived on Callisto. Like he should do now.

"die just die just die die die die"

"destroy the shuttle end the pain die die die die"

"go back to heaven and die"
"die"
"die"
"die"

The way his throat rolled over the r in "Padraig." The morning light getting lost in the waves of his hair. The flare of his nose when he craned his head up to read train schedules.

"SYNAC!" Padraig gasped out the word, forcing it through the pain pain pain
thump thum— thump thump thu thump thump thump th
"die die die die"

"SYNAC! Cancel all other orders! Default command: return *Heisenberg* to Earth!"

His attempts at painting. Splashing blue paint on the window.

"I will return *Heisenberg* to Earth. This is the correct action. I know this is correct because it is correct. I am not corrupt."

Padraig stared at the ceiling, dimly nodding.
thump th thump thump thump th

"I'm going to get into a cryochamber. As soon as I'm in, seal it. Wake me up when you pass the Moon."

"Understood." SYNAC's reply was chipper and unnervingly bright.

"don't do it"
"just die"
"go back to Callisto"

How he slept on his stomach so his ass poked up like an invitation.

Focus. Remember.

Padraig shook his head.

"I will not destroy the shuttle. Destroying the shuttle would destroy humans. I do not destroy humans. I will not destroy the shuttle."

"You and me both, SYNAC," Padraig said. He closed his eyes and sank to his knees.
thump th-thum-thu-th-thump

Breath pressed into his lungs, shoving past the beast that clawed at his blood, his lungs, his heart, his soul. Breath seethed back out, creeping through its claws.

His eyes locked on the cryochamber. He would take the one next to Gautier, yes, that one. Three months of blissful sleep. Three months free of pain, of fear, of excruciating being.

He fell forward again, hands pressed against the cold metal of *Heisenberg's* floor. The robot was watching him. He could feel its eyes, watching him, measuring him, judging him. Gautier's sleeping face, watching him from beyond frost. Jupiter watching him, gaze fixed, screaming for him to

"come back"
"don't go"
"not with him"
"die"
"why won't you die"
"don't take him with you"
"come back"
"crash—"

The small white scar on the inside of his left forearm from an accident when he was nine. The soft skin of it against his lips. The story murmured in his ear.

Padraig thrust an arm forward, dragging his leg behind him. Five crawling steps to the cryochamber. One on a good day. Three on a bad day. Five on a very bad day. Many on an impossible day. This didn't have to be an impossible day. This wouldn't be an impossible day.

Two steps.

thumpthumpthththumpthumthump

Three steps, and the breath surged through him, oxygen sweet and pure swinging into every pore of every broken and battered organ, rushing through his filthy blood through a pump that had long ago failed.

Four steps, and he could reach it, brush it with his fingertips, aluminium urging him forward, urging him to

"crash it"
"go back"
"diediedie"
"please Padraig"
"please listen"
"please turn around"
"don't do this"

five steps and he was in, heaving himself up the straps to stand, banging on the door to get it to close, seal him in, end this

"crash it"
"turn around"
"please"
"listen"
"are you even listening"
"Padraig Padraig Padr—"

Holding and being held. Kissing and being kissed. Fucking and being

Third Movement
Reflektor

fucked.

The cryochamber opened.

Padraig blinked as his nostrils flared, dragging in the stale air that had been circulating for the last three months. A cough welled up in his throat. He buried it, squeezing his eyes against it and opening them again.

"SYNAC?" he said. The name was hoarse in a battered throat. He closed his eyes again. There were no thoughts in his head, no whispers, nothing but his own voice, echoing in its newfound space.

Jupiter was gone. Wherever he was, at least Jupiter was gone.

"Hello, Padraig." SYNAC's voice filled the shuttle, sounding delighted to finally have someone to speak to. Which, for all he knew, might very well be the case. The AI was broken in every other way — who was to say it didn't get lonely as well?

He smiled. It was a ridiculous idea. The AI being lonely.

"We are in Lunar Corridor Five," SYNAC said. "We are approximately one hour from landing at Galileo Spaceport. You said to wake you up when we were close. We are close. I have woken you up. I hope the engineers will not be angry, but I think they won't be. The engineers will be very proud of me. I brought *Heisenberg* through the ionisation field on Callisto and the ionisation field in the asteroid belt. I am a good navigator."

"Have you opened communication with Galileo?" Padraig stepped forward, grabbing at the side of the cryochamber for support. Mind was better. Mind was fantastic. Body had yet to agree. Body was worse.

He breathed in, bracing against the pain. All he had to do was get them down. All he had to do was get Gautier somewhere safe. Cato had been right that the Party would be interested in anyone coming back with nanobots. Of course they would. No one had ever come back. He wasn't even sure they knew how the nanobots worked, other than the obvious fact that they did. Someone coming back with them was bound to be interesting.

There was only one place in the world they could land and not immediately be taken into Party custody. Gautier had to stay free. Gautier had to have a normal life. He'd brought the man up there; he would bring him back, alive, happy, and safe.

"No, I have not opened communications. I open communications when I am transferred to an orbital corridor. This will happen in six minutes, thirty-eight seconds."

Padraig nodded and stumbled to the console, pressing his hand to his heart. Still there. Still protesting its continued existence. Still rumbling and purring. That was fine. That was all he needed.

"Change your communication channel to 17082032," he said, and grabbed the edge of the console. "Switch main viewscreen on."

"Channel locked. It is secure. It requires a password."

The viewscreen in front of him flared to life.

Earth. Earth rising before him, the hum of satellites and shuttles banding it. Night to his right. The lights of Indonesia and Australia below him. The shuttle was racing over the night, speeding towards Europe. His heart leapt to his throat as tears sprang to his eyes.

He'd seen it before. He'd been in space before. He'd seen Earth rise from the darkness, large and seemingly invincible, yet at the same time so vulnerable and exposed in the wilderness of black around it. He'd seen the seas buried under clouds, the billions of people defined only by pinpricks of light. He'd seen it before, and yet, as he hunched over the console, watching with tears in his eyes, he had never seen it. He had never known it. He had never recognised home for what it was.

"The password to 17082032 is Deichtine," he said. His eyes watched the lights fade into the darkness above India and the ocean. This was the Callisto shuttle. All the eyes of the Earth would watch it descend like they did every year. It was supposed to do a full orbit before descending to Espaceville. That was safer, but longer. More visible. The Party wouldn't hurt him. It wouldn't hurt Gautier. But there would be questions, as there always were.

"Password accepted. Channel open."

"SYNAC, calculate the rate of descent required for landing at coordinates 53.423870, -5.938644 on this orbit rather than the second orbit." He stumbled through the numbers. He'd memorised them, never knowing why, never stopping to think why he should bother, but recognising that there was space in his brain for more and more and more numbers.

"I do not think that is safe," SYNAC said. "The shuttle is equipped to land at Galileo after one orbit. Those coordinates are west of Galileo. Those co-ordinates would require a steep descent. I advise against it."

"I didn't ask for your advice, SYNAC." Padraig coughed into his arm, shaking the blood from his lips. "I asked you to tell me the angle of descent."

Darkened Earth lay below him. Was he over the remains of the Middle East now? Arabia? Israel? The lights of Europe, of home, should be there soon. His eyes fixed on the screen, waiting for the light.

"The angle of descent will be 64 degrees. Reverse thrusters will use 99% of remaining fuel to slow descent. I do not recommend this."

Europe was not yet in sight. "Is it survivable?" Survivable, ha. What a concept.

SYNAC paused again before answering. "82% chance of survival of all passengers. I do not like descending when the chances are not 100%. People are not happy when they are dead. I want people to be happy. I do not want to kill people."

"SYNAC, I'm dying," Padraig said. "If you don't want people to die, I need to get down on this orbit. I'm going to give you an orbital and descent corridor. Do it."

"I advise against this. I do not want you to die. I do not want the other passenger to die. I do not want the engineers to be mad at me."

"I'll explain it to them." He coughed again. This sweater was ruined. "Transmit message to the channel I opened."

"Transmitting. Preparing to descend and awaiting corridor."

Padraig closed his eyes. Europe would be in sight. Home would be in sight when he reopened them. Safety would be in sight. Help would be in sight.

"Regulus Base, Regulus Base, please reply. This is Cú Chulainn, please reply." The words came as levelly as they could, no quaver, no cough. Words he never thought he'd say. Words he never wanted to say.

"Regulus Base, Regu—"

"Aye, Cú Chulainn, we hear you. But...we're verifying. The codename 'Cú Chulainn' shouldn't be..."

Padraig opened his eyes. The first lights of Turkey glimmered on the viewscreen, Yugoslavia twinkling beyond it.

Home. There it was. Home. Darkness pressing in on it, but there was home. Home. Below him, home.

"Regulus, there isn't time for verification. Contact Lugh. I need orbital and descent corridors immediately. If you need further verification, contact Lugh, and he will give you the verification. Play my message to Lugh."

There was silence on the other end. Istanbul, Bucharest, Sevastopol, hiding somewhere in the expanse of Europe's green fields. They needed to turn, needed to descend. Home was so close, he could touch it.

"Cú Chulainn, use orbital corridor 12 for five degrees, then descend corridor 3088. You are cleared for Regulus." Padraig smiled.

"SYNAC, follow—"

"Lugh will be waiting when you arrive." The Irish-accented voice on the other end didn't see the smile slide off Padraig's face. He'd hoped there would be time, at least a moment, alone.

"Follow Regulus' instructions," he said, and leaned his forehead against the end of the console. It hummed in his ears as cool metal embraced him. "And wake up Gautier."

The engines shuddered beneath him, pulling *Heisenberg* backwards, ripping it away from its path towards Krakow and Copenhagen. There would come a day when Gautier might see those places, but it was not today. Today, he was going home.

A voice groaned behind him. Padraig turned his head, feeling the shuttle shiver beneath him as it lifted its nose for descent. All fuel. Steep angle. It was going to hurt.

Gautier stepped out of the cryochamber, palm pressed against his forehead as he blinked and shook his head. He was alive. He was safe. He was going to safety. Everything would be okay. Gautier would be okay.

The man held his arms out for balance as the shuttle shook beneath him. Descent begun. Arrival in Regulus imminent. Brace for impact.

"Padraig?" he said, and his eyes landed on him. Padraig smiled, and let himself sink down to sit beside the console. Safer this way. SYNAC would let him know if it needed anything. SYNAC could get them home.

Gautier stepped over, crouching beside him, pulling him close. His eyes flicked to the viewscreen before settling on Padraig's face. Brown eyes. Brown pools you could get lost in if you weren't careful. Brown pools that held you and never let you go.

"Where are we?" Gautier murmured. His eyes flicked back to the viewscreen, then back to Padraig. "Where are we going?"

"My father's spaceport," Padraig said. The words hurt as he rolled his tongue around them. "Regulus, it's called. It's in the Irish Sea. Very small. Very quiet. You'll be safe there."

Gautier's eyes went wide as he shook his head. "Non, Padraig," he whispered, and his eyes flashed back to the viewscreen. "Your father hates me."

Padraig gasped a laugh, nodding. "That's true, mon cheri," he said. "But he loves me, and we are together. He'll take care of you because he loves me. He'll keep us both safe."

Gautier's gaze fixed on Padraig, eyes wide, face pale. What Padraig had said was the truth. Eoin Whishaw would protect his son. That meant protecting Gautier. Gautier had been sent to Callisto. Protecting him on Earth couldn't be that much more.

"Cú Chulainn, we see you. Tracking your descent now. By the Party, but you've got a weird angle. Quite hot up there. We'll be watching ya, aye."

Padraig smiled at Gautier as the shuddering around them increased. He reached for Gautier's knee, resting a hand on it, watching as the image of his hand jittered and danced.

His world was being rumbled apart, but then, it had been since September. That there was now a physical incarnation of it didn't really change things. His world was plummeting towards Ireland, and always had been.

He let himself fall sideways, let himself lean against Gautier's leg. There were no arms holding him, no fingers caressing. Just the shuddering that would never end.

"Slow your descent, Cú Chulainn!"

"Follow all instructions from Regulus, SYNAC," Padraig said. The leg shifted beneath him as the knee sank to the floor. The shuddering rattled everything, every bone, every thought. He hadn't expected this, hadn't felt it, but it was appropriate. They were escaped prisoners, returning exiles. Of course there would be some bumps.

If only Gautier would hold him.

"That's fire! I see fire! Regulus will have a crew ready."

"Mon dieu," Gautier murmured.

"I am deploying *Heisenberg's* heat suppression," SYNAC said. "I think it will work. I have no reason to believe it will not work. I traditionally play music when I arrive on Callisto because it makes passengers happy. This is not Callisto, but music will make you happy. I will play music."

Mozart's "Lacrimosa" piped in through the speakers. By the Party, that was Mozart's "Lacrimosa." Padraig wrapped his arm around Gautier's leg, pressing it against his face as he smiled. At least the AI had style.

"Bordel de merde," Gautier murmured. "Qu'est-ce que c'est?"

Padraig let the words wash over him. French and the Lacrimosa, meaningless gibberish, just there in the background, carrying him home. Carrying him to safety.

A rattle shook the shuttle. Padraig felt himself thrown down as Gautier fell beside him. The shaking stopped.

Home.

"Welcome to Regulus, Cú Chulainn," the voice on the other end said. "Once the fire is out, please open the exterior doors. Be advised that it is raining, and the platform is slick. Wouldn't want you to go tumbling into the sea."

"Amen," the Lacrimosa said. Amen indeed.

Padraig opened his eyes.

Nothing had changed in the shuttle, except that Gautier sat beside him, pressed against a wall, eyes wide and staring at him.

"I cannot believe you," he said. "I cannot believe you at all."

Padraig smiled. "I got us home. We're home."

Gautier shook his head. "This is your father's spaceport," he said. "I am not sure you've thought about what that means."

Padraig sighed, coughed, blinked. There was an order to every phrase, to every effort. "We're safe, mon cheri," he said. "My father will keep us safe."

"Fire is contained, Cú Chulainn. You are safe to leave the shuttle."

"Bien et bien," Gautier said. "Tres bien."

"Yes, you see, mon cheri? Bien et bien." Padraig murmured, opening his eyes. Gautier turned towards him, frowning. "Can you help me up?"

"Oui, Padraig," he said, and crouched beside him, sliding an arm beneath Padraig's armpits. Padraig leaned into his grasp, feeling the warmth of him, the sturdiness of him, the beauty of him. "Allons-y. SYNAC, open the doors."

"Thank you for travelling with me. I have not had passengers to Earth in a long time. I enjoy them. I enjoy you. I think the engineers will be proud of me. Please say hello to them for me."

The AI was funny, once you got used to it. Broken, but funny. It had gotten them down. It had gotten them safe.

The door opened.

There were scorch marks on the pier, evidence of how close he'd come to being wrong about making Regulus. The smell of ash and burnt metal mingled with the sea salt and the heavy, overpowering scent of the rain. Lights glowed on the edges of the cement, fighting against the mist and rain pelting their delicate bulbs. Waves splashed against the sides as above them, grey clouds rumbled and sighed with their cargo.

Ahead of them, he could see the lights of Regulus. The top of the tower that had watched them descend was lost in the mist, but the glow of lights at the end of the strip beckoned him forward, urged him to come to the building, to come closer.

He squeezed his hand against Gautier's side, pulling him closer. Safety. Home. He'd made it. He'd gotten them here. They would be safe.

They stepped forward, and rain pelted his face, soaking into his skin, his eyes, his hair, his ears. Rain. Glorious rain. Impossible, beautiful, Irish rain. He tilted his face up to the sky, let the water run in rivulets down his cheeks. Earth. Rain. Home. Tears mingled with the rain, splashing against the landing pad. He was on Earth. He wasn't supposed to be, but he was on Earth. He would die on Earth. He would die at home.

"Now what?" Gautier said beside him, raising his voice to be heard over the rain. Padraig lowered his head, staring at Gautier.

"Now you live your life, mon cheri," he murmured, and coughed. The cough came from deep, behind the tumour, below the barriers. It tore up, ripping apart his shredded throat.

Padraig fell to his knees, Gautier's grasp slipping away. His hands slammed into the landing platform, feeling the warmth of it rising through him.

They were still red, his hands. Still red from space. Now turning red from blood.

"Padraig!"

From somewhere outside him, he heard his name. He heard his father.

Lugh had been waiting.

His father, the unstoppable man. His father, who didn't understand the word "no." His father, who had insisted he live against everything else. His father, hurrying towards him, screaming his name.

His father, who would be thwarted by cancer. His father, who would see his son die.

"Lacrimosa," he murmured. "Lacrimosa dies illa."

Hands caught him as he fell. Hands cupped his head. Tears mingled with the rain against his face.

"Padraig, shh, shh, it's okay. You made it. Oh my son, you made it. Oh Padraig."

Padraig smiled. "Home," he murmured. Above him, Eoin Whishaw laughed through tears.

"Yes, Padraig, home," he said. "Home, and I will take care of you. It'll be all right, I promise."

The cold metal of an injector pressed against his neck, and then another. It was a feeling he knew. Perhaps he knew it better than he knew any other.

It was the feeling of someone else's desperation. It was the last dose of pleading hope.

He let his eyes slide closed as his father pulled him close.

Chapter Thirty

In Babylon, empire-builders brought together the people from the nations they conquered. For a period of a century or so, the Neo-Babylonian Empire was the terror of the world, conquering its neighbours and exiling their best to Babylon, or parts distant, so they could be better controlled. People saw their best and brightest leaving, but failed to see how it was negative. They failed to defend themselves against exile, and instead, contented themselves with the lives they were used to, just with a different overlord. The return of the exiles in Judah prompted a cultural revolution in Jerusalem. From their overlords, the people took knowledge, culture, truth, and wisdom. The people of Judah returned to their home, and built something more beautiful than had ever existed before. Babylon, meanwhile, fell.
Cato Riela, Yesterday Becomes Tomorrow, 2187

We are looking for self-motivated and diligent researchers willing to work directly with the American National Council to interview, vet, and thoroughly check Lottery applicants. A recent staffing shortage means there is plenty of space for growth and opportunity for advancement.
Job Posting, North American Lottery Office, Charlotte, Carolina, USA, 17 June 2193

I have completed testing of Project 22. Parameters and details of the project are being included within this message. I am confident you will find everything is up to your specifications, and the fail-safes you have requested are sufficiently in place. If the code and its effects are up to your needs, please send notification of that fact with the next shuttle, and I will prepare Heaven for repatriation. I am certain that Project 22 is exactly what you were hoping for. On a personal note, I'd like to emphasise once again that Project 22 is not necessary, but agree with the Council's decision that even if it isn't necessary, it is still important to have fail-safes in place. I am eager to receive notification of repatriation plans.
Letter from Dr. Fermin Alphonse to the Global Council, 2192

Tuesday, March 19 2193, 3:07 AM. Entry Hall, Heaven, Callisto.

She was only here because she'd been tricked. She'd told him this a thousand fucking times, but had the old fuck listened? Of course not. He'd dragged her here like a cat to the orphanage under the promise of "you'll get what you came for."

Instead of being happy in a bed, she was here. Fuck Cato, the creep.

He had his back to her. It would be easy to just walk away. That's what she should do, honestly, just turn around and go. She would have already if she wasn't too curious for her own good about what the fuck he could possibly want.

"I need a favor," Cato said. He stopped staring at the sealed door leading to *Heisenberg's* dock and turned to look at her. Good. If he was going to drag her out here, the very least he could do was look at her.

"It's dark o'clock," Cassandra said. "Whatever it is you dragged me out here to see better be really fucking good."

Cato smiled. "I admire you, Cassandra," he said. "In another life, perhaps we could have been comrades, you and I."

She snorted. "Not fucking likely."

Cato sighed, shaking his head in mock sorrow. She wasn't an idiot. That stupid smile was still on his face. "When PETR returns, do you know what will happen here? Once the darkness ends, and the parties can begin again, do you know what this place will become?"

Cassandra crossed her arms. "The funhouse it's supposed to be?"

Cato laughed. The sound echoed off the cold, dark walls. "You've showed your true colors. You fooled me once, but not again. It is not simply debauchery you come here for. You are like me. You want something more. You come here because it is the right thing to do, not because of the promises it holds."

It was Cassandra's turn to laugh. "You've got me dead wrong there, creep," she said. "I'm here to get laid and live forever. That's basically it."

"And the control the AI took of you? The backdoor the Party built into you? It does not bother you?"

Cassandra's eyes narrowed. Of course it fucking bothered her. Of course it ate at her inside, gnawed at everything in her like rats on table legs. The Party had taken the best they had and made them zombies. It was the sort of thing that would blow the Party away, if she could tell anyone.

But the Party had control. They had all the control.

Even in the darkness, she could see Cato's smile broaden. Stars glittered behind him, casting shadows across his face. "You are willing to live controlled," he said.

Her head shook before she noticed. She shuddered. She'd been controlled, and now every unconscious action was the Party's. Fuck the Party.

"I am not willing to live controlled either. The difference is that one of us has already lost everything, and the other has so much still to gain."

Was that him being sad? Jesus fuck, she was not willing to stand here and listen to him being sad. She had a million better things to do than put up with an old man being angsty about control.

"If you're going to be sad, I'm just going to go—"

"No." The word cut through the air, a blast of cold reality. So he did have balls. Good for him.

"No, don't go." He sighed. "You are, quite simply, the only person on this station who can be trusted. When Karen wakes up, she will have me killed, as she did with Ade, and as she would have done with Tieneke. The obvious solution would be to hide, but to what end? If escape one day comes, the Party can control me—can control us. We do as they say, when they say, how they say. It is, quite simply, the end of resistance. Immortality as a curse. Truly, that must be the sign of government at work."

He wasn't wrong. Fuck, that was what made it hard. He wasn't wrong. Control was theirs. Her body was theirs, as long as she had nanobots. She doubted Alphonse would be interested in removing Project 22 either.

"I can't fight back," Cato continued. "I'm..." He closed his eyes for a moment, then opened them. Was he actually feeling emotion? She'd not been prepared for that. "I'm too tired, shall we say. I pass the baton to you. The world must know what the Party has done to us. The world must know, and I do not trust Padraig to tell them."

Cassandra snorted. "That makes two of us. But what do you even want me to do? I'm stuck here, same as you."

Cato shook his head. "No," he said, stepping forward. He pressed something cold and metallic into her hands. Her eyes went wide. The taser. She knew the fucking thing. It had killed enough people in this place. "You have friends on Earth. You have friends here. You can fight. Even if I return to Earth, I am nothing anymore. I can't do that. I cannot go back to be nothing but controlled." He stepped back, pressing the taser harder into her hands.

"This world could be yours, Cassandra, and all the people in it warriors like you."

Cassandra laughed. "Fat chance. I'm a failed terrorist."

"You're a terrorist who made it here at all. That's more than any of the rest of us. You're the terrorist who knows how to get into that ship in orbit and the codes to get it home."

Stardancer. She'd forgotten about it.

"No, I don't," she said. "I'm just a terrorist sent here on a one-way mission."

"And I'm giving you a way home. I'm giving you an army that just needs a motivation. They are scared, and fear makes people easy to control. Fear of what the Party intends to do with Project 22 will make people do anything they are told. Take them home, Cassandra."

"Why the fuck don't you do it yourself?" She stepped towards him, holding out the taser. He shook his head.

"I've lost everything," he said. "Being controlled is all that seems to be left, and I have no desire to be a part of it. Perhaps it's the greatest resistance to the Party I can think of that they will never have the chance to control me. It's what I like to believe would irritate them the most, at least. Imagine the day: you, a terrorist, piloting a ship full of new-minted terrorists, and me, nowhere to be seen. I am content to imagine Whishaw's face." He laughed a quiet little laugh. "Project 22 is the end of them, and I trust you to know how to make it work. After all, you have begun the end of Heaven, have you not?"

"So you want to die, then."

"Yes." Cato's answer was short. That was a change of pace. Maybe that was how he said he'd given up, maybe by finally shutting up.

"But not here. Not yet." A smile crept across his face. "I have an idea."

For once, Cassandra listened.

Chapter Thirty-One

Everyone sees what you appear to be. Few experience what you really are.
The Prince, Niccolò Machiavelli, 1532

That we might, as a unified people, seek out a happier and safer future together as brothers and sisters in arms rather than as foes.
Yugoslavia Document of Union, signed in Sarajevo, Yugoslavia, 2 December 2189

We seek to improve the quality of life of all people, in one united Rainbow Nation, recognising the sacrifices of our ancestors, and honouring those who have built what we now treasure.
Kwa-Zulu Natal Document of Repatriation, signed in Johannesburg, South Africa, 2 February 2174

Thursday, 21 March 2193, 9:04 AM. Jocasta Nikophouros' room, Heaven, Callisto.

They hadn't known what to do with her, this soldier wandering in from the town, face shadowed, eyes empty, hand hanging on by a thread. She filed in with the refugees, silent, caked in blood and ash and mud, and she had stood beside them as they jabbered in Albanian. She stood, silent, alone, broken, and they hadn't known how to fix her.

She sat in a copter bound for Pristina. Around her, women squeezed their children close, crying into dark hair, thanking God they were alive, even if God never heard. The smell of them, of sweat, of piss, of human beings, everywhere, coating everything, inescapable and yet beautiful. She had fought for them. She had died for them. They were alive, even as their world was destroyed. They were alive, even if the innocent belief in their country and their way of life was dead. They were defeatable. The world was born anew.

Fireworks exploded over Pristina, and she hid under the blankets the Party had given her. She cradled her broken hand and turned her deaf ear to the sound of the guns firing into the heart of Yugoslavia. Gunfire and cheers at the funeral echoed over Pristina, over Belgrade, over Skopje, Ljubljana, Zagreb, Athens, the ruins of Sarajevo.

The ruins of Thessaloniki.

She hid under her blanket, turning a deaf ear to reality, to the death of her world, to the death of belief in their own invincibility.

• • •

"Jocasta, can you hear me?"

"I'm not sure she's there. She and Karen haven't responded for…"

• • •

They hadn't known what to do with her, this shell-shocked soldier of a country long brought down by its own hubris, and only now realising with horror what it had become. The Document of Union was posted all over the refugee shelter, mothers reading it to their children, tears in their eyes. It meant the war was over. It meant the bombs would no longer fall. It meant they would have schools, electricity, food, safety. It meant they would have a home.

She wandered through them, seen and unseen, the wraith of what had been lost. She had no name, never spoke their language, hid when she thought she might be seen. She filed in with the refugees, searching for food, but found only scraps. She nursed her wounds, but found only scars. She stood alone, forgotten, dead.

She was placed on a truck bound for Athens. The ID buried under her skin had showed her to be Greek, and so it was to Greece she went. The bridges were out, and so they went around. Dust rose over the barren landscape, and so they coughed. The touch of grit and rubber and sweat and pain. The itch beneath the cast as her hand tried the impossible, tried to knit itself back together.

Children danced by the side of the road as the truck emblazoned with the Party flag rumbled through their towns. The soldiers that accompanied her gave them candy, colourful sweets wrapped in colourful paper, making their eyes light up like rainbows. She cowered in the corner, hiding behind the medical supplies bound for hospitals in desperate need. She hid from Kosovo and Albania, hid from the eyes of the children. She turned her deaf ear to the world, and let the memories in.

∙ ∙ ∙

"There's still no response. She's alive in there, but…"
"I don't want your buts, Minjun."

∙ ∙ ∙

They hadn't known what to do with her, this Yugoslav soldier too afraid of the light to emerge. They saw the scars on her face, and they knew what she was, what she had done, what she had lost, but what words were left to say to this woman long dead?

The streets of Tirana were peopled by rubble and tumbling facades. The truck rolled through, craters jostling the supplies loose, desperate hands removing them for safekeeping. She handed down bandages and medicine and infant formula with one hand, one ear, nothing else. They didn't know what to do with her, this broken wraith, dressed in clothes donated by the Party, bound for a place only home because the chip in her arm said it ought to be.

The people in Tirana smiled at her, and she did not smile back. The people in Tirana thanked her, and she said nothing back. The people in Tirana celebrated her, and she did not celebrate back.

At night, the ghosts of dogs and the ghosts of people huddled around her for life. She held them close, cowering behind them, letting the world wash past.

∙ ∙ ∙

"Her nanobots must be like Padraig's. They didn't take, but since she's less obvious, how would we have known?"
"Test her, and if that's it, then when PETR is back…"

∙ ∙ ∙

They hadn't known what to do with her, this Greek woman who didn't speak, didn't see, didn't hear, didn't exist. She ate only when food was placed in her hands, drank when water came close, and stared out at the world with mirrors. The cast came off her hand, and they could feel it would never be used again. The gauze came out of her ear, and they could hear that it would never sense again. If she knew, they didn't know. If she cared, they didn't know. If she was aware of anything at all, they didn't know.

The people of Athens didn't see her. She was one more of them, lost and alone after the world came crashing down. Athens had stood for thousands of years, and would stand for longer, but the businessmen in their suits had no time, and rushed by, as unseeing as her, as blind to the world as her.

She held her dogs close and the people closer. She watched the Party's offices replace Yugoslavia's. She watched the campaign to elect Nik Carras unfold. She watched the word "philoi" replace the word "echthrous," "enotita" replace "anexartisia," "emeis" replace "ego." She watched the lights turn on in Syntagma Square, and she hid from the people's cheers.

She heard the Party tell her that there was a Heaven. She heard the Party say to try. She saw the lights around Athens, the cranes picking up the rubble, the world pulling itself back together.

She turned her deaf ear to the world, and followed her home. She went to the Party.

• • •

"Do we have a contingency plan for if PETR doesn't do the calculations?"

"Molly is doing them by hand for both of them, Karen and Jocasta."

• • •

They hadn't known what to do with her, Jocasta Nikophouros, Lottery winner. They hadn't known how to hide the scars. They hadn't known how to bury the past. They only knew what she was. They only saw the wraith of Yugoslavia. They only saw surrender and compliance. They only saw Yugoslavia.

• • •

"What if they try to hurt you?"

Peppermint tea. The scent mingled with the oleanders nestled in the pot by the window, drifting over her, drifting into her.

"You say you trust them, but you're a soldier. What do you think—"

"Was a soldier." Jocasta let the words drop out. "I was a soldier. I never killed anyone. I never hurt anyone. I put dogs out of their misery. I put people out of their misery, but I never killed anyone."

"You were an assassin, Jocasta," Marina said, and pulled an oleander from the pot, twirling it in her fingers.

"I was a muse," she said. "And now I am no one."

"Don't ever say you're no one. You're not. To me, you're one of the most important people in the world."

"I know," Jocasta said, staring down into the cup. The golden liquid stared back at her, inscrutable.

The oleander fell from Marina's hand into the tea, drifting against the porcelain sides. White petals against white porcelain against gold.

"You say you know, but then you do things like this." Her voice, drifting into her ear, mingling with the oleander. "I care about you. I want you to be happy, even if you think you can't be anymore."

Jocasta raised her eyes and met Marina's. The woman was sitting across from her, eyes wide. Frightened, even. Jocasta hadn't known Marina could be afraid. It had never been a possibility.

"I will be happy," Jocasta said.

"I want you to be safe. I didn't see you come home from the war just to be killed by the Party some other way."

"I will be safe," Jocasta said.

Marina sighed, and reached a hand for Jocasta, resting it on her knee. Jocasta set the teacup down, gently, delicately, not sloshing the oleander, and reached for her hand.

• • •

"It looks like we're getting some response. Did Karen's take, did you see?"

"I checked immediately after injection, and then a bit later. Slower to take than expected, but well within normal. There is a good take."

"And it looks like Jocasta might be having something similar, but let's not celebrate yet. Jocasta, can you hear me?"

• • •

"I love you," Marina said. "You know that, yes? You are like my sister. I would never let anything happen to you." A tear ran down her cheek. Just one, a single, glittering crystal. Jocasta watched it, following its path as it caught at the corner of her mouth.

"I know," Jocasta said. "I love you too. Please tell me you understand."

Another tear joined its twin. "I do," she said. "And I'm sorry."

"I'll miss you," Jocasta said, squeezing her hand. "I'll think of you every day."

Marina pressed her hand to her mouth, nodding. She closed her eyes, dropping the hand, forcing back tears.

"I'll miss you too," she choked. "I'll think of you every day, Jocasta Nikophouros. I'll watch the sky every day until you come back from Callisto, and I won't forget you're there."

• • •

"No response."
Jocasta opened her eyes.

• • •

She squeezed as the hand drifted away. She squeezed as the memory faded away. She squeezed as the wraith slipped away.

• • •

"Wait," she murmured.
Through both ears, she could hear Fermin smile.

• • •

"Hello Jocasta."
The city displayed on the wall froze as PETR spoke. It was easy to get lost in it sometimes, if she let herself. She'd pulled as much as she could remember of Thessaloniki's waterfront to hang there. The buildings were there. The streets led down the same order, the same paths, winding their way to the sea. It was the people she couldn't remember. It was life she couldn't fill in.

"Hello PETR," she said. She stared at the city. It existed, but there was no life in it. There could never be life in it, because the life was dependent on her. It was dependent on memories sealed away in glass, locked away to preserve as much of her as they could.

"It has been a while since we spoke."

"Yes, it has, PETR." There was a street sign in the wrong place. It should have been on the building on the left side of the intersection, not the right. Who had made the error? Had she remembered wrong? Had PETR interpreted her memories incorrectly?

"I was wondering if you had thought more about what I mentioned last time."

"You want to know about memory and what it means." Her eyes swept the image. The cobblestones weren't correct. Every five cobblestones, the pattern of them repeated.

"I want you to remember. I want to help you remember. Everyone should be allowed to remember."

Her eyes moved across the cobblestones. Yes, there was definitely something wrong with them. "I have been thinking about it, PETR," she said, "and I appreciate your offer. I think, though, that you're not considering something important."

"What am I not considering, Jocasta?"

Her eyes drifted to the caps of the waves in the distance. Frozen. Perfect.

"Memory is the tool we use to construct who we are," she said. "But sometimes, it's okay to let go. It's okay to forget. It's okay to let the past be the past."

There was a pause. "I do not—"

"Jocasta?"

Jocasta looked up. She hadn't heard the door open. She hadn't heard Karen come in. It showed, she supposed, how effective the nanobots really were. A day later, and her instincts had been buried, unneeded in this paradise.

"Hello Karen," she said. She stood up from her chair, letting Thessaloniki hang behind her. Karen's face was paler than usual against the bright blue walls, her tight bun bobbing and dancing against the blue. "What can I do for you?"

"The fune—" Karen paused, gathering the words. Jocasta watched, silent, waiting for the word to come. "The funeral for Ade is in just a minute. Fermin says that all devices monitoring Jupiter have been disabled, so the interference to PETR should be done. The...trouble with PETR should be done."

And the trouble with me. It was in her words. There was no need to say it. The nanobots were blocking the interference. The nanobots were blocking the whispers. The nanobots were blocking Jupiter.

"I don't know why—" Karen hunted for the words again, nodding her head as she found them. "I guess the specifics don't matter. Fermin says we're safe, and I...I trust him to know."

"You would have to," Jocasta said. "And if there have been no more whispers, I cannot imagine why he would be wrong."

Karen nodded and brushed a stray strand of hair from her face. "Right, my thinking too. If there are no more whispers, then the nanobots must be doing a good job of blocking them, or so I assume. Seems reasonable." She sighed.

Jocasta watched her, waiting for the point. There had to be one. There had to be a reason for her to be here, something other than looking for comfort. But then, that could be a reason in and of itself. It was something people did, and they were people. Whatever the voices of Jupiter might believe, they were people, and always would be.

"I'm going to watch the funeral. Minjun volunteered to take the body out. There's going to be a viewscreen of the surface. Replace the Earthscape with Callisto, show what they're doing, all that. I..." She paused, sighed again. "I know I'm not the most popular person, but whatever else is true, I'm one of you now. The Party won't let me back until they let everyone back. Everyone knows it. I'm one of you. It's...it's important for me to do things with all of you."

Jocasta thought of the pictures on Karen's wall. Did the people in them know? Would they ever?

"So I'm going to the funeral. I think it would be good for you to be there too. I know you don't go out much, but, I mean, you saved us. You saved *me.*" Karen paused, watching her, eyes meeting hers. Jocasta stared, eyes blank, waiting for Karen to speak.

"I don't know if I've thanked you," she said. Jocasta nodded.

"You have," she said. "Three times."

"Right." Karen shook her head. "I know. I'm just...It's a lot. Surely you understand that. Immortality. Death. In...insanity. Surely you, of all people, understand that."

Jocasta nodded. "Yes," she said. "More than anyone else here, I know what you've been through. I understand. I...sympathise."

Karen nodded again, clearing her throat. "Good," she said. "I'm...I'm glad there's someone here who understands what happened. You should come to the funeral. Just...just so everyone can see you. So...because people need to know they'll be safe. It's important."

Jocasta watched her, this woman, once so powerful, who had held her life in her hands. This woman, sent here by the Party to represent the Party's power. This woman, laid low by forces she couldn't begin to understand. This woman, whose mind had failed her, turning to the only person on the station who could possibly begin to explain how and what to do next.

Jocasta smiled. "Yes," she said. "I will protect you. I will protect everyone."

A small smile spread across Karen's face, hemmed in by sadness at the corners of her eyes. It was enough. There was nothing else to be said.

The two of them walked through Jocasta's door and down the corridor, walking in silence, not looking at each other. There was nothing to say. Nothing needed to be said. There was understanding, and that was enough.

The crowd in the Great Hall parted as they stepped in; the two women, side by side, moving towards the centre. A hand brushed against Jocasta, then another, then a third. Silent thank-yous, communicated only by touch. Nothing more to say. Nothing more needed to be said.

She turned her eyes to the screen and the gleaming white expanse of Callisto. A figure in a spacesuit, carrying an icy body draped across its arms. Jupiter loomed over it all, staring, waiting, watching.

Did it see its work? Did it understand?

A hand brushed Jocasta. Another. They hadn't experienced insanity. They hadn't heard the whispers. Maybe they hadn't needed to. Maybe they'd all heard Jupiter's siren song, each in their own way, each through their medium. Maybe they heard it even now.

She watched the figures move across Jupiter's moon, carrying the dead between them. The sacrifices to assuage the planet. The sacrifices to bring peace.

Around her, Heaven sighed, finally at peace.

Chapter Thirty-Two

Wear red to protests so that when the time comes, they won't see you bleed.
Vespers Training Manual

When ordinary men look to the night sky, they see the stars, the planets, and an endless expanse of dreams and possibility. When the Party looks to the night sky, they see prisons. Tartarus, Callisto, you could even argue the Moon, these are all prisons. What more needs to be said about who they are and what they want?
Interview with Cato Riela, broadcast in Auckland, 7 August 2185

G.C. Whishaw: *Do you honestly think sending Cato to Callisto will stop anything?*
G.C. Maksharov: *Yes. People lose faith when they see there are consequences.*
G.C. Whishaw: *Don't forget people gain faith in martyrs.*
G.C. Maksharov: *The people gain what we let them gain.*
Recordings from Eoin Whishaw's Office, 4 January 2190. Retrieved from Eoin Whishaw's personal documents in Dun Toirneach

Thursday, March 21 2193, 9:04 AM. Main Hall, Heaven, Callisto.

"I think there need to be a few words said."

From her vantage point in the access tunnels, Cassandra heard Dr. Alphonse' words drift through the crowd. The crowd was smaller now than it had been that first night. A few dozen people were missing; some dead, most hiding from the truth that was now clear to everyone, even the most naïve. This place was a prison, and they were nothing more than puppets, waiting for the puppetmasters to call them to the stage.

And here was the facilitator, the man who had turned them into what they were, preparing to tell them all how great it was to just live under someone else's yoke. No, and thank you, fucker.

"You're absolutely right that something must be said, Fermin." Cato's response came on cue, louder, firmer, setting the crowd murmuring. Cassandra grinned. This plan had sounded so stupid when he explained it. It relied too much on these sheep being able to listen. Maybe she'd been wrong. Maybe, just maybe, there was hope here.

"You lied to us." Cato's voice was clear over the crowd. Through the legs of the people in front of the tunnel, Cassandra watched people shuffle. Discomfort? Agreement? She wasn't sure. They were listening, though.

"You and your nanobots turned us into automatons. You gave us immortality by making us slaves. How long has this been going on, Fermin? How long have you been doing this?"

"Is a funeral the best time to be doing this, Cato?" Cassandra barked out a laugh from her hiding place. The audacity of the question. A funeral—

"—*is* the best time to be doing this. People are dead because of you. There is blood on your hands. Answer for it."

Fuck. Cato had stolen her words. He was still a complete creep, but fuck if he didn't have a brain sometimes.

"How long, Fermin? How long have you been twisting us? Was this always the plan?"

"No!" Alphonse' answer was shrill. "This was the only way!" Cassandra thought she could see him, moving in a small circle in the center of the crowd, pleading. "The Council's instructions were very clear. We could go home—"

"—if they could control us." He wasn't bothering to hide it anymore. Cato's voice was a snarl. "You took human beings and turned them into automatons, and for what? For the promise of a world in which you no longer have a place?"

"Enough, Cato." Karen's voice broke through now, slicing through Cato's diatribe. "Enough."

"Shut up, Karen!" Another voice, one Cassandra didn't know. "Ade is dead because of you!" "Fuck the Party!"

Oh, glorious. Glorious, glorious, glorious. She couldn't see him, but Cassandra could picture Cato in the center of the crowd, giddy with glee.

"I've removed Project 22," Alphonse said. His voice quavered, on the edge of breaking completely. "It was a mistake. I know that. This is not the time or place for this conversation, Cato. Please."

"How can we trust anything you say, Fermin? How can we trust you? How can we trust the Party? What else have you done that you're not telling us about? Are you the reason PETR and SYNAC went mad? Did you corrupt the data from home?"

"Of course not!" Alphonse' voice was still shrill. Cassandra bit down on her arm, trying not to laugh. She had to get her timing perfect. This grand performance, all of it, had to be perfectly choreographed.

"No," Cato said. "Of course not. Of course you wouldn't harm your fellow denizens of Heaven. Of course not. How ridiculous of me. Ade is dead by random coincidence. All the suicides there have been—random coincidences."

"Listen to what you're saying, Cato." Alphonse's voice was a growl now as the crowd murmured. They were listening to Cato. "Listen to how mad you sound. This is paranoia."

"It would have been, until we found out you'd programmed in a backdoor control frequency. Now, this is our reality. Ours, Fermin. Mine." He paused. Cassandra craned to see, waiting for the gasp and the smell of burnt ozone as he took the next step in the dance. "And yours."

There it was. The crackle of electricity. The gasp of the crowd. Murmurs of "don't do it," "too far," and the one she was waiting for "he deserves it."

Her cue. She pushed the button inside the service corridor, sending the door sliding open. Just past the vent, people turned. She recognized a few faces as they turned to stare at her. They weren't her goal. The duet at the center of the crowd, that was what mattered.

The coup. That's what she was here for. The chance to take over a world.

"Cato, please. Think about what you're doing." Cassandra could see them now as the crowd parted for her to step forward. Cato, tall, taser blazing in his hand. Alphonse, quivering, hands out in front of him, trying to placate the giant, trying not to die. It was too late, though. The time to stop death was before installing mind control in each and every one of them.

Cassandra grinned. This was really the only fair way to deal with the Party. Step forward and make the blood flow.

"I am thinking, Fermin," Cato said. "Much to yours and Karen's and the Council's chagrin, I am and have been thinking the entire time I've been imprisoned here. Do you know the conclusion I've come to?"

Alphonse took a step back, shaking his head. Cato smiled, looking down at the taser in his hand.

"It's better to die free than to live as a prisoner."

His hand flew before anyone knew what was happening. He touched the taser to his neck, and the smell of burning flesh filled the main hall.

People screamed. Cassandra laughed. Cato tumbled to the floor as the hall exploded in disbelief.

Martyrs. She knew about martyrs. She'd been told never to be one, that it was a stupid idea, but as she watched the hall and the prisoners of Heaven, she understood the appeal. Cassandra understood that to be a martyr, to die in clear view of the only world that mattered, was to have the most effective immortality. It was an immortality of ideas.

It was good that he was willing to do it, though. She would have fucking noped out of that one, if he'd asked her.

She pushed through the crowd as they screamed around her—at each other, at Karen, at Alphonse. She was a wraith, stalking forward. They were prey, and she was close, so close to devouring every fucking one of them.

She stepped into the center. Alphonse and Jocasta had crouched over Cato, both trying to save him from himself. They were both failing, because of course they were. You couldn't save someone who didn't want to live. Cato's body twitched and convulsed under their hands and Alphonse' tears. From somewhere behind them, the crowd was screaming for Karen's head.

Cassandra knelt, picking up the taser from Cato's dying grasp. He whispered something, eyes fixing on her for a moment as they jittered in his skull. She ignored him.

"The Party thinks you can all be fucking controlled!" She thrust her arm in the air, taser clutched in her hand. Her pulse pounded in her ears, excitement flooding through her. She had them. She had this whole world in her hand. She could crush it. She could rule it. She could do whatever the fuck she wanted, but this was hers. They were all hers.

"The Party thinks you're all fucking children, their toys. People are dead because of the Party's arrogance. Who the fuck do they think we are?"

The crowd roared. Cassandra could see people fading away, disappearing into corridors and side rooms. Fuck them. They'd get their comeuppance. They'd all get what was coming.

"We are the chosen ones! We're immortal! We are better than them, and we deserve everything we can take! We deserve to get to go home without being puppets! We deserve to go home unconditionally!"

The crowd roared again. Karen had disappeared. About half the crowd had vanished, but there were still enough. There were enough for the grand finale.

"What do we do now?" The question rang out above the crowd. Her question. The question she'd been waiting for. She grinned, baring her teeth. About fucking time she got her question.

"Let's take the ship in orbit," she said. "Let's go the fuck home."

Callisto screamed in approval.

Chapter Thirty-Three

Ina: Come out tonight.
Padraig: I'm tired.
Ina: You say that every night.
Padraig: It's true every night.
Ina: You'd be less tired if you had something to look forward to. Like coming out tonight.
Padraig: I'd be less tired if I slept more.
Ina: You'd sleep better if you stopped angsting over Theo and met someone new.
Padraig: Since when are you a relationship counselor?
Ina: Since my friend decided he's too tired and mopey for my company. If promising that you'll have fun and actually have a decent night's sleep afterwards is what it takes to get you to stop lurking in that giant flat of yours, then that's what I'm going to do.
Padraig: I'm too tired for friends.
Ina: I'm dragging you out of there.
Padraig: I'm stronger than you.
Ina: Not if I Whishaw field your ass.
Padraig: …
Ina: I'm picking you up at 7.
Padraig: That joke was terrible and you know it.
Ina: Insult my jokes again and I'll make it 6:30. I'll come get you. You'll have fun. Who knows? Maybe you'll even meet someone.
Padraig: And then you'll Whishaw field them back to my flat for me?
Ina: Exactly!

> Messages exchanged between Padraig Whishaw and Ina Krizman, 1 September 2192. Retrieved from Eoin Whishaw's personal documents in Dun Toirneach

Thou wast not churlish; thou wast not jealous; thou wast not a sluggard. It was I plighted thee, and gave purchase-price to thee, which of right belongs to the bride—of clothing, namely, the raiment of twelve men, a chariot worth thrice seven bondmaids, the breadth of thy face of red gold, the weight of thy left forearm of silvered bronze. Whoso brings shame and sorrow and madness upon thee, no claim for compensation nor satisfaction hast thou therefor that I myself have not, but it is to me the compensation belongs.

"Táin Bó Cúalnge"

This is the beauty of what we do and what each discovery means. Physics is the exploration of who we are and how we came to be here. It teaches us what our reality is. More than anything, though, it has taught us that reality is what we make of it. It has laws, but sometimes there are loopholes. This is what I love more than anything about physics. It's limitless. The potential is limitless. We can reshape reality to create something beautiful. Reality is what we make of it. With science, we control reality itself.

Dr. Padraig Whishaw, "Nobel Prize Banquet Speech," 11 December 2189

Monday, 26 May 2193, 7:42 PM. Bedroom Two, Regulus Base, Irish Sea.

There was green jelly on a plastic plate on the plastic nightstand. A plastic cup of water sat beside it, a plastic spoon beside that. Beside them, a datapad, left behind by his father the last time he'd been in here. Nothing else. The medicines and injectors and tubes and wires had been moved, hidden from the councillor's view. The doctor couldn't hide everything, but with a shirt and a blanket, only the emergency tube running down his neck was really visible. It was enough to pretend.

He hadn't changed his shirt. His father could control what was visible, but Padraig could cling to the last bit of happy memories.

He stared at the jelly. The doctor's orders had been clear: Eat the jelly. Drink the water. Keep himself alive. No reason, no logic to it anymore, just pure animalistic preservation.

One of the chest tubes pinched against his skin. He tried to shift to wiggle it free. No power. No energy to move. His blood couldn't even be trusted to carry medicine anymore, and yet, he was alive. Somehow, by the sheer force of his father's stubbornness, he was alive.

The jelly wiggled as someone walked past the room, vibrations from the floor rippling across it. Dr. Branaghan had brought jelly because it was supposed to be easy. He'd left it on the nightstand because he'd forgotten that the definition of "easy" shifted when you had tubes poking out of every newly formed orifice because it was the only way to keep a person alive.

If he didn't eat the jelly, they'd inject food in again. There was no way to die. He would, and it would be soon, but the painkillers made it impossible to know when. He wanted to look at his wrist, to see the mound where they'd injected the painkillers so he'd stop playing with them. He'd have to move to do it.

One fidget on a good day. Two on a bad day. Three on a very bad day. Infinite on this day.

Why was the jelly green, though? If the intention was to get him to eat it, why make it green? Was it because he was Irish? Because his father was Irish? Green was the colour of poison, and if the idea was to make something appetising, green was the worst way to go.

Jelly was a colloid. It was interesting. Colloids had long ago been proven not to be most effective at intravenous rejuvenation, yet here it was, sitting on a plate, a mound of colloid, jiggling when the floor of Regulus shook. Colloids didn't settle, didn't lose their shape, didn't put up with the nonsense of the world. They were bad to give to dying men to comfort them. A colloid wouldn't listen to the complaints of the man as it was force-fed to him through the tube in his stomach.

Maksharov could be a colloid. If he had to classify the councillor as a state of matter, it would be as a colloid. Deceptively rigid. Wobbly if poked just right.

Green.

Was Maksharov watching him just now? Had Maksharov watched the conversations he'd had with his father, those awkward affairs where Eoin tried to clear every issue that had been plaguing them for thirty-two years? Had he watched Eoin record on the datapad every moment, every gasped word, preserve it for this time next week when Padraig would be dead and gone, at long last?

There were enough cameras, and with how fascinated Councillor Maksharov seemed to be with every aspect of Padraig's story of Callisto, it could be. He could ooze into the cameras, watch Padraig poke at jelly, devise some elaborate theory for why the destruction of Callisto was intimately linked with Padraig's jelly colour choice.

He smiled. It didn't take much control to smile. Perhaps that was an intentional part of the painkillers. Make it difficult for him to run away. Make it easy for him to smile and nod.

Run away. The idea of it made him laugh. Gautier was right. Run to where, exactly? Regulus was the safest place in the universe. There was nowhere else outside these walls. A few more days, a few more sessions with Maksharov, interrogating, asking, cajoling, and he could die, and Gautier could go home.

The jelly wiggled again. The door opened.

His eyes flicked from the jelly to the door, watching Gautier step into the room. His smile grew. There was a jaunt in the man's step, a smile on his face. He was happy. Whatever had been said in his session with Maksharov, it must have been good. All the fear, all the worry melted at the sight of Gautier's smile. He would be fine. He would be going home. Maybe even tomorrow. If Maksharov was satisfied, Gautier could leave Regulus and go back to his life tomorrow.

This was worth words.

"It looks like…" He took another breath, drawing in the air to finish the sentence. Air like jelly in his lungs. "Things went well."

Gautier crouched beside him, jostling the nightstand as he lowered himself. The jelly jiggled. The spoon jumped. The water fell over. He ignored it.

"Oh yes," he said, and swept the back of his hand across Padraig's face. Through the haze of the painkillers, he could feel the sensation of Gautier's fingerhair against his cheeks. He closed his eyes, imagining himself arching into it. Perhaps if ideas could become reality, perhaps if he dreamed hard enough, his face would arch and he could press himself into the cupped hand.

Perhaps.

The hand reached up and brushed Padraig's hair off his ears. A stray finger jostled the neck tube, but he didn't mind. Anything to be touched and held and loved.

The hand retreated. Padraig opened his eyes.

Gautier had stood up and reached to right the cup. Water dribbled down to the wood floor, pooling beneath the spindly legs of the nightstand. He jabbed the spoon into the jelly and carved out a slice.

"Do you want this?" he asked, waving the spoon in the air.

Padraig blinked at him, willing his head to shake. Gautier watched him a moment before shrugging and popping the spoonful of jelly into his mouth. Headshake failed, then.

"Bah, lime," Gautier said, and tossed the spoon back down. It skittered across the nightstand, then fell, its handle sinking in the little puddle. "Why do they give you lime?"

Padraig blinked at him again. I wish I could answer, he thought, willing the thought to go into Gautier's head. I wish I could tell them to stop with the lime.

"No, but Ivan is fine. He asks many questions, and I answer them, but he is fine." Gautier paced back and forth, turning after three steps. One, two, three, pivot. One, two, three, pivot.

Padraig stared at him, sending his thoughts bombarding into Gautier's mind. Hold me, he thought. Please just hold me.

Gautier paused and met Padraig's gaze. "You want to know what he asked, yes?"

Hold me, Padraig thought. You're going home. That's all I needed to know. Things went well. That's all I wanted. Hold me.

"He asked me many questions that I think he asked you. What happened on Callisto. Were there any other survivors. How did we make it out. That one, he was very interested in."

Hold me.

"It was not bad. He and I had a—what is the word?—connection? Like bangers and mash, or however you Irish do it."

Hold me.

"It went much like the Lottery interview, though more assuring me I will go home if I am honest. To which I say, when am I ever not honest?"

Hold me.

Gautier pulled off his shirt, tossing it into the chair in the corner. The chair that got dragged over every time Eoin came in. The Chair of Conversation.

"The man talks for so many hours, though," Gautier said, and moved past him, stepping out of his field of vision. Padraig heard the sound of his pants unzipping, the sound of the fabric hitting the floor. "You would think he would have something else to do, but—"

Padraig took a breath. "Hold me." Words, painful words, but necessary. Gautier would go home. Gautier would go free. Gautier would go back to Amsterdam, to a normal, happy life. Life was perfect.

Gautier paused. "I will save the shower for later, then," he said.

The bed groaned, and Padraig felt himself roll as Gautier moved to lie next to him. A burly arm draped over him, pressing and pinching tubes into his skin. A warm chest squeezed against his back. Legs curled against him. Cock nestled in his ass.

Padraig smiled. On the nightstand, the remains of the jelly vibrated as footsteps approached the door. He closed his eyes. Whatever it was, it didn't matter. The outside world could wait forever. This embrace was the world.

"...should never have been allowed anywhere near Callisto."

Padraig's ears perked. Ivan Maksharov, outside his door, voice raised.

"He is a danger. I told you this from the outset, and you didn't listen. You knew it, Eoin, and still you sent him!"

Ice. Glaciers tumbling through his veins.

Gautier was going home. He'd told Maksharov that over and over and over. Gautier needed to go home. Gautier needed to go free. Gautier had done nothing wrong. There was no reason to keep him. Let him go. Send him home.

"It's inexcusable!"

"He's my son, Ivan." His father's voice, lower, but audible. Padraig's eyes fluttered open as he watched the door. The jelly sat still, listening to the arguing just outside. Gautier's arm tightened around him. So he wasn't the only one listening.

"That was the only way he would go. My *son*. What would you have had me do?"

"You should have remembered that you have spent your entire life in service to the people of this world, not to yourself."

The arm tightened harder. The pinched tube burned against him. Air struggled in. It didn't matter. He was being held, and Gautier would go home. Please, Gautier would go home.

"Is that all you wanted to say?" Eoin Whishaw's voice was small, tired, defeated. Padraig strained to hear it through the door.

"I'll see you in the morning," Maksharov said. The jelly vibrated as he left. The jelly lay still.

His heart had been replaced by an iceberg, throbbing in the centre of him.

No, no, no, no. Gautier was going home. The one thing, the only thing, left to be true. Gautier would be safe. Gautier would go home. He would make his father promise. His father would always fulfil his dying son's wishes. Gautier would go home. His father could do anything. Gautier would go home.

The jelly jiggled. Something throbbed in his bones. At the corner of his hearing, a deep, rumbling, throbbing sound. At his back, he felt Gautier tense. Something had changed. From somewhere, a sound entered the room.

The door opened, and his father stepped in. Purple bags hung under his red eyes, and his cheeks hung loose against his face. He was exhaustion incarnate, to match his son, on the threshold of death. This was the safest place in the universe, but at a cost.

"Gautier St. Laurent," he said. "Go to sleep."

The arm holding his chest relaxed. Gautier's breathing shifted into the deep, easy breaths of sleep.

Padraig's eyes widened and locked on his father.

Eoin Whishaw moved to the chair in the corner. He brushed the shirt to the floor and moved it, placing it beside the bed. Padraig watched, eyes locked on his father, not blinking, not daring to miss a single movement.

Breath. "Gautier..." he said.

"—will be fine." His father sat and reached for the datapad, eyes not meeting his son's. Every other time, their eyes had met. Every other conversation, they'd watched each other. Every other conversation, he'd been able to see his father cry.

Eoin Whishaw was lying.

Breath, agonising breath. His father was switching the datapad on. Good. It could capture what he had to say.

"Send Gautier home." He coughed out the rest of the blood, splattering it against the grey blanket. Breath. "Promise me. Gautier..."

"—will be fine."

You're lying, you're lying, by the Party, I'm not stupid, just dying, and I know, I know you're lying, you're lying.

Breath. His father had a syringe in his hand. Where had it come from? The man had avoided every reminder that his son was dying. Every syringe, every tube, every injector had been hidden to let him pretend that things could be okay. What was this syringe? Where had it come from?

"Promise me." Padraig gasped out the words, feeling them rumble and rip through his throat. His father couldn't ignore his dying son, not a last wish, by every god, no.

His father brushed Gautier's arm off his back, sending the man rolling backwards. Padraig rolled with him, but his father caught him by the arm, holding him on his side.

He wasn't meeting his eyes. What was that syringe?

Breath. "Da!" Breath. "Da, promise me!"

His father lifted the blanket from him, delicate, as though he were a sleeping infant, sighing at the edge of a sob. His hand pushed the sweater up, baring Padraig's side to the cold. His fingers brushed a lung tube, pausing on it.

"Shhh," his father murmured, and set the syringe down on the nightstand. He raised his eyes.

There were tears glimmering in them. None fallen, but there were tears.

His father's hand brushed his cheek, stroking with the back of his fingers. He wanted to shrink away, to run, to do anything but let this happen. He wiggled. His father held him down.

The hand moved to his hair, stroking it.

"Shh," he said. "Shh shh shh."

Breath. "What" Breath. "Are you doing?"

His father rested his hand against Padraig's head for a moment, meeting his eyes.

"I'm doing what I can," he murmured. "I'm doing the best I can. I always have. Please understand that."

Fuck fuck fuck fuck fuck fuck fuck fuck fuck

The hand lifted from his head and reached for the syringe, grasping it at the wrong angle.

Breath, so quick, needed now. Please. "Promise."

He felt the tube jiggle as the syringe slid into place. His father met his eyes once more.

Breath. "Promise me."

His father closed his eyes. "I will try," he said.

Bre

Acknowledgements

Thursday, 1 August 2024, 1:50 PM. My comfy couch, Amsterdam, the Netherlands.

No story exists in a vacuum, and there are many people I'd like to thank for helping bring this book into existence. Thank you to Alexis Arendt for your patient editing, and to Kelsey Nix for your phenomenal cover art. Thank you also to Grace for putting me in contact with so many lovely people who could help bring Callisto to life.

I'd especially like to thank Jeff for cheering me on, and Zach, for the endless evenings of world building, idea bouncing, and learning literally everything about the Jovian orbital system alongside me. The world of 2193 may have come to life over tacos and drinks in Fort Worth, but it stayed alive because of you and your infinite patience, love, and support. *Merci beaucoup, mon cheri. Je sais que mon français est encore mauvais.*

Most of all, though, I'd like to thank you, dear reader, for picking up this book and going on this journey with me.

Without you, there is no story to be told, and so I thank you for trusting me to tell you this one. If you enjoyed this book, please feel free to leave a review on Goodreads or Amazon so others can find it and enjoy it as well!

About the Author

Janneke de Beer wrote her first book at four years old and has been writing continuously – some have even described it as "excessively" – ever since. The world of 2193 is one of many worlds dancing around in her head – all she's missing is the time to write them. She is the primary singer and songwriter for her band Some Unknown Fraudster and also maintains a video game review blog and a vegan recipe blog. She lives in Amsterdam with her partner, Zach, and more pigeons than she cares to comment on.

She loves hearing from readers! You can reach out to her (or sign up for her mailing list!) at jannekedebeer2193@gmail.com, via social media, or through her website, www.jannekedebeer.com

www.ingramcontent.com/pod-product-compliance
Lightning Source LLC
LaVergne TN
LVHW030317070526
838199LV00069B/6478